PASSION'S MASTER

"Would it make you feel powerful and mighty to crush me—to make me feel your conquering strength? Well, go ahead and do your worst, master." Christy dared him openly.

The captain's senses reeled. His blood pulsed at a dizzying speed. His head pounded wildly—ready to explode. A fever raged within him.

With unquenchable hunger he snatched her to him. Arms of steel encircled her. His fiery lips crushed down on hers, aflame with desire and urgency. The fire of his kiss assaulted her senses, and for a brief moment Christy too felt the spark of his passion pulsing through her veins. But this was wrong!

Panic gripped Christy. He was like a wild, raging animal, driven by lustful desire. "Take your hands off me!" she cried with every ounce of authority she possessed trying to shock him out of his madness.

"No. Not this time, my love," he whispered, low and unswayable. He reached up to free her long black hair, sending the shining mass tumbling down. . . .

EXCITING BESTSELLERS FROM ZEBRA

By Deborah LeVarre

ZEBRA BOOKS
KENSINGTON PUBLISHING CORP.

ZEBRA BOOKS

are published by

KENSINGTON PUBLISHING CORP.
475 Park Avenue South
New York, N.Y. 10016

SECOND PRINTING MARCH 1984

Printed in the United States of America

For all her devoted patience, mighty support, and undying confidence in me, I dedicate this story to Dawnna, my twin sister and very dearest friend.

One

The London harbor was a beehive of activity on that oppressively hot July day in 1758. Sweaty men swarmed over the docks and on heavily laden ships headed for all parts of the trading world.

The men loading *The Merrimer* were no exception. The sun melted down on them as they skillfully manipulated ropes and pullies to maneuver their precious cargo into the hold. Tired muscles strained and tempers flared, but the general mood was optimistic. The trip to Charleston, South Carolina promised to be extremely profitable if they succeeded in reaching port before their arch competitor, *The Rupert.* Hopes were high for their success for they had a skillful, daring captain and a strong crew to supply the muscle.

Earnestly involved in all the hustle of activity, few took notice of a small shabbily clothed fugitive dodging through the crowds. A heavy overcoat, out of place on the hot day, came to the wearer's knees, while oversized gray trousers dragged on the ground.

The figure halted for an instant in the sunlight, panting heavily. A black hat pulled tightly down over a smudged, pale face hid long lush lashes fluttering over expressive emerald green eyes that looked down over a small, dainty nose and full, red lips. Few could guess that the sodden, boyish attire disguised a pretty young girl.

Casting a nervous glance behind her, she sped swiftly to a stack of massive crates scattered along the loading dock and crouched down behind them. Her breath came in jagged gasps as her ears strained for the sound of approaching footsteps. Her palms felt cold and clammy, despite the oppressive heat, as she cautiously peered over the crate.

A scream nearly escaped her lips, but she bit her finger to stifle the cry. Quickly she ducked down behind the boxes. The swift movement engulfed her in a new wave of suffering. Excruciating pain from the scores of gashes covering her back brought tears to her eyes. Again she bit on her finger until the threat of unconsciousness passed.

Her situation was desperate. A brief glimpse had revealed the hideous vision of Henry Slate laboring ever nearer. His beady eyes darted between every box. Saliva dripped unchecked down the corners of his twisted, filthy mouth. He wheezed heavily from the physical strain on his obese body.

She shuddered violently at the vision. He would kill her if he caught her. It was escape or die! But how?

"Let's load these crates here next," came a deep, throaty voice directly above her head.

Her heart stopped! It was over. In seconds she would be discovered.

"No. The captain wants this foodstuff loaded before it spoils in this damn heat," came another voice, farther off.

"Goddamnit. Tell him to make up his mind," grumbled the man as he shuffled off.

The young fugitive swallowed hard and took a deep breath. She'd come too close to being discovered. It was imperative to move.

Whispering a silent prayer, she risked another look from behind her cover. Cold fear sent icicles down her spine. Slate was no more than sixty feet away!

Again she crouched down and bit savagely on her lip. Should she risk an outright dash for freedom and gamble her adversary was too drunk and clumsy to follow? But no; weak and feverish from her wounds, she knew it was sheer folly to even attempt such rashness. Even in his intoxicated condition he could undoubtedly overtake her. There was also the possibility that his exclamations would elicit the aid of some passing stranger to his cause. Outright flight seemed to lead only to guaranteed capture. But what else could she do?

She shifted her weight to ease her discomfort. The oppressive heat was closing in on her. Every noise was magnified a thousandfold as she strained to hear the approach of Slate or the workmen. Her head pounded unbearably. Her muscles tensed. She thrust her hand out to push off against the crate.

A throbbing pain shot up her arm and she stared dumbly at her scraped, bleeding fingers. Could she endure more? Even the crates seemed to be against her. The crates . . .

Suddenly an idea crashed through her mind. Of course, the crates! Why had she not thought of it sooner? She could hide inside one of them until Slate tired of his search—and she could be gone before the dock men began to load. It seemed her only chance.

Spurred by a ray of hope, she hunched down and threaded her way through the confusion of ropes and cartons searching for a suitable hideout.

A ray of sunlight shining on a nearby box caught her eye. Slits in the side revealed neatly folded fabrics with ample space at the top to protect the precious linens from being crushed. Perhaps there was just enough room for a small, thin girl to squeeze in.

She brushed aside irksome tears. Yes! She just might fit. But did she have time before Slate was upon her? How could she climb up and in without being seen? Was this just another dead end? Chewing anxiously on her lip, she ventured another peek over the crate to assess her position. Slate was nearly on top of her!

She pivoted, ready to bolt from the spot. A loud crash halted her flight. She gazed in wonder as Slate, caught up in his own drunken rage, stumbled on a piece of rigging. He fell heavily, evoking a stream of loud, obscene curses. The men loading the ship stopped their work to watch in amusement as he struggled clumsily to his feet.

Seizing upon the diversion, she jumped up, shoved aside the lid, and nestled herself into the crate . . . and waited.

The box was dark and cramped and she lay very still, hardly daring to breathe. Seconds ticked by and false hope tingled her senses. Slate had abandoned his hunt. She was safe at last!

Abruptly her hopes vanished. Heavy footfalls approached and hard, labored breathing sounded directly above her. The rank, pungent smell of whiskey and body odor made her want to gag. Her eyes strained to see through the tiny slits. Would he see her lying inside? Her heart pounded wildly. She dared not even breathe. Every nerve in her body strained and panic churned her stomach into tight knots.

Suddenly his hand came down on the lid. He knew she was there! In seconds he would raise the lid. She'd be trapped. His filthy hands would lock about her neck and he would strangle the very life from her! A scream rose in her throat. She fought it with every ounce of will power she possessed.

But wait. Slate was moving away—very slowly. He had not seen her; nor had he heard her. She was safe!

A slow, deep breath filled her lungs and she let it out with deliberate control, forcing herself to relax. Desperately she wanted to climb from her stifling prison. But prudence warned her to wait a few moments longer, just to be sure Slate was gone and would not come back.

With imminent danger now forestalled, her abused, exhausted body again was racked with misery. Cramped in the uncompromising carton, her back ached unbearably. Waves of nausea and dizziness plagued her. Life was so cruel; so haphazard in dealing out sorrows. Hadn't she already endured far more than her share these past two years? Where would the suffering and sorrow end?

Death had struck her a cruel blow when a freak accident nearly two years ago had snatched away the two most important people in her life. Her father, a well-known horse breeder and racer, had strong convictions concerning the morality of slavery. Numerous times he had been warned against his outspoken condemnation of the buying and selling of Negroes in the Colonies. But as always, little could deter his determination

Despite the rightness of the cause, his zeal had wrought only sorrow. He and his wife had been killed on their way to an anti-slavery rally. Their carriage had lost control and gone plunging over a narrow mountain ravine. The tragedy had been listed as accidental, but the girl knew otherwise. She was convinced her parents had been murdered in cold blood. Hadn't the carriage smith inspected the broken buggy after the accident and found certain unusual malfunctions in the supposedly sturdy rig? It had been concluded that when the carriage reached a high speed, one wheel had given way and sent it rumbling off uncontrollably. The carriage smith had admitted to her that the stage had probably been sabotaged, but he had suddenly been frightened into silence and would say nothing publicly. The death of her parents had been listed as a tragic mishap.

It had all happened so suddenly. One day she had been the carefree, happy daughter of a wealthy merchant; the next, all semblance of that happiness had vanished forever. She was unceremoniously whisked off to the small farm outside London to live with her Aunt Heather and her aunt's husband, Henry, as their ward.

The transition had been swift and devastating. But for the orphan girl, the real tragedy had only begun. The pompous, greedy magistrate, Theodore Joanace, had ordered a thorough investigation into the estate of the late Mr. and Mrs. William Patterson. With the help of some of his elite and equally despicable associates,

Joanace had produced evidence that the Pattersons owed a substantial amount of taxes to the Crown. Any amateur accountant could have seen through the forged figures and accounts they produced, yet no one dared protest the findings. Thus the estate had been completely sold off to settle the supposed debt, and the girl had been sent to live with her relatives as best she could. Her parents had been labeled blackguards and swindlers, and their names forever etched as traitors to the country.

She knew Joanace had been behind the previous threats to her parents' lives. Their refusal to be intimidated only intensified his anger. Anyone who opposed profits at the exploitation of slaves offered a potential threat and made him appear weak and ineffectual ruler before the King. Their elimination rid him of the unpleasant situation and also served as a warning to others who would follow in their stead. The added settlement of the estate in Joanace's behalf no doubt had gone to further appease him. The girl grew purple with rage every time she thought to what great lengths he had gone to dispose of them thoroughly and completely. She prayed that someday he would be repaid for his wickedness and treachery.

She had little time to ponder life's injustices, however, for life with the Slates was painfully hard. They were poor farmers and had barely enough to support themselves, much less a young girl. But she had done her part, working long hours in the fields. Her back ached and her hands bled many a night, but Slate was never satisfied no matter how strenuous her labors. His desire for drink and money was insatiable and caused him to

13

drive her almost beyond endurance.

Her aunt, a frightened, unhealthy woman, pleaded with her husband to ease up on the girl. But he paid no heed and drove her on all the more. For survival she had learned to endure his backbreaking demands in silence. But the mental agony he inflicted by his baiting, demeaning slurs and insults about her beloved parents rankled deeply. Despite her most valiant efforts to hold her tongue, eventually her resolve would weaken and she would argue back. It did not take long, however, before she learned the only response Slate gave to her defense of her parents was the crack of his whip.

After nearly a year of such abuse, she had finally disciplined herself to ignore his taunting and thereby save herself the agony of the lash. But when he drank, as he did more indulgently after the death of his wife, he would become vicious and take out his stick and whip her unmercifully, with little provocation. The past year she was never without gashes marking her bruised, white flesh. Numerous attempts to escape had always been thwarted. His severe punishment after such incidents had petrified her into abandoning any hope of relief.

Last night's drama, however, had given her a new resolve. He had been drinking more than usual and had come home from town in a wicked mood. His cutting remarks about her and her parents had been even more degrading than usual. Despite her courageous efforts, she had given in and fought back his verbal slurs. She had refused to acknowledge that her parents had indeed been traitors. He had become enraged and had beaten her until he fell over from exhaustion in a drunken stupor. She had staggered away, half dead, but with a vow that never again would she listen to his ranting or feel his whip upon her.

It had taken her most of the night to reach London. The girl had to stop several times to fight the pain and unconsciousness which plagued her every step of the way. The delay had given him time to recover and he had doggedly followed her here to the docks. Would she ever be free of his malicious clutches?

The air gradually grew stale inside the self-made prison. Her feverish musings tumbled together in confusion. Voices, distant and indiscernible, filtered in and out of her consciousness from another time; another place. She felt groggy and incoherent. The insistent yet unfamiliar voices grew louder, grating annoyingly on the recesses of her mind.

"This is the last of 'em to be loaded. Hurry it up now. We're running way behind as it is."

Her eyes flew open. The faceless voices were all too real now. Panic pulsed through her veins. She muffled a scream as several men passed by. Should she alert them that she was in the box? Surely it would cause a commotion. What if Slate was still prowling about? She had been a fool to linger overlong and lose track of time. Had she dozed for two minutes or two hours? Her mind felt near bursting. What should she do? A deafening blow rendered the sides of the crate. They were nailing it shut! They were trapping her inside!

Frantically she tried to raise a fist to pound on the crate. But what was wrong? Her arms seemed restrained by tremendous weights. She was paralyzed and powerless to move!

The crate pressed in on all sides; smothering her as they continued pounding nails. Suddenly the crate began to drag along the dock. Fear gripped her anew and frantically she strained every ounce of her being, aching from the effort. Still she could not speak.

In seconds she was suspended in the air. The carton rocked dizzily from side to side. Nausea churned her empty stomach and her head reeled giddily. Back and forth she swung in her suspended prison. Suddenly the crate was falling, faster—faster! Her breath caught in her lungs. Cold terror surged through every vein. Her heart stopped beating. She was being plunged into the sea; or smashed to the ground! Death gripped at her with cold, black fingers. Life was over. Would there be pain?

The box crashed to the deck.

"Take it easy with these crates, Jackman!" yelled the worker. "Those Charleston belles won't be appreciating wrinkled silks and finery."

His reprimand was lost on the young fugitive. Her head slammed against the carton and blackness consumed her.

Two

A dull, persistent pounding throbbed in her head. It was so hot, breathing itself was an exhausting chore. Every muscle in her body screamed in agony. Slowly, reluctantly she pried open her eyes. Her head swam dizzily. A sick gnawing churned in her stomach. This had to be some terrible nightmare. Yet who could even dream of such agony? No, this was all too real.

Slowly her senses began to function once again and she nurtured the resolve to free herself from the crate. The men had no doubt taken a rest from the strenuous loading. She must escape before they returned. With great effort she raised her arms to lift the lid. The temporary paralysis had vanished as quickly as it had come, but a drugged, weakened effect still lingered.

She pushed gently. No response. She pushed again, harder this time. Still the lid would not budge. A new twinge of fear swept through her as she tried once again to free herself. The wooden structure held firm.

Her adrenaline began to pump. Would this box of fine linen prove to be her coffin? Was she to be trapped and suffocate or starve to death; her emaciated body to be discovered when the crate was opened? Had she escaped the clutches of Slate only to die as a trapped animal?

No! She would not succumb to such a demise. A surge of strength sprang to her limbs. Fighting the pain her actions brought, she threw her shoulders again and again at the stubborn lid. The crate offered pitifully little room for leverage. She was pitting her meager strength against the sturdy container—and losing! The thought compelled her to heave all the harder.

At last the bite of the nails into the wood began to loosen. Encouraged somewhat by the splintering wood, she continued to slam her weight against the crate in vigorous determination. Yet the lid held fast. Then a crackling pierced her ears and she pitted her final ounce of strength against the crate. The battered lid cracked from the blow and crashed to the floor.

Free at last! She felt jubilant. Greedily she gulped at the cool, refreshing air which rushed in. Gradually she relaxed as her pain subsided to a bearable level. It was some time before she mustered the strength to rise. The experience proved far more painful than she anticipated. Her cramped muscles protested and nearly refused to cooperate.

Adding to her misery, the great heavy overcoat scraped unmercifully against the bleeding sores on her back. It was all she could do to raise herself to sit on the crate which had held her prisoner for so long. Tears spilled down her smudged face as she prayed for the strength to go on.

At length the pain subsided somewhat and she gingerly swung her legs to the ground. A muffled cry escaped her lips as her shaky legs buckled beneath her weight, toppling her to the hard floor. She gritted her teeth, pulled herself up and tried again. Though still unsteady, her legs held her up and she forced herself to walk. Gradually the feeling returned to her stiffened limbs.

Now that she was at last free from the crate, a thousand questions raced through her mind as she stumbled about the dark, cluttered room. How was she to get out of the hold without anyone seeing her? She had to leave before the ship sailed. She noted the word "Charleston" printed in bold letters on many of the crates. Was that the ship's destination? Regardless, she must disembark immediately lest she find herself sailing for this place called Charleston with an unsympathetic crew. Though the prospects of returning to the London harbor without a penny to her name were disheartening, the idea of being thrust into a strange new world across the sea was even more disquieting. But how could she steal away without being detected?

Further deliberation ceased. With no warning whatsoever, the hatchway burst open, flooding the hold with brilliant light. She sucked in her breath, temporarily blinded. Heart aflutter, she stumbled back, crouching quickly behind a crate. Hardly daring to breathe, she listened closely to the gruff, faceless voices.

"Everything bloody well better go smoothly from here on out, Henderson. Thanks to you and those bumbling fools you hired on, we've had nothing but trouble since we started loading."

"Hey, Nath. It ain't my fault things went poorly. I got the best men I could find on such short notice. I know they're nothing but scum, but you leave them to me. I'll whip them into shape, or kill 'em trying," responded the second man.

She winced at his fierce words. He'd be no man to fool with. The second man again spoke, this time from all too near her hiding place.

"For everyone's sake, especially yours, you'd damn well better. Just look at the way this stuff was loaded. This crate of linens is smashed beyond repair. I warn you, if the captain sees this, he'll spare no mercy. He's in foul humor since we got such a late start. He'll have us all thrown to the sharks. Call down a few of your men, Henderson, and get this mess cleaned up before the captain swabs the deck with our carcasses. I'll wait here. I want to make certain the job gets done right. It's my hide too," added a third man.

Heavy footsteps pounded up the stairs. The remaining two men shuffled slowly about the room, poking, prodding and cursing until her ears stung from their profanity.

She shifted her weight slightly and chewed nervously on her lip. Should she throw herself at the mercy of these two men, explain what had happened, and enlist their aid in helping her reach shore? Surely they would be sympathetic to her plight. But even to her, such blatant optimism seemed doomed to failure. Why should they risk their captain's ire to help a total stranger? No doubt they would enjoy handing her over to him.

She shuddered at the very thought. Their brief yet all too vivid description of the fierce, vengeful man who commanded the ship made her realize he was definitely no one she wanted to run up against. If he had no mercy for his own crew, surely he would spare none on a stranger. But then how could she possibly get away? Even if she somehow managed to create a diversion and slip past these men, there were sure to be many others on deck. Would her masculine disguise allow her enough anonymity to safely ease her way off the ship and back onto shore? She was plagued by burning indecision. A sense of impending doom crashed down upon her taunt nerves. She began to shiver despite the fever which raged in her tortured body.

One of the men coughed. His foot slammed against the crate where she hid.

"Goddamn . . ." he cursed, rubbing his bruised shin gingerly. "Bring that lamp over so I can see what's piled up in this corner without killing myself," he ordered.

She clutched her throat. The lamp! Oh, no! Her heart pounded so wildly she felt it would burst from her chest. Reckless with fear, she jumped from behind the crate and dove toward the stairs.

"Hey! Who's that there?" yelled the man in wild-eyed surprise as she whipped by him. "Stop, now!"

She paid no heed to his command but stumbled blindly toward the stairs. She reached the hatchway in seconds and lunged up the steps two at a time. All life centered on the focal point of light at the head of the stairs. The air burned in her lungs. Almost there! Another three steps!

Suddenly the light disappeared from the doorway. Three grim faces stared blankly at her. Helpless, confused, she plunged headlong into them. "Move away! Move away!" she choked.

"What the hell . . ." blared the recipient of her

swinging arm.

Suddenly a rough hand gripped the back of her coat and yanked her downward. Her feet left the stairs and she was swung around so sharply, she went colliding into a stack of crates and sprawled across the floor. Blinding pain seared her back, consuming her in agony. Someone was firing questions at her. Her head whirled. Her eyes would not focus. Someone shook her roughly.

"Answer me, kid! Who are you? What the hell are you doing down here? I never saw you before. Did the captain hire you on? Why are you lurking about? How did you get here?" His endless stream of questions exploded at her.

What plausible answer could she give these men? She felt suffocated under their intense scrutiny.

"You'd better answer, boy, or I'll whip the answers out of you," threatened another.

The girl cringed in horror at his threat. The lash was a fate worse than death. She tried to speak, but her voice croaked raspily. She moistened her dry, parched lips and tried again.

"I . . . I . . ." she trailed off, easing herself to a sitting position.

The man's eyes turned into tiny slits. "Damnit, boy. Find your tongue or I'll rip it out of your head!"

"No! No! Please wait," she tried again. Fear glistened in her eyes.

"Goddamn!" interrupted the fiercest looking of the group. "The kid's a bloody stowaway. It's written all over him," he growled and shook his fist menacingly at her.

"Is that true, boy?" cried her original interrogator.

22

"Let me explain," she began. Gradually she eased herself up, leaning against the crates for support. Her knees shook violently, but she had to stand. She would not let them see how petrified she was. She would let no one call her a coward.

The men surrounding her grew perceptibly more hostile. "Toss the bloody bastard overboard!" suggested one.

"Yeah. Feed him to the sharks," sneered another.

"That's too good for him. Hog tie him to the masthead and see how long he lasts!"

"Shut up, all of you," ordered her interrogator. "Henderson, go get the captain. He'll be wanting to know we got uninvited company. And he sure as hell won't be none too happy."

She watched in fear as one man begrudgingly disengaged himself from the group and hurried up the stairs. The others turned their gaze back to their hostage.

"I think you'll wish we'd thrown you overboard, boy. I'd say it a far more humane punishment than unleashing the captain on you. He's just liable to tear you limb from limb. He's that despicable when he gets riled. It should be real interestin' to see what he does."

The grim faces of the other men supported his thinking.

"Please, let me go. It's an accident I'm here. I never planned it. I'm not a stowaway. Please, just let me go ashore. I promise I won't bother you again. You needn't tell your captain. This is all a terrible mistake. Let me go and there will be no harm done. Please!"

The men looked at her in open astonishment.

Suddenly their faces softed and they burst out in mocking laughter. "That's a good one, kid," the leader of the group sneered. "Set you ashore, aye? Well, boy, what would you have us do—turn around the ship and head back just to let you off?"

"Head for shore . . . ?" she began in confusion. "I don't understand."

"Yup. Been gone from the London harbor for nigh on three hours now, laddie. You must have fallen asleep," he guffawed. "Did you have a nice nap?"

Her hand flew to her throat. She felt close to choking. "No! No. It can't be!" she cried and shrank back against the crate. Gone from shore for three hours? Oh God.

"Did you think we would sit in the harbor until you were finished with your little nap?" he repeated wickedly.

She savagely fought back the tears that welled up in her eyes. She was trapped—without hope! The room grew deathly quiet. The men watched and waited in anticipation for the imminent confrontation.

"What the hell do you mean, you found some kid hiding in the hold? How the hell did he get there?" thundered an angry voice from above, shattering the stillness like glass. "Who would have the supreme audacity and stupidity to stow away on *my* ship?"

Without waiting for a response, the owner of the voice pounded heavily down the shaking stairway. The raging bull bore down upon the girl. In three long strides he swept across the floor. Men bolted out of his path lest they be trampled beneath him.

He halted not three feet from her, his long legs spread

wide in a commanding stance. Immense hands with the power of three men were locked gravely in his belt. His looming shadow dwarfed her and blocked out the light from the hatchway. "What the hell are you doing on my ship?" His booming voice shook the hold. "Who are you? Answer me, boy." His hands gripped his belt even tighter. He was livid with rage.

She winced from the ferocity of his words. She could feel those hands squeezing around her neck. Unconsciously she pressed even closer to the crates, willing herself to disappear from his angry brown eyes. He expected an answer, but how could she evoke words from a throat that was parched and dry from fear?

"I'm not a stowaway, sir . . . Captain. It was an accident. I . . . I was hiding from someone . . . on shore. I hid in a crate. I must have fallen asleep when it was loaded. I had no idea the ship had set sail. It was an accident, Captain. I'm not a stowaway. I don't want to be here. It is all a dreadful mistake."

Suddenly the wrath of Slate seemed immensely preferable to being trapped aboard this ship with its beastly captain and crew. She shuddered involuntarily. The movement was not missed by his calculating eyes.

"I quite agree. You have made a grave mistake; one I can promise you will deeply regret." His tone held the challenge of an executioner. Her already pale face drained of all color. "No doubt you expect me to believe this story. Tell me, just who was this dastardly fiend?" he stormed.

"No, let me guess and spare you the opportunity of lying to me," he interrupted as she opened her mouth to speak. "Your disheveled appearance clearly proves you were running away from a life of work and poverty to find exciting adventure and riches on the high seas. Admit it, boy. That's why you stole aboard, isn't it?" he goaded.

"No, Captain. No . . ."

He silenced her with his piercing eyes. "Your earnest denials ring false with me. You incite my wrath and insult me with your brazen lies. I can see with my own eyes that you are a stowaway; a bloody, stealthy runaway."

"Captain, you don't understand. You've made a mistake. Let me explain," she tried once again.

"Damnit! How dare you stand there shivering and pitiful and tell me that I have made a mistake. It is you who made the blunder, my boy! No one comes aboard my ship without my permission. No one! I cannot tolerate it. You must be punished—and severely." He bestowed on her an expression of such loathing that she feared he would kill her that instant with his bare hands alone.

She shrank even farther back into the shadows. It was useless to defend herself against this fearsome monster. He would hear no reason but his own.

Her silence and unequivocal terror encouraged him all the more. He eyed her dispassionately. "Do you still claim it a mistake you are here?"

His sudden change in strategy took her by surprise. She could only nod her head.

"Well then, boy, I've reconsidered. I will play the simpleton and take your word on that." He watched her countenance ease somewhat. Then he landed the blow.

"Take heed. There will be no mistake about the way you return to London. You will be sent back to shore the same way you came—in a crate. You will probably return in a day or two, unless of course, the sharks reach you first. Most likely even they will leave you be. There's frightfully little of you. You would provide a sorry meal for them." His eyes openly mocked her. "You do swim, don't you, boy?" he sneered. "Just in case you should manage to get out of the crate?"

"Please, sir, I implore you to reconsider. Do not do this terrible deed. Let me work for you. I'm willing to do more than my share. Give me a chance to prove myself. I may not look strong, but I am, and I will work hard for you. Please, don't throw me overboard." Tears glistened on her pale cheeks, but the sight evoked no pity in him.

"I do not want you aboard my ship. It is as simple as that, my boy. You came here at your own risk. You must now pay the consequences. And as for work, you look as if you can hardly stand much less mop a floor or hoist a sail. You would be totally useless to me; in fact, a complete nuisance. I want you off my ship. That is my final word."

She blinked back tears and stared helplessly, trying to reduce this monster to human form. Not much more than thirty years old, he had a dark, roguishly handsome face of sharp features. Wisps of thick dark hair escaped from the tiny band which unsuccessfully tried to hold it bound. His mouth was set in a hard, unyielding line. His dark brown eyes were cold, demanding, and devoid of compassion. Despite his young age and striking good looks, she saw no mercy reflected in his deep brown eyes—only anger.

His question cut into her reverie like a knife. "What is

your name, boy?"

"I'm not a boy," she cried out in hot retort.

"Pray, then, just what are you?" came his mocking reply. "Do you elevate yourself to the status of a man? Why, there's narry a whisker in sight." His hand brushed her face roughly. "'Tis smooth as a whore's bottom," he said.

She jerked away, appalled by his touch as much as by his words. She'd been a fool to speak hastily, without thinking. So far her disguise combined with the darkness of the hold, had fooled them as to her gender. Did she dare tell him the truth? The decision weighed heavily on her mind. She furtively cast a glance at the faces around her. They reflected the same hard, mean, brutal character of their captain. These men would use her; they would lustfully take their pleasure and then cast her aside as worthless chattel. That would be a fate worse than death.

She glanced again at the man before her. The firm set of his jaw and the cold, vindictive glint in his eyes decided the matter. "My name is Patterson, Captain."

"Well, Mr. Patterson," he said with stilted formality. "On our return to London your family will be notified that they have one less mouth to feed."

"You needn't trouble yourself, sir. I have no family," she replied bitterly.

"I see. Well that only reaffirms my conclusion about your guilt. You can fully expect to pay for your foolhardy actions. I have no pity on liars, stowaways, or orphans," he said dispassionately. "Nath, empty one of those crates and make room for our departing guest."

Without a word the man moved across the room. Obviously disgruntled, he began spewing cloth and linen from the crate onto the floor.

An unbearable pressure descended on the girl's chest as she helplessly watched him. She shot her attention to the captain. His eyes were cold as stone and his intentions were deadly serious.

Fight! Fight for your life, her mind ordered, but no words would come. Her mind whirled in a sea of blank, unconnected thoughts.

The captain shifted his weight. Her eyes caught the light from above. If she could just get past him, if only for a moment . . . it was worth a try. The box was nearly empty. Did she dare? Yes!

"Don't try it, boy. You'd never make it."

All hope was instantly shattered. She began to tremble. Tears trickled slowly down her cheeks. The face of her executioner grew even darker.

"The crate is empty, Captain," said Nath. The words were her death sentence.

"Good. Put him in." His stony countenance never changed.

Two of the men approached her in silence. She saw them coming, but her eyes looked past them to the man solidly blocking the exit. Emerald orbs silently pleaded with him for mercy. He chose to ignore her. Rough arms seized her. Her feet dangled as they easily lifted her between them, carrying her toward the box.

"No! Wait! Please, Captain. Is there nothing I can say that will change your mind? Let me explain. Give me a chance!"

The men halted abruptly at her outburst. Her heartrending cries were terribly convincing. They waited for the captain to respond.

"My boy, I am a busy man. Nothing you could possibly say would change my mind. Now get him into the box, Nath. I have many things to do," he ordered casually, as if discarding an old boot.

Gripped by an overpowering rebellion at his injustice, she wrestled free of their grasp. Lightning quick she raced for the stairway. The captain was quicker. His massive bulk thwarted her escape.

She spun about, running blindly, irrationally about the cluttered hold. Savage, sneering faces flanked her every turn. She ducked and dodged hands thrust out to seize her. Terror swept her on. They closed in. There was nowhere to run. She was trapped!

"No! Don't touch me! Get away!" she screamed hysterically. Her lungs burned. She panted heavily but could get no air. They were suffocating her. A flood of tears poured from her eyes. "Call them off. Get them away!" she shrieked.

Her gasping ceased suddenly as her eyes met the captain's. He stood beside the stairway, watching the chase with utter indifference. She stared at him in total bewilderment.

"And just where do you think you can run? A ship offers quite limited avenues for escape." His words came slowly and with complete unruffled dispassion.

"What kind of man are you? What gives you the right to send me to a watery grave? I told you the truth. It was an accident that I came aboard your ship. I don't want to

30

be here any more than you want me here. You're nothing but a cold blooded murderer!" she cried in anger.

"I'm an inhumane murderer, am I?" he remarked dryly, a little muscle under his right eye beginning to twitch. His cool indifference was rapidly being replaced by anger. Slowly he moved to within inches of her. His voice was deliberately lethal. "I am the captain of this ship. That is all the right I need. Rules of the land and rules of the sea are entirely different. I am the judge, the jury and the executioner. No one questions my decisions."

Anger drained from her. There was no hope. It was useless to argue further.

"Nath, see if you can manage to get this scrawny boy into the crate *this* time. I'd not thought it such a difficult task. You seem to be having a terrible time of it, however."

Nath stepped forward. It seemed no one was safe from the captain's biting tongue.

"No!" she cried loudly and immediately lowered her voice to a calm, controlled tone. "Let me go. I need no one pushing or dragging me. If your decision is final, then allow me to walk to the crate unmolested. Allow me to die with dignity."

The captain raised an eyebrow at the sudden change from frightened, ranting boy to brave, proud young man. He was impressed, but unrelenting. They all watched in surprised silence as she stepped to the box and climbed in.

Without a word, she curled herself up into the crate and lay, barely breathing. Her head rested on her knees, away from the men who moved near to nail the lid into place. She did not want them to see how quickly her brave exhibition had once again turned to cold dread.

"Captain, are you sure you want to do this?" came a voice from above her.

"Yes, I am sure, damnit! Nail it up!" His few brief words completely destroyed her last shred of hope.

"Yes, sir," came the brisk reply.

Within seconds the lid crashed down onto the crate. She hugged her knees as darkness once again surrounded her world. Each thud on the lid hammered through her as if striking her very being. Her knees grew wet from salty tears flowing freely but silently. She made no sound as the crate was lifted onto deck. Muffled, indistinct voices teased her ears. The entire crew had come to watch.

Attached to a heavy rope, the crate swung out over the side of the ship. Again she felt sick and dizzy as it swayed from side to side. The sound of angry, swirling waters filled her ears, then grew even louder. Faster—faster she dropped through the air! Her flesh crawled in panic. She clawed at the lid. It would not move. There was no escape for her now.

The crate splashed into the ocean, jolting her roughly. Frigid cold water licked at her feet. Her ankles vanished in bubbling green. And still the water came. She gulped for air and her hands clutched at the sides of the crate, willing the wood to surrender to her shaking. It held fast.

The water rose to her waist. She could feel death clutching at her—greedy, eager. A scream of terror rose in her throat. Suddenly the cold, salty water touched the open sores on her lashed back. The scream died on her lips. She clenched her teeth and squeezed her eyes closed. The pain was excruciating. The water rose higher. It passed her shoulders. She gasped and struggled for her last breath. It was up to her neck. "Oh, please let me die quickly," she prayed aloud. "It hurts so bad. I can't stand any more."

Pain and fear swept her along into semi-consciousness. Her arms went limp. She no longer struggled for air. Her mind whirled in past and present. Her head dipped to rest against the crate. It was over. She waited. . . .

Bright sunlight burned her eyes. She could not focus. She watched from a distance as her body was lifted from the crate with no volition of its own. She tried to walk, but found her feet only skimming the floor. Who was holding her, carrying her along? Where were they taking her? It seemed such a long way.

The bright sunlight suddenly disappeared and again she seemed to be plunged into semi-darkness. The hands gripping her tightly suddenly vanished. She swayed sluggishly under the weight of her own body. With great effort she forced herself from the languor engulfing her. Slowly her eyes focused and she found herself standing in a small room lined with books and charts. Her gaze wandered slowly about the cabin. Where was she? She was so confused. Nothing looked familiar. How had she gotten here?

Her clouded, bleary eyes continued their slow journey around the room. Suddenly her glance touched upon the cold, calculating face of Captain Michael Lancer. Her hand flew to her lips to stifle an unwilling cry. Harsh memory came flooding back as he regarded her insidiously. His tall, threatening bulk dwarfed her, as if the ocean had shrunk her before this giant of a man. She shivered from a cold, penetrating fear. Why had he spared her life? What did he want of her?

Reading the questions reflected in her wide, pensive eyes, he strolled casually about the room. Finally he spoke. "I have decided to let you live. My intent was to teach you a valuable lesson about the possible consequences of such rash actions on your part. Having accomplished that end, I will permit you to sail with us."

"Thank . . . thank you, sir," she stuttered.

"Oh, don't be so quick in thanking me, boy. The truth of the matter is you may wish I had let you die. You see, I fully intend to make you pay complete retribution for your actions. From this time on you are an indentured servant and you are going to work like you have never worked before. You will labor and toil for me the length of time I designate until your room, board and passage have been paid. You will be no better than a slave and will be treated as such. You will know the meaning of exhaustion and learn to sleep standing up. Oh yes, my boy, you may well not thank me for saving you."

She watched him through emerald eyes clouded with pain, fear, exhaustion. Come what may, she had not the strength or will to fight this giant of a man any longer. "I am no stranger to hard work, Captain," she answered, her voice almost a whisper. "I will work hard for you until my indenture has been paid. You will not regret your . . . generosity."

Misunderstanding her words, the captain stepped toward her threateningly. Was this boy being insolent?

Something about the pale face and shaking hands stopped him. Long lashes fluttered heavily up and down. For the first time he took a good look at his stowaway. The boy really was frail and battered looking, yet possessed an inner strength and dignity. He shook his head in confusion and backed off. There was something totally different and intriguing about this young lad, but he could not decide just what it was.

Fearful of the scowling face before her, Christy stepped back hesitantly. A loud knock on the door broke the heavy silence between them.

"Come in," bellowed the captain.

The girl stepped aside to avoid being hit by the swinging door, but she did not move quickly enough. It struck her back. A groan escaped her lips as she staggered across the room, clutching at a high backed chair to brace herself. The room spun and it took all her control to remain on her feet. Her green eyes dulled even more with pain, regarded the captain through a haze. He and the man who had entered the room stared at her in confusion and apprehension. More was wrong with this lad than a dunking in the sea.

"What's wrong with you, boy? What ails you? You look as if you're sick and ready to drop over. I may well regret my decision to let you back on board. It seems you can hardly stand, much less do a hard day's work."

She could only shake her head to dispute his words. Her voice would not come and she struggled to hold back the tears which threatened to spill down her cheeks. The pain from her back and the encroaching blackness threatened to claim her.

"Send for MacDonough," ordered the captain with renewed concern. "I want him to look this boy over before we let him near the other men. If he has the pox . . ." his voice trailed off at the heavy consequences of such a catastrophe.

At last she managed to find her voice. "No. I'm fine. I don't want anyone to touch me!"

Despite her efforts, she began to shake uncontrollably. Chills ran up and down her aching limbs, yet she felt so hot. It was the heavy overcoat laden with water and salt that caused her agony. She could hardly stand under its weight. If she could just sit down for a moment perhaps the pain would ease up.

"Are you already giving orders aboard my ship?" barked the captain in irritation, still concerned about a possible epidemic. "Do you forget so quickly that I am the captain, I give the orders, and what I say goes! Now, go get MacDonough," he ordered the man without taking his eyes from her.

The seaman in the doorway jumped at the sharp command yet made no attempt to obey; sensing a critical confrontation between the two would soon erupt.

Her mind warned of impending danger. She looked around the room for escape, or at least something with which to protect herself. Tired and sick as she was, she was determined to defend herself against whatever these men threatened. Her eye caught sight of a pistol lying partially covered under a stack of papers on the desk.

With a speed of one acting from sheer desperation, she darted across the room and grabbed the pistol. The man in the doorway cursed loudly as she leveled the gun at the captain. It felt cold, and so frightfully heavy in her trembling fingers. She grasped it with both hands in an effort to steady it. She hoped her total lack of experience did not show. She had never held a gun in her life!

"Captain, I told you that I do not want anyone to touch me. I assure you I carry no pox or contagious disease. I want only to be left in peace."

The effort in crossing the room had cost her dearly. What little strength she had left was quickly ebbing as she concentrated all her efforts on holding the gun up and trying to steady her trembling hands and voice.

"Put that gun down, you little fool!" yelled the captain, infuriated that such a small boy had been quicker and craftier than he, and now stood with unsteady hands holding his own gun at him. "You'll only hurt yourself with that thing. Besides," he took a chance, "it's not loaded." A wicked twinkle crept into his eyes.

Christy took a step back. "I don't want you to move, Captain. Or you either," she said, nodding at the man in the doorway. "You could be right about the gun not being loaded, Captain, yet I hardly believe that you would have it lying around for decorative purposes. Don't tempt me to try to prove my point," she threatened.

The captain grimaced. His little trick had not worked. "Pray, my boy. What is it you want then? Do you plan to hold that gun on me the whole way to Charleston?" he asked sarcastically.

"No, Captain. All I want from you is your word that none of your men will touch me. Do you understand? Promise me that you will not permit your men to lay a hand on me!" She was losing control quickly. Soon the pain and blackness would win. She had to get him to promise before she fainted. His word might not mean much, but it was all she could hope for.

The captain was dumbfounded. He had promised to let the boy live and work his passage to the Colonies. All he wanted was to have someone look at the lad and see what was ailing him. Why was it so important that he promise to keep his men away?

Still bewildered, he shook his head. "I promise to hold off my men. Does that make you happy?" he asked gruffly, not at all pleased at having to make a concession even as small as this one.

His words registered slowly in her mind. Somewhat satisfied she had done all she could to protect herself, and no longer able to support the weight of the gun in her hands, she lowered the weapon slowly. She felt the captain lunge at her and rip the gun from her grasp. She no longer cared. Her fate was now in his hands. There was little she could do but trust in his honor. With blessed relief, the blackness came to free her from the pain.

The captain watched, perplexed, as the disarmed youth tumbled to the deck. With quick reflexes he caught her before she struck the floor. Shaking his head in confusion, he gazed down at the lifeless form in his arms. Suddenly he sucked in his breath.

"My God!" he cried, aghast. In utter disbelief his eyes beheld long, silky black hair spilling out from under the confinements of the cap. He threw a bewildered glance at the man in the doorway, and both gazed down at the beautiful young girl he held in his arms.

Three

Christy lay between sleep and wakefulness. She was comfortably nestled in a bed with warm blankets piled high. Time had lost all meaning. She knew she'd better get up soon, lest her mother come in and gently chide her for sleeping so late. But she felt so warm and content. Just a few moments longer . . .

She wiggled further down on the bed. Timbers groaned. The ship lurched. Her eyes flew open and she sat bolt upright in bed. Searing pain shot down her back. Realization returned immediately and she sank back down onto the pillow until the stinging eased somewhat. She glanced quickly around.

The room was small but something about it had the look and feel of its masculine owner. A small heating stove was placed a few feet from the foot of the bed. A mahogany table sat in the middle of the floor while a rather large desk was placed against the wall. Papers and maps of all kinds were piled high with little semblance of order. A dressing stand with wash basin stood at the head of the bed and in front of it the only porthole in the cabin. A closet door hung open, giving her a glimpse of a few finely tailored suits and some heavy, bulky looking woolen garments. There was little doubt that this was the captain's cabin and with a start she realized she was lying in his bed.

Fear prickled her skin. She reached for the collar of her dingy shirt. A new wave of horror flushed through her body. She was stark naked except for a bandage covering her bruised back!

Who had undressed her and taken care of her wounds? Was it the captain? She shivered when she thought of those cold, calculating eyes raking her body and she cringed to imagine those huge hands touching her. Had he just tended to her wounds, or had he taken himself some pleasure? Christy hoped and prayed that even this cruel man would not stoop so low as to rape her as she lay unconscious. The more she pondered the matter, the greater her discomfort became at lying in his bed without benefit of even a robe to cover herself. Set upon remedying the situation, she eased herself out of bed and wrapped a sheet quickly about her, determined to find her clothes.

The porthole in the room was open slightly as she moved toward the closet, and she stopped to look out. The breeze whipped at her long, silky black hair and sent it cascading down her arms and past her waist. For a moment she forgot her peril and breathed deeply of the ocean air. It cleared her head slightly, as did the sight of the golden sun just rising on a horizon of endless green.

Her serenity did not last long, however. She was suddenly possessed by an uncanny sensation of eyes piercing through her. She spun about quickly and sucked in her breath. The captain, tall and rugged, stared smugly at her.

"I see you've finally come around. You've been unconscious for nearly three days now," he said as he watched the wind whip gently at her hair. "How do you feel, *Miss* Patterson?" He rather mockingly stressed her gender.

"Much better, thank you," she replied cautiously. "And yes, it is *Miss*. Miss Christina Patterson." She felt terribly weak and her back ached, but she had no intention of cowering before him.

"I'm glad to hear that. For a while I did not think you would pull through. Your fever was high and you thrashed about as if demons were upon you. It appeared you were reliving some dreadful experiences."

"What did I say?" she asked quickly.

"Nothing I could make much sense from," he said, but from the terror she had expressed in her delirium, he guessed her life must have been pure hell. "Why did you come aboard my ship and attempt to hide away? Did you really think you could survive the entire voyage without being detected?" he demanded.

Christy's shoulders drooped and she shifted her weight uneasily. She reached out and touched the wall for support, deliberately stalling for time. "I told you before, Captain. It was an accident. I never meant to come aboard, much less sail. I was hiding from someone . . ." her voice trailed off.

"Well, never mind, my dear. I can see you are quite determined to remain close-lipped on the matter. So, we'll save that little story for another time when you are rested and stronger and more of a sporting challenge," he answered, very sure of himself as he gazed up and down at her slender form. "That's quite a fetching sight you make, all wrapped up in my bed sheet. I'm sure you realize that standing in front of the light from the porthole makes your covering practically transparent," he commented with some amusement.

His remark took Christy by surprise. She blushed deeply and pulled the sheet more closely about her full, well-shaped breasts and tried to move toward the shadows of the room. The captain, however, was not so inclined and deliberately blocked her path.

"You needn't move on my account, my dear. As long as you occupy my room, the least you can do is make it somewhat worth the sacrifice." He laughed as she looked fearfully into his eyes. His intense gaze seemed to devour her very being.

"Where are my clothes?" she demanded with all the courage and dignity she could muster.

"Well, I'll tell you, my dear. They were in such despicable condition, I had them thrown overboard."

"Oh, no! What am I to wear?"

Her unmasked dismay brought a grin to his handsome face. "That sheet is fine for now," he said benevolently, yet his eyes were bright and lusty as he spoke. Christy noted his heightened color and again attempted to reach the shadows and some degree of modesty. "I suppose, however, that when you are up and feeling better you may need something a little more . . . discreet. Use one of the robes in the closet for now, however. I can't have my men getting all worked up and fighting over you, though I'm sure you would be well worth the effort. You

42

are very beautiful, you know. It rather wounded my masculine pride to discover I had such a lovely maiden on board my ship, right before my very eyes, and did not know it. I am sure the reason for it will make a fascinating story."

Christy's head began to swim and she leaned against the wall for support. His continued verbal harrassment was taking its toll on her.

The captain took note of her reluctance to answer. His curiosity was sorely aroused by this young woman, and he longed to know her secrets. But he could see she was distressed and in pain. He would have to be patient.

"Well, enough of this idle chatter for now," he said. "I want you in bed, where you belong."

"No. I'm fine, really," she lied, positioning herself so that the table stood between her and the captain. Her back ached, and she felt weak and dizzy, but she was determined to fight this man if he had evil intentions on his mind.

"I said, get into bed!" he boomed and in two strides was around the table and beside her.

She looked up, and up. And there went that twitching on his cheek. She peered stubbornly into his blazing brown eyes, desperately trying to suppress the fear which pulsed through her. "I don't want to get into your bed."

Captain Michael Lancer grabbed her by the shoulders until she winced from the pressure. "When I tell you something, I expect you to obey—immediately!" he bellowed.

His harsh reprimand set her knees to trembling violently. With a choked sob she slowly crumpled down the wall and would have fallen to the floor had he not caught her in his arms. Unceremoniously cradled in his grasp, she could do naught but squirm uncomfortably; feeling completely at his mercy. "You . . . you promised not to touch me. You promised," she whimpered against his chest. He only laughed at her, his gaze devouring a partially exposed round, white breast.

"If you recall, my love, I only promised to keep my men away from you. You made me promise no such thing for myself," he cleverly pointed out.

Christy's eyes widened incredulously as she realized the truth of what he said. "But . . . but I meant you as well," she stammered, trying to free herself from his arms.

"Ah, my dear. It seems that what you said and what you meant are two entirely different things. And besides, the situation is now somewhat changed. I promised a young boy, only to find he is actually a young wench. You appear weak and would be useless to me as a hand on deck. But—" he paused, looking down at the soft black tresses cascading over his arm and the wide, deep green eyes which regarded him with terror—"I am sure I can find another way for you to pay off your debts."

Christy's ears clearly caught his lustful intentions. She struggled again to be free of him, but he held her tightly in his arms, crushing her against his chest until she gasped for breath. Too weak to struggle further, she grew limp in his arms.

"With your great beauty, my men will have trouble keeping their hands off of you. It is a long, lonely trip to Charleston with a ship full of men. Why, it will be difficult enough to keep them at bay, much less myself. Am I to get no reward for giving up my cabin and keeping you safe from the hungry men aboard my ship?"

He paused, enjoying the feel of her soft, feather light body in his arms. "Actually, I am quite pleased with the turn of events. I have little need for another deck boy. On the other hand, a soft, beautiful wench to warm my bed suits my needs and desires far better. It will certainly be my pleasure helping you pay off your indenture, little Christina."

He walked to his bunk and slowly laid her down. "Unfortunately I shall have to appease myself just now with a little kiss, for even I am not cad enough to take you while you are in pain and not at your fighting best." He chuckled as he bent toward her, his breath hot and passionate upon her flushed face.

Enraged beyond speech by his declaration, Christy pummeled his chest with her fists and jerked her head to the side to avoid him. But her furious defiance did little to deter him. In one swift movement, his huge hand captured her tiny wrists and held them tightly. With his free hand he turned her face to his. Lips warm and hungry met hers in a savage kiss.

"Someday, my love, your back will be healed and I will take great pleasure sharing my bed with you and helping you pay off what you owe me," he prophesied. He released her hands and stood gazing down at her, enjoying her reaction.

A tear of anger trickled down Christy's silken white cheek. "I hate you! You'll never touch me. I will fight you with all my strength," she cried defiantly.

DEBORAH LEVARRE

He grabbed her again, easily pinning her arms to her sides. She struggled in vain against her strong warden. "And do you think your strength any match for mine, little one? Could you hold me off if my intent was set?" he mocked.

Christy ceased struggling, realizing it only made him angrier and was, in fact, totally useless. She was certainly no match for this tower of strength.

Abruptly he released her, yet his eyes continued to hold her captive. His gaze floated freely along her slender form and back up to her face. He had never seen eyes so vivid; so strikingly similar to the color of a raging, stormy sea. They fascinated him, as did the rest of her. Her subtle curves promised to be truly exquisite. This surely would be an unforgettable voyage.

Even after the door slammed behind him, Christy could still feel his piercing brown eyes boring into her very soul. She turned to the wall, her body shaking with sobs of fear and anger. How dare he treat her that way? She would never let him touch her—never—she vowed as she wiped the passionate kiss from her still warm lips. She fumed on at him, yet her anger did not last long. Exhausted from her suffering and ordeal with him, she finally fell into fitful slumber.

It was nearly dark when a light knock on the door roused her from her sleep. With trepidation she wondered if it was the captain back to humiliate and frighten her more. "Come in," she managed with all the authority she could muster.

As the door opened slowly, she peered over the blankets with dread. Instead of the captain, however, a

46

large man about fifty years old and on the heavy side walked into the room and stood hesitantly in the doorway. "You feeling better, lassie?" he asked shyly.

"Yes. Thank you," she answered, wondering who he was. His green eyes twinkled shyly and the blush on his cheeks only accentuated the fiery red of his hair and heavy beard. Surely there was little doubt about his Irish heritage.

"May I come in then, and speak to ye, if yer feeling up to it?" he asked politely; quite a different approach than his captain's earlier entrance.

"Yes, of course. You may come in," she answered. She still felt exhausted from her bruises and her bout with the captain, but this man seemed gentle and polite. It was indeed a contrast to her first visitor. On impulse she decided she was going to like this Irishman, and she could sure use a friend right now.

"Me name is Patrick, ma'am. Patrick MacDonough. I'm originally from Dublin, but now me home is Charleston, whenever we set ashore, that is."

"Hello, Mr. MacDonough. I'm pleased to meet you. My name is Christina Patterson."

"Oh, let's have none o' this 'Mr. MacDonough' stuff. Most people just call me Paddy," he corrected her.

"Very well, Paddy," she replied with a smile. Yes, she was going to like MacDonough. "Fair is fair. My mother used to call me 'Christy.' I'd be pleased if you'd call me the same."

"Very well, Miss Christy," answered Paddy with theatrical formality. He paused a moment. "You said your mother used to call you Christy. Have you outgrown it then, in her eyes?" he asked, trying to find out a little about this girl.

"No, she is dead," whispered Christy. "So is my papa."

"Oh, I'm so sorry, lassie," answered Paddy, admonishing himself for forgetting the captain had told him she was orphaned. She looked so young and defenseless to be without kin. But who then had whipped her so?

"I hope your back is feeling better," he began again after an awkward pause. There would be enough time later to find out more about her. "It was me that dressed your wounds," he blurted at last and scratched his stomach nervously.

Christy's face went scarlet, matching Paddy's, but he hurried on to cover their embarrassment. "I cleaned and dressed your cuts. Put some cream on yer back then. Should heal nicely in a week or two, with rest," he explained.

Christy's face felt red from embarrassment at the thought of this man undressing her, but after another look at Paddy, she decided since someone had to help her, she didn't mind it being this soft-spoken Irishman. At least it had not been the captain who had handled her unconscious body. The thought of him made her shudder again.

"How about a little hot soup? You are so frightfully thin and weak. I don't doubt it's been days since you ate last, so we'll start out with something easy," he prescribed.

"That would be fine, Paddy, although I have no

appetite," she admitted.

"Don't worry, lassie. It will come back in no time," he reassured her and disappeared from the room.

A short time later he returned carrying a huge bowl of soup. Very gently he propped her up in bed and watched her eat, slowly at first but with increasing gusto.

"I'll bring you something a little more substantial later; something that will stick to your ribs," he promised as she finished the last spoonful. "You just lie down now and sleep."

Christy could only nod in agreement as she sank down into the covers. The soup had warmed and relaxed her. She was totally drained and was asleep almost before Paddy shut the door and shuffled down the hall.

Three hours later a knock at the door woke Christy from her peaceful slumber. As promised, it was Paddy carrying a tray of steaming beef stew and biscuits.

"Did you sleep well, lassie?" he asked as he eased her up and put the tray on her lap.

"Yes, I did, Paddy," she answered, wiping the last bit of sleep from her pretty green eyes. "I feel much stronger already," she said proudly and turned her attention to the tray before her. "This stew smells delicious."

"I expect you to eat every morsel, too," Paddy ordered paternally. "'Tis the only way to get your strength back." He sat back to watch her eat.

Christy dug in with relish, finding she was really quite hungry. The soup had awakened her long inactive appetite and she had to force herself to eat slowly, enjoying every bite. A short time later she finished the last mouthful and, wiping her lips, she turned to compliment her host.

"The stew was very good. And see, I ate every bit. Did you make it yourself?" she asked.

"Heavens no, lassie. I'm no cook though I love to eat as you can see," he added, patting his large stomach contentedly. "I supervise the working of the starboard sails, help read the charts, and do a little doctoring now and then when needed," he expanded.

"Sounds impressive, Paddy. How long have you been sailing?"

"Well," he began, leaning back in his chair and stroking his beard thoughtfully. "I reckon nigh on thirty years now," he calculated. "Yeah, been that long. The sea is all I know. I tried to be a landlubber once, but the sea kept beckoning me, pulling at me heart strings. I just couldn't say no. So here I am and here I'll stay till the sea is done with me," he said as if quite content with his fate.

"Have you never been married or wanted a family?" asked Christy as he pulled out a corn cob pipe and began the tedious process of lighting it.

"I was married once, 'bout twenty years ago," he said between draws on his pipe. "Becky was her name. She was a fine woman, though terrified of the water. She wouldn't so much as set foot on a ship. Scared her into the vapors. But we were happy, Becky and me. I got me a job with a livery and had a little farm of my own. I missed the sea, but I loved me Becky too much to leave her alone." He had finally succeeded in lighting the pipe and puffed contentedly.

"What happened, Paddy? What made you decide to return to the sea?" she asked gently, and then quickly added, "I don't mean to pry, Paddy. It's none of my business."

"Oh I don't mind, Miss Christy. It's logical for you to ask. Becky, she died giving birth to our little girl. It was too hard on her. She was not a strong, healthy woman." He paused, tears filling his eyes. "Little Melinda, she died too a few days later. I found the cabin too big and lonely for myself after they died, so I returned to the only thing I really know—the sea."

"I'm so sorry, Paddy. You must have loved Becky very much to give up the sea for her," commented Christy sympathetically.

"Yes, I loved her dearly. I visit their graves when we dock at Charleston." He paused, remembering. "I guess me Melinda would be about your age now—'bout eighteen," he muttered half to himself as his pipe sent up tiny clouds of smoke above his red head.

"May I ask you a question?" he suddenly asked. It was his turn to find out a little something about this beautiful young girl who had been so badly abused.

"I suppose so, but I cannot guarantee you an answer," she responded warily. She had an idea of what his question would be and was not sure she could answer him honestly.

"Who whipped you so cruelly, child? Why would anyone do such a terrible thing?"

Despite her efforts, tears filled Christy's eyes and trickled slowly down her cheeks. "Paddy, you've been very kind to me. I really do appreciate it. But it's too painful a memory to me right now. I cannot put it into words just yet. I'm sorry," she sobbed and turned to face the wall.

Paddy jumped from his chair in concern at having distressed her so with his prodding. He handed her a rather soiled handkerchief which she gratefully accepted, blowing her nose and dabbing at her eyes. He said, "There, there, child. I understand. Must be terrible things to make you so upset. You needn't feel obligated to tell me. But," he added, "if you ever need to talk, remember, lassie, I've got a good, sympathetic ear."

Christy smiled up at him, grateful for his understanding.

"Now, little miss, you must be getting your rest. But would you mind terribly if I saw to them bandages of yours first?" he asked timidly.

"No, Paddy. Go right ahead," she replied and rolled over onto her stomach so he could remove the bandages and apply more cream.

He approached cautiously, feeling shy and uncomfortable. "'Tis already looking better than it did four days ago when you come aboard. We'll have you up and around in no time," he commented optimistically, and Christy marveled at how gently this large man rubbed in the soothing cream. It took the burn and sting from her bruises.

Just as he finished and was preparing to reapply the bandages, there came a sudden knock from outside. Without waiting for a response, the door burst open and in strolled the captain. "Excuse me," he had the decency to say, though obviously without sincerity.

Christy felt acutely aware of her exposed back and longed to snatch the blankets up from her hips. Her awkward position, however, prevented her from reaching down without exposing herself further. It was obvious the captain was quite aware of her dilemma yet deliberately stood across the room, openly admiring the roundness of one smooth, white breast pressing out at her side, her tiny waist and small, delicate hips. He also noted the horrible whip marks covering her slender back.

"Yes, sir?" coughed Paddy rather nervously.

The captain raised an arrogant eyebrow and then walked slowly to the closet. "The air is cool tonight. I have need for a sweater or something to warm me. Please forgive me for intruding into my own cabin."

He was gone as quickly as he had come, but the damage was done. Christy began to shiver, remembering his threats to bend her to his will. Paddy hurriedly finished applying her bandages, seeing her distress.

His doctoring complete, Paddy gently helped her roll over on her back and tucked the blankets around her shivering shoulders. "I'll be right back, lassie," he murmured and hustled out of the room. In a few minutes he returned with a large mug of piping hot tea. "You drink this down, Missy, and it will warm you and help you sleep." Christy began to protest, but he would hear none of it. "'Tis my special potion," he responded, answering the surprised look on her face as she tasted the brew. He'd put a drop or two of brandy in it to calm her down and help her sleep.

When she had finished, he took the cup from her and she nestled down to let the hot drink slowly warm her. It worked like a tonic and in a few minutes he had satisfied himself that her breathing was slow and regular and she was sleeping peacefully. Without a sound he slipped from the room.

Four

Christy awoke early and slid out of bed. She shivered as the chilly morning air turned her smooth skin into goose flesh. Wasting no time, she hurriedly pulled on the captain's robe which she kept lying at the foot of the bed. Despite the fact that it dragged on the ground and nearly drowned her in the extensive yards of wool, she felt warm and snug wrapped in its massive folds. The pleasant aroma of tobacco clung faintly to the fabric, serving as a constant reminder of just who owned the robe. Her only consolation was her certainty that no light could penetrate through the cloth and thus reveal her rather scantily clothed form.

She cheerily hummed a little tune as she splashed cold water on her face and finished washing. Paddy would be in shortly with her breakfast and to check her bandages. This had been the routine for four days now. He had taken absolute charge of her, from bringing her meals to tending her wounds. She was progressing very well under his careful eye and feeling like her old self again. With her renewed health and spirits, she felt she was ready to be up and around.

The captain had, for the most part, stayed away from

his cabin, only coming now and then for some article of clothing or a chart. When he did intrude into her little world where only he and Paddy ever entered, he was barely civil to her. She knew he hated her for having disturbed the life aboard his well-organized ship. She also knew he resented sleeping in a small bunk partitioned off for him in the crew's sleeping quarters.

A short time later she was sitting eating the breakfast of hot cereal and tea that Paddy had brought when the captain gave his usual sharp knock and barged in.

"Good morning, Miss Patterson," he said as he moved to a position directly across from her and stood contemplating his stowaway bundled in his robe. Even in its huge folds she looked beautiful with her long black hair falling loosely about her shoulders. The front of the robe bulged from her swelling breasts.

"Good morning, Captain," she answered, peeking up at him between spoonfulls of cereal, returning his close scrutiny.

She had to admit he was the handsomest man she had ever seen. His large frame stood proudly at well over six feet tall. His body was lean and hardened by the strenuous life at sea. His shoulders were broad, his stomach flat, and his legs long and muscular. He seemed to embody perfectly the descriptions of strong, rugged men who she had heard inhabited these wild and untamed lands across the sea.

His finely sculptured face was tanned from the wind and sun, and his noble chin was firmly set beneath a mouth which was stern yet revealed the slightest trace of softness. Christy's face grew warm remembering the feel of those lips upon hers. She knew he was a man not easily reckoned with, who took openly and with little effort what he wanted, regardless if it was given freely or not. She decided that meant women, too. She suspected he had many lady friends who he no doubt treated with careless abandon one minute, showering them with kindness the next, and always demanding their affections. He would want everything his own way, too. Now, contemplating this magnificent man over her cereal, Christy was sure he would be an impossible mate.

As if aware of her close scrutiny and her innermost thoughts, the captain finally spoke. "I'm sorry to disturb your breakfast, but I've need of some charts and calculations on my desk. There's a storm brewing and I must see if we can sail around it." He turned and began searching through the drawers of his desk.

Christy sat and watched his fruitless search, and mounting agitation. "Perhaps I can help, Captain," she volunteered, moving toward the cluttered desk. "I found a book of charts, bound in blue, kicked under the chair. It was filled with nautical terminology, maps, wind velocities and other similar information. I leafed through and found it very fascinating and informative," she said and picked it up from the corner of the desk he had neglected to search. "Is this what you are looking for?" she asked sweetly.

"Yes. Yes it is. Thank you," he mumbled.

As he took the book from her their hands touched. Christy felt something electrifying in the brief encounter. She pulled her hand away in haste, yet he had felt it too. He looked down at the gently swelling breasts partially visible between the folds of his dressing down. A loose black curl had made its home in the soft valley between her breasts. Seeing his gaze upon her, Christy blushed hotly and pulled the robe more snuggly about herself.

He raised an eyebrow at her modest reaction but ignored it for the moment. "I was not aware that you could read. I should have known you were educated from the manner in which you speak. It is not the speech of the lower classes."

"I was not always poor, Captain," she flared. "My papa knew the value of education and insisted I learn to read, write and calculate at an early age. I have always felt it was one of the most important things he did for me. I feel everyone should have had the opportunity to be educated, whether rich or poor. Don't you agree, Captain?" she asked boldly.

Again the captain raised an eyebrow. "Why, that is quite a profound and revolutionary statement coming from such a young woman," he responded in open astonishment.

Christy again took his words as an attempt to belittle her and continued her defense. "I have lived and learned much in my few short years, Captain. And may I remind you that just because I am young, and a woman, does not mean that I cannot think and feel and question."

The soft, proud tone of her voice impressed him even further. "Well, perhaps when you are feeling better and I have the time we can discuss the matter. There is much I have to learn about you, it seems. You are the most unorthodox stowaway I have ever encountered."

"Thank you, Captain. From you I consider that a compliment," she replied with dignity.

The captain paused thoughtfully as an idea suddenly struck him. After mulling it quickly over in his mind, he put his thoughts into words. "Perhaps you may be of some use to me after all. My books and accounts are in somewhat of a mess. Mayhap you can make some sense of them."

It was Christy's turn to raise a shapely eyebrow. Perhaps he was not such an ogre after all; perhaps she should give him another chance.

A knock on the door broke the moment and sent the captain hurrying off, but not before he turned, tipped his cap, smiled at her and wished her a good day.

Later, when Paddy came in to clean up her breakfast dishes, he found Christy full of energy and enthusiasm and couldn't help but comment on the fact. "You're looking bright and chipper this morning, Miss Christy. Did you sleep well?" he asked.

"Yes, thank you, Paddy. I did. And I feel so much better and stronger," she proclaimed and to prove her point walked spiritedly around the room, dragging the robe behind her.

Paddy was in good humor as usual, and their conversation was light and cheerful. At last, however, Christy broached a subject which had been on her mind for a few days. "Paddy, you've been so good to me, I hesitate in asking yet another favor of you. But I must admit I feel like a caged bird being stuck in this cabin all day and not being able to move. I dare not venture out in the captain's dressing gown. Isn't there anything aboard this ship that I could wear?"

"Well, miss," said Paddy, eyeing the petite form of the girl in front of him. "You're such a tiny, little bit of a thing—it's doubtful. But I'll see what I can do. Now you let me take a look at that back of yours and then we'll see about some clothes for you," he answered.

"Thank you, Paddy. You're too good to me." She moved to a chair and slowly slipped the robe off her shoulders. After close inspection, Paddy was very pleased with the progress of her bruises.

"I don't think you need these bandages anymore, lassie. Let the air finish healing them sores," he said as he gave her a little pat on the head. "I guess you won't be needing me to look out after you anymore once you're well and up and about." His tone held a detectable note of sadness.

"Oh, Paddy. You've been so wonderful to me. You won't stop coming to see me, will you?" she asked.

"Oh, now don't you worry, lassie. I'm just joking with you. Just let anyone try to keep me away from my little Christy." He winked merrily at her. "Now, let me scrounge around and see what kind of get-up I can find for you to wear. I'll be back as quick as I can," he promised and disappeared through the door.

True to his word, a short time later Paddy returned carrying a plain gray shirt with an even grayer, more worn pair of trousers to match.

"Lassie, I'm afraid all I could find was these work clothes the men wear on board ship," he said, holding up the nondescript outfit. "I had trouble too finding a get-up that might even come close to fitting you. Most of the men aboard are big gorillas like me who can pull their weight without a struggle." He paused as Christy reached out to take a better look at the worn clothing.

"They're clean, I guarantee you, though they've seen plenty of wear. I'm sure you won't have any use for them, but I thought I'd let you see I tried anyway," he apologized and started toward the door. "'Tis nothing suitable for a lady like you."

"Wait, Paddy," she called him back. "Let me try them on. Unsuitable as they are, at least they're better than nothing. I cannot make the entire voyage in Captain Lancer's robe. This way I'll look more like one of the men and be less conspicuous. Besides, I did come aboard disguised as a boy. I have an image to uphold," she laughed despite her disappointment, and took the shirt and pants from Paddy's unwilling grasp. "I'll try them on. Come back in a few minutes and you can see for yourself," she chirped with much more optimism than she actually felt.

Once he was gone her gay attitude quickly vanished. She looked in dismay at the dingy outfit. How desperately she longed to have a dress to wear. It seemed like ages since she truly felt and looked feminine. With a shrug of her shoulders, she decided she would just make the best of what Paddy had brought.

Crinkling up her button nose in slight repugnance, she slipped into the shirt and pants. As Paddy had feared, they were terribly big on her. The shirt nearly came to her knees; the sleeves fell past her fingers by inches. The trousers proved even more of a problem. They simply refused to stay up. She nearly tripped on the long hem as she searched for a rope to act as a make-shift belt. The sash from the captain's now discarded dressing gown had to suffice, and as she tugged a secure knot into place she heard a sound behind her.

"Oh, Paddy. I'm afraid your misgivings were well founded. These work clothes were made for a frame far larger than mine. I feel lost in them. What think you?" she asked laughingly as she held her arms high, eyes sparkling with mischief, and turned to display the outfit. The smile on her lips slowly faded and her arms fell to her sides as if weighted down. Instead of finding Paddy's jovial grin, she was confronted by the scowling face of the captain.

"Oh, Captain . . . I . . . I had thought it was Paddy who'd come in," she tried to explain but her voice trailed off. He looked upset and angry.

"That's quite obvious, Miss Patterson. You don't seem to object to his presence as you do to mine. Do you prefer older men then?" he said cuttingly; his tone was jealous and defiant as he glared at her.

She fumbled lamely with the low neckline of the shirt in an effort to camouflage her trembling fingers. What had upset him so? He'd been very amiable not two hours ago. Had she done or said something to disturb him? Unsure of him and of herself at this point, she knew not how to respond. "No . . . I mean, he has been very kind to me." Again her voice trailed off as his scowl deepened.

"Oh, is that to say that I have not been kind to you? Have I not kept my men away from you as promised? Have I not let you completely occupy my quarters, having to ask permission to enter as if I were the intruder? You came aboard this ship uninvited and I have given up my room for you and have had someone attend to your every whim and comfort. Besides that, you have done nothing to earn your keep or pay your debt as yet. And now you have the audacity to tell me Mr. MacDonough is kind?" His voice shook with anger.

Christy stepped back fearfully, at a total loss to comprehend his reasoning. Before she could tell him her accommodations had been entirely at his own discretion, he ranted on.

"Where did you get those clothes?" he bellowed.

She winced from the force of his question. "I don't know where Paddy got them," she muttered. "I needed something to wear other than your dressing gown, now that I am feeling better. I asked him to find me something suitable."

He moved to within inches of her. The twitch in his eye was very noticeable as he gazed down at her. Though the outfit was far too large for her, it signaled her desire to be up and about and out of his total control. With nothing to wear but his robe, she had been forced to remain virtually his prisoner; for his enjoyment alone. Now, unattractive as the clothing was, she would be free to come and go as she pleased. These thoughts only intensified his anger at himself and at her.

"If you want something aboard this ship you are to come to me. Do you hear me? I am the captain. Now take off those ridiculous clothes until you can find something that fits. As slight as you are though, I doubt you will have much luck. That being the case, you may have to remain here for the remainder of the voyage—with one minor change. You will be sharing the room with me for I tire of my present accommodations," he boomed at her.

Christy looked up into his angry brown eyes. Tears threatened to spill down her cheeks. His unfounded anger confused and frightened her and she took a shaky step backward to put some distance between them. Sensing her intent, he grabbed the collar of her shirt and tugged at it roughly. A lump of fear formed in her throat that he would rip it completely off her body. After another penetrating glare, however, he turned abruptly and left the room, slamming the door behind him.

Christy stared numbly at the closed door. She felt totally shaken from his unexplained anger, and the dammed tears she had held so bravely flowed unchecked down her pale cheeks. In hopeless defeat she turned her back to the door and sobbed softly.

"I just saw the captain in the hallway. He was in a foul temper. You'd better steer clear of him today, Miss Christy," came Paddy's words of warning interrupting her weeping a few moments later.

"Thank you, Paddy," she answered, trying to swallow her tears. She quickly wiped them away, hoping he would not notice her puffy, red eyes, but when she turned he saw her tear-stained face.

"What happened, lassie?" he exclaimed.

Ignoring his question, Christy clutched at his arm and pleaded desperately to him. "Please, Paddy. Please! Find me someplace to stay. Get me out of *his* room. I don't care if I must sleep in the hold. Just find me a place where I will be out of his sight."

"What has he said to you?" asked Paddy angrily.

"He's no right upsetting you so, lassie. I just don't understand. I've always had great respect for him, till now. He's so fair with his men and popular with the ladies. He's no right treating you so badly. I'll tell him so myself!" ranted Paddy

"No, Paddy. You mustn't say anything to him. He will only hate me more. I am the intruder. I don't belong here. Please, just find me a little room to stay in. I will be out of his way and everyone else's. Please, Paddy, promise me you will say nothing to him except that I am moving," she beseeched.

"I won't say nothing to him. I promise. Though it will be hard to hold my tongue," he admitted. "Now you calm down before you end up sick," he ordered paternally. "Here, look. I brought you a needle and thread to take in them clothes I brought you to fit a little better. Busy hands quiet disturbing thoughts, my mother always used to tell me—especially when she had some unpleasant chore for me to do." He chucked to himself, trying to perk her up. "Now dry those eyes, lassie. I can't bear to see a woman crying. Gets me plum riled up, it does."

"Thank you, Paddy. I do appreciate all your kindness to me. I don't know what I'd have done without your friendship," she said, quieting somewhat.

The corners of her mouth turned up slightly as he winked cheerfully at her. Satisfied that her tears were over, he headed off to find her another place to stay. He doubted the captain would be pleased, but he would rather risk his wrath than face her tears again.

For the rest of the day Christy worked diligently stitching the shirt and trousers to a more accommodating size. The sewing made the hours fly by, and when Paddy visited her later that evening he found her in improved spirits.

She stood for his inspection of her redesigned attire. "Well, Paddy, what do you think? Do they look any better now?" she asked as she pirouetted before him. The pants seemed to accentuate her tiny waist and round buttocks while the shirt clung just tightly enough to reveal the fullness of her breasts. Despite the manly attire there was no mistake the garments covered feminine curves.

"They look just fine, missy. Just fine. Though it's a shame you've got no dress to wear. Don't seem right, females in pants," he said.

"You're right. I never liked wearing pants either, even when I worked on my uncle's farm. But since I have no dress, these will simply have to do. Besides, the less conspicuous I am aboard this ship the better. The captain finds my presence distasteful enough. I wish to provoke him no further."

She paused. Her own mention of the dreaded captain again reminded her of the mission she had sent Paddy on. "Did you find me a place to stay?" she asked eagerly.

Her hopes were quickly deflated, however, by the regretful look which flickered across his face. "Well, Miss Christy . . ." he began slowly, unwilling to look her in the eye. "I looked everywhere and just couldn't find nothing suitable for a lady," he explained apologetically.

Despite her sinking hopes she had to laugh at his liberal use of the word "lady." "Oh, Paddy, you're so sweet. No one would believe I was a *lady* in these clothes," she chuckled.

"I'll hear none of that now," scolded Paddy. "I know you enough to see that you are very much a lady despite the manly clothes. It's what's inside that counts, not outside. But don't you fret, now. We'll work something out about your room," he promised.

Christy had the distinct feeling he had dismissed the idea already. She, however, was not so willing to give up. "Is there no place at all I can go, Paddy? Surely on a ship the size of this one a small nook or cranny could be found," she persisted.

"Well, there is a small storage closet full of junk just down the hall. But it would never do, Miss Christy," he said, hoping to squelch any hopes she might have.

Christy, however, could sense a small glimmer of weakness in his resolve and pursued her determined assault. "Show me this storage closet, Paddy. Let me be the judge of its fitness. No matter how bad it is, at least it will be a place to sleep so that the captain can have his room back. You don't realize just how important this is to me," she coaxed unremittingly.

"Oh all right, lassie. I know when I'm beat. But you're not going to like it," he condescended at last, seeing she was determined to be out of the captain's quarters.

He heaved a heavy breath and led her slowly down a long dark corridor, stopping in front of a rickety wooden door. "Here 'tis, Miss Christy, but as I told you it's not much."

Christy gently pushed open the door and held the lamp high to peer inside. The closet Paddy now presented her with was just that, and no more. It was large enough to walk into, large enough to put a cot, but no larger. Dark and very dirty, it was filled with various discarded items of all sizes, shapes and in sundry forms of decay.

"This will be fine," she said with more enthusiasm than she felt. "A little scrubbing and no one will know it. I'll get to work on it tomorrow." Without giving him a chance to argue or dissuade her resolve, she turned and headed back to the captain's room for what she hoped would be her last night there.

Paddy shook his head as he watched her retreating figure. He never claimed to understand women, but this one had him completely baffled. She was as stubborn as any man, yet as beautiful and gentle as any woman could be. She certainly was a mystery to him. With a sigh of defeat, he hurried away to finish his evening chores.

Five

Christy's nails cut her palms as she clenched her hands into tight fists. Choking sobs rose in her throat to strangle her. Every nerve was tense to the point of breaking. Again the searing pain ripped her tender flesh and threatened to tear her asunder. Chilling, fury-crazed laughter pierced her ears as the whip hissed through the air. She steeled herself against the next blow. It landed with lethal precision on her bleeding back. "Please, Henry. Please . . . stop! Stop!" But again came another punishing blow.

In desperation she tapped some deep reservoir of strength and spun to confront him. A horrified gasp escaped her lips. She blinked in utter disbelief at the incredulous vision. Her fat, drunken uncle was gone. But there in his place loomed a monster, face twisted grotesquely in hate, and eyes, black as coals, boring into her very soul!

Terror such as she had never experienced clutched her. "No! No!" she cried, but the creature only grinned hatefully. He raised the whip clutched in his massive hand. Tears stung her cheeks. "Stop! Stop!" But she knew it was useless. Hate radiated from the beast. Death!

She could see it, smell it, feel it closing in. Her eyes burned at the sight of him and she spun away from him. "No! No! No!" she cried, pounding her fist against the wall.

"No! Stop! No!" The words rang out loudly. Pain throbbed in her hand. In the midst of her cries her eyes flew open. She gazed at her hand, raised to strike. She blinked repeatedly and spun about. Still quivering, a final tear trickled down her cheek as she fell back wearily onto the pillow.

The terrible nightmare was always the same—leaving her frightened and tense. Her initial recollection of it was during those first few days aboard the ship as she fought the forces of her fever. But as she recovered, the dream had not vanished. Instead it grew more frightening with each passing night until she feared sleep itself. Relentlessly Slate came after her with the whip in his hand and cornered her in a small, dirty room. In pain and fright she would turn to face him, only to see his place taken by a looming monster grasping the whip in maniacal glee, consumed by hate and anger and the promise of revenge. It was terrible, and what made it even more terrible was that it had a marked resemblance to Captain Michael Lancer. No small wonder the nightmare served to nuture her fear of him.

In a desperate attempt to dispel the disturbing thoughts of her nightmare, she rose, still shaken, and washed the tears from her face. She dressed quickly in her shirt and trousers for the room was cold and her spirits exceptionally low this morning.

When Paddy greeted her with the usual steaming hot

breakfast, he did not fail to notice the rather pale and haggard appearance of his charge.

"It's nothing, Paddy. I guess I'm too eager to get started on my room," she hedged, trying to make little of her appearance.

Paddy's comments broke her reverie and she listened attentively.

"I talked to the captain, Miss Christy. He was none too happy about your moving. Especially since you said nothing to him about it. But he was busy and didn't protest too much. I just can't figure him out." He pulled on his heavy beard in bewilderment.

"Well, I'll be out of his way now and he can move back into his room. I don't blame him for wanting it. Perhaps we can both be happier now."

Finishing her tea in one swallow, she forced herself to think positively. "All right, Paddy. I'm ready. Just find me a bucket and mop."

"You don't plan on cleaning out that closet yourself, lassie!"

"Why, I certainly do. Why shouldn't I?"

"The captain said he'd assign someone. You shouldn't be doing heavy work like that."

"Oh, dear sweet Paddy. I have labored far harder in the past than cleaning out a closet. It is no trouble at all."

Paddy could see there was little point in arguing. "Lassie, for as little as you are you sure have a mind of your own and I'd be afraid to cross you. I'll find you a bucket and mop," he laughed, though half-heartedly.

Christy ignored his hint of playful criticism. "Good. I'll meet you there," she said with finality and started off down the hall. Paddy shook his head and followed after her.

Christy worked all day cleaning and scrubbing the little closet. It was quite a job, being filled with dirty, discarded items. By nightfall she felt exhausted and dirty, and her back ached. But as she surveyed her efforts, she felt a sense of accomplishment and contentment. The make-shift room would suffice until they reached Charleston, and the captain could return to his cabin.

She was arranging the blankets on the floor which would serve as her bed until a cot could be found when she sensed someone's presence behind her. Forcing her limbs to respond with unhurried movements, she rose and turned. "Good evening, Captain," she said with forced politeness.

"Good evening, Miss Patterson," he replied with gravity to match hers. "I see you've done a thorough job in here. I would not recognize it as the same place. Had you waited, however, I would have enlisted one of my men to help you. As usual you seem to take much upon yourself."

Christy sensed that his tone was forced, but as yet not threatening. She also noted the unmasked intensity with which his eyes took in every detail of her frame, so well outlined in the remade shirt and trousers. Self-consciously she brushed aside the stray strands of velvety black hair which hung about her face and neck.

"I didn't want to trouble anyone, Captain. I saw no need to take your men from their work. It's nearly finished now, and you can return once again to your cabin." He made no reply, continuing to stand in stony silence. Feeling some word of gratitude was due, she proceeded. "Thank you for letting me stay there. It was very kind of you."

"Yes, it certainly was kind of me," he agreed in mock gravity as he nodded absently, surveying the tiny room once again. At length his gaze rested on the make-shift bed of blankets on the floor. "Is that to be your bed? Have we no extra cots?"

"Paddy was busy today and I did not want to trouble him. I am sure he can find one for me tomorrow." The captain's lack of response puzzled her. He just stared at her with cold, penetrating eyes. "It will be fine, Captain. I've slept in worse places than this."

Hearing it spoken, Christy blushed at how it must have sounded to the captain. He must think her a real trollop. She hurried on to correct her mistake. "I mean, when I was staying with my uncle I slept in the shed with the cow."

Had she really said that? She stuttered on, blushing wildly. Why did this man make her feel like a bumbling child? "What I mean to say was, there wasn't much room in the house, so I slept in the shed . . ." her voice trailed off. Why should this man care about where she'd slept? She chastised herself for being such a fool.

"My dear, you needn't explain to me your past sleeping arrangements. It is your present one which concerns me." A slightly mocking smile flickered across his face.

"Oh, this will be just fine, as I said before." She backed away nervously.

"No woman has ever slept on the floor aboard my ship.

Most of them slept in my cabin, and enjoyed it I might add," he boasted, smiling rather devilishly. He lifted his hand and stroked her cheek, looking very sure of himself.

Her eyes narrowed in agitation, unimpressed by his egotistical gloating and she pushed his hand from her face. Undaunted by her gesture of rejection, he went on. "Since you deem myself and my room unpleasant and unworthy, and wish your own accommodations, you force me into finding you a cot. I will have no woman on my ship, invited or not, sleeping on the floor. My reputation as a gentleman would be ruined."

Christy suppressed her strong desire to laugh at his inflated self-esteem. Thus far his behavior had been anything but gentlemanly. But, prudence warned her to keep silent.

When she made no response, he continued. "I'll see what I can come up with. If I am unable to find anything by the time you retire, you will have to spend another night in my cabin." A protest sprang to her lips but he silenced her with his raised hand. "There will be no discussion, madam. If a cot is not secured you will sleep in my cabin until one is found, or made. But don't look so glum, darling. Most women would jump at the chance to stay in my bed," he added.

"Captain, may I remind you that I do not typify most women," she replied with cool dignity. "And at the risk of being overly bold, it is my opinion that you, sir, are a conceited braggart."

The captain turned from the doorway to regard her but kept his cool stance, choosing to ignore her cutting insult. "You definitely are unlike most of your gender," he agreed. "My problem remains, however, to determine just exactly what kind of a woman you are." His tone was derisive and sarcastic as he stood in the doorway, openly devouring her with his eyes.

How quickly he had again turned the tables on her, thought Christy. His heated perusal made her feel as if she stood naked before him. "Do I pass inspection?" she flared in angry indignation under his scrutiny.

Christy could almost feel his pulses racing as he pressed her lightly against him. Fire burned in his intense brown eyes and his grip tightened perceptibly. She began to squirm nervously. To her dismay, however, he did not let her go just yet.

"It seems I am forever coming to your rescue, my lady. I have dried those green eyes, and wiped the dirt from that smooth, soft cheek. I saved you from whatever fiend took pleasure in letting the lash fall upon you. I rescued you from being eaten by sharks, for much a pity that would have been. And I have saved you from the eager eyes of my crew, though you wish to display yourself to all now," he accused, motioning to her new accommodations. "Yes, my little dove, you owe me much, aside from your passage and board, and I grow frightfully tired of waiting for your payment."

Christy writhed in fury at his words, but his iron grip held her firmly. "I owe you nothing, Captain. I told you I never meant to come aboard your ship," she spat at him. "But as is rightful, I give you my word that I will not renege on compensating you for my passage, but not in the manner you deem appropriate," she fumed. "And as far as your saving me from the sharks, if you recall it was you who would have fed me to them. Given the choice, I believe their teeth would cause far less pain than yours, my lord!"

The captain raised an eyebrow at her heated outburst. "I had not realized my teeth so sharp, love, but perhaps we should put it to the test, aye?"

Infuriated by his mocking, Christy threw her arm up to strike him. Before she could land the blow, however, her arm was seized and pinned roughly behind her back. A hot retort sprang to her lips but she found her protestations abruptly silenced with his fiery, passionate kiss.

Stunned, she could not summon the strength to fend him off. Her paralysis, however, did not last for long. As his lips burned hers with their fire, she swung her boot fiercely into his shin. But being an experienced fighter, he sensed her assault and quickly sidestepped the blow. His grip tightened on her arms and, undaunted by her retalliation, his lips again covered hers, nearly singeing them in his ardor.

A fist pounding steadily into his chest did little to deter his onslaught and, in fact, only seemed to incite his appetite for more. To stay her attack, he lifted her from the ground and crushed her to him, squeezing the very breath from her struggling body. His advances grew bolder. An insistent hand tested the soft roundness of her buttocks.

"No! No!" she choked, knowing the fight was useless. She was utterly helpless and completely at his mercy!

"Excuse me, Captain. I must speak to you," a voice called from outside the door. "Are you in there, sir?"

The door shook from the heavy pounding and at last penetrated the captain's consuming advances.

He released her abruptly and took a step back. His breath came in short, rasping gulps and with great effort he forced himself to gain control. "I'm coming, damnit, man. Hold your peace!" he bellowed to silence the intruder.

Regaining his composure at last, he addressed Christy. "Some day, my love, duty will not call me away, and you will be mine. Then, without interruption, I shall take what is mine by right. For now I must be about the business of sailing this ship." With a brief nod in her direction, he turned and stalked through the door, slamming it as he went.

"I'll sleep where I want to," pouted Christy bravely from behind the closed door. "He treats me like a child, or his pet dog!" She stamped her foot in defiance, then laughed at herself. Now she really was acting like a child. Although she loathed and feared the captain, it was hard to overlook his handsome face and tall, lean, muscular body, especially when he held her so close. Her own blood began to race in a new yet exciting manner when his lips met hers in fiery passion. But, she reminded herself, she hated and loathed him and would fight him with all her strength. She would not succumb to his passion or her own. She did not want him. He was a cruel and wretched man interested only in his own pleasures.

Her anger cooled somewhat and she focused her attention on finishing her room. It took her mind from the maddening yet confusing drama with *The Merrimer*'s domineering captain.

The hours passed swiftly, yet as time drew on Christy feared the worst. Her patience was rewarded at last, however, when Paddy and two men appeared at the door, a small cot held between them.

"Oh, Paddy, you found a bed for me. You'll never know how happy you've made me!" she cried in unmasked delight.

"I had a bit o' trouble finding it, but this one finally turned up," he replied with a twinkle in his eyes. "You done a right remarkable job in here, lassie," he complimented as he glanced around the now spotless room.

"Oh, Paddy. Thank you. I am rather pleased myself," she admitted, her infectious smile lighting up the room.

The fact did not go unnoticed by the two men carrying the cot. Few had really gotten a good look at the girl since she'd come aboard, but it was rumored that she was indeed a beauty. Now, standing in the glow of a candle, with her dark hair spilling loosely out of its captive bun, eyes sparkling, lips red and full, she was enough to quicken the pace of any man's blood.

Christy, unaware of their lustful stares, chatted happily with Paddy. "I hope this is not one of the crew's cots."

"No, lassie, 'twas an extra one, hid away, to be sure," he smiled at her. "You seem to be happier about it than the captain. He wasn't so pleased when I showed him the cot, though it means he'll be back in his own cabin. 'Tis strange indeed he's been acting lately."

A small frown crossed Christy's brow, but was quickly replaced by a smile. The captain would again have to be satisfied with an empty bed. Such a shame!

Paddy's glance fell on the two men who had put the cot in place and were now openly regarding Christy. He didn't care for the way they looked at his little lassie. Perhaps she'd be safer in the captain's room after all. He must speak to the captain about getting a guard for her.

He dismissed the two men curtly and then turned to go himself. "I know you must be tuckered out from all the work you done today. You sleep well now. And, lassie, do me a favor and latch the door when I leave. I put a lock on it last night for you. Some of the men may not know, or forget, this is no longer a storage area. Don't want anyone accidentally walking in on you."

Christy gave him a grateful smile and closed the door. He listened outside, however, waiting for her to latch it. No need alarming her about the real reason he wanted her to keep the door locked.

Christy was tired from her strenuous day's work and her bruises were not a little irritated by the activity. When at last she sank into bed, she immediately fell into a deep, exhausted sleep. But as usual, her dream returned and she awoke, hot and frightened, pounding her fist into the pillow. It seemed it would take more than being free from Henry Slate and out of the captain's way to free her from her tormented nightmare.

Early the next morning she got up and dressed in her shirt and trousers. It was nice knowing she was in her own room and did not have to worry about the captain barging in.

Paddy brought her breakfast, as usual, and presented her with a small piece of mirror. She accepted it gratefully, and afer he had left she turned to regard herself in the glass.

It had been a long time since she'd seen herself. Her uncle had broken every mirror in the house in one of his drunken rages, accusing her of being nothing more than a conceited slut. Now she gazed at her long black hair, in complete disarray, and at her pale, thin cheeks. She had changed remarkably from the carefree little girl when her parents lived, to a thin, pale woman. She was not displeased with what she saw, but regarded herself passively and with little vanity.

With renewed determination to gain back some small bit of femininity, she brushed her long tresses until they shone. Then she pulled her glossy hair high on her head with mischievous curls falling here and there in utter defiance. She pinched her cheeks for color and regarded her image again. That's better, she decided.

It was in this greatly improved frame of mind the captain found her as he knocked a short time later. "I trust you are happy with your new accommodations," he said as he studied her closely. She looked more lovely than he remembered.

"Yes, Captain. It's fine," she replied. This morning she felt strong and ready to match his strength if the need arose. She met his intense stare with her own. After a moment he went through the door and returned with a small chair and table.

"I thought you might find use for these."

"Why, thank you, Captain. How kind of you," she replied, taken aback by this small display of generosity.

"Actually they were collecting dust in the hold and

getting in the way. You may as well use them."

Christy's grateful smile faded. Did he have to ruin his thoughtfulness by making it appear as if he was simply getting rid of old, useless furniture? She was grateful, however, and vowed not to let him anger her. Not today.

Seeing the determined set to her jaw, he sat himself down in the chair and studied her closely. After some time, he spoke. "Have you any plans as to what you will do when we reach Charleston?" he asked abruptly.

Christy was never prepared for his questions. She eyed him warily. She had given it much thought, but knowing little about this new land she could only surmise what it would be like. She often chided herself for not taking more of an interest in what her father had said about the Colonies. "I have given the matter some thought, Captain. I am hoping, perhaps, to acquire a position as a governess or teacher," she answered hesitantly. "I can repay you for my passage a little at a time."

"And where do you plan on finding such a position? Have you any credentials to offer? Any references?" he questioned, knowing very well she had no such documentation.

"No. I have no real experience. But," she hurried on, "I'm sure I could teach, or perhaps be an assistant."

"My dear, it is shameful how little you know about the place we are headed. It is very difficult for anyone to get a job, much less a woman. There are few families who can afford the luxury of a governess. And if you happened to find a wealthy family, it is unlikely they would hire someone like yourself with no credentials, no references, not even a dress to your name. As for teaching in a school, there are few such institutions, and they are run strictly by men. I suggest you direct your thinking to some other field altogether." The ridicule in his voice cut like a knife.

A lone tear trickled down her cheek but she angrily brushed it away. She would fight for her own integrity against this man who was so determined to defeat her.

"Then, Captain, if I cannot occupy a position in education I will hire myself out as a scrub woman or work in the fields. I have a *great deal* of experience along those lines and I am not afraid of hard work. I *will* find something! You needn't trouble yourself with me after we arrive. I can take care of myself. I will pay you for my debts as soon as possible. You have my word on that!" she said defiantly, with more courage than she actually felt.

"Your sense of responsibility is commendable, madam, yet your naivety is appalling. Find a job and take care of yourself? Both are doubtful. Alone and unprotected, with your great charm and beauty, you wouldn't get past the flesh peddlers waiting at the docks. You'd better make more positive arrangements or you may find yourself walking the streets looking for clients. In which case, I might add, I have no desire to gain my compensation by your roving from man to man."

"And just what would you suggest I do, oh mighty liege lord?" choked Christy, filled with anger at him and at herself for playing into his hands.

Taking advantage of her stunned silence, the captain graced her with a response to her question. "Of course, my dear," he said, lifting her chin with his hand so that she was forced to look him in the eyes, "you could always move in with me. I would take good care of you. You would be a welcome companion and you would find it a much more pleasurable way of repaying your indenture than working your fingers raw."

Christy reached up and slapped his face as hard as she could. "Oh, you despicable wretch!" she seethed at him, nearly blinded with fury at his suggestion. She reached up to strike again but found her hand imprisoned in a deadly grip. Undaunted, she raged on. "I will never be your mistress! You'll spend all eternity alone in a cold bed if you wait for me to sprawl beside you. I don't need you or your clear-cut, simple solutions. I'd take my chances with the peddlers before I'd ever submit to your lecherous pawing," she declared as she vainly tried to free her hand from his grip. "I promise you you'll get your blood money, but that's all—nothing more!"

Furious that she had struck him, both with her hand and with her words, the captain gripped her shoulders and shook her roughly. But anger only intensified her beauty. In a mixture of rage and passion, he desperately wanted to throw her on the bed and himself on top of her, and thus teach her who was master here. His conscience would not permit him that luxury, but at least she would not have the last word.

"Very well, my dear. The flesh peddlers can have you. I offer you a good, comfortable life with me, and ask little in return. I see now how disdainful the idea is to you. It seems you prefer the life of a slut," he snapped and abruptly released her as if she were scalding to the touch.

Christy, however, did not see it the same way. "You

offer me nothing more than the life of a kept whore!" she screamed back at him, still burning with anger.

"Call it what you will. It is better than what awaits you. You are a little fool!"

"Better a fool with dignity than a whore with nothing but disgrace," she flung after him.

He regarded her angrily. Did she have any idea just how close she was to being raped? Only sheer will and determination kept him from taking her. The door slammed behind him as he marched from the room, no longer trusting his rage, or his mounting desires.

Alone again and with the echo of his receding footsteps, Christy slumped in the corner and cried. He was a monster; a man with no feeling or warmth. But despite her mental tirade against him, she was forced to admit that all he had said was true. What chance did a lone, penniless woman have in a strange, barbarian new world?

Six

A few days passed and Christy remained busy making her room as comfortable as possible. Though these activities kept her busy, they did little to dispel her doubts. She had not seen the captain, nor had he come to her room. She thought often of him and what he had said, and worried constantly about what would happen to her when they reached Charleston. Paddy had said she needn't worry, he would help her find a place to stay, but as much as she liked and respected Paddy, she doubted he could be of much assistance to her. She was sitting in such a reverie of doubt and uncertainty, with the shirt she was stitching crumpled and forgotten on her lap, when a knock on the door brought her back to the real world.

"Look what I have here for you, lassie," Paddy said, smiling as he held out cloth of bright green.

Christy stood looking at it in amazement. "Where did you get this, Paddy? It's beautiful!"

"The captain went rummaging through all the boxes of fabrics and finally pulled this piece out. He told me to give it to you to make yourself a dress. He said it would go nice with your eyes."

Christy's expression was thoughtful. Why the sudden

change in heart? Had the captain felt guilty for his rude behavior to her?

Christy's first impulse was to send Paddy back with the fabric and tell the captain she wanted no gifts from him. But she looked longingly at the cloth and imagined how wonderful it would feel to have a dress again and look like a woman. And the cloth was so beautiful! She just couldn't send it back to him. She would find some way to repay him when she got a job. But for now she would have to swallow her pride and accept the token of good will.

"Oh, it really is beautiful," she said again as she held the cloth up against herself. "How do you think it will look on me?" she pivoted with the cloth draped around herself like a child with a new toy.

"The captain was right, missy. It sure will look nice on you and match those green eyes of yours. He's not such a bad man after all, lassie. Just a little moody and hard to understand at times."

Christy could only agree with the latter. He certainly was moody and hard to understand. But right now he was her knight in shining armor for he had sent her a bit of salvation. "I'll get started on it right away. I know just the type of dress I want," she said with genuine enthusiasm.

"Well then I'll be going so I won't be in your way." He turned again and looked at her beaming face. She should be a grand, rich lady with servants and maids to wait upon her instead of being poor and having to beg for every little thing. 'Twas not fair; not fair at all. He smiled at her again and softly closed the door behind him.

Christy was glad to have such a pleasant task and

worked on her dress all day. The next morning when she awoke the weather had turned cold and the sea was terribly rough. Paddy said they were heading into a storm and everyone was busy lashing things down, checking sails, and making everything as safe as possible.

Christy worked again on her dress, but the rough seas, rocking ship and whistling winds made her task difficult. By late afternoon there was no doubt that they would be heading directly into the storm, hitting the worst of it very soon.

The prospect of such a violent tempest caused Christy much anxiety. Even as a little girl she had run with fright into the arms of her mother, seeking protection from the lightning and thunder that seemed to strike her very being. Now, surrounded by an angry mass of frothing fury, there was nowhere to hide and no one to comfort or protect her.

She paced the floor uneasily, wringing her hands in despair. When Paddy came to collect her dinner tray a short while later, he found it untouched.

"Why, lassie, you've not touched a bit. What's the trouble?"

"Oh, I just wasn't very hungry, Paddy," she lied.

"You've got to eat or you'll not fit into that pretty dress you're making. Have you tired of working on it already?" he asked in concern.

"Oh no. I enjoy the sewing. It's difficult, though, to use a needle with the ship bouncing so. I pricked myself more times than I cared to, so I decided I'd better put it away till the storm passes." Her face was white and she wrung her hands again despite her efforts to appear brave. Paddy turned to go when her faint, childlike voice stopped him. "Will it be a very bad storm, Paddy?"

"I'm afraid so, lassie. Looks black out and the winds are frightful. But," he went on, seeing the fear in her eyes, "don't you worry none. We've weathered many a storm. This is a good, sturdy ship. We'll make it through with no problems a-tall," he comforted, hoping his words sounded more confident than he felt.

Not wanting to lie, and anxious to avoid any more of her frightened questions, Paddy made a hasty excuse. "I've got to be off now. There are many things need done to batten down the ship. Will you be needing anything else now, lassie?"

"No. I'll be fine." She gave him a smile and he rather hastily departed, looking guilty but relieved.

"I'll be just fine," she said again to herself as the ship tossed and rolled in the murky darkness. She sat down on the bed but was up and pacing again in seconds. Time seemed to stop as the storm grew more and more intense. She didn't want to be alone in this little room. Terror was rapidly taking hold of her. She must fight it. If she kept busy it might take her mind off the anguish of the storm.

Determined to be of use somewhere, she opened the door of her room and peered out into the dark hallway. The ship pitched back and forth dizzily; she found her way with difficulty to the captain's room. It was dark and empty. The ship suddenly leaned precariously to one side, groaning in protest at the storm's abuse. A scream escaped Christy's lips and she was knocked into the wall.

Without further hesitation, she set off down the dark hallway. She was brutally jostled back and forth against the walls, but little else mattered to her now except finding someone—anyone.

Reckless with terror, she pushed ahead despite the rocking ship, not knowing where she was going but unable to stop. She was totally unfamiliar with the ship except for the captain's cabin, her own room, and the hold. Both the captain and Paddy had warned her that walking about alone might be courting trouble, so she had remained in her little cell. Paddy had installed another latch on her door with strict instructions that it was to be kept locked at all times. She had smiled at his unwarranted concern, but obeyed his request. Now alone in the dark, tossing hallway, she regretted her lack of knowledge or direction of the ship's layout.

She turned the corner and was confronted by a short rampway which led to another dark hallway, and a closed door. Not wanting to go down into the darkness, Christy pushed the door gently, but it would not budge. A sudden gusty draft swept through the passageway, carrying loud, strained voices. The sound was music to her ears. Without hesitation she threw her weight against the heavy door. There were men on the other side.

She heaved again. Suddenly the door burst open and she was flung through it. Just as suddenly the door slammed shut, leaving her trembling on the open deck as rain and wind whipped mercilessly about her. A sob rose in her throat at her folly. Her thin shirt whipped around her shivering body as rain pelted against her face. Violent gusts of wind threatened to knock her to her knees.

With slow, painful efforts, she forced herself to turn and lunged for the door. Her hands clutched the knob in a death-grip. She yanked with all her might. The door remained immovable. She yanked again. It would not budge! Horror rattled in her throat. She was trapped! Her meager strength was no match for the ravaging wind. It held the door shut like a giant vice.

She stood clutching the railing with both hands. Through squinted eyes she looked through the rain and howling wind, hoping to catch sight of one of the crewmen. If someone was there, however, she could not see him through the gale.

"Help! Help!" she called out, but the wind tossed her cries back into her face.

Her grip on the rail began to slip as rain seeped between her icy fingers. Tears mixed with rain as the wind caught her breath and whipped it from her. How much longer could she hold on? "Please . . . please . . . someone help me!" she sobbed aloud as the wind knocked her down on one knee.

With new determination, she struggled to her feet. She shut her eyes and whispered a silent prayer. Her life was hanging on a single thread. Slowly, ever so slowly, she eased her way to the railing end. Swallowing the lump in her throat, she reached out and gripped the doorknob with one hand. Rain made visibility nearly impossible. It was strictly guesswork and luck that helped her reach her target.

Both hands were wet and cold as ice. But now came the crucial test. Inch by painstaking inch she slid the hand on the railing as close to the door as possible. Gently, ever so gently, she pried her fingers loose from the railing. At the last second she released the railing and lunged for the doorknob. A thankful sob rose in her throat as she felt the metal against her palm. She clutched the knob with two trembling hands.

She paused a moment, trying to gather her strength and brace herself against the wind and rain. Ready at last, she gripped the door tightly and pulled with all her strength.

At that precise moment the door came flying open. Unprepared for the sudden thrust, she lost her balance and slipped on the rain-soaked planking. The ranting wind caught her unbraced body, sweeping her headlong across the deck and toward the raging, angry sea.

"My God!" cried the captain as he watched the small gray form skid across the ship about to be swallowed by the sea. His heart in his throat, he dove after her with lightning speed. Three more feet and he'd have her!

He lunged at her flailing arms—and missed! Her foot slipped over the rail. A scream rose from her very core. Wind and rain blurred his vision. Again his arm stretched beyond endurance to reach her. Another inch—only one more inch. Suddenly his fingers locked about her wrist. With superhuman strength he snatched her from the clutches of the raging sea back onto the rocking ship. Her arms flew about him and she clung to him in desperation.

Battling the wind and rain and the constant pitching of the ship, he guided her slowly and with immense difficulty back across the deck and thrust her roughly through the door and back into safety. Protected once again from the ravaging tempest outside, his relief at saving her immediately erupted into anger. "What the hell were you doing out there? Are you trying to kill yourself?" demanded the captain as he glared down at her.

Christy began to cry, sobs racking her shivering body. Her hair was plastered to her pale face. The frightening ordeal, coupled with the still raging storm and the captain's wrath were just too much to handle. She squeezed her fingers into fits, trying to choke out an explanation.

"I . . . I was looking for you . . . I . . . I got lost." Her shoulders shook and her words came in short, choppy gasps.

"Your thoughtless actions could have gotten you drowned, and me along with you, you silly fool. What the devil did you want with me that couldn't wait? Can't you see I'm busy?" he shouted angrily above the roar of the storm.

Christy could sense that the captain's anger matched the fury of the tempest as the ship continued to roll and pitch precariously in the angry water. She was, however, far more frightened by the storm than she was by the captain's anger. "I . . . I just wanted to help, Captain. I . . . thought maybe I could do something," she sobbed.

Suddenly a flash of lightning lit up the hallway with terrifying clarity. A loud crash of thunder pierced their ears. It was too much for the petrified girl. She gasped in horror and flung herself into the astonished arms of Captain Lancer.

"I'm sorry. I'm really sorry," she cried, burying her face into the folds of his heavy sweater. "I was so afraid. I didn't want to be alone. I'm afraid of the storm and I don't want to die."

Michael Lancer looked down at the frightened girl clinging to him as if her life depended on it. Despite himself he wrapped her closer into his strong arms to protect her from the fury that raged about them. His anger subsided. How could he remain irate when she clutched him in utter terror? She was like a frightened lamb, yet her exquisite body, so well outlined by the wet clothing, belied her childlike demureness.

"Captain, you'd better come quickly. The starboard sail beam's broken free. It's smashing up the deck. We lost Miller. He was hit and thrown overboard," came the urgent tidings from the darkened hallway.

"My God!" cried the captain as he abruptly released Christy. "Call every available hand on deck. Make sure everyone is securely roped together. We don't want to lose any more men. I'll be there in a moment," he ordered.

"Yes, sir," came the man's sharp response as he darted off to assemble the men.

The crewman's tragic tidings had succeeded in staying Christy's tears. "Captain, is there anything I can do to help?" she asked timidly, wiping the last tears from her eyes.

"What? What?" he muttered harshly, almost having forgotten she was there, so deep in thought was he.

"Can I do anything to help?" she repeated, gazing at him through her laden lashes.

"Yes, there is something you can do, Miss Patterson," he said. "Go to your room and stay there. You're only in the way. I've got work to do and you'll be nothing but one more worry. You've caused more than enough trouble already. Now get back to your room and stay there!" he bellowed more harshly than he meant and pushed her down the hall.

With care she picked her way back to her room. Her heart ached for the unfortunate Miller, yet she thanked God that her close call had not ended in a similar fate. A burst of thunder made her cringe, but she hurried to her room seeking safety there.

Her room, however, offered little comfort to her bruised body or taut, frayed nerves. She sat on the bed to rest but found the bolts holding it in place had broken loose. It began to bounce from one end of the room to the other with the rocking of the ship, crashing into the walls as it slid. The noise and jerky movements only intensified her terror, and as time passed the storm seemed only to worsen. The cot slammed into her leg once again. She kicked it away angrily.

Suddenly with no warning, a small crack opened in the wall of her room. As the ship dipped to the left, water poured in, soaking her in an icy shower. The flow ceased abruptly as *The Merrimer* rolled right. Seconds later, however, the flood returned as the ship continued its rocking.

Christy watched in horror as the small room quickly filled with water. With frozen fingers she grabbed the mattress on her cot and shoved it against the small crack. She could not believe such a miniscule opening could produce such a flood of water. The water ceased pouring in, but the padding would not hold for long. She must get help.

Shaking with cold and terror, she waded through the icy water toward the door. She braced her feet and pulled with all her strength. The door eased open, pouring water out into the hallway. Soaked and shivering, she ran from the flooded room, not knowing where she was going, but hoping just to run into someone. If the ship was sinking she wanted to know.

She ran blindly, as one possessed, through the pitch dark. Was there no one left aboard? Was she all alone? The crashing waves muffled all other sounds, and before she heard him, she had run straight into the captain.

"What the devil are you doing out of your room?" he screamed at her above the noise of the wind and storm, greatly irritated that he should find her running about. "I told you to stay put and not move. Are you hell bent on getting yourself killed?"

"No! No, Captain," she cried. "There's water coming in through a hole in the wall. I stuffed it with my mattress, but I'm sure it won't hold," she tried to explain.

The captain heard only part of what she said. He was terribly impatient with her. He had enough on his mind without worrying about her running about the ship.

"I'll check on it. Now go and get out of the way. I don't care where you go, but find a place and stay there until I tell you to come out. Do you hear me?"

"Captain," ventured Christy bravely, at last voicing her fear, "is the ship sinking? I want to know the truth."

"The ship? Sinking? Don't be ridiculous," he barked.

"But the water . . . in my room . . . I thought . . ." she began, but he cut her off sharply.

"Every ship takes on water during a storm. That's only natural."

"But I . . . I . . ." she began again.

A clap of thunder silenced further conversation. She cringed but she knew the captain would be impatient with her unfounded fears. She would have to deal with her terror alone. She would receive no comfort from Michael Lancer.

"Captain, where should I go?" she asked, but her words were lost in the storm.

"Goddamnit, woman! Move!" he screamed and without waiting rushed past without giving her another look.

Christy brushed away irksome tears. The man had no mercy. It mattered not to him how terrified she was. Couldn't he at least offer some small word of consolation or comfort? He had said the ship was in no danger of sinking, but could she believe him?

Heavy footsteps sounded in the distance and she jumped in fright. She decided it would behoove her to disappear until the storm ended. She had no desire to further incite the captain's wrath upon her. In his present state of mind, she had no doubt that he would carry out his threat and physically restrain her on deck. The thought did little to dispel her anxiety and, in fact, sent shivers up her spine.

Where could she go? Her own little room was out of the question. Yet if she went to the captain's cabin she would surely be in the way. Where then?

Suddenly the answer came to her. "Of course, the hold! It should be safe there and I will surely be out of everyone's way," she said aloud. Decision made, she carefully made her way down the stairs and below deck. The door was very heavy, but she finally managed to pull it up enough to slide through. She waited at the top of the stairs until her eyes adjusted to the blackness. She heard no rushing water so she made her way slowly down to the darkness. She stepped down and to her surprise found a small amount of water covering the floor.

Finally she decided to sit on the stairs. If the water did rise, she could make a quick exit. She sat down and tried to steady herself as the ship continued its rolling. The thin shirt and trousers clung to her, wet and cold. She sat shivering and frightened, listening for the storm and sounds of rising water.

What seemed like hours passed as the storm tossed the ship roughly. It was all she could do to retain her place on the step. Thunder crashed violently and filled her heart with cold dread. Without warning the ship dipped precariously, sending her falling to the floor and into the icy water below. Slowly she picked herself up. The water level seemed no higher than when she had arrived, and she decided it might be safer and easier if she found a box out of the draft and away from the steps to sit on. Her muscles ached from the cold and damp as she moved through the water, trying to find a dry spot.

Finally she found a crate that appeared partially dry and perched herself on it, leaning against the wall for support. She had never been so miserable in her life.

Cold and exhausted, she finally dozed off, but her sleep was fitful and she finally gave up. She was shivering uncontrollably. Every muscle in her body seemed frozen. Her head began to swim. She felt faint and began to pass in and out of consciousness. Visions of her parents, her uncle, Paddy and the captain flickered through her mind.

Suddenly the door to the hold burst open. The light was so bright, Christy was temporarily blinded. She heard footsteps pounding down the stairs, but could not focus on who or what approached. Her senses were numb, and objects whirled in slow motion. Someone yelled, "She's over here!" But the words sounded distant, obscure, and muffled by the chattering of her teeth.

Strong arms lifted her from the crate and set her on her feet, but her cramped legs would not hold her and she crumpled to the floor, whimpering softly. Slowly she raised her eyes and looked up into the angry face of Captain Lancer.

"What the hell are you doing down here? I've been tearing this ship apart looking for you. When I couldn't find you I thought you'd fallen overboard!" he said angrily as he slowly helped her to her feet. "Whatever possessed you to come here?" Though his words were harsh, his tired, haggard face revealed his relief at having found her at last.

"You told me to get out of the way . . . and to stay put until you came to get me. I didn't know where else to go . . . so I came here. I was only following your orders," she stuttered, barely able to speak through her chattering teeth.

The captain dismissed his men and carried her up the stairs and to his cabin. The morning sun shone brightly through the porthole, yet it offered little warmth. He threw a heavy blanket across her shivering shoulders and continued his questioning.

"Why didn't you come out when the storm was over? I had no idea where you'd gone." He eased her into a chair and fumbled to light the stove at the foot of the bed.

She felt tired, so very tired, and so very cold. Talking was such an effort. Why did he not understand?

"You explicitly told me to get out of the way and not dare move until you said I could. You threatened to tie me on deck if you caught me in the hallway again. I didn't want you to yell at me again so I did exactly what you said. I was obeying your orders. You are angry at me when I don't listen and now you are angry at me that I followed your instructions. Can I do nothing to please you?" she sobbed, feeling tired, cold and miserable.

The captain studied her closely, sitting hunched beneath the folds of his heavy blanket yet shivering still. He must have frightened her terribly to cause her to freeze to death in order not to cross his orders. "Why didn't you just come to my cabin? It is warm and dry here."

"I was afraid I'd be in your way here. I didn't know where else to go and after this morning I was afraid to go exploring. The only other place I knew of was the hold, so I went there," she said through chattering teeth. Exhausted, and fearful of the captain's fury, she could not control the shivering nor the tears which trickled down her cheek.

The stove finally lit, the captain turned to Christy. She looked totally drained and near frozen. He experienced a deep pang of remorse at having been the cause of her suffering. He should have been more patient and understanding with her.

"We've got to do something about your shivering," he said at length, and rose to tower above her. No wonder she's freezing to death, he thought to himself, wearing only the flimsy, soaking wet shirt and trousers, and sitting for hours in the cold, drafty hold. Only a miracle would keep her from coming down with a serious illness. And how could he ask for another miracle? He'd already used up more than his share of luck the past two days fighting the worst storm he'd ever been through.

"Take off those wet clothes and get into bed," he ordered.

"Is my room dried out then?" she asked miserably. She knew she was at a disadvantage, but she was simply too exhausted to care.

"No. You can't go to your room. It's been flooded and must be pumped out. It will be a few days before we get around to making it suitable for you. Get into my bed."

Christy eyed him warily but made no move to obey his orders; partially from fear of what he might expect, and partially because her muscles would not respond. It was like they were cold, dead weights upon her that would not be moved.

He waited but when she made no effort to respond, his anger returned. "I said take off those clothes and get into bed!" He was exhausted himself and knew he was irritable, but he could not help himself from yelling at her.

"Captain, I would prefer . . ." she began, but to her horror he leaned down to within inches of her and spoke in a low, lethal tone.

"I'm not going to tell you again. I will be back in a few minutes and if you are not fully undressed and in bed, I will do it for you."

Christy could tell from the tone of his voice that he certainly was not above carrying out his threat. He would have no qualms about unceremoniously disrobing her. The thought made her shiver all the more.

"When I return I expect you to be rid of those rags and in bed." With that final threat, he disappeared behind the closed door.

Christy was too cold and exhausted to fight with him further. With great effort she persuaded her limbs to act and took off her damp clothes, tossing them across the chair to dry. She found a shirt in the captain's closet and quickly donned it. It might serve to soothe her modesty somewhat if the need arose. Satisfied, she climbed into bed. But, the heavy blankets seemed not to help. She was still shivering when the captain returned a few moments later.

"Here, drink this down. It will help to warm you," he ordered and thrust a glass into her hand.

"What . . . what is it?" she asked meekly.

"Never mind. Just do as you are told," he answered shortly.

Christy took one look at his face and decided it unwise to argue. Gingerly she took the glass from his outstretched hand and swallowed. Immediately her throat felt as if it had been ignited. She coughed and choked, gasping for breath. "Oh this is terrible," she finally managed.

"Drink it all!" he ordered as she went to put the

glass down.

"Oh, I can't," she protested, but again decided it best to follow his orders. This time, however, she sipped at it slowly.

Satisfied she would drink it all, he turned and began unbuttoning his shirt. A smile crossed his face at her reaction to the whiskey—and he had given her his best!

A short time later he took the glass from her trembling hand. "Did the whiskey warm up your stomach?" he asked with a smile as he slipped off his shirt and began to unfasten his pants.

"Yes. Yes it did, Captain," she replied, only half-heartedly as she watched him disrobe with mounting trepidation.

"You needn't look so worried, my dear. I will tell you right now that you are going to share that bed with me. I am exhausted. I have been up fighting the storm for two days now and I refuse to be forced from my room and comfortable bed. And as for you, the quickest way I know to warm someone is the use of body heat." His eyes twinkled devilishly, despite his fatigue.

"I'm not cold anymore, Captain. Really," she lied. "You can have your bed to yourself. I will sit in the chair." She made an effort to rise. Desperately she tried to control her trembling. His quick eyes missed nothing, however.

"Is that so, my dear?" he said, raising an eyebrow sarcastically. "Why, I can see you shivering and your teeth still chatter. Now be a good little girl and move over," he said. In an instant he had removed his pants and slid into bed beside Christy. "As you can see, I have left on my under shorts. It would be difficult indeed to take advantage of you with such a hinderance. So rest easy," he consoled with a tone cold and mocking.

His words, however, did frightfully little to appease her. She was horrified to be trapped in bed with this man. She drew herself as far against the wall as possible and watched him cautiously.

"Oh come over here. That incessant shivering will keep me awake," he said rather irritably at her reaction. "You needn't worry about that precious virtue of yours right now. I am, sorry to admit it, simply too tired to give a damn. We will both have to wait for a more opportune time."

She looked at him, biting her lower lip, but refused to budge. His patience at an end, however, he slipped his arm under her back and pulled her close.

"'Tis definitely a shame, my lovely lady. A dreadful shame indeed to waste such a golden opportunity. I have finally gotten you to my bed and find myself too drained to react. Alas, I need my rest and you need someone to warm you. We will both have to settle for that just now." With that, he closed his eyes and was alseep in minutes.

Christy lay stiffly beside him, watching his chest rise and fall with each rhythmic breath. She was determined not to sleep, but to keep vigil against the strange, yet handsome man. His hairy chest tickled her back, and his strong arms held her tightly in his sleep. His close proximity frightened her, yet at the same time thrilled her. How could her body betray her so?

Still confused, she felt the whiskey warm her insides, and the heat from his body at last stilled her shivering.

Against her will, she closed her eyes and soon drifted off to sleep. . . .

"No. No. Please don't!" cried Christy, flinching in pain and terror. "Please don't hit me any more! Please!" she pleaded and began striking the pillow again and again.

"Christy. Christy. Wake up. You're dreaming!" came the captain's alarmed voice as he shook her gently. "Wake up!"

He had been sleeping peacefully when the sound of her crying out in terror had awakened him. Only his quick reflexes had saved him from being the target of her pounding fists.

Eyes wide and filled with terror, she focused on him standing above her, hand raised to strike. "No! Please don't!" she pleaded, burying her face into the pillow. "Please!" she sobbed.

"You're dreaming, Christy. Wake up. It's me . . . Michael," he said and reached down to gently pull her black hair from her flushed face and neck.

Heart pounding and still unsure of where she was, Christy blinked repeatedly and turned to gaze up in bewilderment at the captain. Seeing her confusion, he knelt beside her.

"It's all right, Christy. It was a dream. You are safe now," he said, allowing her to regain her bearings.

"That must have been a terrible nightmare you were having. You nearly knocked me out with your flying fists. It wasn't anything I said, now was it?" he asked, trying to make light of the incident.

"No. No. It was nothing you said," replied Christy seriously. It was something you were about to do, she thought as she drew in a deep, calming breath.

"Would it help to tell me about it, little one?" he asked gently. She looked so small and defenseless lying tightly curled in his large bed. Her hair lay fanned out on the pillow. A tear still glistened on one soft, flushed cheek. Her eyes were a sea of deep green protected by long, fluttering black lashes. He longed to take her in his arms and soothe away the hurt and terror he saw mirrored in her wide eyes and trembling lips, but he felt sure she would not trust or understand such tenderness from him. He wisely kept his distance.

"It is a dream I have quite frequently, Captain. You would think after having it so often I would get used to it, but with each night it becomes more terrifying. A man has me trapped and is whipping me again and again." She shuddered from the memory.

"Who is this man? Is he the one who beat you before? Were you running from him when you hid in the crate?"

"Yes," replied Christy, turning her face to the wall. She did not wish to remember her terrible ordeals, yet the dream brought them back all too vividly.

Seeing her unwillingness to divulge more, Michael Lancer turned his attention to dressing and shaving. Perhaps someday she would trust him enough to confide in him. He decided it must have been a terrible life for her to relive it so vividly in her dreams.

"How do you feel this morning? I must apologize for my lack of gallantry in not waiting until you were warm last night. I felt it best, however, to concentrate on sleep and not you beside me. If I had set my attentions on you, I may just have found some excess energy." His brown eyes danced merrily as he shaved the dark stubble from his handsome face. "Did you finally get warm?"

"Yes, I did. The whiskey did the trick," she said, smiling rather cockily.

"And I did nothing to help your condition?" he demanded indignantly, and then, seeing her sly smile, laughed aloud. "You're a little vixen, you are. I have half a notion to prove to you just how much warmth I am capable of giving," he threatened as he wiped the last bit of soap from his face and stood smiling down at her.

Christy blushed hotly, acutely aware of him towering over her. "That won't be necessary, Captain. I'm really quite comfortable now, and you must have many things to do."

"It seems my duties are forever standing in my way," he grinned. "And you are forever pointing the fact out to me. But someday . . ." He deliberately left his sentence unfinished.

A retort sprang to Christy's lips but was drowned out by a sudden sneeze. "Excuse me," she murmured.

"Are you feeling all right? I would not be surprised if you got a cold, sitting in those wet clothes for such a long time. Have you a fever?" he asked and was beside her in a moment.

The slight touch of his hand on her forehead sent her temperature soaring. She fervently hoped he did not guess the cause of her flushed cheeks. The memory of him beside her, strong and warm, was still too fresh.

"You've got quite a temperature, my dear. I suggest you remain in bed all day and rest. I will send Paddy in to have a look at you. Perhaps he can recommend something."

Christy was about to object, but was seized by another sneeze. She did feel a little feverish and congested. Perhaps the captain was right. "Very well," she said.

The captain looked at her with an amused grin. "My dear, I do believe that is the first time you and I have agreed on anything. It will be a day to remember."

Still smiling, he collected a few charts and headed for the deck.

True to his word, Paddy arrived a short time later. Though her cold proved minor indeed, Paddy fussed and worried over her. She submitted to his gentle ministrations, but remained adamant about returning to her room.

And so, as soon as it was pumped and dry she abdicated the captain's cabin and sought privacy in her own quarters.

Seven

Christy sat humming to herself as she stitched her dress. It was nearly complete and the thought of once again looking like a woman was a very pleasing thought indeed. She had not worked on it since the storm and her slight illness. Now that she felt better she took up the task with renewed vigor.

A sudden slip of the needle caused her to prick her finger, bringing a frown to her face and an end to her humming. Oh how careless, she thought to herself as she sucked on her finger to halt the bleeding. Not wanting to stain her new gown, she got up and searched for something to hold on the cut. The bleeding finally stopped, she turned to resume her seat when a scraping noise caused her to glance toward the door.

"Who's there?" she called. No one answered, but she knew someone was outside.

Fear suddenly caused her skin to prickle. Her eyes flew to the latch. It was open! She had forgotten to secure it when Paddy had left with her dinner tray. She sped across the room. Before she had a chance to slip the lock into place, the door burst open and in rushed two men, the latter fastening the lock behind him.

"What do you want?" demanded Christy angrily, eyeing the two swarthy intruders.

She recognized them as Sam and John, the two men who had delivered her cot some days before. John, the shorter of the two men, was bald and reeked of digusting body odor while the other man was big, clumsy, and awkward with eyes that held a vague, moronic look filled with animal lust.

Neither man answered. Instead they stood smiling lewdly at her. "What do you want?" she tried again, her pulses quickening. "The captain will be very angry if he finds you here," she threatened bravely as panic churned her stomach.

The little man took a step forward. "Oh, I ain't worried about him. The way I figure it, he must be done with you beings he put you out of his cabin and all. It's the crew's turn now, and I aim to be the first."

"Get out!" Christy screamed, her fists clenched and her heart pounding painfully.

"What's the matter? Ain't we good enough for you, Miss High and Mighty? You think once you let the captain have his pleasures, the crew is not good enough for you? Well, he's no better a man than me, and I aim to prove that fact to you," he sneered.

His face broke into an ugly grin and he lunged at her. With brutal force he pinned her against the wall. She screamed and struggled to free herself, but he held her tightly, nearly breaking her arms. He leaned forward and his rough beard scratched her delicate face as he thrust his tongue between her clenched lips.

With every ounce of strength she possessed, she

snatched her hand free and aimed for his face. Her long, sharp fingernails raked his cheek. "You wretched animal!" she seethed in open hatred as he jumped back, swearing profusely and holding his bleeding, stinging cheek.

"So, that's the way it's to be, is it, missy! You'll pay for that," he spat.

The blow knocked her to the floor. She felt a little trickle of blood run down her chin. "Get out!" she screamed at the two men. Her heart beat so rapidly it felt near bursting.

"We ain't ready to go just yet, missy. Not till we git what we come for," he hissed. "Now let's have a look at just what you have to offer, my fine lady." He stepped closer and yanked her to her feet. Grimy fingers clutched the cloth of her shirt. In seconds the worn garment hung in shreds about her heaving chest.

"Ah, now that's a sight to behold," admired John hungrily.

"Stop it! Stop!" she moaned in agony. Red, inflamed patches covered her neck and arms where the shirt had burned her flesh as it was ripped from her body.

"Oh no, little lady. I'm just getting started," laughed the revolting little man. Anticipation bloomed in his eyes.

Tears poured down Christy's cheeks as he forced her arm behind her back and began dragging her across the room to the cot, nearly breaking her arm as he pulled her along. "Help me, please! Someone help me!" she tried to scream, but her voice only came in a choked whisper.

In one swift shove, John spun her about and tossed her

onto the cot. "Now, my little wildcat, we'll see how well you can satisfy a real man," he declared. With brutal force he ripped the trousers from her body and gazed with crazed lust at the sleek, sensuous lines of her naked form.

Christy's head spun dizzily. Hot tears scalded her face. "Stop! Take your hands off me!" she screamed.

"Shut up, bitch. There's no one there to hear," John sneered. He fumbled at his pants to loosen his belt.

Suddenly the room exploded about them. The door crashed to the floor as a deadly kick ripped it from its hinges. All eyes turned, riveted to the source of the intrusion. No one moved. No one breathed as the livid form of Captain Michael Lancer filled the room.

A desperate sob ripped from Christy's throat, triggering the captain into terrifying action. With deadly intent, he seized Sam by the shirt, jerked him to his feet, and swung his fist into the vacant face. Sam smashed against the wall and slid to the floor, knocked more senseless than before.

John gaped in abject terror as his captain spun and turned a vengeful gaze upon him. Warm water trickled down his legs as he backed toward the wall. "Captain . . . please . . . We were just having a little fun. I . . . we . . . thought you were done with her . . ."

He never finished his explanation. A thunderous fist smashed into his ugly face. Consumed by anger, the captain heaved him against the wall and drove his knee forcefully into the man's groin. John doubled over in pain and whimpered for mercy, but Lancer was not done with him. Again and again he drove his fist into the man's face until it was nothing but a mass of battered flesh. His anger was nearly beyond control, and he seemed bent on annihilating the little man. Only the intervention of two other crewmen saved John from being beaten into a coma.

"Take them away before I kill them both. I'll deal with them later," Lancer stormed as they dragged the bleeding man and his brainless friend away. His fists were clenched in a tight ball as he spun about and gazed at the whimpering form before him.

Suddenly all anger drained from him and he was filled with concern for the wounded girl on the cot. She lay on her side, staring at the wall. His brow furrowed in a frown as he noted the various patches of red showing where the two men had bruised her soft, white skin. Her full round breasts, tiny waist, and shapely round hips and buttocks stirred his senses though her shoulders shook with muffled sobs. He was filled with rage that his men should do such a thing, and felt personally responsible for the tragedy. He should have warned her, posted a guard at her door, or done something to have prevented this.

The silence in the room grew deafening. Christy could feel his eyes upon her and was acutely aware of her nakedness. An overwhelming shame pulsed through her and finally stayed her tears. With great effort, she stifled her sobs and glanced over her shoulder.

She blinked her wet lashes in horror as she turned to see him looming above her. The captain was unbuttoning his shirt! Her heart pounded wildly in renewed fear. He had beaten the other men unmercifully for attempting to rape her. Was he now going to finish the job himself?

"Oh, please, Captain. Please don't." The tears

streamed down her face as she tried to pull the tattered shirt about her naked breasts. "I beseech you. Do not degrade and shame me further," she pleaded.

"What . . . ?" he began in confusion. His puzzled expression transformed to one of patient compassion. "Don't worry, little one," he said reassuringly. "I am not going to hurt you. I only want to help."

He stroked her silky hair and ever so gently wrapped her in his shirt, succeeding somewhat in covering her slender, quivering body in its massive folds.

She looked up at him through long, tear laden lashes. "Oh, Captain . . ." she sobbed as her head slipped onto his shoulder.

He swept her up into his strong arms and held her tightly. "I won't let anyone hurt you ever again," he whispered into her ear as he carried her down the hall and into his cabin. She sobbed quietly into his massive, hairy chest, clinging desperately to his neck. She felt drained, empty, and utterly at his mercy.

He kicked open the door to his cabin with one foot and laid her gently on the bed. As she gazed at him with trusting emerald eyes, he tucked the blankets around her chin and poured her a huge glass of brandy.

Christy accepted it with trembling fingers, but enjoyed the warmth it sent through her bruised body. Her eyelids grew heavier and heavier. The captain's face above hers soon became an indistinguishable blurr.

Michael reached down and gently brushed the tresses of black silk from her face, and caressed her cheek. He placed a cool cloth on her forehead and wiped away the blood from the tiny cut on her lip. He watched her long lashes at last rest upon smooth, white cheeks. Her lips parted slightly and her breathing became slow and regular.

Satisfied that she slept, he slipped quietly from the room and headed for the hold. When he finished with his men, not one of them would ever dare lay another hand on her again.

Eight

Christy awoke to brilliant sunshine streaming through the porthole. The brightness hurt her eyes and she turned away, covering her face with the blankets. With a sigh, she closed her eyes and attempted to drift back into blissful slumber. A soft chuckle brought her fully awake. Eyes wide, she turned to the source of the disturbance.

Captain Lancer sat at his desk with paper scattered everywhere in mass confusion. At the signs of her waking, he turned, arms across his chest, and regarded her fondly. Seeing her startled gaze upon him, he chuckled again.

"Pray, good sir, what amuses you so?" she asked, a little annoyed that she should find herself under such intense scrutiny.

"Well, my dear, it seems that I again find myself a stranger to my own bed. While I must sit in great discomfort upon a hard chair you lounge leisurely in my bed. Should you grow too accustomed to this comfort, I may well find myself bruised and exhausted and forced to make you share what small comfort it provides." His voice was bright and full of mischief.

Christy gathered the blankets around her chin and sat

up against the headboard eyeing him warily. He made a stunning picture. His skin, darkened from the sun, contrasted sharply with the white of his shirt. His arms, covered with dark hair, rippled with muscles grown hard from strenuous labors. She knew, however, that those same strong arms were capable of tenderness as well as violence. She remembered how he had beaten John and Sam, and she also remembered his gentleness last night as he carried her to the safety of his room and tenderly comforted her. The sudden memory of the horrors of that night filled her with dread. She shuddered at the thought and pulled the blankets more closely about her.

The captain noticed her shiver, along with the heightened color of her cheeks, but made no comment. If she wanted to talk about it he would let her do so in her own good time.

Christy stared at the captain's broad shoulders. She owed him more than she cared to. He had spared her life when, by rights, a stowaway deserved a fatal punishment. He had surrendered his room to her on more than one occasion. And because of his generosity, Paddy Mac-Donough had not only doctored her back to health but also served as her closest and only friend. Yes, her indebtedness to Captain Michael Lancer seemed to grow with each passing day. And on that dreadful night, through sheer instinct, he had spared her her virtue. That act in itself had put her forever in his debt. How could she ever begin to repay him for all he had done for her?

With a new determination at a peaceful alliance, she took a deep breath and softly spoke to the man before her.

"Thank you, Captain, for helping me . . . last night."

The words came with difficulty to her. The dreadful memory was vividly etched in her mind. Would she ever again feel clean where the two despicable men had pawed her? She did not want to see anyone. Even Paddy. All men were the same. She hated them all.

But that wasn't quite fair, she realized. Paddy had been nothing but kind to her. And the captain? Well, she could not be angry with him. He had a right to his cabin. Besides, she owed him too much to be upset. Why, if not for him, the two men might actually have . . . She shuddered again at the very idea.

"Miss Patterson, you needn't thank me. Actually I only wish I'd come along sooner. I hated to see someone else beat me to such a delectable prize. I had hoped to save that little pleasure for myself."

The impact of his words struck her like a knife. Her face became livid with anger. She snatched the sheets about herself and sprang from the bed. It was just more than she could tolerate.

"You are vile and utterly contemptable. You turn my appreciation into mockery," she spat at his smirking face. "Is that all you men ever think of? Women were made for more than satisfying the pleasures of men. There is a mind that goes with this body, Mr. Lancer. It can serve you well and willingly. My body does not come willingly."

Her breasts heaved heavily up and down in anger as she clutched the sheet tighter about herself. She glared at him, hoping for some reaction to her biting words. His smile only broadened. "Oh, you monster!" she growled in utter consternation at his continued silence. Had there been something suitable nearby, she would have thrown it at his arrogant face.

"Your muteness injures more deeply than your cutting tongue," she flared and turned her back to him. She no longer trusted the emotions raging within her and all too clearly revealed by her tearing eyes. She breathed deeply for some time, trying to get herself back under control.

The room grew strangely quiet. She decided he must have gone, disgruntled by her tirade. She began to relax slightly.

"My dear Miss Patterson," came his voice from directly behind her.

She whirled in surprise. He'd been standing there all along watching her. Her guard returned anew.

He raised her chin and looked deep within her flashing green eyes. "It is quite obvious that you are completely ignorant of the ways of the masculine gender. I've no doubt that before the other night you've never sampled a man's love."

"'Tis more like lust!" she interrupted, trying to pull away in contempt.

He nodded his head, conceding the point. "A man's lust then, if you like. I offered myself as a willing teacher, but," he raised his hand to her lips as she began to protest, "you were unwilling to learn. No doubt it was a rather harrowing experience for you. I only hope it does not turn you completely against the art of lovemaking. It can be quite enjoyable, you know," he said.

Christy lowered her gaze and tried to pull away in

humiliation. "Oh, have you no compassion at all? Must you continue to degrade and humiliate me? Have I not been abused enough for one day?" she cried as he lightly stroked her soft, smooth shoulders.

"You are quite right, my dear. I do apologize," he agreed, with little conviction, however. "I have no intention of embarrassing you further. You have been through enough. Please forgive my arrogance," he said, suddenly regretting his spiteful tongue. He turned repentant yet refused to release her.

"Then what is it you want of me?" she snapped roughly and pulled herself from his grasp. The effort nearly cost her modesty as the sheet slipped lower on her naked breasts. Hastily she retrieved it and stood to await his response.

He took his time in replying, being content to look upon her defiant radiance. When he spoke, his voice was low and serious.

"I have not the time at present to explain, but I will be back later to discuss just what it is I expect of you. We will see just how willingly your mind will take on what I give you. Good day, madam," he replied and was gone before she could question him further. She gaped after him in confusion. One moment he was cruel and heartless, the next gentle and kind. Just exactly what sort of man was he who claimed himself her master?

She stormed about the room angrily, trying to work out her frustrations. Suddenly a patch of bright green caught her eye. With a little cry of delight, she hugged her unfinished dress to her. She'd forgotten about it since her attack. Who'd brought it here? The captain? No matter, she decided as she picked it up and began working on it in earnest. She would not appear again before Captain Michael Lancer wrapped only in a bedsheet.

Christy worked in earnest the rest of the day to finish her dress. Her fingers flew as did her thoughts, which remained confused and troubled. Her debt to the captain seemed to grow day by day, yet her position seemed to acquire more and more uncertainty as time passed. He refused to treat her as a slave yet his attitude toward her was usually harsh and threatening. She was constantly reminded that he craved her as his mistress, yet he pushed it no further. He was totally confusing, arrogant, egotistical, mysterious and—magnificent. Yes, she had to admit that physically he carried an aura of dignity and authority and demanded respect and obedience. Whatever it was, she desperately wanted to please him. She wasn't sure why, but the need was there and could not be ignored. It always seemed, however, that the harder she tried to gain his respect the more angry and arrogant he became. He was exasperating, to say the least.

Her mind and fingers thus occupied, time flew. With a thrill of excitement, she stitched the last seam in her gown a few hours later. She had worked long and hard on it and now held it up for her inspection. It was lovely— more lovely than any she'd had in the past two years. Though it was simple, it fit her perfectly. No one would challenge her femininity wrapped in its rich folds. She held it up before her and danced merrily around the room, reveling in the anticipation of once more regaining some measure of femininity.

She washed herself slowly, taking special care with her

hair. She brushed it till it shone and then piled it high upon her head. A few soft curls escaped their confinement and dangled mischievously about her long, slender neck. Satisfied at last, she slipped into the dress, giggling in delight. Her cheeks needed no pinching today. They were painted with a soft, rosy blush. For the first time since her attack she felt clean and confident and looked forward to a visit from Paddy when he brought her evening tea.

She danced around the room, humming a lively little tune to herself as she dipped and swayed gracefully. A sudden knock on the door halted her playful antics. She giggled at her own silliness, hoping Paddy had not heard her. She smoothed her skirts, raised her chin, and glided across the room to answer the door.

Her eyes opened wide in surprise to see Captain Lancer standing in the hallway, a steaming mug of tea held in his large hands.

Her surprise was minimal, however, compared to his. Her drastic yet delightful change in attire left him speechlessly gaping at her in the doorway.

"Is this tea for me?" she asked at last, pleased by his reaction yet slightly embarrassed.

When he made no effort to respond, she lifted the cup from his fingers, smiled coquettishly at him, and opened the door wider so he could enter.

"What's the matter, Captain? Has the cat got your tongue?" she asked, turning her back to him as she set down the hot tea.

"Why yes . . . no . . ." he floundered. "What I mean is . . ." he began again, desperately trying to collect his thoughts. At last his composure returned, yet his voice, when he spoke, was decidedly husky. "You look simply beautiful, Christy," he said with real feeling.

She took note of his use of her familiar name, and dimpled all the more. "You approve of my dress then, Captain? You do not regret giving me the cloth?" she teased.

"On the contrary, my dear. I believe it well worth the price," he replied, his manner once again returning to self-assured composure.

His gaze openly reappraised her lest he'd missed some minute detail. Her beauty was breathtaking. He had thought her lovely before, yet now she looked like a goddess. The fabric of bright green accentuated the emerald of her sparkling eyes and the blackness of her silky hair. Her waist, above gathers of swaying green cloth, appeared so tiny, he mentally calculated he could encircle it with both hands and still have room to spare. The bodice fit snugly, revealing a tempting valley between two enticing, creamy breasts. The garment was simple, with no laces or frills, yet the beauty of its wearer and its perfect fit made it look as if a talented dressmaker had created it solely for her.

Christy blushed prettily and walked toward the desk, hoping to distract him from his intense scrutiny. "Was there something you wanted to discuss with me?" she asked seriously as she fingered a pen lying on the desk.

Those hips. Those damn swaying hips, he thought to himself. How they do sorely tempt me. She's a little vixen and knows it, trying to pay me back for accusing her of knowing nothing about men. He shook his head in exasperation and moved slowly toward her.

Christy knew a twinge of fear when she looked into his dark brown eyes. Perhaps she had played the vixen all too well for her own good. A little nervously she repeated her question. "Was there something you wanted me to help you with?"

"Yes. I need these damn—excuse me—these accounts posted and tallied. Unlike my father, I despise the chore and seem to be forever putting it off. As a result I am far behind."

"How can I help, Captain?" she asked, moving to his side. She glanced down at the scattered papers and casually scanned their contents.

"You said you could read and figure. Do you think you could make some sense out of this mess?" he asked, glad to occupy his mind with some concrete matter.

"I will certainly try, Captain. I have never attempted anything like this before, but if you will explain the details of the process, I will do my best," she answered in earnest.

The captain brought an extra chair and they sat side by side, working together in close proximity. He was impressed and amazed at how easily she understood the procedures. Most women were concerned with stitchery and had little interest in reading and calculating. Again she proved far different than the majority of her gender. When they had finished for the evening, he commented on the fact.

"As I told you, Captain, my father was a strong advocate of education. I found my studies totally enthralling and far more challenging than cooking or stitchery. My mother insisted on equal time for the more feminine arts, but my first love was books."

"Well, if this works out, I too owe your father a great debt. You may be my salvation," he said, gazing with renewed respect at this young woman. Being a typical man, however, his respect for her intelligence soon wandered to his respect for her more outstanding assets.

Christy noticed his sudden change in attitude and decided it best to make her exit.

"I am very tired, Captain. It has been a long day. If you will excuse me, I think I will go to my room. I can continue with these accounts tomorrow. I believe I understand them well enough to continue on my own," she said, standing and smoothing her skirts.

He quickly rose and stood at her side. "Are you sure you want to return to your room? I had Paddy clean it up. But will it be too uncomfortable after . . ." he began then started again. "I mean, it may bring back unpleasant memories. You are more than welcome to stay here," he offered.

His concern was really touching, thought Christy. She longed to reach up and gently stroke his distinguished jaw, but instinct told her she would only be courting trouble. Instead she smoothed an imaginary wrinkle from her dress. "I appreciate your generous offer, Captain. It is kind of you to be so concerned. But I overheard Paddy say it will be another three or four weeks before we arrive in Charleston. I would not force you to return to your former uncomfortable accommodations in the crew's quarters. I will be fine, but thank you again for your offer."

A heavy silence fell between them as he walked her to her room. It had been an enjoyable evening for them both and each was sad to have it come to an end. A mutual feeling of expectation and need hung in the air. Neither would admit openly to it, however.

Michael pushed open the door, yet did not miss her unconscious shudder as she glanced at the bed. Again he felt remorse that she should have learned so brutally the ways of men. "I would like to tell you again how lovely you look, Christina. You grace my ship with your delicate beauty," he complimented sincerely.

Christy was touched by his unsolicited compliment. She blushed softly, suddenly feeling very shy. "Thank you," she murmured and lowered her eyes, confused by the sudden racing of her pulse.

The hallway was dark and quiet except for the soft glow of the candlelight and the beating of their hearts. On sudden impulse, he raised her chin and ever so lightly pressed his lips to hers. Christy's eyes flew open in surprise yet she did not pull way or strike out. The experience was all too thrilling.

Encouraged by her response, he pulled her closer and his kiss grew more bold. A warm, tingling sensation washed over her. Almost against her will she felt herself responding to him and to her sudden longing for love and tenderness.

The thought was all too sobering and she pulled away, embarrassed by her own passionate display. "Good night, Captain," she whispered, and before he could protest she closed the door and slid the bolt.

Nine

Two weeks passed quickly and pleasantly for Christy now that she had a definite purpose and goal. Each morning she would go to Captain Lancer's room after he had gone and work on his accounts. In no time she had them nearly in perfect order and current to the day. She was quite pleased with her accomplishments, as was he.

She also enjoyed Paddy's nightly visits when he came to collect her dinner tray. He would tell her about his home in Ireland and how, at an early age, he had run off to sea and eventually made Charleston his home port. He also began giving her some insights on the life and customs of her new home. She stored away all that he said, hoping that the information would serve to ease her entry into this new world.

He made no mention of her ordeal with John and Sam, but she knew it had upset him. He hovered paternally and constantly reminded her to keep her door latched. As if she needed to be told again! It had been a terrifying experience and she shuddered to remember John's filthy hands covering her body. It was best forgotten by all, so she made no further mention of the incident.

When Paddy came to visit her a few days later, he was

surprised to find her back in her masculine attire.

"I washed my dress, Paddy, and it is drying," she explained, indicating the garment hanging behind the door. "Since I have only the one dress I am forced to wear the shirt and trousers until it dries."

Accepting her explanation, glad her outfit was a temporary one, he seated himself and began his ritual of asking how her day had gone and then going into minute detail about his own.

"We've been having trouble with one of the main sails. The storm tore a hole in it and the patching work keeps giving way. The captain's been at it nearly two days straight now, night and day. It's causing us to lose precious time. And in this business time is money," he said.

Christy had wondered why she had not seen the captain the past few days. The malfunctioning sail explained his absence.

"I'm plum tuckered out myself," Paddy admitted a few moments later. With a yawn and an apology, he excused himself and stumbled off to bed.

Christy, however, was still wide awake and not in the least sleepy. She paced restlessly, wondering what she could do to occupy herself for a few hours. On sudden impulse she headed for the captain's room. Earlier in the week she had noticed a book on his shelf describing the major cities in North and South Carolina. She had made a mental note to read the book when she had time. Now seemed the perfect opportunity. She assumed the captain would be away at dinner. He usually dined late in the evening, between 8 and 9 o'clock. Thus, she was quite surprised when he responded to her soft knock.

"Good evening, Captain. I didn't mean to disturb you. I thought you would be at dinner."

He made no response but glowered at her from across the room. She was slightly alarmed by his unusual behavior and determined to secure the book and make a quick exit.

"I noticed a book on your shelf the other day which appeared quite informative on Colonial living. I thought I would like to read it." She waited, but still he made no response. "May I borrow it, Captain?" she finally asked, point blank.

"What? Yes. Take it. It's yours," he said, preoccupied and sounding tired, irritable, not at all like himself.

Without delay she secured the book under her arm and turned to slip out quietly. Again she noticed how withdrawn he seemed and the dark circles beneath his eyes. "Is something wrong, Captain?" she ventured, concerned by his sullen attitude.

"No, of course not, Miss Patterson. What makes you think something is wrong?" he snapped.

Christy jumped at the unexpected rebuke, suddenly sorry she had asked. "Oh, nothing, sir. Paddy said you've been working hard trying to repair one of the sails. Were you able to get it mended?"

"Damnit. Must he spread my problems to all?" Lancer demanded angrily. "Is nothing private or confidential?"

Again Christy flinched at his unwarranted anger. "I'm sorry, sir. I didn't mean to pry into your business," she apologized softly. "Thank you for the book." She quietly headed for the door, anxious to leave him alone with his problems.

"What the hell are you doing in those rags again?" he barked suddenly.

Christy's hand froze on the door. She had never heard him speak with such venom. It frightened her more than a little. Very slowly she turned to face him. "I washed my dress, sir. It is drying. In the meantime, I put these on."

"Well, I don't like it. I never want to see you in them again. Do you understand?" he demanded.

"But, Captain, I need to wash my dress . . ." she began to explain.

"I won't hear any more about it. That is an order!" he interrupted rudely.

"Yes, sir," she answered obediently, biting her tongue to hold back an angry retort. She turned and once again reached for the door.

"I did not give you leave to go!"

Christy stood mutely, unsure of how to respond. Was she to play along with his game and humor him? A twinge of foreboding tugged at her thoughts. "May I then have leave to go, Captain?" she asked meekly.

"No! I wish to go over the books with you," he snarled.

"But, Captain. It is late and you are tired. It is best to wait until tomorrow."

"Must you forever quibble with everything I say? I have told you before. I am the captain aboard this ship. Do not forget who gives the orders, madam."

"No, sir. I will not." Her temper was beginning to flare at his continued harassment. She walked across the room and stood beside his chair. "Which accounts did you wish to look at?" she asked, pulling the ledgers from the desk drawers and spreading them on the table.

"Please, sit," he ordered, indicating a chair. She complied and waited patiently for his answer.

"What tally have you arrived at for the tea?"

Christy noted he held a large glass filled with rum. He gulped it down and immediately reached to replenish it. Again he swallowed the contents and stared listlessly at the empty tumbler. She wondered how much he had taken before she arrived. Perhaps the strong brew accounted for his erratic behavior.

Christy began to rattle off the figures she had tallied, but each time she glanced at him he looked bored and disinterested. She sighed and continued on, afraid to do otherwise.

The captain listened absently to her monologue. He was dog tired but did not want to be alone. He enjoyed having Christy close, listening to the sound of her soothing, lilting voice. It was a pleasant contrast to the harsh, rough voices of his crew. Perhaps it was the rum that made him so lethargic. He had consumed far more than his normal share in an attempt to relax after the past two grueling days. But he didn't want to think about the ship right now, and least of all the blasted books. He wanted to concentrate his energy on the soft curves of a woman—this woman.

"Enough of that rubbish. Put the books away. I've heard enough," he blurted out irritably and reached for more rum.

"But, Captain. It was you who asked to see them," she flared.

"Don't question me, girl. I said I've heard enough!" he

snapped and smashed the glass down on the table.

Without a word, Christy gathered the papers and put them neatly back in the drawer. Her patience was beginning to wear thin. If it was an argument he wanted she would be more than willing to oblige. But she would try once more to be calm and rational.

"Would you like me to continue doing your books when we reach Charleston? I believe I have a good grasp of the system now. Perhaps I can pay off my indenture in that way?" She had been toying with the idea for some time, and finally had decided to voice her suggestion to him.

Her words brought an ugly frown to his face and his eyes grew dark and deadly. "Is that what you think? You have it all figured out, don't you?" he snarled, his voice slow and slurred. "Well don't delude yourself, my dear. I have repeatedly told you I have something else in mind in way of repayment."

Caution suddenly vanished. She was tired of his continued threats and insinuations of forcing her to be his mistress. It must stop right now! "I see you are drunk and in an ill temper this evening. I have no desire to subject myself to further abuse. Therefore, I am going to my room right now, with or without your leave!" She headed for the door, then whirled around for her final assault. "And as far as my indenture goes, I have repeatedly told you. I refuse to work off my debts in your bed!"

With that she spun about and jerked the door open. But the captain was too fast for her, despite his drunken state. He jumped to his feet, knocking his chair over in his haste, and flew across the room. Before she could make a quick getaway, he slammed the door shut and blocked her exit.

"You'll do exactly what I tell you to do!" he stormed. "By rights of your illegal presence aboard my ship, I am your master and you will obey me! If I order you to sprawl on your back and play the whore, that is what you *will* do!"

Christy was consumed by her own anger. She wanted to wipe his face clean of its hateful gaze and claw those deep brown eyes that leered down at her. With no regard for caution, she flew at him, fists flying. She pounded fiercely at his chest and stomach, swinging with all her strength.

"Are those feathery blows meant to hurt and cripple me?" he jeered, trying to hold her at bay.

Humiliation only added fuel to her already hot anger. "Oh I hate you. You are a vile, detestable animal!"

"An animal, am I?" His amused smile suddenly turned dark and ugly. "Well, since you think me an animal, then I may as well act the part."

The overpowering exhaustion he felt from the past two grueling days suddenly left him. His consumption of rum made his temper explode and his self-control vanish. With a horrifying growl, he seized her shoulders and held her at arm's length.

Christy continued to swing at him, though she hit nothing but air. "You are a cruel, heartless, pompous lech," she hissed, still swinging. Too late she looked up into his face. Too late she realized there would be no holding him off this time.

Her struggles ceased abruptly. She swallowed hard. Her own anger suddenly drained into pulsing fear. "Captain . . . I . . ." she choked. "I forgot myself. Let me go to my room. I'm sorry I lashed out at you. I'll get out of your sight. I won't ever bother you again," she pleaded.

"Oh no, my little stowaway. It's not that simple. You'll not get away so easily this time," he promised.

His hands moved from her shoulders to caress and stroke her neck. "I told you once before I could break your exquisite neck with a single hand. Do you think that is true?"

Christy shook her head slowly. There was no doubt in her mind he had the strength and the inclination.

He read the look of fear in her eyes, and drunkenly enjoyed terrorizing her. He continued to run his fingers on her neck in a tantalizing fashion. "Yes, it would be easy. Oh, so easy," he murmured, mesmerized by the soft fresh scent of her skin, the silky shine of her hair, and the warm softness of her flesh.

Possessively his hand slipped to her heaving breasts and Christy's eyes flew open. Something in her suddenly snapped at the way he fondled her, clearly enjoying the anxiety it brought. It reminded her too vividly of the other wretched seamen and their brutal pawing. She drew herself up straight and spoke boldly.

"Yes, I suppose it would be very easy for you." Her teeth were clenched as she spoke. "Would it make you feel powerful and mighty to crush me beneath your feet—to make me feel your conquering strength? Well, go ahead and do your worst, master. Break my neck and be rid of me at last. That's what you want isn't it? You're a bully, Captain Lancer. A spoiled bully," she labeled him openly.

The captain's senses reeled. Shining black curls captured his hands. Ripe, heaving breasts smothered his senses. Hips, round and demanding, trapped him in their wake. His blood pulsed at a dizzying speed. His head pounded wildly—ready to explode. A fever raged within him.

With unquenchable hunger he snatched her to him. Arms of steel encircled her. His fiery lips crushed down on hers, aflame with desire and urgency. The fire of his kiss assaulted her senses, and for a brief moment Christy too felt the spark of his passion pulsing through her veins. But this was wrong!

Panic gripped Christy. He was like a wild, raging animal, driven by lustful desire. "Take your hands off me!" she cried with every ounce of authority she possessed trying to shock him out of his madness.

"No. Not this time, my love," he whispered, low and unswayable. He reached up to free her long black hair, sending the shining mass tumbling down across his arm.

"No! No! Stop!"

He silenced her protests with his searing lips. In desperation she struggled to pull away but his grip grew tighter as he bent her to his will. His hand wandered up along her back to slip the shirt from her trousers. Her skin felt smooth beneath his touch. Slowly his fingers closed about a firm, heaving breast.

"No! You've no right!" she gasped in horror, wildly trying to be free of him.

"I have every right!" he corrected. His arm jerked outward. Buttons flew about the room as the shirt ripped open. A low, terrified moan escaped her throat as he pulled off the tattered garment and threw it across the room.

Christy's arms flew up to cover herself but he pulled them away, eager to behold her beauty. "Stop. Please, stop!" she pleaded as he again cupped her breast in his hand and taunted her with his thumb. Her senses reeled as a strange need began to burn within her.

"You're a beast—a vile and brutal animal!" she cried, fighting him desperately. But her struggles only heightened his passion. He pressed his hardness insistently against her and silenced her protests with his lips. His hands moved to her waist and with swift determination, he pulled the rope from her trousers and they slid to the floor at her feet.

She tore herself free of his grasp at last, gasping in horror at his demanding advances even while she fought to control the urges his toying evoked.

"Ah, you are truly beautiful!" he breathed as he stepped back and gazed in awe at her naked radiance. He hardly noticed her tears of shame and fear as she continued to struggle against him.

Her body glowed temptingly in the dimly lit room and all too soon he grew discontent beholding her beauty from afar. With mounting excitement, he scooped her protesting form up into his arms and carried her to his bed. Christy watched in paralyzed fear as he removed his shirt and trousers. His searing brown eyes never wavered from her glowing skin, and the fine, full curves of her hips. His breath came in short, rapid gasps as he kicked his pants across the floor and leaned over the bed, once again taking full possession of her trembling lips.

"No! No!" she chocked in hysteria as his lips traveled to the soft peaks of her creamy breasts. Her head spun dizzily and the room grew stifling. In final desperation, she hurled herself from the bed and lunged toward the door.

Her fingers clawed frantically at the door, trying to free the latch. But they shook uncontrollably. Why would the lock not move?

"No lock or door on this ship will stand in my way this night. There is no escape for you, my love," he murmured low and huskily behind her as he calmly watched her feeble efforts.

Anxiously he gripped her shoulders and spun her to face him, putting an abrupt end to her attempts to escape. He devoured her nakedness in ever-mounting excitement. She regarded his with unmasked terror.

Her lips moved in protest, but no sound emerged as he swung her easily into his arms and once again returned her to his bunk. She pounded his chest weakly, her strength waning as he once again smothered her with hot, passionate kisses.

Her breasts were crushed against his furry chest. Though he protected her tiny body from his full weight, she felt suffocated beneath his massive form. She panted and writhed beneath him, yet her struggling movements only intensified his desire. His hand roamed down her back and across her flat stomach. She gasped at the sensation of his touch, her blood pounding as fast as his, yet steeled herself against this bewildering sensation. She bared her deadly nails to strike at his face, so handsome yet so close to hers. He sensed the danger and quickly gripped her wrists, once again pinning them tightly beneath her.

"You fight well and hard, my lady. But have no doubt as to who will win this match. Sweet victory will be mine. Relax and you may enjoy it also," he breathed and once again sought the sweetness of her honeyed lips.

"No!" she cried as he pressed down to once again crush her beneath him.

Her pleas meant nothing to him. He forced her tightly squeezed legs apart with his knees. Skillfully he ran his hands down along her taut stomach to the warm tangle between her legs. She gasped again in bewilderment, but before she had time to protest, his body moved to possess hers and he thrust himself deep within her.

Her choked cry filled the air as he nearly rent her apart. Burning, searing pain coursed through her rigid, unyielding body. Tears poured down her cheeks as he hesitated only for a moment—shocked at finding her thus untouched. But his passion was at its peak, and he could contain himself no longer.

Again he thrust and again the pain pulsed through her. She clenched her fists, contracting them again and again with each new drive. She ordered her mind to overcome the pain, and as her body became less rigid, so did the hurt. Numbness overcame her, and she cursed both Michael and her own sinful flesh.

At last the captain's passion was spent, and he withdrew from her. He eased himself beside her and tried to cradle her in his arms.

Christy pulled away and hugged the edge of the bed, sobbing in utter mortification. She hated him not only for what he had done to her physically, but also for filling her with confusion and shame at the response he had evoked in her.

She vowed that he'd never touch her again. Never again would she let her heart flutter at his glance or touch. Never again would she let him inflict such pain upon her. Her flaming senses had not prepared her for the brutal pain of his assault; they had promised sweet fulfillment. Instead she had felt only burning, searing humiliation. She had learned, too late, where innocent longings could lead.

The captain contemplated her quietly. Her slim, white shoulders shook with sobs. Again he reached over to gently pull aside the damp black curls that clung to her neck, but she jerked away and withdrew further into the corner of the bunk. "Don't touch me!" she whimpered, full of pain and humiliation.

It was not Michael Lancer's custom to force any woman to bed against her will, especially a virgin. He had never had the need before. His lovers had always been women of the world, only too willing to satisfy his needs and their own. Yet this young woman, so tempting, so beautiful, and yet so aloof to his advances, had aroused in him a passion he found difficult to control. But it was more than a physical longing to possess her that set her apart from the rest. He refused to admit, even to himself, that his attraction to her could be more than physical. But there was an unknown element here. It could not be love, for he loved no woman. But what then? Whatever it was, she would hate him now and he felt a deep sorrow at that. In a single heated moment, he had taken this untouched flower and carelessly broken her stem. He had every right to feel ashamed.

He sighed heavily and rose from the bed, tormented by remorse, yet aching for the feel of her. Throwing on his robe, he sat down on the chair and awaited her attack. It was not long in coming.

Christy, feeling him leave her side, ceased her tears and valiantly tried to regain her lost dignity. Pulling the sheets about her, she sat to face him. Though the room was still dark, she could see him silhouetted against the light of the moon. She spoke with slowness and control, yet the anger in her voice was unmistakable.

"You are evil and loathsome. I hate you with my whole being. You have taken from me what was mine alone to give. You have taken the last thing I had left to give a man. I have no family, no money, no dowry, no possessions. They were all forcefully taken from me. But at least I had myself to offer. Now because of you, I have nothing left. I hope you enjoyed your passion, for the price it cost me was a dear one."

She slipped from the bed and with quiet determination headed toward the door.

"I am truly sorry I hurt you. I was tired and the rum gave me the resolve to carry out what I had longed for since I first met you. I am but a man, and your beauty tempts me beyond control."

"Your apology does little to comfort me now, or right the wrong you have done. There is nothing left for me

139

now but the life of a whore! What decent man will take to wife a woman used and soiled?"

Unfortunately her words only pricked his anger. She spoke as if, in one unthinking moment, he was to be blamed for the ruination of her entire life. He would not sit back and accept such guilt. "Actually I only took what was rightfully my due in retribution for your passage. No man would fault me for it," he said.

He leaned back in his chair and continued in his own defense. "I do not believe your life ruined because I have made a woman of you. You are young and beautiful and many men would overlook much to have you as their own. In fact, I may have added to your value, for now at least you have some knowledge of a man's needs. At any rate, my offer still stands. Perhaps now you will give it more favorable consideration. I would be very good to you as my mistress. But do not expect me to marry you merely because I took my pleasure of you but once. A man does not usually wed his mistress."

A tear trickled down Christy's cheek at his words. He simply could not fathom how she felt. "You wound me not only with your force, but with your words as well," she muttered and bent her head to hide her pain.

"As I said, I am sorry I hurt you. But it would have happened sooner or later. You are far too beautiful to have remained untouched for long. A body like yours was made for a man's pleasure. Someday you may even realize it can bring you pleasure as well."

His statement rankled her no small amount and she bristled with indignation. "Made for a man's pleasure, am I? Does that mean I am to submit to every man who desires me? You are no better than the two fools who nearly raped me the other night. In fact, in all respects, sir, you are far worse. You knew my situation and my feelings as they did not, yet you took me anyway as you would any common whore. I will despise you forever!"

"Forever is a long time, my dear. And besides, I thought Sam and John had already done their worst to you. Perhaps I may have been better able to control myself had I known the truth."

The more she thought about it, the angrier she became at his callous lack of concern for her and the things she believed in. Her fingers clasped the wash basin beside her and she hurled it at the shadow before her. Not waiting to see if it struck her target, she dashed for the door.

Only quick reflexes saved him from being struck by the flying weapon. He jumped from his chair and lunged for the door. Grabbing her flying arms, he pulled her back into his room.

"You silly fool! Should you run through the halls naked you would have more than me to fight off! Now go back to bed. In the morning I will fetch your dress."

"No! I want nothing from you. Nothing! Do you hear me? Let me go. I never want to see you again!" she cried, incensed anew by his restraining arms.

"My dear, do not press me too far again." The warning was as equally applicable to his rising anger as it was to his mounting desire. Her naked, struggling form pressed tightly against him did much to weaken his resolve. Without giving her the chance to respond, he picked her up in his arms. Once again she found herself lying naked in his bed as he gazed down greedily.

"You monster!" she screamed, kicking and flying at him with fists bent on inflicting pain and suffering. Her anger suddenly stuttered to a halt. She looked into his eyes. Again they were ablaze with hunger. She drew in a quick breath and lay very still, hardly breathing, yet watching him intently.

For a moment his eyes caressed her and then he ran his fingers along her slender body. She closed her eyes and tried to pull away as his burning fingertips simultaneously sent waves of panic and excitement through her. Her mind screamed of her hate for this loathsome beast all the while her body tingled at his practiced touch.

Michael saw the confusion mirrored in her smoky green eyes and gently yet insistently moved her to face him. His lips touched her long black lashes and traveled slowly down to her lips. Her breasts felt soft and smooth beneath his touch.

A tear trickled down Christy's pale cheek and she began to tremble despite her vow to be brave. It was useless to struggle against him. Regardless of her efforts, he would again have his way with her.

"Damn!" he swore softly to himself as he read the mute fear reflected in the tiny teardrop. It had been sporting battle when she fought against him. He could handle that. But the quiet, quivering form lying in resignation and defeat beneath him, and the terror mirrored in her emerald eyes were enemies too difficult to cope with. He could not inflict more pain on her for his own selfish pleasures.

Christy felt him rise from the bed and move away. In a

moment the door creaked softly and she knew she was alone. The quiet of the room was marred only by her soft crying. This handsome wretch had ripped from her the flower of her womanhood and left in its place a growing, exasperating need for him. Her hate for him was without bounds.

Ten

The morning was filled with shouts of good tidings as everyone aboard hastened to secure the ship for its final docking in Charleston. The men aboard *The Merrimer* were happy to at last be home. It had not been an exceptionally rough trip, but seeing the familiar coastline dotted with shops and houses sent everyone's heart to a quick and light beat of anticipation. Thanks to the strategy and daring of Captain Lancer they had made good time and would be nicely compensated for their efforts of the past three months. The toils of the day grew more stringent, but muscles worked in harmony with each league bringing the ship closer to the shore.

Everyone aboard the ship seemed filled with anticipation. Everyone except Christy. She stood gazing upon the distant shoreline from the deck of the massive ship. The wind whipped gently around her head, making the glowing black curls dance merrily about her face and shoulders. She pulled her shawl closer about her neck and shivered, though the morning air was warm. What life would she have here in this new land?

Michael had enlisted her aid in putting his books in order, but he had ignored her suggestion of continuing as his secretary once they reached Charleston. Perhaps it was not suitable for a woman to hold such a position in this land, or perhaps he already had someone taking care of his finances. Whatever the reason, her face grew hot at the memory of what had followed her innocent suggestion.

Since that night his attitude had changed somewhat toward her. Though she could still read the look of lust in his searing brown eyes, he kept himself distant. It was no secret he still contemplated the idea. She knew she had only to consent to be his mistress and her life would be safe and secure, at least for a time. But that was a price too high to pay for security. She would find some other way.

The past few weeks she had grown to understand him a little more, though he still frightened her at times. But what plagued and confused her more were her own feelings toward him. She remembered with vivid clarity the night he had crushed her in his arms and forced himself upon her. She despised him for it. Yet, with the passing of time, the memory of his burning lips upon her sent a tiny thrill through her body.

She knew little about this big, handsome man, except that he had left his mark upon her body and was playing havoc with her mind. She had lain awake many a night trying to sort out her confused feelings. Why should she care about him? At times he made her feel low and miserable with his verbal abuse. Yet hadn't he given her the beautiful fabric to make herself a dress? He told her she would be of little use to him with duties aboard the ship, yet he had trusted her to organize and tally

145

his accounts.

For some unfathomable reason she longed for his love and respect, yet knew not how to win them. Every time they were together it seemed her temper flared and they ended up with harsh and cutting words tossed like knives at one another. Some of his words cut her more deeply than the lashings bestowed upon her by the drunken Henry Slate. How long ago that seemed, yet how vividly she still remembered his brutal assaults. Well, she was free from him at last, and perhaps here in this new land, her position and feelings would all become clearer. Hopefully she might even find some small measure of happiness.

Her gaze settled on the sandy white beaches which stretched for miles before her. It was truly a beautiful sight to behold after nearly three months at sea. Dense forests of cypress, cottonwood and oak reached to the cloudless blue sky and rolled gently back as far as the eye could see, broken only by an occasional house. The breathtaking sight did much to relieve her trepidation. She breathed in the fresh salty air as the ship drew nearer to the harbor.

Taking one last look at the tranquility before her, she returned to her little room to gather up her scanty belongings. She wore her only dress, the bright green one which she had made. The assorted shirts and trousers she had made to fit went into her sack, along with a few other personal items she had accumulated. With a sigh, she sat on the bed and waited for the docking of the ship.

She tried to envision what Michael's family was like and how they would react to her presence. Michael had impetuously informed her that she would live with him and his family until her indenture was over. He still refused to enlighten her as to what her status would be in his home, but she expected to assume responsibilities in the line of servant or housekeeper. Would his family understand and approve of her or would they ultimately despise her?

He spoke very little of them. She knew his mother had died approximately eight years ago. His father he described as a stern, crusty old fellow. He had one brother who traveled abroad, involved in financing and merchandising, who seldom darkened the doorstep of Penncrest. He also had a younger sister who was away in London at school. She would not return home until her studies were complete. Other than those small tidbits, Christy had no inkling of what awaited her.

Shouts from above brought her from her reverie. The ship jerked and ground against the dock and she realized they had at last reached Charleston Bay. It had been a long voyage, but she was glad it had finally come to an end, no matter what lay ahead for her.

After some time had passed, she decided to venture above and see what was happening. If Captain Lancer saw her, then surely he would tell her his wishes. She pushed open the door to the deck and gasped in surprise at the sight that met her eyes. After nearly three months of nothing but endless green waves, she was hardly prepared for the mass of converging humanity that appeared before her. Other large ships, similar to *The Merrimer*, were docked up and down the harbor with men laboring under the hot sun loading and unloading cargo.

Orders, curses, singing and greetings filtered through the air, blending into indistinguishable calamity.

Christy stood in rapt attention at all the activity before her. The streets running along the harbor were lined with men, women and children. Some were in wagons, some in luxurious carriages, but the majority of the crowd milled around on foot. People waved and shouted to one another and strained to see all that passed, fearing to miss the slightest activity. Old men and women pushed carts laden with all types of ware and fruits in an attempt to earn a pittance or two. A strong salty breeze swirled around her face and limbs as she watched in fascination. It seemed to lift her sagging spirits. This place would be her home and perhaps some of these people would be her friends.

For the first time since their departure from London she relished the adventure of what was to come. Even though Michael had told her Charleston was the most important and prosperous city south of Philadelphia, she had still imagined it to be scarcely populated with savage people living in dingy huts and tents. She was in no way prepared for such cultured, energetic civilization.

So intent was she on the activities before her, Christy failed to notice the crate swinging through the air headed straight for her. A warning shout from Paddy caught her attention, barely saving her from being struck. She glanced around, taking note of the hustling activity aboard the ship. It would be safer to remain below until called for, she decided. She turned, about to descend to the quiet of her room, when a familiar figure strolling down the gangplank caught her eye. She moved closer and called after the captain, but his attention was focused on a small group of people directly ahead. She walked slowly toward the ramp in patient pursuit of her master.

The captain hastened his pace down the rampway and wound his way through the crowd toward an elegant carriage drawn by two exquisite white horses. An enormous black stallion was tethered behind the buggy. Christy smiled. It would only be fitting that he ride such a magnificent beast.

The smile on her lips faded and her steps froze in midstride. With an elated smile, Captain Lancer reached out his arms and found himself wrapped in the strong and passionate embrace of a beautiful woman. Christy watched as he warmly returned her greeting. A twinge of jealousy hit her. He had made no mention of a woman in his life. And yet, as she watched the woman snuggle possessively beside him, she could not help but realize that this woman certainly held some claim on his affections. Their embrace was far too intimate for them to be simple acquaintances.

Christy sighed and tried to fight the feeling of jealousy. He was a handsome man. It was ridiculous to think he had no female ties. She would just have to accept the fact, though it made her feel all the more awkward than before.

She was about to turn away when she saw the woman wave into the crowd. In no way was she prepared for the sight of two small, blond-haired children—a boy of about eight and a girl of about six—who scrambled toward Michael and threw themselves into his waiting arms. They smothered him with hugs and kisses of delight until he gently held them off in order to keep his balance. She could not hear their excited exclamations, but it was obvious from their greeting that he was much more than a friend to them.

Christy turned away, tears of hurt and anger ready to spill down her cheeks. How dare he? How dare the man rape her, repeatedly attempt to persuade her to be his mistress, when all the while he had a wife and two children? She clenched her fists to fight off the tears. Pivoting quickly, she stalked below to her cabin. How could he expect her to live in his home, right under the eyes of his family, and play the tempting whore? How would the poor woman feel, greeting her husband with such love and devotion, only to be introduced to his new mistress? Or, she wondered, was she to be cloistered in some shabby hut, away from the public eye, to sit and await his passions and pleasures? What a dreadful, disgusting man he was, she thought, and slammed the door to her room with such force the whole ship seemed to vibrate.

She threw herself on the bed with a sob of anger. Well, she would not play his game. Somehow she would find a job and repay him with money—not labor. A plan began to formulate in her mind. She brushed away the stinging tears impatiently and rose from the cot. Driven by a new determination, she hurried to the captain's room and scribbled him a note. Boldly she explained that she fully intended repaying her debts and would be in touch with him as soon as she got settled. Satisfied, and not stopping to contemplate the possible consequences, she placed the note conspicuously on his bunk and returned to her room.

She grabbed her few belongings and hurried up onto the deck. A quick look around assured her that everyone was occupied with unloading the ship. She would not be missed for some time. She threw a quick glance at the scene on shore. The captain's attention was fully occupied with his family. No doubt he had completely and conveniently forgotten all about her. Just as well. It would give her time to slip away.

With a deep breath, she clutched her bundle to her and made a hasty retreat down the gangplank. In seconds she was swallowed up in the milling crowd. Only Paddy saw her rush past. Though he yelled for her, she paid him no heed but pushed her way through the crowded street. She had no idea where she was going, but little mattered except putting as much distance as possible between herself and Captain Michael Lancer.

Christy pushed her way through the crowded maze of people, carts, children, dogs and trash in hopes of getting as far away from the harbor as possible. She ignored the curious stares directed toward her; a woman alone with tear-stained face, clutching a small bundle tightly to her bosom.

At last her angry momentum eased. She stopped for a moment to catch her breath. As she did so, a middle-aged man approached and placed a dirty hand on her arm, smiling a toothless grin at her. His words, however, left anything but a smile on her face. She pulled away in haste at his obscene offer and hurried on. Apparently the captain had been correct in warning her of the flesh peddlers that frequented the docks. It was not safe for a young girl to be alone and unescorted. She would have to be more careful. Shaken but still firm in her resolve, she hastened toward what she hoped was a calmer section of town.

An hour later, hot and exhausted, she finally stopped and looked around. The mass of hurrying humanity had thinned, and she stood contemplating the street before her. Away from the crowded and noisy harbor, the town looked quite tranquil and orderly. The main street was wide, lined with numerous shops, stores and hotels. Wagons rolled up and down cautiously, sending clouds of dust into the hot, dry air. Elegantly dressed men meandered slowly down the walkways, tipping their hats to parcel-laden women. Horses galloped down the street, their riders in a hurry to be about their business. A sleepy, rather mangy looking dog stopped to regard Christy. Assessing her as an unlikely prospect for food scraps, he sauntered on down the street and disappeared into an alley.

Christy was at a loss as to just where to begin. Should she secure a room for the evening with a promise to pay later? Or should she begin searching for employment immediately? Not relishing the idea of having to beg for lodging, she decided to try her luck at finding a job. If she had work, it might be easier securing a room than if she had no job and thus no likelihood of payment.

The sun beat down hotly. She had no hat to shield her pale cheeks from the burning heat and they were becoming a bright pink. Rather self-consciously she patted her curls into place and smoothed her skirt. Drawing a deep breath, she entered a tiny dress shop at the far end of the street. A cheerful bell tinkled invitingly as the door opened and closed. She waited nervously for an answer to the bell, and a moment later a short, painfully thin man of forty or more years appeared from behind a curtain.

"Good day, madam. May I help you?" he asked politely, eyeing her slightly disheveled appearance.

"Good day, sir," she responded, trying to sound cool and businesslike. She looked slowly and deliberately about the little shop. Faceless mannequins were dressed in gowns of extraordinary beauty, while sketches of other creations lay scattered about tables around the room. The shop was neat, clean, and looked quite expensive.

"I've recently arrived here from London. My family sent me ahead to get established and will join me in the near future." The little man waited patiently. Though she looked rather bedraggled, he had hopes of acquiring a new client.

Christy consoled herself about the slight lie. It had been partially because of her uncle, Henry Slate, that she found herself in this strange new place, and someday she did hope to have a family and settle down. Gaining a small measure of courage, she continued. "Unfortunately, after having just arrived, I found myself robbed of a good portion of my monies. It will be some time before they hear of my dilemma and can send me financial support." She paused.

Disappointment showed clearly in the little man's eyes. He felt sure that, as before, he would be asked to make some garments with offer of generous payment when money could be had. He nodded his head dispassionately. It was truly a pity such a beautiful girl should have to beg for clothing. It would have been a real pleasure to design and fit such a magnificent figure instead of the floppish, matronly women who made up a large part of his clientele. But he was weary of charity cases. One did not survive long on flimsy notes and empty promises. Besides, he was not a man who overly enjoyed female attentions.

"I am sorry to hear that, madam. 'Tis a terrible shame honest people should suffer so sorely at the hands of criminals and highwaymen. But," his voice became stern and almost unfriendly, "I fear I cannot create and fit a gown for you without proper payment. I am a simple shopkeeper and could scarcely remain in business without financial resources. I am sorry. I cannot help you." With a nod, he turned to go.

"But, sir," replied Christy, realizing her error in not making herself clearer. "I did not come here to ask for your charity."

The shopkeeper turned in surprise and raised his eyebrow dramatically. "Then, madam, just what is it you wish of me?"

"Well . . . I . . . I have come seeking employment."

"Pardon me?" he sputtered, shock registering on his rather delicate features. "Let me understand you correctly. You wish to work for me? Here?"

Christy was slightly miffed by his reaction. "Yes, sir. As I told you, I was beset by bandits and find myself financially embarrassed. I wish to find employment to support myself until I send for my family."

"But, madam. This is highly unorthodox. I never

heard of such a thing. Why, what could you do for me, girl? I certainly run no brothel here!"

She bristled slightly at his rude assumption. "I seek respectable employment, sir. This is why I came here. I do have some experience as a seamstress. I designed and sewed this gown." She indicated the bright green dress she wore. His rather dubious look sparked her to explain further. "I had very little to work with as far as threads and decorations. But it is not bad, is it, sir?" She had never found it necessary to sell anything, much less herself. The experience was new, and rather humiliating.

He looked critically over the superb fit of the full bustline and tiny waist. He had to admit that though it was simple, she had done a fine job. "My dear lady, 'tis indeed a nice, simple dress, and fits you quite well. Yet I cannot judge your talents by one single garment."

"If you would give me a chance, I could prove myself."

"I am sorry, madam, but even if your talent proved satisfactory I have an adequate staff. I have no need for additional help."

Christy's face fell but she would not give up. "Then perhaps, sir, you may have need for someone to sweep and clean up, or run errands, or even post your accounts." She was desperate.

Again he was aghast at her forwardness. "I have no need of any such person," he said rather hastily. "Now, madam, if you will excuse me, I have work to be about."

"But, sir . . ." she began.

"No!" he repeated firmly. "I am sorry. It is out of the question. Good day!"

Christy sensed his decision was final. Despite the

feeling of failure, she raised her chin proudly and smiled at him. "Very well, sir. I thank you for your time. You have been very patient. Good day."

With a nod, she turned and glided from the shop. The smile she gave him belied the tears welling in her eyes.

The shopkeeper watched her leave, shaking his head in cold apathy. With her striking beauty she would soon find a wealthy man to take care of her. Such was the way of things. With that, he shut the door and promptly forgot her.

Christy continued down the street. She stopped at shop after shop, yet had no better luck anywhere else. People were appalled to find a young woman openly seeking employment, despite her story of woe.

As the afternoon wore on, her spirits as well as her appearance began to wilt. It seemed no one was willing to give her any type of help. Even the hotel had turned her down as too thin and pale, saying she would not be strong enough to last two days as a chambermaid. The hotel manager had suggested night work, but she flatly refused and hurried on her way.

Her hopes were finally buoyed when a sympathetic general storekeeper agreed to let her help around the store. He said he was getting old and a pretty face might help boost business. She nearly kissed him in her relief at finally securing a job. But her hopes were short lived. When the stopkeeper's wife took a look at Christy, she decided she wanted no beguiling young girl underfoot her husband's nose all day. She rudely informed them so and unceremoniously ushered Christy out of the shop.

Back on the street again, she noted with a sinking heart

that the sun was beginning to dip into the horizon. She was exhausted, and the continuous growl in her stomach reminded her that she had not eaten since the previous evening. She had only one more place to try and what if they would not take her in? What would she do then? She shook her head stubbornly and refused to consider final defeat. With her best and last smile, she entered a tiny tobacco shop on the edge of town. She was met by a middle-aged man behind the counter.

Christy felt his eyes openly taking in every inch of her body; not missing the slightest detail. Good sense told her to turn around and leave immediately, but the knawing in her stomach and the ache in her heart made her swallow yet more pride and accept his raking perusal. She told him her plight, much the same as she had told the others. The man grinned and winked at her.

"Well, missy. I have nothing for you in the shop, but I'm sure we can work something out. I may be able to find something for you out back. With a face and body such as you've got, we could be rich in no time."

The disgust Christy felt showed on her lovely face and in her snapping green eyes. Much the same suggestion had been offered to her throughout the day. Now, however, tired and hungry, her patience was at an end. "I've no interest in the type of work you suggest, sir. I will not sell myself for you or anyone else!"

With a huff of disgust she whirled and fled from the store, nearly knocking over an elderly gentleman in her haste to leave. His entrance had stopped the loud and vulgar comments that the shopkeeper had hurled after her fleeing back.

She walked quickly down the street and passed the boisterous gaiety coming from a saloon. High pitched feminine laughter filtered through the air and she caught the sight of the crowded, smoke-filled bar. She brushed past drunken men who yelled obscene invitations in her direction and hurried on, blocking out their vulgarity. Her spirits were near breaking. Was the life of a whore all that was left to her? She had tried everything else with absolutely no success.

The captain and his crew had done a thorough yet painful job of opening her eyes as to what life could hold for a single, defenseless girl. She had been totally wretched under the hateful abuse of Henry Slate, yet the sexual abuse she now suffered seemed almost more unbearable. She could suffer the sting of the whip, yet how could she fight the passionate nature of the male being?

On the verge of despair, she stopped, panting heavily, and found herself at the far end of the town. A small church stood off the road surrounded by a cluster of trees. She spied a nearby bench and dragged her weary body to it. Exhaustion was quickly overtaking her, along with misery from a lack of food and drink.

She glanced up at the little church. Perhaps she would find a haven there. She had no other alternative but to try. Reaching deep within herself for strength, she mounted the steps to the church. The door was locked so she knocked softly. There was no response. She knocked again, louder this time, but the noise only echoed through the empty building.

Darkness was swiftly approaching and she had to face

reality. All three hotels had informed her that payment, at least partial payment, in advance was mandatory before a room was rented. Since she had no money they would give her no room. She stared at the huge church door, weighing her alternatives. She had two choices. She could either spend the night in the dark forest or return to the ship in defeat.

The ship offered a sheltered haven against the cold and dampness. She certainly did not relish the thought of wild animals creeping up on her as she slept in the forest. But would the ship be safe? Captain Lancer had, no doubt, gone home by now with his family. She would be alone on the ship and at the mercy of whatever crew remained. With him gone they would no doubt have few qualms about seeking her out. But where else could she go?

With a heavy heart, she decided to return to the ship and worry about the captain tomorrow. She was just too tired and hungry to care any more. Turning dejectedly, she gasped in surprise as an elderly man with gray hair, and of no small stature, stood directly in her path.

"Excuse me, my dear. I did not intend to startle you," apologized the old man. Despite his age, he had a stately bearing, and the thick gray hair which covered his head in neat profusion added to his vintage. His eyes were a soft, gentle brown, and his lips were partially covered by a huge gray mustache. He leaned lightly on his expensive walking cane and regarded Christy with curiosity.

"'Twas my fault, sir. I did not see or hear you. I . . . I was looking for the parson."

"He is out of town for about a month, tending to a sick

relative." He eyed her closely. "'Tis rather late for one so young to be out alone. May I offer you an escort? It is not safe at this hour for you to be by yourself. Too many ruffians about."

"Thank you kindly, sir, but I will be fine. I've not far to go," she lied. She knew only too well it was dangerous enough in this town during the day, much less at nightfall.

"Very well," he said, unconvinced, as she turned to go. He noticed a slight hesitation on her part as she headed into the darkened street. She glanced back to see him frown slightly at her obvious uncertainty. Not wanting to appear as lost as she felt, she began walking with determination down the street. She certainly did not wish to be caught in town when the sun disappeared completely from the already darkening sky.

Chin up, eyes forward, she concentrated on making her way up the street. Yet in her haste to reach the ship before darkness fell, she failed to cross the street to the safer side. Hurriedly she passed the brightly illuminated, crowded saloon. At the precise moment she passed, a drunken man in old, dirty clothing tripped from the doorway and collided directly into her. Taken by surprise, she stumbled and fell into the street.

With unsteady hands, the drunk attempted to help her to her feet. It was all he could do to stand himself, however, and thus was more of a detriment to her than anything else. She struggled to rise, shocked and embarrassed, as he breathed heavily. His mouth was open and he gaped at the soft, ample breasts swelling beneath the tightly fitted bodice.

"Hello there, little lady. Out looking for a little romp?" he slurred drunkenly.

"No! No!" she cried, appalled by his suggestion. Her skin crawled at his touch and she attempted to pull away. The drunk, however, apparently thought her some trollop and disregarded her protests. Even in his intoxicated state, he held her tightly, dragging her toward the brawling saloon doors. She grew wild with panic yet had not the strength to free herself from his grip.

Suddenly a voice came from behind. A hand was placed lightly on her arm. "My dear, what seems to be the problem? Is this man bothering you?"

Before she could answer, the drunken man squeezed her arm tighter. She winced in pain.

"The lady's with me." He yanked her roughly in his direction.

"I think not, sir, for the lady is with me," replied the elderly gentleman with quiet authority.

The drunk looked at the man confronting him with a jaundiced eye. "She's with you, aye, guv'ner?" he slurred. "Well I found 'er wandering alone. You git yerself 'nother wench to warm yer bed. This un's mine."

"Sir," said the elderly man. His voice was no longer soft but held a note of forced control. "I told you this lady is with me. As you can see, my carriage waits." He indicated a handsome buggy parked across the street.

"And what if I don't let 'er go?"

"Then, good sir, I will have to call my driver over to help you see it my way." He again indicated the carriage, but this time they noticed a huge man with bulging muscles and a mean, dark glare casually leaning against the doors.

The drunk thought over the situation. At length he released her arm and glared with open contempt at them both.

"'Ave it yer way, guv'ner. She's too bloody scrawny fer my tastes, anyway," he said to soothe his pride. Uttering an oath at them, he headed for the saloon and the safety of his cups.

Christy shuddered involuntarily as he disappeared through the swinging doors. Once again she had been forced to cope with a drunken, disorderly man. This time the outcome had been considerably less violent, however. Her musings ended abrutly as the elderly man lightly touched her arm and guided her toward his carriage. His grip was gentle but firm, and despite her feeble protests he gave her no choice but to enter the carriage. Seeing her seated, he entered himself and closed the door behind him.

"Excuse me for being so presumptuous, my dear. I did not mean to interfere but I could see you needed to be extracated from that bumbling fool." He eyed his companion closely as she sat uneasily in the shadows.

"I am in your debt, sir. I don't know what I would have done had you not offered your assistance. You have my deepest gratitude."

"You need not thank me, my dear. It was my privilege to offer my services. Now since you are in my carriage, allow me to drive you home. Where shall I direct the driver to take you?"

A combination of tears and shame pricked Christy. What could she say to this kind gentleman? How could she tell him she had no place to go? The silence became heavy as she frantically debated with herself as to what to say.

"Come now, child. I want only to help you."

"I . . . I was on my way back to the harbor. I just arrived from London and was looking for a place to stay. I have not found anything as yet, so I am forced to return to the ship for the night."

"But, my dear. There are many inns along the harbor and here in town. Have you not tried them?"

"Well, sir," she squirmed uneasily. She hated lying to this man yet found herself repeating the same story she had told all day.

"I find myself very low on monies," she began. That was indeed an understatement. "I was set upon by thieves when I arrived and cannot afford lodging. I have tried all day to find employment but nothing is available." She was dangerously close to a flood of tears and only fists tightly clenched in her lap stayed them from spilling out.

The man took note and questioned her gently. "But, my dear. Are you all alone? Have you no family or friends to take you in? Surely one so young did not come so far all alone and unprotected, with no contacts?"

The day of humiliation and defeat closed in on Christy. She could no longer hold back the grief and exhaustion. Tears spilled unchecked down her cheeks. She nodded lamely, shame keeping her from lifting her eyes to meet his. "'Tis a long story, sir. But I am indeed all alone."

"That's incredible!" He paused in shock as he listened to her weep. His thoughts once again collected, he tapped

163

the roof with his walking cane. "Morgan, home please," he ordered. The coach set off with a jerk. He pulled a handkerchief from his coat and pressed it into her trembling hand. "Dry those pretty eyes, my dear. I shall see you have a place to stay for as long as need be."

Christy wiped her eyes with the cloth. "Sir, that is very kind of you, but as I said, I have nothing to pay you for your kindness. It would be far too presumptuous to accept your generous offer under the circumstances."

"Bah. That's pure nonsense, my dear. It would be an honor to have you grace my humble abode. You will be welcome in my home as a guest and no payment will be required." He paused, contemplating his passenger. "I will ask one thing of you, however."

Christy looked up, suddenly unsure and frightened. Would he too demand payment for his kindness in the form of physical retribution? Such seemed to be the way of things for her.

Her mind was quickly put to rest as he continued. "I would like to know your name. One as lovely as you must surely have a name."

Christy smiled at his humor through her tears. He was so kind. Why was she suddenly so quick to expect the worst from people? "Sir, my name is Christina Patterson." As soon as the words left her lips, she realized her error. Surely Captain Lancer could trace her. Perhaps she should have given a fictitious name. But there was no point in worrying now. She had already sealed her fate by revealing her true identity.

Unaware of her trauma, he continued. "Ah, Christina. What a charming name indeed," he complimented. "And let me introduce myself to you. You may call me Sir Phillip." He lightly touched her hand in a formal gesture.

"I am pleased to meet you, sir." There was silence as she again debated with herself. She could not involve this kind man into her troubles without at least giving him fair warning. "Sir, before we venture any further, I think it best I admit something to you. You may wish to return me to the harbor, after all."

"Nonsense, my dear. Why would I do a thing like that?"

"I must tell you. I owe a man a good deal of money." She continued quickly at his shocked expression. "I could not pay in full for my voyage here and owe him a considerable sum for my passage. I fully intend to repay my debt. That is why I searched so diligently today to find employment. But alas, I found nothing."

"How much money do you owe this man?"

Christy's look was one of puzzlement. "I really don't know, sir. For some reason he has been quite evasive when I have posed that question. But I am sure it must be a goodly sum. I fear he will extract payment for my debt . . . in his own way . . . and I prefer to pay him back in cash. That is why I ran away when we docked. I suppose I may be considered a fugitive." She turned for a moment to gaze out into the blackness. Night had fallen and the outside world looked black and ominous as they bounced along toward their destination. "If I accept your hospitality I fear I will make you an accomplice. My benefactor may be quite upset with anyone who would interfere and help me. He has a rather violent temper and I would not want to subject you to any harm." Again she stopped and regarded the darkness. A shudder passed through her as she imagined Michael Lancer's rage when he found her gone.

Sir Phillip regarded her with interest. Despite her desperate plight, he sensed in her an inner courage and deep concern for others. Usually a good judge of character, he wanted to know her better. She was anything but an ordinary young woman and her story was definitely intriguing.

With genuine kindness, he touched her arm. "We will worry about your debts and this man tomorrow, my dear. Do not concern yourself with my welfare. I am sure I can handle him with no harm to myself. What is important now is to get you something to eat and a good night's sleep. On the morrow we will discuss this other matter."

"You are indeed kind, sir." She smiled at him and settled into the corner. She felt fairly safe and comfortable with this man, and she was tired; so terribly tired. Despite her efforts to remain awake and alert, her unbearably heavy eyelids fluttered closed, and she dozed fitfully.

Some time later, the coach stopped and she found herself being led into what appeared, through her sleepy eyes, to be a huge, magnificent house. Without a word she was handed over to a big black woman and a young maid, who lead her to a room. Without delay they had her undressed and steaming in a hot bath.

Christy thought it strange the woman had taken charge without a word from her elderly employer. It was almost as if she had been expected. But her tired mind refused to contemplate this strange occurrence further. She relaxed in the tub, letting the exhaustion drain from her body.

A short time later she found herself tucked comfortably beneath warm, soft blankets, her stomach pleasantly full. With a sigh of contentment, she drifted off into exhausted slumber.

Eleven

The sun was just beginning to filter through the window when Christy awoke. The rich blue drapes dressing the windows swayed leisurely in a gentle breeze. With a yawn of contentment, she propped herself up in the huge canopied bed and gazed at her surroundings.

The medium-sized room was tastefully decorated in varying shades of blue and brown. A large dressing table stood on one end of the room, complemented by a smaller version, complete with wash basin, hair brushes, and fresh linen. At the far end of the room was a sofa of delicate blue, green and brown brocade with a tiny footstool placed to one side. Various scenic paintings of the surrounding countryside graced the walls, adding a touch of quaint cheerfulness. The room was certainly pleasant and seemed like real luxury to her after living in the barn at the Slates, and then being so long cramped aboard the dark, musty ship.

. She slipped from the bed and shivered slightly as the cool morning air tickled her bare feet. She settled the small shift upon her shoulders and tiptoed about, making a closer inspection of her room. She strolled about, touching this, examining that.

The fresh linen placed neatly beside the wash basin reminded her of the rather stout black woman, called Bertha, who had tended her last night. Though she had been thorough and efficient, Christy sensed that Bertha neither liked nor trusted her unexpected guest. Small wonder, she thought, coming in the middle of the night with nothing but the clothes on her back. It certainly must have appeared unusual.

Yet Bertha had taken it in her stride, as if accustomed to such occurrences. Was Sir Phillip in the habit of bringing strays home, or had she, in fact, been expected? She could not rid herself of this eerie feeling that somehow Bertha and the serving girl had known she was coming. But how ridiculous to suspect anything. Even she herself had not known from one minute to the next what she would do. How could a total stranger have guessed her moves?

She strolled to the window and out onto the balcony. From her side vantage point, she could see a good portion of the spacious mansion quite clearly. A tree-lined road wove gently up to four large pillars decorating a flight of marble stairs leading to the entrance of the house. Her gaze traveled beyond the house and out to the yard. She wrinkled her brow as she noticed the unkempt appearance of the large flower beds which were scattered around the plush green lawn. It seemed a shame to let such beauty go untended. Perhaps the gardener had been ill.

Well away from the house, yet still slightly visible from her window, she glimpsed two large red stables. Even from this distance they appeared clean and well kept. The sight pricked her curiosity. How many horses did Sir Phillip own? What breed were they? Would he let her see them? Her enthusiasm suddenly vanished. Thinking of horses brought back a flood of memories—good memories, but all too many painful ones. She forced herself to once again study what lay around her. It was not hard to guess by the house and surroundings that Sir Phillip possessed considerable wealth.

A door slamming somewhere in the house brought Christy from her reverie. With a sigh she slipped on her dress and sat before the mirror to brush her long black hair into shining splendor. With deft fingers, she tucked it up on the top of her head, securing all the loose curls. She felt so much better this morning after a hot bath and good night's sleep. Her cheeks had a rosy hue from the brutal sun of the previous day. Perhaps they were a bit too red to be fashionable, but her critical eye consoled that they gave her a healthy, glowing appearance.

Ready at last, she stood and smoothed her dress wondering what to do. Should she be so bold as to find her own way to the breakfast room? Or would Sir Phillip send someone for her? She paced the room fretfully. The growl of her stomach finally decided the matter. She opened the door and stepped out, taking a wide, richly carpeted staircase down to the first floor.

A door to her far right stood slightly ajar and she glided across the immaculately polished floor to venture a peek inside. Sir Phillip sat behind a large, exquisite desk completely engrossed in stacks of papers and ledgers. She knocked softly, feeling shy and unsure of herself.

Sir Phillip glanced up. A smile softened his features as

he spied her in the doorway. "Come in, Miss Patterson. Come in," he called cheerily, rising quickly to greet her. "You're up early, my dear. Did you sleep well?"

"Yes, I did. Thank you, sir." In the light of day, Sir Phillip appeared even more stately and distinguished than she remembered from the night before. In fact, he looked similar to someone else she'd met. But who? She dismissed the thought quickly, feeling silly. She knew no one here in the Colonies. Her mind was playing tricks on her.

Sir Phillip, in turn, regarded his guest from behind slightly tilted spectacles. After a bit of rest and freshening up, her beauty was astounding. She seemed to have regained her poise and confidence somewhat and walked toward him with head held high. Despite the circumstances under which he had found her, there was no doubt in his mind that she was a well-bred young lady.

"Have you had something to eat yet, my dear?" he asked.

"No, sir, I have not," she replied.

"Well, if you don't mind waiting just a moment or two until I tally the last of these figures, we can breakfast together," he said indicating a seat across from his desk.

Christy picked up a copy of the *South Carolina Gazette* lying on the chair and placed it on the corner of the desk.

"Thank you. That would be very nice. Oh but I did not mean to intrude if you are busy. I can certainly wait in my room," she said, rising.

"Nonsense, my dear. 'Tis just some figures I post each morning before I enjoy a hearty breakfast. I'll be finished before long. Just make yourself comfortable. As I said, I

171

am nearly finished."

Christy nodded and smiled, settling herself back into the chair. When Sir Phillip had resumed his work, she let her gaze wander about the room. The study was large and unquestionably masculine. Heavy wooden furnishings dominated the room yet it was spacious enough to tastefully accommodate them. Beautiful dark paneling reached to the high ceiling and rows of books lined a dark wood book shelf. She was immensely impressed by the wealth displayed.

On the far side of the room two large paintings hung above the fireplace. The vivid colors brought the power and fury of the tossing, foamy sea into the room itself. A portrait behind Sir Phillip, above a beautiful carved mantel, caught her interest. It depicted a middle-aged woman of breathtaking beauty. Her smile was demure, yet her dark brown eyes seemed to beckon to Christy; as if the woman actually sat before her, living and breathing, and reading her every thought. There was something magical about those eyes and she immediately felt a strange kinship to this unknown lady. Was she Sir Phillip's wife, perhaps? Christy looked forward to meeting her.

She tore her eyes away and continued looking about the room. A table with carafes of bourbon, brandy, and stronger brews was positioned beside the desk where Sir Phillip sat. Behind this was another table holding various pipes and tobaccos. Christy's glance fell upon Sir Phillip and she was startled to find his attention focused on her and not on his papers. Unperturbed at being detected, he closed his ledgers, took his spectacles from his nose, and rose with a thankful sigh. "'Tis finished for another morning." He smiled at her. "And now shall we see what delectable tasties await our starving palates?" he said dramatically.

Christy smiled and rose. "Your eloquence is delightful, sir," she complimented, charmed by his manner.

"Why thank you, my dear. Your flattery is much appreciated by this old man," he answered, offering her his arm. "Shall we go?"

"Good morning, sir, and madam. I hope I am not interrupting anything?" A third voice suddenly interrupted their departure. The voice was all too familiar to Christy.

The smile died on her face and her flesh prickled. She turned toward the door. There was no doubt the voice belonged to Captain Michael Lancer.

The silence hung like an ominous cloud as they stared at one another.

"Ah, Michael, you're just in time for breakfast," Sir Phillip called with slightly too much enthusiasm. He took Christy by the arm in a possessive, slightly guilty manner as if expecting her to bolt from the room. He could not however, bring himself to continue the light banter.

Again the silence was deafening as she stood regarding the two men before her. Sickened by her betrayal, she pulled her arm from Sir Phillip's grasp and drew back. His mere touch scalded her. Her emerald eyes openly accused him of trickery, yet no words condemned him.

Sir Phillip frowned to see her regard him thus. He had wanted to tell her gently of his association with Michael but had not had the opportunity. Now it was too late. He had lost the trust of the suddenly pale woman at his side.

At length, Christy composed herself and addressed herself to the man in the doorway. "Good morning, Captain. What a surprise to see you here. I had no doubt you would find me but I did not think it would be quite so soon. Apparently your informant wasted no time in telling you of my whereabouts."

She looked directly at Sir Phillip in accusation, and then suddenly turned and walked to the window. She did not wish either man to see or know the depth of her despair. Her knuckles were white as she clutched the sill with trembling hands. Her shallow, ragged breathing revealed her efforts to remain under control.

Sir Phillip frowned at Michael and walked to the window beside her. "Please don't think too badly of me, my dear. I was asked to be a part of the little charade and found it difficult to refuse Michael. I had no idea you were so vulnerable. I am deeply sorry if I hurt you."

"Hurt me! Why should I be hurt? I only gave you my trust. I thought you were my friend. It seems all along you were plotting against me. No doubt you both had a good laugh at my naivety." Tears of frustration slipped down her cheeks.

Then Michael spoke: "Come now, my dear. Don't be so hard on Father. It was my idea, after all. He only agreed to the plan upon my coaxing. He meant you no harm. Nor did I."

The astonishing revelation nearly knocked Christy over. "Your father!" she cried, relinquishing her place at the window and whirling to face the two men. No wonder Sir Phillip had looked so familiar!

"I presume then, sir, that your full name is Sir Phillip Lancer? I thought your introduction odd last night. If I had been less tired and more alert, and less trusting, perhaps I would have guessed the game. What a fool I was to trust anyone," she chastised herself aloud.

A sudden knock on the door caused a momentary truce. Sir Phillip strode impatiently across the room to admit the intruder. The man who entered was almost as dirty as his trousers and shirt. His black hair was in wild disarray and in need of washing. He glanced first at Sir Phillip and then to Michael. Finally the beady eyes he focused on Christy held open curiosity, and perhaps a bit more.

"What is it, Hoffman?" asked Sir Phillip, rather roughly. It was untimely enough for an intrusion, and he cared not for the seedy little man. But he did his job and did it well, and Sir Phillip could not find a replacement without just cause.

"I need a word with you, sir," answered the man rather self-importantly, dragging his eyes from the beautiful girl back to his employer.

"Can't you see I am busy right now. Surely it can wait."

"No, sir. 'Tis important."

"Very well, Hoffman," he grumbled. He turned to Christy. "Excuse me, please. I will return as quickly as possible." With that he hurried out, closing the door behind him.

As soon as his father was gone, Michael turned his full attention back to Christy. He had been greatly worried when he had found her gone from the ship, without a clue as to her whereabouts. It was far too dangerous for her to be roaming alone about Charleston. Now, gazing on her angry beauty, he was grateful to again have her at his side.

"Now, my dear, I believe you were accusing us of plotting against you," he began, strolling leisurely in her direction.

Christy watched him approach with increasing misgivings. To hide her apprehension, she began firing questions at him. "How did you find me so quickly? Was it necessary to involve your father in my capture? How did you know where I would go? What I would do?"

Michael waved his hand in her direction. "One question at a time, madam." His tone was mocking as he casually strolled to the smoking stand and lit a cigar. He puffed appreciatively for a few moments before beginning his narrative.

"Paddy saw you rush off into the crowd and immediately came to inform me. It seems he was concerned about your welfare and hurt that you did not stop to bid him farewell. I returned to my cabin and found your note. It was easy to guess you intended trying to find a job. Knowing you as I do, I presumed you would first attempt something respectable. I had a few of my men keep an eye on you as you visited shop after shop. Without much luck, I must surmise."

Christy grew hot in humiliation. It was bad enough she'd suffered rejection after rejection. But to discover others had watched her lack of success rankled her deeply. "Why did you not just send your men to fetch me back immediately, then, if you knew where I was and what I was about?"

"What? And ruin your adventure? Ridiculous. Besides, if I'd interrupted, you may have been inclined to run off and try again. At least now you know that route to be hopeless and have not much choice but to remain with me."

His tone was cruel, cutting her more than any lash ever could. She was furious with him and with herself for being such a fool. "You are despicable," she growled at him.

"So you have told me on more than one occasion. It also seems you shared the description with my father. Now let me think. How did he say you put it? Ah yes. 'He has a violent temper and may subject you to harm.' Indeed, madam, I had thought my anger well contained when dealing with you."

"Well then think again, sir!" she interrupted. "Your idea of temperance and mine seem entirely different."

"Actually my father only mentioned the incident as a chastisement for treating you so cruelly. You must have painted a very black picture of me, indeed, my dear. But aside from that, he has, for some unknown reason, taken a liking to you. He regrets his part in your entrapment. He told me so last night after you were in bed. I had to tell him the whole story, you see, in order to get him to agree to help. I did not want to cause a scene by dragging you off, so I had him appear at your darkest moment and rescue you. Quite gallant of me, don't you agree?"

"Sir, your gallantry could only be exceeded by your abundant modesty," she replied coldly.

His humor suddenly vanished as he strode to loom

before her. "My dear, I don't think you realize just how lenient I have been with you. Do you know all the time and trouble you have caused me? Do you realize it is a criminal offense for a bond slave to run off? It is my legal right to have you bound to a post and publicly whipped for your attempted escape." He watched her cringe in fear at his threat.

"As we both know, you are well acquainted with the feel of the lash upon you. I fear you are far too spirited and headstrong for your own good. Someday you may find yourself in deep trouble if you do not curb your will." He paused and regarded her skeptically. Her shoulders squared even as he spoke. "I see my words fall on deaf ears. Is a whipping the only means to break your spirit and make you docile?"

Christy raised her chin and faced him proudly. "Sir, many men before you have tried long and hard to break my spirit—without success. If, as you say, it is your right and desire to use the lash as punishment, then I cannot stop you. But be warned, sir. You may break my back, but you will never break my spirit! Never!"

He raised his brow at her courageous rebuttal. She had a grit and determination that he admired and, at the same time, found slightly infuriating. "Very well. I see the lash will not tame you. I had no intention however, of further scarring your exquisite flesh. One does not destroy or mar beauty such as yours. The law, however, does allow me another recourse in dealing with runaway slaves. I am permitted to increase the amount and length of your bondage in retribution for your attempted escape. I believe that will be more satisfactory to me, though perhaps more torturous to you."

"But I did not run away from my debts. I fully intended to repay you every last shilling! I told you so in the note I left!"

"Ah yes. The note. Without a witness and my authorizing signature, it would certainly not stand up as valid in any court of law. You should have checked more thoroughly before taking such rash action. You've no one to blame but yourself."

"And I am sure you would have signed and approved my note had I handed it to you before I left," she quipped indignantly.

He smiled benevolently down at her, his answer quite clear from the look on his face. He put out his cigar and tried a new approach. "Whatever possessed you to run off in such a hurry? Did I not indicate that I would find a place for you here and that you would be taken care of?"

"With your lustful proposals you only too clearly indicated how I would be taken care of. Did you honestly think that after taking me once against my will, thereafter I would willingly submit to your passions once we arrived? I thought I made my feelings clear to you on that point. But now, finding you have a wife and two children; the situation is even more revolting. You pride yourself and your desires too highly, my lord!"

His eyes flashed in anger at her insult. A moment later, however, he burst into laughter. "My wife! Did you say my wife? And two children? My goodness. Why, my dear, whatever gave you the idea that I was a family man?"

"The woman at the harbor . . . the two children. I thought . . ." Her voice trailed off in sudden confusion.

"Is that why you ran off? Because you thought I was married and had a family yet still wanted to cool my passions upon your slender form? You could have saved yourself much time and embarrassment had you but asked before taking flight. The woman you saw at the harbor is my sister-in-law, Matilda Lancer. The two little ruffians belong to her. She is certainly not my wife and, to the best of my knowledge, I have no little bastards running around the continent."

Christy's face was scarlet. "But the way you embraced; the way the children behaved. They seemed so pleased to see you. And, you never mentioned them."

"My sister-in-law is quite an aggressive woman, and rather enjoys such open displays of her affections."

"But does not your brother take offense to such behavior? Surely no man would consent to his wife openly running about seeking masculine attentions, even if the man is his brother."

"No doubt my brother would object strenuously were he here. But alas, he has been dead some three years now."

"Oh, I am so sorry," she murmured. The pieces were at last falling into place. "It must be difficult for her and the children without a husband and father," she commented to conceal her embarrassment.

"Matilda would like to remain an active member of the family, stressing her need for the companionship you suggest, and the children's need for a father. But widowhood seems to agree with her. Henry left them very well provided for upon his death. They live quite comfortably in a large home not far from here. She leads a free and exciting social life now. But I fear her valiant efforts to gain my affections may be distantly based on her slowly dwindling financial resources. Her excessive spending may soon get the better of her. As for me, I have no desire to tie myself down to any one woman. There are too many opportunities out there to be saddled down with one female.''

Christy's eyes narrowed at his arrogant, belittling tone, but she kept her mouth shut and let him go on.

''The children are a different matter. I fear they suffer from the absence of a father. I spend as much time with them as possible. They are truly the most conniving little darlings you ever want to meet. The open display of affection was smothered in demands to see what I had brought for them. But for all their mischievous ways, they are dear to me.'' His tone grew soft. Perhaps there was a bit of humanity and tenderness deep down inside this man, Christy thought. As if sensing her thoughts, his face turned dispassionate once again.

''Perhaps her excessive spending and carefree manner are just an act to cover her loneliness. Money cannot replace love and companionship,'' Christy volunteered in defense of a woman she didn't even know.

''There was little love and companionship, as you call it, between Henry and Matilda. Theirs was strictly a marriage of convenience, combining the wealth of the Stovingtons and Lancers. They never got along particularly well together. Both were too stubborn and could never agree on anything. I doubt Matilda grieved long over the death of her spouse.''

''Oh, Captain. That's a terrible thing to say! How could anyone not be deeply affected by the loss of a husband?''

''It is obvious you do not know Matilda, or you would

not doubt the truth of my words. I believe she found marriage a heavy burden to pay in exchange for her expensive tastes."

"How did he die?" she resumed her questioning, still not comprehending such a cold and unaffected attitude. The loss of her parents had crushed her deeply. Would not the loss of a husband be even more traumatic?

"Oh, it was a rather strange occurrence. Though we were not particularly close, I did feel the tragic impact of his untimely death. He was killed in a rather freak carriage accident. His body was not found for some time. We can only guess what really happened."

Christy's face suddenly drained of color. She gripped the chair before her tightly in an effort to support her trembling knees.

The captain was quick to notice her sudden faintness. "What is it? Are you ill? Let me get you to a chair," he offered in concern.

"No . . . no. I am fine. It's just your brother's death must have been tragic. I mean, 'tis a terrible thing when loved ones are taken so quickly," she stuttered, trying to cover her involuntary reaction.

"You speak as if from experience."

"Yes. My own parents were killed in a so-called accident of the same sort."

Captain Lancer watched her closely. He had known from his first meeting with her that she was orphaned. Now perhaps he had an opportunity to find out a little more about her. He knew that somewhere along the line of her short life she had come from a home of wealth and refinement. How she had come to live in terror and poverty was a mystery which plagued him still. "You say it was a 'so-called accident' as if you don't believe their deaths were completely an act of fate."

"I have no concrete proof of my suspicions, only the confidential opinion of a man who later refused to be questioned. But hopefully someday, Captain, the truth will emerge."

He did not doubt the conviction in her voice. "What makes you believe their deaths were no accident?"

"Political convictions, sir. My father believed strongly in a cause which others found distasteful. I believe he proved to be an embarrassment to certain officials and had to be removed." She turned away to again take a stance at the window. She fervently hoped she had not revealed too much about her parentage. It would not do to have her secret publicly known.

The captain, however, had gained little from her admission. It was completely noncommital, giving no clues as to what her father's cause had been or whom he had displeased. She seemed all too anxious to keep her past a secret.

Before he could question her further she changed the subject. "Captain, now that I find myself with an extended indenture to you, I would very much like to know what my duties will be and how long I will be in this bonded state. You have refused to gratify me with these answers before. I believe it my right to know."

"You are, of course, quite right, my dear. But I have not yet specifically decided upon either." He paused and looked deep into her sea green eyes. "My original offer still stands," he said softly. "Now that you know I have no family commitments, perhaps you will reconsider? I would be very good to you, fitting you in the best gowns and living like a queen. It would not be a bad life, and I am not such an ogre, after all."

Christy looked up into the serious brown eyes regarding her. She was filled with dismay and defeat. Tears glistened in her eyes, ready to spill any moment.

"You have not listened to one word I ever said, have you? My parents brought me up to be a dignified lady, despite my present circumstances these past years. Though I was forced to live like the most wretched of creatures, I have never lost my spirit or pride. And now, after everything I have been through, you expect me to give up all and roll on my back to play the brazen harlot! Well, Captain, no matter how bad the circumstances, I simply cannot change what I am and what I was raised to be."

"I thought as much," he said, stroking her cheek lightly with his fingertips. Her withering glare brought his hand swiftly back to his side. "I did not realize you felt so strongly about it. Since that is the case, however, I will have to find something useful for you to do to occupy your time. I am sure your talents are many." He glanced down at the soft swell of her creamy white breasts, plainly visible beneath the confines of her bodice. "I am sure I can find something for you. Be patient, my dear. Perhaps I can yet persuade you to my way of thinking."

"Never! Never!" she rasped, backing away. A single tear made its way slowly down her flushed cheek.

"Never is a long time, my little beauty. We shall see."

She was about to hurl another protest at him when the

door burst open and Sir Phillip entered. Observing the high color in Christy's face and his son's mock smile, he determined to make peace between them, if only for the time being.

"As usual, Hoffman was upset about nothing. Something about one of his men," he explained, and then cast a penitent look at Christy. "Would it be too much to hope that all has been explained and I have been exonerated?"

"Well, Father. I believe all has been explained. As for your acquittal, you will have to await Miss Patterson's decision," replied Michael.

Sir Phillip's eyes requested leniency yet her silence echoed reproof. With a sigh, he decided she needed more time and concrete proof that he truly wanted to be her friend and could be trusted. "Well, I don't blame you for delaying your decision, my dear. Give us time to prove ourselves. In the meantime, shall we eat? I am famished," he said, offering her his arm.

"Thank you, sir, but 'tis not the place of a bond slave to sit at her master's table. I will eat with the other servants."

Sir Phillip threw his son a quick glower. "Is this son of mine filling your head with such dribble? 'Tis still my house and I will have sit with me who I choose. Now come along, my lady, before I die of hunger."

He again offered Christy his arm. Begrudgingly she placed her hand on his. Angry as she was with his part of the deception, she believed he offered a small amount of friendship and protection from his unswayable offspring.

After the rather fiery prelude, breakfast itself passed with relative ease. Everyone, including Christy, munched with relish on the eggs, ham, potatoes, hot cereal and muffins set steaming before them. Juice and hot coffee flowed freely in each cup as Sir Phillip told Christy a little about his parents and his own life in Charleston, and Penncrest, her new home.

"My parents were one of the first families to arrive here. They sailed on the ship *Carolina,* landing at the Port Royal River on March 17, 1670. Eventually they moved to Charleston and built this house. It took time, but gradually my father built up his shipping business to a profitable size. He was a merchant and exported deerskins and furs to England. A few people tried to convince him that the real money was in slaving, but he was staunchly against such dealings and stuck to furs and naval supplies."

Christy swallowed hard at his mention of slavery. It seemed others shared her father's hatred of the trade. Sir Phillip seemed not to notice her lassitude and continued on.

"My father had good cause for his concern about slavery. Though he did not live to see it, there was a great slave insurrection led by a Jimmy Cato in 1739. Scared the hell—pardon me—out of us, since blacks outnumber whites by nearly 10 to 1. The situation is little improved now, despite all the legislation passed. Anyway, thanks to Lieutenant Governor William Bull, the slave rebellion was put down and we've had relative peace since then."

"I've heard, Sir Phillip, that Negroes were not the only people to be enslaved. What about the men with the red skin—Indians I believe they are called?" asked Christy.

"Oh, yes, my dear. Indians were also bought and sold

as slaves. They finally revolted against such immorality. While I do not condone slavery of any kind, I myself served under Governor Charles Craven to fight off the Yesasse tribe in 1715. The main fighting took place around Port Royal. The only thing that saved us was the support of North Carolina, Virginia and New York. We finally succeeded in driving them south to Florida. Let me tell you, we all counted our blessings when it was over. Some settlers were so afraid of Indian attack, they went so far as to arm their own slaves. Yes, as I said, it was a terrifying time and those who remember it still wake up at night in cold fear."

Talk turned to a lighter vein, and Christy laughed at Sir Phillip's tales of the fun that had taken place in the huge, spacious house, due in the most part to his youngest son's penchant for mischief. Michael good-naturedly denied the blame for any wrongdoings, but Christy could guess that as a child he must have been a real torment to his parents.

The subject soon turned serious and both men grew somber and reserved as Sir Phillip recounted the death of his beloved wife, Eleanor, some eight years past from influenza. A tear trickled down her cheek at their loss. It was obvious Lady Eleanor had been a much loved and respected woman. Her presence was still sorely missed despite the length of time since her death. Christy recalled the magical brown eyes and tender smile of Lady Eleanor, so exquisitely captured in the portrait. She felt their loss and a loss of her own at never having had the opportunity to meet such a wonderful person.

The conversation retained its serious tone as Sir

Phillip spoke about the death of his eldest son, Henry. "It was a terrible shock, to lose him so swiftly. But he left behind two beautiful children. Those scamps bring much joy to this old man. I only wish Matilda would surrender them to me more often. I think she fears I will spoil them more so than they already are. Bah! That's ridiculous. What else is a grandfather for, if not to spoil the little imps and send them home for mother to cope with." His eyes twinkled merrily as he spoke of them with such fondness.

Glancing quickly at his expensive time piece, Sir Phillip rose and bowed formally. "It has been an absolute delight having such a beautiful, charming lady grace my table. I thank you for listening so politely to my tales and hope to see you for dinner. Until then I will leave you in the patient hands of my son, for I must be off on some business. Good day to you both." He smiled at Christy, yet gave his son a silent warning to keep the peace. With that, he departed.

Christy smiled after him and then turned her attention to Michael. Alone again and without the support of Sir Phillip, she felt uneasy. "Your father is very witty and clever; not at all the stern, crusty fellow as you described him. He has a way with words that makes me feel at ease."

Christy suddenly blushed at her own bold appraisal of her master's father, but Michael took no notice. He had been somewhat skeptical of bringing her to Penncrest. He knew his father would accept her with open arms. He was not so sure, however, of just how she would adjust to the strange environment. However, her behavior had, thus far, proven his doubts groundless. Her quick wit and easy, relaxed manner impressed him anew. She was truly a remarkable young woman.

"Yes, he can be quite charming and vivacious when he has a mind to be. Not at all like his vile and arrogant son, eh?"

"It seems you do lack a few of your parent's virtues." Her voice was a whisper and her thick lashes fluttered over her lowered eyes. Yet a mischievous smile flickered on her warm, red lips.

"You agree too readily, my dear. But no matter. Perhaps you will permit me to practice some show of hospitality. May I show you about the house and gardens?" He rose quickly and held her chair.

"Why, 'twould be sheer delight, kind sir," she quipped in return and curtsied low, offering him her hand. Too late she realized the error in her action. He gently squeezed her fingers and raised her hand to his lips, planting upon it a light yet warm kiss. The feel of his lips upon her hand as his eyes gently caressed her features sent a quiver of fire and delight cascading through her slender body. She blushed hotly and pulled her hand away, wondering that his simple gesture could elicit such a strong reaction within her.

Michael said nothing, but as he stood aside for her to precede him from the room, he took note of her heightened color and quickened pulse. Perhaps the iceberg was not as dense and unmeltable as she would have him believe.

They strolled slowly about the house and grounds. He walked with ease and obvious pride as he spoke freely of himself and his home. She noted the subtle, calming effect Penncrest had upon him. The rough, domineering exterior he had exuded on the ship had greatly diminished. Would his hatred of her lessen as well?

Their final stop was the stables Christy had seen from her window. She openly admired the fine line of horses owned by the Lancers. Apparently they took great care in selecting only the finest breeds. She patted each horse and ran an approving hand down their flanks.

At the far end of the stables stood a young filly. Christy's interest was immediately aroused by the golden brown horse who tossed her blond mane vainly at her visitors. She laughed happily and reached to stroke the horse's nose. "Oh you are a spirited beauty, my young one, and well aware of the fact. I pity the man who broke you. He must still be sore from the battle."

As if the horse comprehended her statement, she whinnied and again shook her magnificent mane.

"You seem to know a good deal about horses, my dear. Do you ride?" She seemed perfectly at ease with these creatures, and a picture of her riding freely through the meadow, silky black curls streaming in wild disarray behind her, flashed through his mind. He smiled at his mind's picture despite himself and forced his attention back to her words.

"Oh, I used to ride a little. My father owned and raced many fine horses and I helped him with their grooming. I've not ridden in some time, however." Her sigh was genuine. She longed to ride with free abandon, to feel the wind in her face and the powerful beast beneath her. "I loved the task of helping my father, though my mother constantly worried I smelled more like a horse than a lady. On my tenth birthday, my father surprised me with a little filly of my very own. Oh how I loved my little Stardust. We were practically inseparable and grew up together. I still miss her." A stray tear trickled down her cheek. She brushed it away quickly lest Captain Lancer notice.

"Whatever happened to your horse?" he asked.

"When my parents were killed, she was sold—along with everything else."

He sensed a need to draw her from her unhappy reminiscing. Her beautiful green eyes were clouded with pain, and he longed to bring the sparkle back. "You may feel free to ride any time you wish, Miss Patterson. The horses are at your disposal. However, I would be wary of this young filly. She is quite spirited, as you say, and needs a firm hand," he cautioned. "Though, now that I think about it, you exhibit much similar characteristics, my dear."

"Do we indeed, Captain?" She raised a shapely eyebrow at him. "And would you attempt to tame me with the same techniques?"

"I believe the trick in taming both of you is getting you on your backs," he replied without thinking, and immediately regretted his coarseness.

To his surprise, she rallied to the cause. "Well, sir, if that be the case, then you had better pray that luck be with you for you will have a fierce and difficult battle on both accounts."

He's a persistent cad, thought Christy, growing warm under the intensity of his gaze. Seeking to cool her senses and his, they sought the shade of a mighty oak tree. She sat on a clean, whitewashed bench and looked up as he leaned lightly against the tree and related a few details about the family business.

"When my father was old enough, he took over his father's shipyard business. It had started out small, but over time it has grown and now comprises two large enterprises—import and export. The bulk of our business is in shipping rice to England and the West Indian Islands. We also ship tar, pitch, turpentine and the like. We bring back rum, window panes, furnishings, and other commodities scarce here. Our main source of competition was a man named Joseph Wragg, but he too has recently succumbed to the profits of dealing in human flesh and brings in slaves from Africa and Barbados.

"Father is still very much involved in the business. He goes into Charleston quite often though he now prefers leaving the day to day responsibilities to his highly competent overseer. All major decisions are still under his control and he is sole manager of the accounts."

Michael paused for a moment and chuckled at some private memory. "His trips are quite sporadic and unpredictable these days. No one ever knows when he will appear, so they must be constantly on their toes. Why, it's not uncommon at all for him to be seen strolling about the docks, talking amiably to the men who work for him. He is a well-liked and respected employer, and often settles disputes on working conditions, wages, and employee disputes. He is considered a fair and just man, and therefore usually has little trouble with his people.

"With my love of the sea and the challenge of trade, I too find the business fascinating. Father continually urges more and more responsibility my way. It was originally planned that Henry, my eldest brother, would inherit the business. Fate, I fear, was unkind in that respect—taking his life at such an early age. But, one must not ponder overlong on such tragedy."

Michael paused and then went on. "Eventually I will take over the business from Father. But for now, my main interests lie in a little venture I started nearly a year ago—a small timber mill. I built it up from nothing and trained the workers myself. It has panned out far beyond my expectations in such a remarkably short time. I am anxious to ride out tomorrow and see how it has fared in my absence."

"A timber mill? That is quite removed from shipping and merchandising, is it not, Captain?" asked Christy.

"No, not really. In fact the two have more in common than you realize. Timber is plentiful here with our immense forests of pine and cypress. This timber provides us with pitch, resin, tar and turpentine used in constructing ships. And, the tall pines are perfect for sturdy masts. So, you see, the two businesses can be quite complementary," he explained.

"I'd not thought of that, but you are quite right," answered Christy, impressed with her new knowledge.

They were still enjoying the comforts offered by the shady branches of the oak tree when the foreman, Hoffman, appeared, demanding Michael's attention on some matter. He raked Christy with his gaze as he had done earlier in the study, and then hurried off with Michael.

She watched as the two men strode across the lawn together. Everything about them was in sharp contrast. Hoffman was short, thin, and definitely unconcerned with the more social graces of washing. His filthy clothing hung limply upon his scrawny frame and the many frayed places attested to the extensive wear they received.

Michael, however, presented a much more pleasing image. His tall, lean body was held erect, and his stylish attire fit his muscular frame to perfection. The image of his naked form pressed tightly against hers brought a blush to her face. If only his manners were as neat and cultured as his appearance, she felt she would have no further cause for concern. But it was clear he was a man of strength and strong passion, and as long as he remained thus she had better be wary. . . .

Later, with a sigh, she strolled through the yard and up the wide, richly carpeted stairs to her room. Ah, would it not be marvelous to be the mistress of such a grand house? To give parties and teas? She vaguely remembered such grand affairs her parents had given or attended. Though she'd been too young to be included in the festivities, she would sit huddled on the stairway and peek down at the beautifully clad ladies in their long, exquisite gowns. And the men! Oh, how strong and gallant they all appeared before her youthful eyes. The mixed laughter and music would keep her awake yet dreaming throughout the night. She prayed that someday she, too, would waltz about the floor in a stunning gown in the embrace of a handsome gentleman.

Eyes closed, she imagined the scene and spun around the room in an imitation waltz. She smiled coyly at her debonair partner, who quite without conscious effort materialized into Michael Lancer. She looked down at her dress to smooth some imaginary crease, and reality returned sharp and cold. How could she even imagine herself a grand lady, standing proudly beside the captain? It was ludicrous. She owned one simple dress. Besides that, she was not even a hired servant but rather a bonded slave.

An angry frown clouded her face at her own impertinence. She must accept her meager status and be content with it. With a heavy sigh she removed her dress and lay down to rest. With little effort sleep overcame her and cleared her mind of the disquieting thoughts. . . .

It was nearly dusk when Christy was awakened by a light rap on the door. Bertha entered, followed by two young serving girls carrying hot water for her bath. As she supervised the pair, Bertha regarded the young woman before her with mixed curiosity and mistrust. She was not much older than the two silly maids who carried the water, yet somehow this one seemed mature for her years.

Master Michael's homecoming had been looked forward to with great anticipation. He was loved and highly respected by nearly everyone at Penncrest. Yet the well-planned festivities had suddenly been cancelled. Little explanation had been given, other than Sir Phillip would be detained in Charleston. When he returned he would be accompanied by a relative of the family—a cousin of sorts. Preparations were to be made at once for her coming, yet no one was to breathe a word to the girl about anyone or anything at Penncrest.

The entire household was abuzz with curiosity to begin with at such mysterious doings, yet when Sir Phillip arrived escorting a pale young woman, tongues wagged. That her "luggage" consisted solely of a few tattered shirts and trousers was enough to set the servants gossiping. Bertha herself had been somewhat put off by the whole thing, though she tried to quiet the other servants.

After she had put the bedraggled girl to bed she had overheard Sir Phillip and Master Michael heatedly discussing her circumstances and rightful place in the household. She certainly was not fool enough to believe their explanation of the girl being a distant cousin. Yet it was equally difficult to fathom Master Michael bringing a mistress to live in his own home. It was out of character for him to flaunt his passions, though she knew he engaged in frequent overnight flings. Yet, even if that was the case, this Christina Patterson was hardly more than a child; and to be openly engaged in such an occupation was both sad and disgusting. What was even more curious was the fact that she herself seemed uncertain of her status. The whole business was mighty peculiar. It would certainly be interesting to find out the true reason for her presence here at Penncrest.

When the tub had been filled and the two giggling girls dismissed, Bertha addressed herself to Christy. "Dinner be served shortly, ma'am. You be needin' help in dressing?" she asked. Until the truth emerged Bertha planned to exercise all due caution.

"Thank you, no, Bertha. I can manage fine on my own." Though she did not want to put off Bertha, she had no desire to undress before her and reveal her scarred back. The black woman made her feel shy and ill at ease. Behind those large, dark eyes, which gave no hint as to her feelings, was a mind as alert and quick as her own. Christy had observed the respect the other servants had for Bertha, and knew that the Lancers trusted her completely in running the household. This woman's friendship and trust might be an asset well worth the effort of gaining.

"Very well, Miz Patterson." Bertha nodded and turned to leave.

Christy felt reluctant to lose this opportunity to speak to the woman and draw her out. The sooner she let Bertha know she intended to pose no threat, the better. But could she get through the black woman's stony defenses? "Have you been with the Lancers long?" she asked.

"I reckon you could say so. Been close to thirty-five years in all." The pride in her voice as unmistakable.

"Oh, my, Bertha. That's a long time. Why, I am sure you are an indispensable member of the family."

Her compliment worked, for Bertha puffed with pride. "Why, I helped raise every one of them young uns, I did. 'Specially Master Michael. He was always off galavantin' and wantin' his own way. It's a mystery how he be able to sit after all the lickin's he got." Her chuckles caused her whole body to shake merrily. When she again regained her somber state she eyed Christy warily, fearing she had overstepped her bounds.

Christy, however, laughed right along. "Sir Phillip expressed the same musings at breakfast this morning. But the captain—Master Michael—strenuously denied he was anything but a perfect child."

Both women laughed and then Bertha became serious once again. "Seems like jist yesterday I bounced them children on my knees. Now some of 'em got children of their own. 'Tis a shame Lady Eleanor could not live to see her grandchildren. She'd a been proud. But I guess then she'd a suffered too when poor Master Henry was kilt. The whole lot's a shame, it is, and unfair. Both to die so young."

Christy, too, silently mused on the same line of thinking. Her parents had also been snatched away at their prime. It was terribly unfair as Bertha had said.

"Yes, it surely was a shame, but we got high hopes for Master Michael and Mistress Ann to find good partners. Mistress Ann be too young for such things now, but someday soon, and we all got hopes the young Master'll find hisself someone worthy to add to the family. He should be thinkin' on such things 'stead of traipsing 'cross the ocean and back. It's high time he settled down with a nice lady and had children."

Christy sensed a touch of warning from Bertha's tone. It was apparent the stout housekeeper had higher hopes for Michael than what Christy, a penniless girl with no social name or background, could offer. She had to conceal a smile at the very idea. She could hardly blame the woman for her concern, yet there was little cause for worry.

Anxious to change the subject, Christy moved the

discussion to safer ground. "I was not aware that the captain—I mean Master Michael's older brother was married. I was under the impression he traveled extensively and returned home only seldom."

"You be right about him never comin' home. But Master Phillip, he found hisself a young bride in Ireland of all places. Said British girls are too dull. Never even brought the girl home to meet us till they were married nearly two years, with one wee babe and another on the way. The girl seemed nice enough, come from good family. But 'fore we had chance to get to know her they were off again and we've not seen 'em since."

"That is too bad. But, perhaps one day he will return to his native home." Again there was a pause, but Christy decided to push on. There was still much she wanted to know about the Lancers. "And what of Mistress Ann? Has she been away at school long?"

"Been away in England nearly three years now, and her only now turning seventeen. I tried to tell 'em was not good sending off a young girl alone, but no one would listen to old Bertha. They all said she needed proper schoolin' in the more refined arts, being brought up with three brothers and no mother and all. Last time she come home she was a real lady and made us all proud. But she likes school in London. I even overheard Sir Phillip say she was serious over some young fella learnin' to be a doctor. Seems she'll beat Master Michael to the altar after all!"

Bertha finished, lost in thought for a few moments. A loud crash from below brought her from her musings. "You'd best get yourself dressed and down to dinner. Sir

Phillip and Master Michael don't like being kept waitin' when it comes to eatin'." She sampled the water in the tub. "And here, your water's turned cold. I'll send Minnie up with more hot water."

"No, thank you, Bertha. That won't be necessary. There's little time and a cool bath may be refreshing on this warm evening."

"If there's nothing you be needin', then I best check on that crash we heard. Probably some careless ninny broke somethin'." Bertha's voice broke into her musings. Christy nodded absently and she hustled off. It seemed that for a servant, Bertha had no fear of speaking her mind.

She counted herself lucky in learning some additional interesting facts about the Lancers from Bertha. The woman was still distant and aloof, but perhaps with a little care and luck, Christy might yet win the house-keeper's trust.

Twelve

The first few days in her new home passed slowly for Christy. An early riser and with little to occupy her time, the hours seemed to crawl in an agony of slowness. When boredom threatened to weaken her grip on sanity, she would approach the servants with an offer to assist them in their daily tasks. Most of them looked at her with apprehension and mixed curiosity but declined her offer. With her own uncertainty as to her status in the household, it was understandable that they were uneasy in turn as to where she stood. Besides, the others took their cue from Bertha who still reacted with a measured degree of aloofness and guard.

So with little else to challenge her mind, Christy would stroll along through the grounds and sit, hour after hour, under the shade of the rose trellis, or walk through the woods to a clearing and sit beside a cool, refreshing stream. She ached to saddle a horse and take a long ride. Michael had given his permission, yet she felt because of her lowly station it was not the thing to do. She fretted at being treated as a guest when she knew, in reality, she should be earning her keep. Each passing day only increased her indebtedness to the captain.

The highlight of her day was joining Michael and Sir Phillip for the evening meal. They would discuss the day's problems and events, either at the shipyard or timber mill, and plan for the morrow. But after the meal the two men would retire to the study to smoke, and she would again be left to her own resources. Usually she would curl up on the sofa with a book from the study. Often she would wake to find the candle out and the moon shining brightly upon the floor. Then she would crawl into bed and drift off again to sleep.

After her first week of such inactivity at Penncrest, she rose reluctantly, fearing that this particular morning would be no different than the others. Though she in no way missed the grueling pace set for her by Henry Slate, she longed for some purpose, some goal in which to submerge her energies. Sir Phillip seemed not to notice her dilemma and Michael only laughed at her boredom. "You do have an alternative," he would suggest playfully. "I would see to it your idle time is kept to a minimum." She would storm off in renewed anger determined not to let him wear her down. But after only one week, it was proving a difficult challenge.

With a disgruntled sigh, she finished dressing and went to eat breakfast. This morning both men were absent as usual. Michael was at the mill and Sir Phillip in Charleston. Neither promised to return until quite late in the evening. Their joint absence made her feel even more listless and pensive than usual. She nibbled absently on a freshly baked muffin, contemplating thoughts of another long day. Even the weather seemed as overcast as her spirits.

With a tiny pout she put down her half eaten muffin. Today would be different. She would make it that way. Since no one seemed the least bit inclined to ease her listlessness, she would boldly take matters into her own hands.

Despite her earlier resolve, she decided to saddle one of the horses and ride through the meadow. It would do her good and give her an opportunity to see the countryside. Already in better spirits, she headed for the stairs, deciding her shirt and trousers would do fine as riding garb. The sound of an approaching carriage sparked her interest. Perhaps Sir Phillip had changed his mind about going into Charleston. She headed for the front door and pulled it open eagerly. The expensive-looking carriage which pulled up in front of the house was definitely not Sir Phillip's. Newton, the stable boy, ran to open the door and offered his arm to assist the blond woman Christy had seen at the dock. As soon as her balance was secure, she drew her hand abruptly away and nodded absently to the boy as she sauntered up the stairs, looking for all the world as if she were mistress here.

Christy held the door for Matilda Lancer, noting her rich attire. The woman brushed past without so much as a glance in her direction and stood in the vestibule removing her gloves and looking about in carefree abandon. Seeing no one else about, she turned to Christy who stood somewhat in the shadows.

"Well, well. You must be the poor, unfortunate relative Michael found in London and brought home to enjoy his money. He has a habit of taking care of those less fortunate than himself," she commented cattily.

"Come out here where I can get a look at you."

Matilda had heard from a few people that Michael's so-called cousin was quite lovely, but she would not believe it until she saw for herself. The girl in front of her moved slowly from the shadows, subjecting herself to Matilda's haunty appraisal. The tiny frame, shining black hair and finely detailed features of the woman before her, set off by the loveliest green eyes she had ever seen, caused Matilda no small twinge of jealousy. This was certainly no homely school girl who would be easily reckoned with.

She gave Christy a cold, demeaning look. From that first glance both realized they could never be friends; only bitter rivals. "By what name do you call yourself, dear?" Her tone was definitely condescending.

"Christina Patterson, Mrs. Lancer."

"Humph! Just how is it you are related to the Lancers anyway? I've never heard them speak of anyone named Patterson."

Ruffling in defense, Christy returned Matilda's intense perusal. The slightly older woman was quite lovely, she had to admit. Though taller than herself, she was pleasantly slender and her light blond hair curled purposefully beneath a sweeping feather bonnet. Wide brown eyes looked down at her as if she were a mere child. Her finely tailored suit fit her superbly and no doubt she could distract the attention of any man with her swelling and clearly discernible cleavage. "We are very distant cousins, Mrs. Lancer, and have not been in touch for some time. In fact, the relationship stretches so far as to make us more acquaintances than relations." Deliberately she kept her answer cool and noncommittal.

She had no intention of leaving herself open for attack by this snobbish, ill-mannered woman.

"Well then, however did he manage to find you, my dear? Or perhaps you found him?" The raised eyebrow was by no means an accident.

"The meeting was purely accidental, Mrs. Lancer." You've no idea just how accidental, thought Christy.

"Well, you'll have to tell me all about it sometime, child. It must be a fascinating story," said Matilda. She could see the girl had no intention of telling her anything she didn't already know, and she was becoming bored with the subject. Patting her hair lightly, her eyes wandered about the room toward the study. "Where is dear Michael? I have something to discuss with him."

"He is at the mill today and Sir Phillip is in Charleston."

The other woman's face fell in disappointment. "Oh, what a shame. I wanted to invite him to tea. It's been so long since we've had some time together, what with him so very often at sea. Besides, he's such a dear and takes such good care of myself and the children. Why, he's nearly taken the place of Henry since he died. I sometimes fancy he would like to permanently adopt us. Other women just don't seem to interest him anymore; he's so content with us." It was clear Matilda wanted no doubt left in the girl's mind that she was claiming Michael as her own property.

"Yes, it is very kind of him. No doubt he feels a certain responsibility to his dead brother's wife and children," replied Christy sweetly.

"Oh you needn't feel sorry for him. He enjoys our

company and is more than adequately compensated for his attention," Matilda fired back. There could be little misunderstanding the implication of her words. But Matilda was not at all pleased with the way the conversation was going and decided to cut it to a quick close. "Well, my dear child, I must be off since there is no one here I wish to see. Tell Michael I was here. I am sure he will be deeply mortified he missed my call. Good day," she said and strode out the door without another word.

Christy fumed as she stood at the window watching the cloud of dust that rose from her departing carriage. She knew she would be hard pressed to remain cool and subservient when Matilda Lancer was nearby. It was obvious the woman cosidered her some sort of threat and had taken an instant dislike to her. Again she had been subtly warned not to push her attentions on Michael, and again found it amusing that so many should take such concern over a bond servant.

"Is that woman gone?" demanded Bertha, startling Christy from her musings.

"Yes, she just left, Bertha. She was looking for the captain—Master Michael."

"Humph! That woman is always comin' and goin'. She'd like to be mistress of this place. What's more she'd do anything to get it too." She suddenly paused and looked directly at Christy. "Guess I've said too much. But even the lowest maid can see Matilda Lancer would stoop to pretty near anythin' to keep other females from her brother-in-law. The last young lady he brought here left in a hurry. Master Michael was plum confused, but those of us got eyes and ears know Mrs. Lancer threatened her somehow. Stay clear o' that lady. I'm giving you fair warnin'."

"Thank you, Bertha. I'll do just that," Christy replied, watching the woman bustle about her duties. She hesitated, then took a chance. "Is there anything I can help you with, Bertha?"

"No. No, child. I've been taking care of things since dear, sweet Lady Eleanor passed away. Somebody had to take charge after she died. Didn't need any help then and don't need any now. I got things runnin' smoothly and till a new mistress joins the family I reckon I'll keep on doin' things like always."

Christy quickly masked the hurt brought by Bertha's words. Was her reply another snub as to her own unwelcome state? Shoulders sagging slightly, she headed for the door. The day had turned even more dreary, she noted, as she left the confines of the house and headed for some fresh air.

As she descended the marble steps she was filled with an overwhelming desire to flee from this place and the people who cared little for her. She served no useful purpose and each day found herself owing Michael more and more. Yet she knew from her episode in town that it would be nearly impossible for her to support herself. What could she do? She was trapped, forced to bide her time and await the bidding of her master.

She strolled listlessly past the colorful gardens noting with dismay the weeds which were beginning to strangle the bright profusion of fragrant yellow jessamine, peonies and anemones which graced the grounds. She had overheard one of the servants say that Hickman, the gardener, had gone to take care of his sick mother and would probably not be back for a few weeks. Apparently neither Sir Phillip nor Michael had secured a replacement for the man. Hickman would certainly have his work cut out for him when he did return. But in the meantime the lovely blossoms were suffering from neglect.

Christy knelt absently to pluck a weed which had firmly wrapped itself about a brilliant red zinnia. Freed of its captor, the flower seemed to gain strength and stood again tall and proud. Another weed met its demise at her hands, and then another. Soon she found herself totally involved in picking weeds, discarding dead plants, and cleaning up the flower beds. She worked at a crisp, energetic pace, happy to occupy her thoughts and keep her hands busy. In less than three hours the flowers stood tall and strong, free from weeds and thistles that would have choked and eventually destroyed them.

At last she stood up and stretched. Her back ached slightly from the unaccustomed bending. But the slight discomfort was a small price to pay. She admired her cultivational efforts. She loved flowers and was glad to have restored the flower beds to their original multicolored splendor. She bent to pick one last weed and straightened, well pleased with herself and her day's work. She finally felt as if she had accomplished something of purpose.

Her nose wrinkled slightly as she gazed down at her muddy hands and soiled dress. Though her spirits were high her body definitely needed some cool, cleansing water.

A movement from the front of the house caught her attention. She waited patiently as the captain strode across the lawn toward her. He presented a striking picture—tall, lean, and quite handsome in his leisurely working clothes. His sleeves were rolled up past his elbows and his shirt hung open to the waist. No wonder Matilda wanted him for herself.

She felt rather drab and dirty after her work and quickly dusted her skirt and patted her falling curls into place. It was unfortunate Michael should catch her looking thus, but there was little she could do now. A smile came to her lips as he neared. She opened her mouth to bring his attention to her day's accomplishments. As he drew close however, the look of rage on his face sent her heart to pounding. She waited fearfully to discern the cause of his anger.

"I came home early from the mill expecting to have you join me for tea at Matilda's, and Bertha informs me you are out working in the garden. Just look at you, appearing for all the world like some simple peasant. Who told you to do such a thing? We have a gardener who tends the grounds. We are not destitute that we must stoop to having a woman laboring in the gardens."

Confused by his anger, she began to tremble. "Why, no one told me to work in the gardens, Captain. I overheard that the gardener was gone, and noticed the weeds taking over. I had nothing to do and only wanted to help."

"You take too much upon yourself, madam. I did not bring you here to act as my gardener. Do not ever dare do anything like this again. Do you hear me?" he boomed down at her.

"Yes." Her voice was hardly above a whisper.

"I said, do you hear me? Speak up, girl!"

"Yes. I hear you. But I don't understand. I only wanted to help," she choked as tears streamed down her upturned face.

He glowered down at her ashen complexion and trembling red lips. Her eyes were opened wide in terror and confusion. Why had he lost his temper and come storming at her like some madman? No wonder she was petrified of him. He chided himself sternly at seeing her thus because he could not control his temper.

A longing coursed through him to wipe her lovely face free of the tears, and cover her trembling lips with his own. Oh how he ached to wrap her in his arms and show her just how loving and gentle he could be, instead of a brute. There was a soft side to him despite the anger which so readily manifested itself when she was near. But no doubt his gentleness would result in only frightening her further.

Without giving him further opportunity to berate her, she bounded for the house, hoping for the safety of her room.

Suddenly a man came galloping up the road on an old, wheezing horse, flapping his arms and shrieking wildly. The captain and Christy looked up as he galloped toward them. She stopped in mid-flight as he nearly crushed her beneath the horse's hooves in his haste.

"Master Lancer! Master Lancer!" he began breathlessly, almost falling from the horse as he reared in sharply. Michael lifted his hand to steady the exhausted animal.

"Please. You've got to help me! My son . . . he's fallen into an old well and we cannot get him out. Milly is frantic with worry and threatens to throw herself down the well after the boy. Can you come?"

One look at the man's overwrought and disheveled appearance was all Michael needed to convince him the situation was serious. Turning quickly and waving at the man to follow, he headed toward the stables, hurling questions over his shoulder. "Of course I'll help, man. When did this happen? Is the boy hurt?"

"Nearly an hour ago, sir. Johnny cries a lot, but I can't tell if he's hurt. I told them children time and time again to stay clear o' that old well. They just don't listen. Now little Johnny's gone and fallen. I'll never forgive myself if he's . . . if something happens to him," he muttered as he followed behind the lengthy strides of his boss.

Michael reached the stable and in record time had his horse saddled and a rope secured. In minutes he was mounted and ready to ride. "Lead the way, man," he ordered as the worker hastily remounted his own tired horse.

"Captain. Wait!" called Christy as they prepared to ride off. "May I come along? Perhaps I can be of some help." She ran to his side and called up to him in the saddle.

"I doubt you could be of much assistance. 'Tis no job for a woman," he said, reining his horse around.

Undaunted, she touched his leg boldly to stay him. "But, if the boy is hurt I may be able to help. Especially if his mother is too distressed to think clearly."

"Sir, please. I beg of you. If she thinks she can help let her come," cried the distraught father, eager to be on their way.

"Very well. Come along then. But we've no time to saddle a horse for you. Ride with me," he said. Before Christy could protest, she found herself being lifted from the ground and placed unceremoniously on the saddle in front of him. He kicked his horse and they galloped off at such a pace, she clung to him tightly, fearing she would be thrown to the ground.

The muscles in his arms felt hard and strong as they encircled her jolting body. She doubted he felt their closeness as she did, but beneath the scowl on his handsome face, his anger at her was all but forgotten. It was hard to be upset with her when she clung so near. He urged his horse on, trying to forget her closeness and concentrate on the task ahead. He would deal with her and his feelings later.

In only a short time, they reached the crest of a hill and raced down to a small cluster of people standing fretfully about an old, dilapidated well. As soon as the great black stallion came to a halt, Christy jumped down and waited as the captain swung himself down and ran to the well. The boy's father was close behind, and Christy brought up the rear.

A small, tidy house stood a short distance away from the well. A rather shaggy-looking dog barked furiously at the great intrusion and ran back and forth nervously among the gathering crowd, confused by the great commotion.

Michael Lancer frowned as he gazed into the dilapidated old well. He tested the edge of the structure for sturdiness and his scowl deepened as the rotted wood crumbled in his hands. He spoke not a word but it was obvious from his intense concentration that his mind was conjuring up every possible alternative. Suddenly a small, exceptionally heavy young woman with red, swollen eyes and tear-stained face separated herself from the gathering crowd and stumbled forward to paw at his arm. She recognized him as the owner of the timber mill and had heard he was a man of action and honor.

"My baby is down there. Please get my baby out!" Her nails bit into his arm in her frenzy.

Christy's heart ached for her, yet the tension on Michael made her realize the heavy weight placed on his shoulders. Gently she pulled the woman away to give him freedom to think and move about.

"Can the boy tie a rope about himself?" Michael demanded.

"Nay. Nay. He's just a baby. He'd fall for sure!" the boy's mother cried, ready to again throw herself on the well. Christy was hard-pressed to restrain her, but at last she ceased struggling and again reverted to wailing in her hands.

Captain Lancer looked to the father for a more coherent response.

"'Tis unlikely, sir. He's hardly four and if he should not tighten it properly, could be bad for him," he answered soberly, echoing his wife's trepidation.

"Very well. I shall have to go down into the well and get him."

He took the rope from his saddle and wrapped one end about a sturdy maple tree some eight feet away. This looped end he then tied to the horn of his saddle. The other end he securely tied about his waist. As briefly yet clearly as possible he instructed two men to ease his horse slowly forward at his command, until he reached the bottom of the well.

Preparations complete, he raised himself onto the well and swung his feet over the side. At his signal the men led the huge animal forward. Slowly, ever so slowly, he eased himself down into the well. The silence was incredible. Everyone waited expectantly.

"Easy, boys. I've hit something here!" he called up suddenly.

The horse reared slightly as his bit was pulled roughly. The rope jerked, wood snapped, and suddenly a terrified cry came from below.

"Damnit! Hold that horse," he cursed. Silence followed as everyone waited expectantly. "Bring me up, slowly," his order came up a short time later.

The men complied, guiding the horse backwards, rope taut, until Michael's hands clasped the sides of the well and he pulled himself out. Beads of perspiration trickled down his face and neck from the stress of the climb. In frustration he unfastened the rope from his waist. "There's an obstruction blocking the way—broken boards and planks. I cannot get through without dislodging the whole mess and sending it crashing down on the boy." In disgust he tossed the rope against the well. "It's just too risky to try to get through without hitting the damn mess!"

"Oh no. My baby! My little Johnny!" shrieked the boy's mother and broke free of Christy's grip. She raced toward the well and had to be physically restrained from throwing herself into the gaping black hole. "I'll find a way to get through!" she cried as Michael handed her over to her husband.

"Don't be crazy, Milly. You're far too heavy to fit if even Master Lancer cannot make it." With a rather pensive look at his wailing wife, he spoke softly to Michael. "What can be done now, sir? Surely there must be another way to get him out?"

The captain ran his fingers through his mop of thick brown hair. "I'm just too big to get through without hurting the boy more."

"We've got to do something! We can't just leave him down there to die! There's got to be another way!" It would not be long before the boy's father was as hysterical as his wife.

Michael walked around the well staring intently into the depths below. "Give me the rope. We'll just have to hope the boy can fasten it himself and hold on. I don't see any other way."

"Oh, my baby! He'll fall for sure. He'll be killed! My poor baby!" wailed the distraught mother, hugging herself and swaying back and forth, unconsolable.

Christy's heart ached for the poor couple. Surely there was something that could be done to save the boy. She regarded the wailing mother and then Michael. The well looked dark, foreboding, as did Michael, but she'd made up her mind.

Stepping to the side of the crumpling stones, she retrieved the rope. With stiff fingers, she slipped it about her legs and waist. Silently she secured the make-shift cradle tightly in place. Satisfied it would hold her, she stepped toward the well.

"What the devil do you think you're doing?" demanded Michael as he spied her securely bound by the rope.

"You said you were too large to get through. I am smaller. Perhaps I can make it safely. I'd like to try."

"That's ridiculous! It's much too dangerous. You wouldn't have a chance."

"Why wouldn't I make it? I have as much a chance as anyone else," she argued, insulted by his lack of confidence in her.

"I'm telling you. It's out of the question. I'll not have you climbing down and breaking your neck. The matter is closed. I'll find another way," he said with finality and turned his back on her.

"Captain, you may be stubborn, but so am I. 'Tis my life I risk and my choice to do so. You may have a legal right to my service in payment for my passage, but you do not own my very life. I am going down into the well and try to rescue the little boy. I cannot stand by and do nothing."

"But no one expects you to take such a chance."

"Look at the boy's mother. Do you think she cares if I am man or woman, grand lady or slave? Now, will you help me or shall I enlist the aid of one of these other men?"

She watched his face grow flushed with anger. His brow twitched. Sweat streamed down his face. By offering to try to save the boy she risked more than her life. She risked the captain's fury at her for her blatant disobedience. Well, she would just have to ignore his fury for now and devise some means of coping with him later.

With a sigh of resignation at his continued silence, she turned her back to him and slowly and deliberately climbed up onto the rim of the well. The men held the captain's horse, ready to lower her.

With an angry growl he strode to her side. "You may have your way now, my dear, but remember, you must deal with me later. And I warn you, I am not a sporting loser."

Christy smiled nervously at his warning. "I've no doubt you have little experience with losing. You usually get what you want. But though my flags of victory are few, do not underestimate me as an opponent, my lord." Before he could retort, she turned her attention to the well and a shudder possessed her. It looked dark and eerie. What a horrid experience for such a small child, she thought.

"Johnny, I am coming down to get you out of there. Can you hear me, Johnny?"

There was no response from below. Christy's eyes met Michael's in silent concern. Unwilling to contemplate the awful possibilities, she continued to talk reassuringly into the darkness. "Johnny, I must get through some loose boards. I'll try to be very careful, but some of them may fall. Cover your face with your arms and keep your head down low. Don't be afraid. I'm coming down now. Can you hear me?"

A low, frightened whimper filtered up to them. The sound was reassuring. At least the boy was alive and conscious. She took a deep breath and gave Michael a trembling smile. Ever so slowly, he guided his horse toward the well. Her head disappeared as she went deeper and deeper into the blackness below.

Half way down her foot stuck the wedged debris. Gingerly she tested the opening. It appeared large enough for her to get through, provided she was very careful. She gathered her skirts about her to keep them from catching on the precarious boards.

A low, steady whimpering from below told her she was nearly to the boy. The sound gave her the courage to go on. To cover her own fear she spoke reassuringly to him. At long last she stepped beside him and felt his cold, quivering body. The rope slackened as her feet sank into slimy water. It smelled rank and stagnant. Slowly she reached out and took the small boy in her arms. He clung desperately to her, nearly choking her in his gladness to find human companionship.

"There, there, Johnny," she soothed, stroking his damp hair. "It's all right now. Are you hurt anywhere?"

"My arm hurts real bad," he choked, holding it toward her. The intense darkness kept her from seeing the little boy's arm, but she took it between her fingers and gently probed up and down. "Ohhhh!" he screamed out in pain and pulled away as she lightly touched the break in his tiny limb.

In the darkness she lifted her skirt and began ripping

her slip which would serve as a temporary sling. As she worked she called up to reassure those waiting above. "Captain, I made it safely. Johnny is fine. I'll be sending him up in just a few minutes."

Her long bandage ready, she turned to Johnny. "Be a brave little man and hold your arm across your chest while I tie this." Quickly she proceeded to immobilize it with the cloth. It was difficult because of the extreme darkness and cramped condition, but when the bandaging was complete she praised him for his perserverence. "That was a good, brave boy, Johnny. Now, I'm going to tie this rope around you and then Master Michael will pull you up!"

"No. No!" he cried, trying to pull away. "I'm afraid to go by myself. You come with me."

"I can't, Johnny. The opening is not large enough for both of us to get through together. You must go by yourself."

"No. I won't go without you!"

"Oh, but, Johnny. Your mother and father are up there waiting for you. Don't you want to see them? They are very worried about you."

"No. My pa will be real mad that I was playing round the well. He might beat me. If you come with me you can make him not be mad at me."

"Your mama and papa care very much for you. They will not beat you. I promise," she said, hoping such was the case. The boy remained unconvinced, however, and she was forced to come up with a new tactic. "I saw a little, shaggy dog up there running about and barking. Is he your dog?"

"Scruffy? That's my puppy!"

"Well, Johnny. Scruffy is up there looking for you. Don't you want to see him again, and take care of him? Maybe he's hungry?"

Suddenly the little fellow broke down. "I want my mama. I don't like this place. I want to see my mama." He began to cry softly.

"There, there, sweetheart," she said. Without waiting further she reached around the tiny boy and began securely fastening the rope about his legs and waist. Better get him up before his fears returned.

"Are you all right down there?" came Michael's worried voice.

"Yes. Fine. I'm sending Johnny up in a minute. I think his right arm is broken so be careful lifting him." She tried to keep the tension from her voice, but it was beginning to wear her down. "Now Johnny, I have tied you very tightly so you will not fall. All you have to do is hold very still and they will pull you up. But you must stay very still and not bump the boards on your way up. Do you understand, Johnny?"

"Yes, but I don't want to go by myself," he whimpered, his fears returning.

"I know, but the sooner you go the sooner you'll be with your mama." She gave him a reassuring hug and tugged on the rope. "Captain, pull him up slowly."

The rope grew taut. Johnny's feet lifted. A frightened cry escaped his lips as he struggled uneasily.

"Be still, Johnny. You will not fall," came her harsh command. He quieted somewhat.

Gradually he moved farther up the well. The process

was slow and it seemed to take forever. But extreme care was required, especially since the boy was hurt. She was glad Michael was exercising caution and taking it slow.

The lengthy wait did little, however, to ease her own fears. The darkness seemed to close in about her, and now that she did not have the boy to reassure, she felt frightened and uneasy. She shivered from the cold water and slime trickling down her back.

A warning shout from above drew her attention. Johnny, in his excitement at seeing the top of the well, struggled and squirmed to hasten his ascent.

"Be still, Johnny!" cried Christy sternly.

"Mama! Mama!" he screamed in a combination of joy and fear.

From the sound of his voice, Christy guessed him to be better than half way up—right about where the lodged debris rested precariously. "Be still!" she called again. Her warning cry went all but unheard. His swinging foot struck a loose plank, and then another. Christy gazed up into the darkness in horror as the sound of falling debris filled her ears. With a terrified cry rising from her throat, she covered her head with her arms. Seconds later boards and heavy planks tumbled down upon her. . . .

The sound of crashing boards filled the air above the well. With a stream of cursing, Michael quickly pulled the astonished boy up the rest of the way and set him in the arms of his mother. Both clung tightly to one another, tears of happiness flowing freely.

Frantically he leaned over the well. Particles of dust trickled up. "Christy! Can you hear me? Are you hurt?"

Only deadly silence met his frantic calls. His blood

turned icy. If anything happened to her he would never forgive himself for letting her go down there. Damn the boy for not holding his eagerness, he thought, yet he could hardly blame the lad for wanting to be free of this dank prison.

"Christy, can you hear me?" Again he received no response.

"Is the young miss all right?" It was Johnny's mother. "What happened, sir?"

"The boy accidentally knocked the boards on her. Either she is hurt or cannot hear me." He responded absently, his mind a whirl of indecision.

Damn her for being so stubborn and refusing to listen to reason. She had known it was dangerous to go down yet she had taken the chance anyway to save the boy. Surely they would have come up with some other plan to get him out. He should have forced her to listen to reason. But no doubt she would not have obeyed him anyway. She had a mind of her own.

"Is there anything we can do to help, sir?" offered the boy's father. He too felt sorry that his son's safety had been at the cost of a stranger's life.

"I just don't know what to do. But take care of your son, man. There are others here who can help if it's needed." The boy's father had suffered enough anguish already. Besides, no one else could be of much help.

Again he leaned over the well and yelled loudly. Again no sound came from below. Well, he could wait no longer without knowing if she was hurt. He had to save her.

With sweaty hands, he quickly tied the rope about himself. Easing himself onto the edge of the well, he called to the men to begin his descent. A slight movement from below stayed him. He strained his ears, trying to discern any sound.

Consciousness slowly returned to Christy. Dazed from the avalanche, she lay very still. Pain ripped through her body. She tried to move only to discover that a heavy weight lay across her shoulder and chest, pinning one arm. Another large board lay across her partially bent leg. She shook her head to clear it of the fog and dizziness. Tiny chips of wood fell to join those already piled in her lap.

"Christy? Can you hear me? Please, answer me! Are you hurt?"

The voice seemed to drift slowly down to her. Was she dreaming? She listened to it as if from a far off place. Where was he, the owner of this faceless, formless voice? Why did he hide in the darkness? She reached up to grasp the source of the intrusion. A sharp pain gripped her. Her eyes flew open wide as her desperate situation struck her full force.

"Captain." The word was a whisper, barely audible to her own ears. "Captain," she forced herself to speak louder. The board crushed her chest, making the very act of breathing difficult.

"Christy, are you hurt? Can you make it by yourself?" called Michael.

"I'm pinned beneath a heavy plank . . . and cannot . . . move," she gasped with much effort.

"If I throw a rope down, can you hook it around the board so I can pull it away?"

"I don't know." Pause. "My right arm is pinned." She

223

gathered breath. "I'll try." An overpowering fear was beginning to seep into her veins. Suppose this did not work? What then?

She was filled with panic. Crazed with cold terror, she struggled savagely to move the obstruction. The heavy board only nestled tighter against her. She wanted to scream. The slimy walls were closing in—crushing her! She couldn't breathe; she was suffocating. "Help me. Please! Don't leave me. Please don't leave me!" she pleaded, tears pouring down her face.

"Don't worry, Christy. I'll get you out. I promise," he vowed, sensing her terror by the panic in her voice.

His reassuring words placated her slightly. She gulped repeatedly, trying to suppress the panic which had almost overcome her. Of course he would not leave her. She would be out in no time.

"Here comes the rope. I have looped the end. See if you can slip it over the end of the board. When I lift it, pull yourself free."

An eternity seemed to pass before she felt the stiff rope touch her hand. Slowly, ever so slowly, and with great difficulty, she eased the rope toward the end of the board which held her prisoner. Another inch. Just another inch and it would be over.

She gritted her teeth and stretched her fingers almost beyond endurance. It hurt so bad. Oh God, she prayed; just a little bit more. So close. Inches separated her from life and death. Stretch! Another inch. You can do it. You must!

Tears of joy and relief dampened her face as the rope at last slipped over the tip of the plank. She closed her eyes, reveling in success. Her breath came in jagged gasps. She must rest. The worst was yet to come.

"Did you manage to hook the board? Are you all right?"

"Yes. Go ahead and pull."

Ever so lightly she felt the weight of the board being lifted. With the weight off her shoulder she was able to use both arms to guide it away and along the wall of the well. "I'm free," she called a few moments later. Tears streamed down her dirty, streaked face.

"Good. I'm going to let it down now. Stand clear."

With painstaking care she used her hands to slide herself up the side of the well to a standing position. With the weight of the plank gone, she could more accurately estimate the extent of her injuries. Her shoulder and arm hurt badly, as did her ribs. A steady throbbing pounded in her head and she reached up to rub it. A warm, sticky substance clung to her fingers. Was it blood, or slime from the wall? She couldn't be sure. It was too dark to see. She couldn't tell if any bones had been broken, but she felt terribly bruised and sore, and each breath made her wince in pain.

"Can you make it up now?" he called from above.

"Yes, I think I can manage," she lied.

With a great deal of difficulty she tied the rope about her waist and legs in much the same fashion as she had done for Johnny. The pain in her shoulder made the process slow and agonizing, but finally she felt herself secure and ready. She took a deep breath.

"Are you ready?" called the captain.

"Yes. Go ahead!" Her throbbing fingers clutched the

rope in a tight grip.

Ever so slowly she felt it tighten about her waist. Soon she hung limply in the air. The pressure on her torn and injured body was tremendous. All her energies were focused on remaining conscious and keeping a secure grip on her lifeline. She longed to hasten her ascent, yet knew the folly in this. Her hands guided her up the walls of the well toward light, safety, and Michael. His face towered not far above, outlined in sunlight. He had never looked more handsome or dear to her.

"Hang on. You're almost up. Only a bit more now."

A sense of urgency filled her. She lifted her arms high and gropped for him frantically. With one easy movement he dragged the rope up and pulled her from the well. "Thank God. Thank God," she cried, tears of pain and joy burning her face. She clutched him tightly, her legs shaking and unsteady.

"Oh my God!" exclaimed Michael as he held her frail, quivering body close. Her dusty hair lay tangled about her shoulders. A large, bloody lump protruded from one side of her head. Her face as well as her arms, dress and boots, were smudged with dirt and grime. One bruised, red shoulder lay exposed, marking the resting place of the heavy board. Looking down at her he marveled at her strength of will.

"I was so frightened. It was so dark and cold. I was afraid you'd leave me," she cried into his chest.

"You needn't have worried. I would never have left you." He placed his arms about her as much in comfort as for support. His mighty limbs seemed to pass their strength to her. It was over. Both she and little Johnny were safe. Her tears slowed, and she relaxed against him. "Where is Johnny? Is he all right?"

Michael looked down at her tear-stained face. "The boy is fine. One of the neighbors is tending him. No doubt he will be up and playing again tomorrow. 'Tis you I'm worried about now. I've already sent someone for the doctor. He will meet us at Penncrest. Do you think you can make it back? If not, the boy's parents have offered to care for you here."

"I'll be fine. I can make it."

"Well, then, can you stand here while I bring my horse?"

She nodded. Her head spun dizzily. Just as she was regaining her balance she was suddenly besieged by the boy's mother.

"Thank you so much, miss. You saved my boy's life. I can never repay you. Thank you. If you ever need anything, anything at all, just let me know. I'll do whatever you want, I'm that grateful."

The stout woman squeezed Christy heartily, heedless of the pain her gratitude caused. The captain was quick to assess the crisis and only his immediate intervention in pulling the thankful woman away saved Christy from dropping to the ground.

"Miss Patterson is well aware of your gratitude, madam. I suggest you permanently barricade this well so such an accident does not happen again," he admonished the boy's father. "And now if you will excuse me, I am taking Miss Patterson home."

With extreme care he swung her into the saddle and mounted behind her. Waves of dizziness entranced her.

Unconsciously she reached a small, trembling hand out to grip his large, steady one. He drew his arms more securely about her and gently pressed her swaying head against his chest. Kicking his great steed, they started off at an easy pace.

She relaxed slightly in his safe embrace, trying to ease her aches and pains. After some time, she opened her eyes to regard her torn and filthy dress. "What am I to do, Captain? My only dress is now damaged beyond repair. I fear I shall have to go back to wearing my shirt and trousers," she teased in an effort to lighten the worried frown on his face.

He glanced down at her torn sleeve. The gaping cloth gave him a satisfying view of her partially exposed breast. He longed to reach down and gently wipe away the dirt which rested there. His eyes traveled down to the large rip in her skirt. A shapely thigh rested close against him. "I suppose I will be forced to see you properly dressed. You cost me more money already, and not having paid me a shilling back as yet. I shall have to add it to your account," he teased back.

She stiffened, about to retort, but the movement jarred her shoulder and she winced in sudden pain. Her fingers clutched his arm tightly until the shooting ache eased somewhat.

"That will teach you to talk back to your master," he chided softly. He eased her head back to rest against his chest, where it remained for the rest of the journey.

News of the accident had already reached Penncrest, for when they arrived anxious shouts greeted them at the gate. Michael slowed his horse and jumped from the saddle. Calling for Bertha, he slipped his arms around Christy and gently lowered her to the ground, careful not to let go lest she fall.

"Oh, Lordy!" cried Bertha upon seeing her disheveled state. "You come with me, child. Let me get you into the house and up to bed. Doc Littman will be here in no time."

She grabbed Christy by the shoulder in an attempt to assist her up the stairs. Unfortunately it was her injured side. With a muffled cry of pain, the girl crumpled at the feet of an astonished Bertha.

She was only partially aware of the strong arms of Captain Lancer as he gently scooped her up into his arms and carried her to her room. She closed her eyes, relinquishing herself to his care. How strong he was, and how safe she felt in his arms. If only he could find a small place for her in his heart. As she drifted into semi-consciousness, she was oblivious to the look of concern written all over his handsome face.

Thirteen

Michael watched as Dr. Littman slowly, almost painfully, descended the stairs. The old gentleman had tended to the family throughout their years in Charleston. He was both family physician and close friend. But it was sad indeed to see what age, overwork, and rheumatism had done to the once-energetic doctor. The years were certainly taking their toll on him.

"How is she, Doctor?" Michael asked anxiously as the elderly man stopped for a breather at the landing.

He waved to Michael to be patient. Puffing heavily, he slowly made his way to a chair in the study. After a brief rest he directed himself to Michael's question. "The girl will be fine, Michael. She is young and strong. With proper care and rest, she will be up in no time. By God's good graces she has no broken bones. Her left shoulder and her ribs are badly bruised, however, and will give her a substantial amount of pain. I offered to give her some laudanum to ease her discomfort, but she refused. She's got grit, I'll say that. But it's the lump on her head that has me slightly concerned. She could have a slight concussion. I told Bertha to keep a sharp eye on her for the next few hours. But at any rate, she should stay quiet and rest for some time." The doctor paused for a few moments and looked directly at Michael. "'Twas a brave thing the girl did; going down into the well to save a total stranger's child."

"Brave or foolish. I'm not sure which," growled Michael. He filled two glasses with brandy and offered one to the grateful doctor.

"Why foolish, Michael? I understand you tried yourself and failed?"

Michael was slightly ruffled by his provoking tone. "I failed because I was too large to fit safely through the opening. Her only asset was her small size. One look at her should tell you how foolish she was for taking such a chance. It was just too dangerous. I ordered her to forget the crazy idea. But, she wouldn't listen—as usual. She's damn lucky both her and the boy made it out alive." He took a few gulps of the brandy and paced the room in agitation.

"Well, both are safe now and that's the important thing." Dr. Littman had to smile to himself at the scowl on Michael's face. Did he detect a wee bit of jealousy that a woman had succeeded where he had failed? Or, was his gruff manner a ploy to hide his concern for the life of this girl? His curiosity sparked, the doctor pressed on. "How long have you known Miss Patterson?"

"Close to three months, Doc. Since we set sail for Charleston."

"Where is she from? How do you come to know her? It's not your common practice to transport people, just goods. What made you change your policy?"

"Wait a minute, Doc. Why all the questions?"

Michael asked suspiciously.

"Come now, Michael. We've known one another for many years. You don't expect to call me here to tend an injured girl, one new to these parts, and have no questions as to who she is or why she's here. Bertha told me you're claiming she's some distant relative. I don't buy that story. It seems too farfetched for me, especially since your father's people came from Germany and your mother from the other end of England. What's the true story?"

"I guess your questions are justified, Doc. But there's something bothering you. What exactly are you driving at?"

Dr. Littman fingered his glass. "Well, I'll tell you. When I examined the girl I found some old and some not so old scars literally covering her back. Many of them have faded away and will soon disappear. But the traces that still remain prove the girl was badly abused. I would place the worst of it back to about three months ago. Do you know anything about it?"

"What the hell are you driving at?" demanded Michael in fury, jumping to his feet. "Do you think I whipped the girl?"

"Please. Calm yourself, son. I'm implying nothing of the kind. I've known you for all of your thirty-two years. I know you have quite a fondness for the ladies. You also have a violent temper when crossed. However, I have never known you to abuse a woman nor have I heard any evidence to the contrary. So, calm down. I am just curious as to what happened three months ago in relation to you and this young woman."

Michael relaxed somewhat. He certainly did not like being put on the spot and accused in any way of harming a woman. He'd done his share of fighting and brawling with men, but he'd never layed a violent hand on any woman. He may have used some friendly persuasion, but never violence. His conscious did prick him sorely, however, at the memory of the struggle Christy had given him on the ship. Yes, he did feel bad about that, but he intended making it up to her as best he could.

"Would you care for some more brandy, Doctor?" He refilled the glasses and began. "What I am about to tell you is strictly private and confidential. Only you, myself and my father know the story. For her safety, I believe it should remain that way."

"Yes, of course, my boy. I understand. Go on."

"When I left London three months ago the ship was not far out when we discovered an uninvited guest aboard."

"You mean the girl stowed away? But why?"

"Please. Let me continue."

"Yes. I am sorry. Do go on," coughed the doctor apologetically.

"One of my men found the girl hiding in the hold. She claimed she'd been playing some sort of game with a friend and hid in one of the crates. Said she must have dozed off and found herself aboard my ship. The peculiar part of it was, she was disguised as a boy. I did not discover the truth until she collapsed in my cabin. Paddy McDonough took a look at her and that's when we found she'd been badly beaten. Neither of us thought she would live. Only his constant and gentle care saved her."

Michael told the old doctor everything that had happened—including the sea-dunking he had given the stowaway.

"That was rather harsh treatment, Michael. Though I know the laws governing punishment at sea are different than on land. But, don't blame yourself too harshly. No doubt the healing and cleansing powers of the salt water did much in saving her life." The doctor paused to mull over the interesting story. "'Tis strange she did not reveal her true identity in an effort to save herself," he muttered, half to himself.

"Yes. I've often wondered the same thing myself. But, I believe she was too frightened to risk disclosing herself. Even now she refuses to tell me about her past. I think she still fears I might return her to London and to her tormentor."

"So, you've no idea who beat her?"

"No. Not really, though I do know it was not her parents. They are both dead; killed in some sort of accident about two years ago. She seems terribly frightened and reluctant to divulge any of her past. As I said, I think she fears being linked with her tormentor and returned to suffer the consequences of her escape." He paused in his reflections, remembering her vagueness and quick changes of subject when any mention was made to her past. "I do know, however, that at one time her parents were quite wealthy. She is very well-educated and has the airs of one well born. Other than those tidbits I have no clue into her past."

Both men were silent for some time, contemplating the complex young lady who now lay resting in the room above them. Finally the doctor spoke. "Why the charade about her being your distant relative? What exactly is the girl's position here?"

"I hardly think it would be beneficial for either of us if the truth were known. She would have no chance at a happy future if everyone knew she was a stowaway. Besides that, gossip mongers might press her for details. I feel somewhat responsible for her safety and well-being since it was my ship she sought as refuge. She is very much alone and needs someone to look after her. Besides, until I find out who it was who abused her so badly, at least I know she will be safe and well cared for here."

"You've a point there, Michael. And it's kind of you to take her in, especially since you know next to nothing about her. How long will she stay? Does she have any plans?"

Michael coughed and nervously paced the room, careful not to face the doctor. His conscience was plagued by a slight degree of guilt that his real reason for keeping her here was, for the most part, quite selfish and had little to do with gallantry. She was a beautiful young woman and he enjoyed having her near.

"What is it, Michael? Is there something else you're not telling me?" asked the doctor at the younger man's obvious discomfort.

"You may as well know the truth. When I pulled her out from the sea, I was still convinced she was a boy, running off to sea to find fame and fortune. To teach her there was a penalty for her rash, impetuous actions, I declared her an indentured servant—a bond slave, and ordered her to work under my orders to pay for her passage. I have not lifted that debt from her."

"That's preposterous, Michael. How do you expect her to pay you back?"

Michael knew the doctor would be even more angry if he knew just what he did hope for. "The money means nothing to me. But if I give her her freedom, where would she go? She is very strong willed, Doctor, and would not continue to accept my hospitality if she were free. Nor would she take any money I might offer her. In fact, I've no doubt she would find some way to eventually pay back the money she feels she owes me, though I would clear her debt completely. Until she finds some way of taking care of herself, I will not have her wandering around Charleston with no finances or a place to stay. At least by keeping her here, though under false pretenses, I can see that she is safe and has food to eat and a roof over her head."

Somewhat placated by his explanation, Dr. Littman went on. "That's commendable of you indeed, sir. But do you not think she will soon become suspicious if you give her no opportunity to work off her debt?"

I've given her many opportunities, thought Michael, but said instead, "You are quite right, Doctor. Even while we were on the ship she pestered me for some way to begin her duties. I was hard-pressed to keep her occupied and out of trouble aboard a ship full of healthy men. Now, she has been here in Charleston less than two weeks and already nags me for some job or chore to keep her busy. She has much pride and determination and is anxious to clear her debt. But, I cannot have her doing menial tasks. I know she is a well-bred lady and she should not be forced into physical labor to pay off her debts," he said, remembering his anger just this morning at finding her working in the garden. "But I will definitely have to come up with something soon, for she grows impatient."

"Well, don't make it too soon," said the doctor, rising from his chair with considerable effort. "The girl needs plenty of rest. She's been through a brutal experience and will need time to recover." He lifted his worn medical case and hobbled toward the door. "I'll be back tomorrow to look in on her." He paused and looked straight into Michael's eyes. "Striking girl, isn't she? I'm sure you have not failed to appreciate her delicate beauty. It is quite rare these days. Be kind and gentle to her, will you, son? She's apparently been through quite a bit in spite of her tender youth. I believe she could use some friendly compassion and understanding."

Michael grinned in spite of himself. The doctor's meaning was quite clear. "I will be good to her, Doctor. But I am a man and she does sorely test my control."

"'Tis good for your character to practice self-control, my boy," he returned with a twinkle in his eyes. "If I was thirty years younger I might have the same problem myself. Well, take care now. I'll see you tomorrow," he said and labored down the stairs to his waiting buggy.

Michael watched him drive slowly off. A grin still touched his lips. Oh how right the doctor was. She was indeed a rare and beautiful gem.

When his coach had disappeared from sight, Michael turned and hurried up the steps and down the hall to Christy's room. He was about to knock when Bertha exited, carrying Christy's torn dress. She pulled the door shut behind her.

"How is she, Bertha? I'd like to see her for a moment."

Bertha stubbornly blocked his path with her rather massive bulk. "Now you listen to me, Master Michael. Miss Christy is just fine now. Doc Littman and I took real good care of her. Poor child's been through a terrible ordeal. She don't need to see you or anyone else. Now you just leave her be. She needs her rest."

"I just want to see her for a minute," he insisted, but she was not to be dissuaded.

"I took care of her just fine. Now you leave her be. She's sleeping."

Michael knew it was hopeless to argue with her further. With a sigh of resignation he preceded her watchful eyes down the hall and went to relay the events of the day to his father. He would get his chance to see Christy later.

In the morning, a knock on the door roused Christy from her rather fitful slumber. Most of the night she had been tormented with nightmarish images of her uncle's huge, drunken face looming above her, whip poised and ready to strike again and again. She would run and run, only to find herself trapped in a dark, damp prison with something pinning her body. More than once she awoke, hot and feverish, to find Bertha shaking her gently to rouse her from the fiendish dream. Now Bertha stood before her, breakfast tray in hand, and looking a little tired and worn herself.

"Good morning, Miss Christy. I brought you some breakfast, child."

"Thank you, Bertha." She brushed back a tangle of black curls. She winced unconsciously as she gingerly pulled herself up to a sitting position. Bertha watched sympathetically as she settled herself and then set the tray laden with eggs, fried potatoes, ham and muffins covered with jam on her lap. It was a hearty feast, yet she had no appetite. She nibbled on a muffin and sipped orange juice as Bertha watched maternally.

"You got to eat, child, to build up your strength and heal those bruises," she said, trying to encourage Christy's appetite. She stood back and regarded this tiny, frail young woman in a new light.

The events of the previous day had done much to dispel some of her earlier feelings of apprehension. Though Christy's efforts in the garden yesterday had been entirely unsolicited, it proved to Bertha that this young woman was not above helping out and soiling her dainty hands. And then, of course, there was her heroic rescue of the Miller boy. Surely someone who would crawl down into a dark, horrid well to save a child could not be all bad.

But what had really weakened Bertha's disdain was the sight of the ugly, fading scars covering the girl's tender back. She had definitely been badly treated and her terrified dreams last night attested to the fact. How in the world had Master Michael gotten involved with such an abused girl? It was not unlike him or his father to help out the less fortunate, and this young woman appeared to need all the assistance available. Yet the fact that she seemed rather terrified of her benefactor was still a puzzle, along with the fact that she displayed the airs of one well bred.

Christy's rather humble apology interrupted Bertha's musings. "I'm sorry, Bertha. I know you've gone to much trouble to prepare such a nice breakfast, but I am not hungry now. Perhaps later I will be able to eat."

"Very well, child. I don't want to force you. I'll have the cook make some soup for you later. The doctor will be back this afternoon to have a look at your bruises, so you just take a little rest till then. Maybe those nasty dreams won't bother you today." She took the tray and tucked the blankets about Christy.

"Thank you, Bertha, for all your help. Especially for sitting with me last night," came the girl's trembling voice. Suddenly a lump formed in her throat. Tears flowed freely from her eyes and slid down her pale cheeks. She turned away, ashamed of her weakness before this stranger.

Bertha quickly placed the tray on the table and hustled to the bed. With strong yet gentle hands she gathered the sobbing girl into her arms and rocked her gently back and forth. "There, there, child. You go right ahead and cry. Get out all the hurt," she soothed, stroking Christy's head gently. "You cry on old Bertha's shoulder. She'll listen to you, child."

Two years of bottled up heartache spilled down her cheeks. Her body shook with rending sobs. The dammed up pain overflowed in a flood of sorrow.

At last the emotional pressure eased and her sobs died away. Tears spent, she lay exhausted and quiet in the comforting black arms of the housekeeper. How much she missed the companionship of a woman these past few years. Bertha reminded her of her own former nanny and friend, Elizabeth. She relished the sensation of once again being consoled and cared for. She seemed to be constantly fighting for her very existence.

"You feel better now, child?" asked Bertha as she held Christy at arm's length and regarded her with a practiced eye. Christy nodded weakly. "Good. Now you just lie back and take a nice long sleep. You'll feel much better when you wakes up."

"Thank you, Bertha, again," Christy whispered weakly.

"No need to thank me, child. You come to old Bertha any time you need to. That's why I'm here. Now go to sleep."

Christy smiled and shut her eyes. Whatever had changed the housekeeper's attitude toward her was a mystery, but she was certainly glad for the transformation. She needed an ally. . . .

She was sitting in a chair out on the balcony of her room a few days later watching the sun dip slowly over the horizon. The evening air was blissfully cool and soothing. She felt completely relaxed and at peace as she marveled in awe at nature's magnificent artistry. The vibrant pinks, blues and oranges of the setting sun filled her being with tranquility. So entranced was she by the crimson sunset, Captain Lancer's soft knock went all but unheard. He pushed open the doorway and stood gazing at the silhouetted perfection before him.

The soft, colorful beams of the fiery mass sinking behind the earth made her hair shine as it fluttered gently about her face and shoulders. Her young, tranquil body was clothed only in a pale, thin chemise. She was a moment in time, caught by a romantic painter's brush. She was a picture of serene beauty, an image enough to stir even the most cold of hearts. He was greatly moved and hesitated breaking the spell of her quietude. After a few moments, he took a deep breath and knocked loudly on the door. "Good evening, Miss Patterson. I trust you are feeling better?"

"Oh, Captain. You startled me!" she cried and jumped from her seat to face him.

With slow, deliberate strides, he joined her on the balcony. Her heart beat wildly as she noted his broad shoulders and muscular arms, bronzed from the sun. The blue shirt he wore was only partially buttoned, revealing his hard, muscular chest and a mass of thick black hair. Spotless trousers molded tightly to his lean torso and legs. She was acutely aware of his nearness and his intense masculinity, and also that she was covered by only a rather light dressing gown.

Regaining her composure, she responded lightly. "Yes, Captain. I am feeling much better, thank you. The doctor stopped by a short time ago and said I would be up in no time. No bones were broken and the lump on my head has gone down considerably. He insisted I continue to rest for another week before tackling anything strenuous. I thought that rather humorous since I've really done nothing of consequence since I arrived here." Her laugh was nervous. "It seems I am forever costing you money and aggravation. I have been totally useless to you thus far as a servant and, in fact, seem to have done nothing but rest and recuperate since our first meeting. It may take me a lifetime to repay you what I owe at this backwards rate."

"Perhaps you are right, my dear. But all that will soon change. As soon as you are well again I plan on putting you to work. Your leisure days are over."

"Oh that's wonderful, Captain. You've found something for me to do!" she exclaimed, hoping he had abandoned the idea of her being his mistress for some genuine assignment. "What is it you want me to do?"

"One moment, my dear," he said and disappeared from the room. A moment later he returned, a box held lightly under his arm. "Whenever you feel up to it I want you to go into town to the dressmaker for a complete wardrobe fitting. Your only dress was completely ruined in the well. Besides, you must look presentable in your new position. Until that time, however, perhaps you may feel more comfortable in this than the dressing gown." He withdrew the box and placed it into her hands.

"I don't understand, Captain. What sort of work would require a suitable wardrobe?" she asked, bewildered and hesitant as she looked up into his teasing brown eyes.

"Open the box, my dear," he ordered.

Her fingers tore anxiously at the parcel and she gasped in astonishment at the lovely dress which spilled from the box. She grasped it tightly and held it to her. "It's lovely, Captain. Just lovely! You are far too generous with me," she murmured, her eyes a dancing sea of green.

"You needn't thank me, my dear. Actually I have my own selfish designs in mind. You see, I've given your suggestion considerable thought and if you are to be my secretary and accountant, it certainly would not be practical for you to go about dressed in trousers or a dressing gown. It would create quite a disruption, I fear."

"Your secretary, Captain? Did I hear you say your secretary?"

The look of complete surprise and delight reflected in her eyes pleased him. "Yes. You did such a splendid job on the ship I am sure you are capable of handling my affairs here. The work will be far more involved and detailed than my shipping ledgers, since as you know, I own and run the timber mill. It requires more and more of my time and I find less time and inclination to sit down and do the paperwork and figuring. Do you think you can handle the responsibility?"

"Oh yes, Captain. Yes. I am overwhelmed. How can I ever thank you? You will not be disappointed. I will work hard for you!"

He smiled down at her. For all her happiness a stranger would have thought he'd given her a priceless gift instead of a job. "You may well not thank me. The job entails much work, long hours. It is not an easy chore, as I well know." Though his tone was less than enthusiastic, he was happy with his decision. He knew she could handle the responsibility and it would free him from a task he had come to loath. Eventually he would have been forced to hire a secretary, anyway. This was killing two birds with one stone. He would have an excuse to keep her here, and at the same time get his bookkeeping done.

"I will work hard, Captain. I promise I will not let you

down. You will not regret your decision," she reiterated happily.

I regret it already, he thought to himself as he gazed upon her youthful beauty, so well outlined in the sheer gown she wore. He longed to take her into his arms and crush her to him. After having once tasted the sweet fruit of her flesh, he ached to sample it again. But he remained strong in his resolve to keep his distance until she came to him. He would not allow himself to weaken as he had once before. But how long would she keep him waiting?

"I will explain the necessary procedures to you before I go."

Christy looked up in confusion. "Are you going somewhere, Captain?"

"The mill requires more and more of my time of late, as does the shipping business of father's. I plan to set sail for the West Indies in two weeks and make one more short trip. I should be gone only about a month. When I return I will sell *The Merrimer* and settle down to take full responsibility for the mill. I can no longer leave its upkeep entirely to the overseer." A hint of sorrow edged his tone.

"Will you not miss the sea?" she asked. She remembered the vision of him standing tall and strong on the bridge of his ship, enjoying his pipe and looking like he belonged there.

"Yes, I will miss it dearly. But I have other responsibilities and I cannot remain at sea forever. I have served my time and will turn it over to younger men. Besides, after having such a unique stowaway on my last voyage, any other trip would be anticlimactic."

Christy blushed, feeling his hot gaze upon her. Embarrassed by his comment, she lowered her head to contemplate her wiggling bare toes. The captain followed her gaze downward, again taken by this dainty creature who could set his senses reeling by a mere glance. He touched her chin and lifted her face to meet his. "Yes, your presence certainly made the trip interesting." His tone had turned husky, and there was a hint of hunger in his eyes.

She blushed again and held the dress tightly against her chest in sudden apprehension. She had seen that look in his eyes before, and it both frightened and excited her. A sudden knock on the door broke the spell. It was Bertha carrying a tray heaped with delicacies.

"Why, Bertha. You will make our guest plump and round and send us to the poor house if you continue to feed her thus," Captain Lancer teased.

"Nonsense. What do you know?" she shot back. "The girl is thin as a rail. She hasn't eaten a bite all day. And besides, it would take more than a few such meals to put meat on her bones. You let Miss Christy be. Bertha will take real good care of her."

Christy stood in embarrassment as they bantered back and forth about her physical state. A little self-consciously, she sat at the table and was very glad when both finally left her to enjoy her meal in peace. She ate every bite.

Fourteen

The momentum of Michael's welcome assignment carried Christy through the worst of the recovery. Under Bertha's watchful attention, she regained her strength and her bruises healed nicely. It was remarkable how the housekeeper's attitude had improved toward her. She was not sure why, but was definitely grateful for the new way Bertha treated her. Perhaps she had taken the cue from the captain, for he too treated her with far more respect.

Sir Phillip dropped in at regular intervals during the day to check her progress. As her strength returned, he escorted her on slow, leisurely walks through the gardens. During this time together they grew quite close. They talked of England, and she found herself more than once coming close to confiding in him. But she feared they would scorn her if her true identity were known, and the terror of being returned to her uncle was still too strong. She staunchly determined to remain mute on the subject of her past. Sir Phillip, however, though he could not draw her out on that subject, did marvel at the knowledge and wisdom she possessed for one so young. He had no way of knowing just how deep a role politics had played in molding her future.

Even Paddy McDonough unexpectedly stopped in to pay his respects. It was a nice reunion. Christy had missed this Irishman since the ship docked and felt she owed him an apology for running off without saying goodbye.

Her happiness was short lived, however, when Paddy informed her that he had hired on with *The Beacon*. He explained that it was among a new fleet of ships in need of experienced navigators. It was a good opportunity for him to use his talents at charting seas. His visit was all too short, and it was a rather tearful farewell. But he left with his promise to stop in whenever he docked in Charleston.

After the days of rest and visiting, Christy enjoyed the evenings as well. After dinner she and Captain Lancer would retire to the study and pour over the accounts. She caught on quickly and looked forward to some day actually seeing the mill. He was patient and thorough in explaining the details of the ledgers and procedures involved, and she realized just what a mammoth job she had undertaken. Once she was fully recovered her new duties would keep her very busy.

Well pleased with her speedy recovery, Dr. Littman made his final visit and released her from his care. The following Saturday she found herself rumbling toward Charleston in an open carriage between Michael and Sir Phillip. At Michael's insistence she was to purchase a suitable wardrobe for herself. She looked forward to the prospects of having some new things, yet still felt uneasy about the added debt it would place on her. Would she ever be able to stand on her own and face him as an equal?

It seemed too distant and far-fetched even to contemplate.

The countryside was lush with greenery as they neared Charleston. A salty sea breeze tickled their noses long before they reached the town. With the captain and Sir Phillip at her side, it looked far less threatening than she remembered from her first visit.

The captain pulled the carriage up in front of the little dress shop and helped her down. Then he and Sir Phillip discussed a meeting time. Both had errands to run and knew Christy would be quite some time with her fittings. Arrangements complete, Sir Phillip sauntered off, cane in hand. Michael turned and offered his arm to Christy. The little bell in the doorway tinkled cheerfully as they entered the shop together. Mr. Kramer rushed out to meet them.

"Good day, Mr. Kramer. How are you today? May I present my cousin, Miss Christina Patterson," he said in a businesslike manner.

"Your . . . your cousin?" muttered the astonished shopkeeper. "Ah yes. Enchanted, my dear," he quickly covered his slip.

Christy hid the blush on her cheeks by bowing deeply.

"Yes. We are fortunate to have her visit us from London," replied Michael absently, taking no notice of the little man's astonishment.

"Of course," he muttered again. This girl had certainly done well for herself. She had wasted no time in finding an eligible, wealthy bachelor to look after her. But Michael Lancer! He nearly whistled to himself. The Lancers were one of the wealthiest and most influential families in all of Charleston. This girl had definitely started out at the top.

He looked at them closely, standing side by side. They certainly did make a fine-looking couple. Her tiny, delicate beauty contrasted sharply with his tall, rugged good looks. He did find the "cousin" pretext a bit amusing, however. No doubt it was socially more acceptable than "mistress."

"I am delighted to meet you, Miss Patterson," Mr. Kramer finally answered, fully enthusiastic for the captain's benefit. No doubt he would spend no small amount on his new amusement. "And what can I do for you today, Mr. Lancer?"

"My cousin is in need of some new clothing. Those things she brought from London are unsuitable to our climate here. You were highly recommended to me by my sister-in-law, Matilda Lancer. Can I leave it to you to outfit my cousin completely and stylishly?"

Mr. Kramer puffed with pride. "Oh yes, Mr. Lancer. You've come to the right place. It will certainly be an honor to fit Miss Patterson. Would you care to see some sketches?"

"No. No. I have business to attend to. I will leave selection to Miss Patterson's discretion and your own recommendations. Will two hours be a satisfactory length of time for you to select the wardrobe and take appropriate measurements?"

"Yes, Mr. Lancer. That should be sufficient." He paused, wondering how to broach the matter of price. "Ah, sir, may I inquire as to the limit you wish to set?" he asked delicately.

"Whatever the lady likes. Within reason, of course," replied Michael.

"Very good, sir." Mr. Kramer was quite pleased. He guessed this young lady would spare no expense, especially since her wealthy keeper was footing the bill. "I am sure we can find something to please the young lady."

"I shall see you in a couple of hours then," said Captain Lancer. He nodded to Mr. Kramer and tipped his hat to Christy before disappearing into the street.

Mr. Kramer was too much of a businessman to make a comment to Christy, but as he showed her to a table and spread out some sketches, his smug look both embarrassed and infuriated her. She knew what he was thinking and yet could not defend herself without telling more than she cared to. Well, let him believe what he would. His concern lay in her wardrobe, not her personal affairs.

A thrill of excitement tickled her as she viewed Kramer's sketches. It had been years since she'd seen such lovely gowns. But, when it came to actually choosing, she again felt at a loss. She did not know how much Michael wished her to spend. She did not intend to buy too much, yet she was sure if she did not buy the items he had in mind, he might be even more furious. Naturally, Mr. Kramer was only too enthusiastic about the most costly of items.

At length she decided to remain as thrifty as possible, and chose three simple yet stylish gowns with matching accessories and undergarments. She noticed Mr. Kramer was hard pressed to conceal his disappointment at the modest sales, yet she did not want to put herself even

251

farther into debt by buying costly clothing. She owed Michael Lancer far too much money as it was without adding to the price.

Her decision complete, she absently leafed through additional sketches. In her own mind her selection was complete, yet Mr. Kramer continued to tempt her with his inventory of elegant wares. She praised his talents yet remained steadfast in her resolve. Her battle was nearly won when, in a last effort, he approached with a gown of exquisite cut and flair. An involuntary cry of delight escaped her lips as he spread before her the deep green velvet cloth, edged and trimmed with soft white lace. Her eyes were bright with longing to own such a magnificent gown and he increased his persuasive measures. It took all her willpower to dismiss it. But, she argued with herself, it was hardly appropriate or practical for a bonded servant to own such a gown. Besides, when would she ever have need of such a dress?

"The three gowns I selected will do quite nicely, Mr. Kramer. I wish to see no more. Shall we proceed directly with the measurements? It grows late and I do not wish to keep Mr. Lancer waiting."

"Very well, madam," replied Mr. Kramer with a sigh to match her own. Reluctantly he showed her to a back room and began taking her measurements. To her it was a long and labored process, and she was quite relieved when the ordeal was over. Mr. Kramer bustled off with the sketches and measurements, leaving her to dress in peace.

She had just finished and was patting her hair into place when she heard the shop door tinkle. Thinking it must be Michael, she pulled aside the curtain and stepped out.

"Dear Mr. Kramer. How are you today?"

Christy stopped short. The voice belonged to none other than Matilda Lancer. She was dressed to the hilt and followed closely by her two children.

"Ah, Mrs. Lancer. As always it is a pleasure to see you. You grace my humble establishment," he bubbled. "I suppose you have come to pick up little Michele's dress? Here it is. I have it all ready for you," he said and handed the neatly wrapped box to the little girl. "Mademoiselle will look stunning in her new gown," he said benevolently and patted her head.

Little Michele was not at all taken with his show of overaffected enthusiasm. She snatched the box and turned away. Mr. Kramer reddened slightly but continued on, undaunted by her rebuff. "And how are you today, monsieur?" he questioned the boy, obviously trying to impress their mother with his friendliness and affected French mannerisms.

"Do you have any candy?" came the child's reply. He too was little impressed by the shopkeeper's airs.

"My dear Oliver. It is not at all polite to ask Mr. Kramer such a question," Matilda said in gentle reproach. Yet she glanced sweetly in the dressmaker's direction with a look that said she fully intended him to jump and fetch the boy some candy.

Obviously flustered and caught off guard, he bowed at the little tyrant in an effort to conceal his reddened face. "Why, I always have candy for you and your charming little sister," he said and excused himself to look for the sweets.

In his haste, he almost knocked Christy over as she stood quietly beside the curtained doorway. The near collision caught Matilda's eye and she arched an eyebrow in surprise at seeing her.

"Why, my dear Miss . . . What was the name, child? It seems to have slipped my mind," she began snobbishly.

"Christina Patterson."

"Ah yes. Miss Patterson. Michael's little cousin. What brings you to Kramer's shop. 'Tis quite expensive, you know."

"Mr. Lancer has asked me to outfit Miss Patterson," replied Mr. Kramer before Christy could respond. He held a gaily ribboned box of assorted chocolates which he offered to the two children.

"Mr. Lancer is purchasing some gowns for you? Well, how perfectly sweet of him," Matilda exclaimed, yet found it nearly impossible to contain her jealousy. This little mite must mean something to him that he should lavish such expensive gifts on her. She did not like it at all. She was having enough trouble cajoling Michael's affections without the interference of some young nobody.

"Isn't it just like Michael to look out for those less fortunate," Matilda answered, her brown eyes flashing.

"Yes, Mr. Lancer has indeed been more than kind to me," Christy said quietly and left it at that. Let Matilda think what she would.

Mr. Kramer moved to offer Matilda a chocolate, but she waved him off carelessly. "No thank you, Kramer. I do not care for anything but the finest sweets. But perhaps Miss Patterson would enjoy some. She certainly could use some weight to fill out her figure."

Christy blushed hotly. She had never come across anyone so blatantly rude. She shook her head at Kramer's offering and was about to retort to Matilda when the door chime tinkled and Michael sauntered easily through the doorway.

"Well, Matilda. This is a surprise." He tipped his hat.

"Michael, darling. How marvelous to see you," she began, but before she could continue, Oliver and Michele intercepted her greeting.

"Uncle Michael. Uncle Michael!" cried the two children, forgetting the candy and throwing themselves into his arms. Their greeting was barely complete when the door chime sounded again and in walked Sir Phillip. He nodded politely at Matilda, yet there was no warmth in his greeting. There seemed to be little love loss between father and daughter-in-law. The children, however, were a different story. With obvious delight, they bombarded their grandfather with hugs and kisses.

"This is indeed a pleasant surprise, darling," Matilda continued as she placed her hand possessively on Michael's arm. "I came to pick up little Michele's dress and who do I find here but your little cousin. She tells me you are buying her wardrobe. You are indeed overly generous, my dear. Why, leaving such a young and obviously impressionable girl to pick through all these lovely creations. You may well find yourself a pauper," she proclaimed wickedly and glanced cattily at Christy.

A worried expression came over Michael's face and he politely disengaged his arm from hers. "Is that true,

Christina? Have you indeed sent me to the poor house?"

Christy's face burned hot with embarrassment as they all turned to regard her. Matilda had deliberately put her in this uncomfortable position and was now enjoying the results of her accusing words. What really hurt was the fact that Michael had taken the bait. Before she could defend herself, Sir Phillip took up her cause.

"Why, I'm surprised at you both. Can't you see Miss Patterson has a sensible head on those lovely shoulders. I am sure she used good judgment in choosing a wardrobe." He sensed Michael was in foul humor, and Matilda was clearly at her humiliating best. Wisely he deposited a coin in each of his grandchildren's hands and sent them off down the street for a treat. No need for them to witness such pettiness. When they were gone, he moved to stand beside Christy and placed a reassuring hand on her arm.

She smiled up at him, flattered he would take such a stand on her behalf having only known her for such a short time. She blessed her good sense in keeping her selections to a bare minimum. Her congratulations were a bit premature, however.

"Well, Mr. Kramer. Will you settle the debate and enlighten us as to just how much I owe you," began Michael, becoming slightly perturbed by all this needless banter.

Mr. Kramer sensed the heavy undercurrent. He knew he must be cautious in his reply lest he lose either of them as customers. Since this Miss Patterson was actually only the third party, her feelings could be spared. "As a matter of fact, Mr. Lancer, the lady was extremely modest in her selections. She chose only three of my simplest gowns." Though he tried to hide it, he was obviously piqued at the scanty sale.

"What?" boomed Michael. His temper was growing hotter by the minute. "Must you women make everything so damned complicated? I said spare no expense. I can certainly afford to see you properly dressed. Let me see what has been chosen." Though he had been distressed at the prospect of a high bill, he was even more upset that she should be so modest in her selection. Did she think him too cheap or poor that he could not afford to buy her decent clothing? It made him appear stingy before this mealy little shopkeeper.

Hoping to increase his profits, the little man presented the sketches of the three dresses. "The young lady decided upon these. They are nice of course, yet plain and simple. I could not persuade her to chose something more . . . chique . . . shall we say?"

Michael glanced at the sketches in growing agitation. "These are quite common. Was there nothing more comely you could have chosen, Christina?" he growled at her.

"I'm sorry, Captain. I thought you would prefer the simplicity of these gowns to something more elaborate."

Taking advantage of his dissatisfaction, Mr. Kramer pressed on. "Miss Patterson was immensely tempted by this green velvet, sir. I am sure she would like to have it despite her negative response." He spread the lovely gown before them. "I believe with madam's slender figure and emerald green eyes, she would look lovely in this gown."

Matilda regarded the dress with fained displeasure. It was exquisite. She would love to have it. But her larger, fuller figure would not do the gown justice. Since she knew she could not look good in the dress, she resented the tailor's suggestion that Christy's slender form would.

"I am sure Miss Patterson did right in declining this gown. Why, where in the world would she wear such a dress? The other three are far more practical for her simple needs. This velvet is certainly too extravagant for such a young and immature girl."

Christy flushed scarlet at Matilda's biting words. She despised Matilda and Michael both for openly humiliating her in front of Sir Phillip and this shopkeeper.

"Enough of this prattle. I've lost patience with the lot of you. We will take these three dresses Miss Patterson chose, but definitely add the green gown to the order. I have not the time or the patience to be bothered further in picking out gowns. In the future, however, I see I will have to choose my cousin's gowns for her since her tastes are far too modest to suit me." With that, he drew Mr. Kramer aside and paid him.

Christy was again made to feel the incompetent child. She had tried to spare the captain expense and now he had insulted her for her thriftiness. He was impossible to please. She bit her lips to still their trembling. To hide the flush on her face, she bent to smooth an imaginary wrinkle from her skirt. She was immensely relieved when the tinkle of the bell signaled the return of the two children.

"Though no one asked my opinion, I believe Miss Patterson's taste impeccable. But since all is now settled, shall we leave Mr. Kramer to his work and have some lunch? I am famished," said Sir Phillip in an obvious effort to break the uncomfortable silence.

"Why, Father, what a marvelous idea. Shall we go to Maxwell's? Their crabmeat devonshire is divine!" cooed Matilda, suddenly bubbling and enthusiastic. Too bad Michael had given in and purchased the velvet. But she would get her way later. "Don't you agree, Michael? Maxwell's has the tastiest food in town."

"Yes. Yes. Whatever you say, Matilda. Maxwell's is fine," agreed Michael as he concluded his business with Mr. Kramer.

The little entourage filed through the door with Sir Phillip and Christy bringing up the rear. Once outside, Matilda took a firm grip on Michael's arm and cooed brazenly in his ear.

Sir Phillip snorted softly and offered Christy his arm. "Actually, the crabmeat at Maxwell's is the worst I've ever tasted. They spare little, however, on atmosphere and price, for most of the wealthy, influential gentry of Charleston dine there. 'Tis why I think Matilda fancies it. She is easily impressed with such pomp and flashy extravagance. But today we will humor her."

Despite her despondent mood, Christy had to laugh at the devilish twinkle in his eye. What a dear he was for trying to ease her discomfort. For his sake she must try to overcome her melancholy.

The little procession had nearly reached the expensive restaurant when a carriage came thundering down the street and screeched to a halt only a few yards away. Billowing clouds of dust settled slowly back into the street after the disruption. The huge black driver of the carriage jumped down, placed a footstool on the ground, and opened the door to help his rather portly master alight.

"Such a commotion!" exclaimed Michael indignantly. "Who does the man think he is, riding about town like a madman?"

Sir Phillip adjusted his spectacles and took a better look. "Why, that's Joanace. It took me time to recognize him through the dust. He's the new lieutenant governor working with Governor Glen. Rumor has it the two don't get on well together. They disagree on treatment of the Indians. This Joanace still believes in enslaving them and taking their lands. Glen is all for peace."

"Have you met him yet?" Michael wanted to know.

"Yes. The Businessmen's Guild held a welcoming luncheon in his honor. I met him there. I believe you were in London at the time. It it said he was sent here quite against his wishes. He has a strong aversion for our fair land and is totally unsympathetic with our causes. I found him quite pompous and disagreeable. I really question the king's wisdom in sending him to govern here. He has riled not a few of the merchants and townspeople in only the short time he has been here."

"Well perhaps you should introduce me, Father. I would like to judge for myself what type of man he is. He certainly has not obtained my confidence with his rather rude behavior thus far."

"Very well," sighed Sir Phillip.

The little entourage carefully picked their way across the crowded street and presented themselves before the lieutenant governor who was giving instructions to his driver. Matilda pushed ahead with Michael, anxious to make herself known to this influential politician. Christy trailed along behind with the children.

"Good day, Governor. My name is Phillip Lancer. We met at your welcoming reception in July."

"Ah yes, Mr. Lancer. You are in the shipping business, I believe," said the official with a quick, calculating glance. Both men remembered their rather heated argument concerning the heavy taxes and tariffs being levied against the merchants.

"Yes, you are correct." He turned to Michael. "Governor, may I present my son, Michael Lancer. Michael, this is Lieutenant Governor Joanace."

Christy's heart skipped a beat. Surely Sir Phillip had not said *Joanace?* She must have heard wrong. It was not possible. . . . A lump formed in her throat. She strained to see over Michael's shoulder.

She saw the man with her own eyes. But she could not believe what she saw. Horror nearly strangled her as a sharp gasp ripped from her throat. She blinked frantically, trying to dispell the hideous sight. The blood in her veins turned to ice, and her hand flew to her throat as she fought for breath.

"Are you all right, my dear?" asked Sir Phillip, concerned by her peculiar outburst.

"Yes. I'm sorry. I am fine," she murmured, trying to still her wildly beating heart and gain control. "Please excuse me."

She conquered the impulse to turn and flee and gulped air greedily, trying to regain her poise. Her eyes were glued to him, yet it took her a few seconds to realize he had turned his gaze upon her. Suppose he recognized her? What would he do? Would he humiliate her in front of these people? Would he send her to jail, or worse yet, back to Henry Slate?

"And who is this charming creature, Mr. Lancer? Your daughter, perhaps?" She heard him ask as he studied her from head to toe. "She graces this barbarian world of yours."

"Permit me to introduce my cousin, Christina Patterson," offered Sir Phillip. He was puzzled and concerned by Christy's sudden pallor. Was she overtired by the long day after her recent injuries, or did her paleness have something to do with this overweight official?

"I am charmed indeed, my dear," he said, taking her hand and planting a wet kiss upon it.

Her skin crawled at the feel of his slimy lips upon her flesh. She eased her hand away nervously and clutched her handbag tightly. Knowing a response was in order, she attempted some courtesy. But the lump in her throat made her all but mute.

Matilda watched the proceedings in mounting agitation. She coughed slightly, furious at being left out of the introductions. The lieutenant governor's open admiration of Christy did little to sooth her indignation. "Why, Governor Joanace. You mustn't judge us all as barbarians. Some of us are quite civilized," she cooed and batted her eyes at the robust man.

"Oh, excuse me. I am so sorry. This is Matilda Lancer, my daughter-in-law," said Sir Phillip hastily, perturbed by his own lack of courtesy in introducing Matilda. Christy's actions had made him forget his manners.

The man turned his attention to Matilda. With equal gallantry he kissed her hand also. "What a lovely wife you have, sir," he said in way of a compliment to Matilda as he glanced at Michael.

"My wife? Oh, 'tis an honest mistake, sir. Mrs. Lancer is my sister-in-law," explained Michael.

"Then pray tell me, my dear, how your husband lets such a fair jewel fend for herself?" he complimented.

"Alas, dear Governor. I am alone, for my husband is dead three long years," she replied with far more remorse than necessary.

"Oh, I see. My most heartfelt apologies. And my condolences to such a lovely widow."

"Oh you are too kind," responded Matilda prettily, eager to retain control of the conversation. Unfortunately the man's attention had already wandered back to Christy.

"And you, my dear. Are you also without a husband?" he asked boldly.

"Yes," Christy choked, but was saved from further reply by Michael.

"My cousin is unmarried as yet," he replied stiffly. The man was certainly rude to even ask such a personal question.

"Oh, please forgive my lack of manners. I meant no harm. May I just say that you are indeed lucky to have such a lovely cousin," he drooled.

Christy lowered her eyes to the ground lest he see how his leering comments sickened her beyond endurance.

She wanted to scratch his eyes out. How dare he stand there and play the benevolent magistrate, showering her with compliments, after cold-bloodedly murdering her parents?

"Yes, we feel extremely honored. She has only just recently come to us from your fair land, Governor," replied Sir Phillip, hard pressed to remain civil and contain the contempt he felt for the pompous ignoramus.

"Oh, really? Your gain was surely England's loss." He paused, and fluttered a lacy handkerchief beneath his nose. A strange expression suddenly crossed his face, and Christy caught her breath in trepidation. Surely he now recognized her.

"Hmmm. I vaguely recall a family named Patterson. They lived in London a few years back. Perchance you are some relation?" he asked cautiously.

Her heart skipped a beat as Joanace studied her closely in a new light. She swallowed hard, knowing she must weigh each word carefully, and hoping to hide the tremor in her voice. "No, I think not, sir. I do not come from London originally. I have no living relatives of whom I am aware." You murdered them all, she added silently.

"My mistake, my dear. It must have been someone else then. I surely would have remembered a lovely young woman like yourself," he said without conviction. Christy could not help but feel she had not totally convinced him.

Matilda was eager to draw the attention back to herself and engaged Joanace in relating information about life in London. He directed his comments to her and the two men since Christy made no effort to join in the conversation. Yet more than once she glanced up to find his eyes upon her. Had he believed her explanation? Or did he recognize her? It had been nearly three years since she had confronted him with the murder of her parents. She was only fifteen years old then; just a child he had dismissed without a second glance. Surely it was highly unlikely he recognized her now that she was a woman. She sincerely prayed that was the case, yet determined to stay as far away from him as possible.

Michele and Oliver, bored at this grownup talk, skipped around the group of adults. Their play became overly boisterous until a loose stone caused Michele to trip against Christy. Shaken from her reverie, she helped the little girl up, murmuring concern for the child's welfare. She glanced at Matilda, hoping the woman would not scold the children, but was quite unsettled by the peculiar way Matilda was regarding her. Had Matilda noticed the tremor in her voice when she denied heritage with the Pattersons of London? Did she suspect there was more to her story than met the eye? Or was it only womanly jealousy which caused her to stare so intently? Christy smiled pointedly at the woman, thus breaking her intense stare, but she still felt uneasy.

Taking advantage of the diversion, Lieutenant Governor Joanace said his goodbyes. "If you will excuse me I must be about my business, dear people. It was certainly a pleasure meeting all of you. I hope to see you again." He nodded politely to the group, yet his gaze lingered for a moment on Christy.

"Good day, sir," replied Sir Phillip formally.

"It was so nice meeting you, Governor. I do hope we

can get together again soon. Perhaps for lunch some-time?'' called Matilda as the little group resumed their trip to the restaurant.

During lunch Sir Phillip and Michael exchanged some rather heated discussions concerning Joanace. Both agreed he was a pompous man and extreme care would have to be used in dealing with him.

They were both curious about Christy denying she had come from London, but neither pressed her for details. It was obvious, however, that for some reason the sudden appearance of Joanace had deeply upset their guest. Either she knew him from some dealings in London, or else merely feared any form of the law. It was puzzling and both men silently determined to find out more about Christy and the past she hid so secretly.

During the meal, Christy contributed little to the conversation. She feared if she spoke at all her voice would reveal the turmoil she felt within. Her head spun from seeing her most hated enemy. The horror of her childhood had again manifested itself in the form of the fat Governor.

"The crabmeat is delicious today, as usual. You should have ordered it instead of the steak, Father. I told you how superb it always is," said Matilda, itching for an argument.

"The steak is fine, Matilda. And I do not care for the crabmeat here," answered Sir Phillip.

Slightly miffed that he should not agree with her, Matilda sought out someone she knew would knuckle under her fire. "Whatever has happened to your appetite, my dear Miss Patterson? You've not touched a

thing. Do you not like the crabmeat I suggested?"
Matilda asked with mock concern. Behind her question
was an open challenge to say the fish was anything but
delicious.

"Oh, it is very good, Mrs. Lancer. I suppose I am tired
from all the fittings of this morning," she answered, yet
kept her eyes on her plate.

"Yes, I suppose it might be tiring for one not
accustomed to such things," Matilda granted, being
aware of Christy's obvious impoverished circumstances.
"Kramer knows my measurements exactly and I need
only show him a design I like without going through all
that fuss."

"Nonsense, my dear Matilda," piped in Sir Phillip.
"Christina is still recovering from injuries suffered while
saving one of the mill worker's sons. It is perfectly
understandable she would be tired. Besides, after today
Kramer will know her requirements and will be able to fit
her in anything without all the 'fuss' as you put it. And
might I add, if you continue to eat those sweet desserts,
you may need your measurements adjusted," teased Sir
Phillip.

Matilda was quite indignant he should make mention
of her weight. Though he had insulted her, she would
gain her revenge by making this puny cousin squirm in
discomfort. "You needn't worry about my weight, sir. I
am in perfect shape and intend to remain that way. If you
must concern yourself with such mundane matters, I
suggest you direct your criticisms to your little cousin.
The girl looks half-starved."

"Really, Matilda. Christina looks fine to me," defended Sir Phillip. "Don't you agree, Michael?"

"Miss Patterson's weight is her own affair," he replied curtly, yet he remembered all too well her unclothed, slender form and its pleasing attributes.

Christy was acutely embarrassed. After suffering humiliation and abuse from both Mr. Kramer and Matilda at the dress shop, and then coming face to face with the hateful Joanace, she felt ill-prepared to cope with further attacks on her person. She would have liked nothing better than to sink to the floor and disappear from sight. But instead she forced back her tears. "I have always been thin, as were my parents. Thus far it has never hindered me in any way. In fact, my size proved a definite asset in maneuvering through the debris in the well. I see no reason to change." Again she lowered her eyes, hoping the subject of her person closed.

Matilda did not take her cue. Instead she seized upon this new opportunity to further belittle her adversary. "Oh yes. I'd forgotten about that episode with the boy. But really, my dear, crawling down inside a well after a timber worker's child was rather foolish. You could have been killed, and who knows what problems that would have created." Her tone clearly indicated the fatality would not have been a cause for much sorrow on her own part.

"Really, Matilda. Though I wasn't there I do know it took a tremendous amount of courage. We should all be very proud of Christina. Isn't that right, Michael?"

"Yes. Christina was very brave, and very lucky," replied Michael. "And so were we. It would have been a tragedy to lose such a newly acquired cousin."

Christy sensed his words held a different meaning for her than they did for the others. She blushed hotly at his intense gaze and returned her attention to her plate.

Matilda was again disappointed that she had been unable to provoke Christy. Instead the girl had ended up looking like a saint. A change of tactics was in order. "Dear, wasn't it odd the lieutenant governor should know people in London named Patterson. 'Tis not a very common name. Funny you did not know them," she baited.

Christy felt the color drain from her face. Her hands dropped to her lap to hide their trembling. So Matilda had, after all, noticed her shock and anxiety in the presence of the Governor and now meant to capitalize on it.

"Yes, it was rather odd, wasn't it? But as I told him, I lived outside of London and as far as I know I am the last surviving member of my family."

"Why, my dear. Aren't you forgetting Michael and Sir Phillip here? Don't you claim them as your cousins?" Matilda was quick to catch her slip.

"I'm sorry. I was referring to my immediate family, Mrs. Lancer." The effort to remain cool and aloof was almost more than Christy could bear. Joanace's sudden reappearance had shattered her world. And now Matilda's relentless probing was gradually weakening her defenses. If help did not come soon, she knew she would completely break down in front of them all.

Matilda conceded, yet her tone implied victory. "Tell me, just what part of England did you come from then, if not from London?" she probed on, greatly encouraged by the anxiety written all over Christy's face.

"Matilda, I believe that is enough questioning for now. Christina has admitted she is tired and I do not believe you should press her for details which do not concern you," scolded Michael, all at once aware of Matilda's game and Christy's extreme paleness.

"Well, I should think you might be interested in where she hails from since she claims she is related to you," seethed Matilda indignantly.

"We are well aware of where Christina comes from, Matilda. But she has decided to make Charleston her home now. Her past is inconsequential to you," said Michael, coming to her defense. "Now if we are ready, I suggest we go. I fear an impending storm and would like to get Father and Christina home before it strikes."

Matilda's eyes flashed in anger as Michael rose and held Christy's chair for her. A wan smile was all Christy could muster in light of the past few hours' traumatic events, but she was relieved Michael had spared her the ordeal of having to explain her origins to Matilda.

Still upset by her putdown, Matilda jumped from her chair and grabbed for Michael's arm. She was angered by his strong reproach yet unwilling to surrender his attention; especially to Christy. He found himself in a rather awkward position, with a lady on each arm. He was saved the embarrassment of choosing when Oliver spied a shaggy dog in the street and went scurrying off after him. Matilda called after her son angrily, but he paid no attention. She had no choice but to run off after him.

"Are you all right, Christy?" Michael asked with concern after they had at last bade Matilda and the children goodbye and were settled in their own buggy, homeward bound.

"Yes. I am fine. Just a little tired. I suppose the accident has left me weaker than I anticipated," she evaded.

"Just relax, my dear. We will be home shortly," comforted Sir Phillip, also quite perturbed by her frail condition.

Little was said on their ride home in deference to her fatigue. When they finally arrived, she immediately excused herself on the pretext of a nap. Alone at last, she slowly undressed and lay on the bed. But despite her incredible exhaustion, her mind was a frenzy of activity. What had brought Joanace to Charleston? Had he recognized her? Would he check further into who she was and how she had come to this faraway place?

Dinner that evening was exceptionally quiet. Michael and Sir Phillip made an effort at small talk, but for the most part the meal passed in silence. She tried to lighten her spirits and join in the conversation, but the cold, empty terror she felt could not be dispelled. She was close to tears and found it supremely taxing to appear calm and at ease. She only nibbled on her food, and at last gave up any pretext of an appetite. When the dishes were finally cleared, she excused herself with an apology of a headache and disappeared up to her room.

In an effort to distract her troubled thoughts, she tried to read. Yet all too often the faces of Lt. Governor Joanace, Henry Slate and Matilda leapt at her from the pages. At last, in resignation she put the book aside and blew out the candle. Perhaps sleep was the only answer to ease her troubled mind. But exhausted as she was, sleep would not come. She tossed and turned, becoming more frustrated by the hour. The darkness itself became her enemy and she prayed for the light of day.

With a groan of despair, she rose from bed and stood out on the balcony, looking out into the quiet, peaceful night. Perhaps a stroll in the evening air would soothe her. She slipped on her robe and slippers and glided silently down the stairs of the quiet house. Everyone seemed to be asleep so she felt safe in venturing out.

The clear, full moon lit the way as Christy strolled leisurely about the gardens, breathing the fresh, cool air. Stars winked playfully at her while crickets sang their shrill serenade. The burdens of the day gradually eased, and when she at last reached the flowered trellis at the rear of the house she felt far less troubled.

Hungrily she breathed in the fragrance of the beautiful red roses. Their soft, silky petals clung stubbornly to the arches and wound their way among the braces to finally droop tantalizingly down the sides of the metal frame.

She plucked a tiny red bud from the vine and sat down on the bench positioned in the center of the little enclosed area. The moon cast its full magical brightness upon the tressle. She closed her eyes and sniffed the heavenly aroma.

Transfixed by the beauty and tranquility of her surroundings, she failed to hear the approaching footsteps or see the large shadow falling across the archway. The figure hesitated and stood back to regard her in silence. The intruder was captivated by how the moonlight highlighted her long, silky black curls as they fluttered softly in the evening breeze. The soft glow penetrated her sheer robe hanging limply from her narrow shoulders to reveal the shapely curves beneath. She sat perfectly still, almost like a statue, oblivious to all but the sight, touch and scent of the perfect red rose.

Christy studied the delicate beauty of the flower she held and carefully stroked its velvety soft petals. Again she raised it to her nose and breathed in the sweet, enjoyable aroma. The hour was late, yet she was reluctant to leave this haven of peace and return to her room to once again struggle for sleep. She cupped the rose in her hand and held it in her lap. Studying it closely, she marveled at nature's perfection. Again she filled her lungs with the sweet smell. But—what was this? Another scent, less desirable, tickled her nose. She looked up with mild irritation to find out what was intruding on the delicate fragrance. A huge shadow fell across the archway.

"Who's there?" she gasped, jumping to her feet in sudden fear.

"Do not be afraid. It is only me," came a voice from the archway.

The frightening shadow immediately materialized in the person of Captain Lancer. Illuminated by the moon, she saw him leaning against the trellis, puffing slowly on a cheroot. Her heart resumed its normal beat. "You . . . you startled me, sir," she admitted, trying to inflict a slight laugh to her words.

"I am truly sorry, my dear. My intent was not to frighten you. I happened to be out strolling and saw you come this way. I found you sitting there lost in thought.

You seemed so content I hated to disturb you." His handsome face was briefly illuminated by the flaming red tip of his cigar as he took a deep puff and eyed her closely.

"I did not hear you come up. It was the smoke from your cheroot which gave you away."

"Yes, I suppose it ruined the fragrance of the roses. I am sorry," he apologized and immediately tossed the offending tobacco into the trees. "I often find myself troubled by insomnia, but I am indeed surprised to find you suffering from the same condition. Did the trip into town overtire you, perhaps?"

"Perhaps. It was a busy day, was it not? But I was feeling a little restless. I ventured out onto the balcony and couldn't help but be mesmerized by the beauty of the night. The temptation for a walk was too great to resist."

"Yes, it is a lovely evening, is it not," he agreed as he stepped forward and placed his foot upon the bench. He gazed into the heavens at the mass of twinkling diamonds and at the large, brilliant moon. But his attention did not linger overlong in what was above. His real interest was in the beautiful young woman before him. The moon bathed her in a light that gave her the appearance of a lovely Greek goddess. He longed to take her into his arms and prove to himself that she was real and not a product of his dreams. Instead, however, he curbed his desires and rested an elbow upon his knee. "What did you think of our lieutenant governor? His attitude seems rather strained and pompous. I dare say he will bear close watching."

Christy's tranquility suddenly shattered at his reference to Joanace. Color drained from her face and her hands began to tremble. To cover her shaking, she moved into the shadows.

When she volunteered no comment, Michael continued. "I suppose he must have some good points, however. He was greatly captivated by your beauty. He found it difficult to keep his eyes from you. Surely he cannot be all bad to appreciate quality when he sees it."

Christy blushed at his compliment and gripped the robe tighter about herself. She was acutely aware of his physical magnetism and thèir all too romantic setting.

"Thank you, Captain. You are too kind. But one cannot judge a person's character by how he perceives beauty."

Again Michael noted Christy's acute uneasiness when he mentioned Joanace. He and his father had discussed it at length after dinner and both agreed there must be something about the man that caused her to react so violently. His curiosity got the better of him and he prodded her gently, hoping to gain some insight into the secrets of this complex young beauty.

"I hear this Joanace is a very wealthy man. I have also heard from various sources that a large amount of his capital has been taken illegally from those brave or foolish enough to speak against slavery. Perhaps you've heard something to that affect, since you came so recently from London?"

Christy saw stars of her own. His words were like salt on an open wound. "Oh he is truly vile and the most wretched of men!" she cried without thinking.

"You know him then, after all?" he asked surprised by the intensity of her outburst.

Too late she realized the error of her heated words. Tears welled up in her eyes, and she began to tremble despite the warmth of the evening. "I am sure I don't know, Captain. It is what I heard from those who knew him, from those who suffered under his rule."

Her knees began to shake. She was losing control. She had to get away from him and his questions before he cornered her; before she inadvertently revealed more harmful information about herself. "Please excuse me, Captain. I must be getting back to the house. It is late and the evening air has become chilly of a sudden."

"Oh forgive me for standing here rambling while you are cold. Let me offer you my jacket," he said.

Despite her protests, he wrapped her in the folds of his light gray smoking jacket. Her trembling, however, only increased as his hand touched her shoulders. He gazed down into the deep emerald of her eyes. Her closeness was so sensual. It stirred his whole being.

In the glow of the moon, Christy all too clearly read the look of desire reflected in his eyes. She was filled with the nearness of him and was nearly overcome by his male magnetism. Her heart began to beat rapidly and a pink flush rose to her cheeks.

Panic at his pointed questions about the lieutenant governor seemed dim when compared to this new, threatening sensation. She could feel a fire within her being kindled as he gently stroked her head. She ached to throw herself into his strong, protecting arms and pour out the entire miserable story to him. She longed to have him soothe away her sorrows and transport her to a world where love and passion would wipe away life's ugly realities. Surely there was such a place. Her tingling senses and Michael's persuasive petting promised such paradise.

The temptation was nearly overpowering. Her mind beckoned her flee, while her senses demanded satisfaction. Her pounding head and heart felt ready to explode from the conflict.

"Christy, my love . . ." began Michael as his hand ever so lightly brushed against her breast.

"No! No!" the tortured cry burst from her soul. "No!" she cried again, though her words were not meant for him but for herself. She couldn't let herself be weak. She must not allow herself to be seduced.

Without another word, she grabbed the jacket about herself and bolted toward the house, leaving Michael to stare after her in utter astonishment.

She did not stop until she reached her room and had the door securely locked behind her. Her legs shook and her breath came in ragged gasps. How close she had come to surrendering herself to her own passions and his. The horrifying encounter with Joanace, and now her appalling weakness before Michael's magnetic sensuality shocked and sickened her. Long into the night Captain Lancer heard her muffled sobs of self-doubt and rebuke.

Fifteen

Captain Lancer would be leaving in two days on his final trip to the West Indies and Christy worked diligently bringing his accounts to order. This morning he was at the mill giving final instructions to the overseer as to the scheduling and production of the timber. If all went smoothly with the voyage he would be returning in less than a month.

Christy sat back for a moment to clear her head. She felt dizzy and slightly nauseous; a malady which of late seemed to plague her until well after the noon meal. She attributed it to the shock of seeing Joanace. Since that day, fear of discovery was always on her mind. Though Michael and Sir Phillip held strong convictions about Parliament's heavy suppression of Colonial trade, she knew them to be staunch British subjects. Should they discover she was the daughter of branded traitors they would, no doubt, want nothing more to do with her. Though the charges were false, they would send her back to again live in fear and humiliation at the hands of Henry Slate. These ponderings caused her enormous anxiety yet, try as she would, she could not strike them from her mind. If only there was someone she could share her secrets with; someone to comfort and advise her . . .

The dizziness finally passed and she again bent intently over her task. A short time later she posted the last entry and tucked the ledgers away. The day was warm and sunny, and after sitting so long at the accounts, she decided a brisk walk in the sunshine might be just the answer to lighten her frame of mind.

The sun felt warm and soothing, and she ambled toward the stables. The Lancers owned some fine animals and she enjoyed walking through the stables and petting them. The love of horses was an inborn instinct to her from the days, which now seemed so long ago, when her father owned and trained them. Though she longed to ride, she felt it too presumptuous to be entrusted with one of their prized mounts.

As she strolled toward the stables, she noticed Sir Phillip taking his usual afternoon constitutional. The elderly man insisted on daily exercise and enjoyed his walks about the grounds. She waved cheerfully and headed in his direction. She was very fond of him and today she could use some friendly companionship. She felt particularly low and did not wish to be alone.

She was about to cross the road when suddenly, from out of nowhere, came the flurry of horses' hooves. She turned in time to see a carriage barreling down on her. Without a moment to lose she threw herself to the ground and out of the path of the wheels which nearly crushed her.

Sir Phillip swore loudly and rushed to her side. "Are you all right?" he asked in concern as he helped her to her feet. Both were shaken from the near tragedy.

"Yes, Sir Phillip. I believe so. Just a little dusty," she answered, brushing the dust from her skirt.

"Damn fool woman!" he exclaimed in disgust. "She should have more sense than thundering up the drive like that. You could have been hit!" He was clearly upset with Matilda and meant to tell her so. Cane in hand, he stormed up the drive and waited as she and the children scrambled from the carriage.

"Wasn't that fun, Michele?" cried Oliver in excitement. "Did you see how fast we went? Let's do it again."

Matilda laughed breathlessly. "Oh that's enough for now. We shall race again later," she said and straightened her hat.

"What do you think you're doing, racing up the drive like a maniac? You could have killed Miss Patterson with your carelessness," reprimanded Sir Phillip sternly.

"She shouldn't have been standing in the road, Father. She should be more careful," laughed Matilda at his anger.

"Don't be cross, Grandfather. The lady is not hurt and it was great fun," said Oliver, grabbing his grandfather and demanding a healthy greeting.

Michele joined in, asking for absolution. He could not stay angry with his two grandchildren for long, but he certainly intended to have a word with Matilda about her wild conduct.

"Come on, Grandfather. We brought a new game Mama bought for us. Come play. It's great fun," the children chorused together.

"Very well. Let's see what this game is about," he said,

still cross but rapidly weakening. He gave Matilda a stern look, tucked the game under his arm, and followed the children out onto the lawn.

"I've come to see Michael. Where is he?" Matilda asked Christy with a condescending tone as she patted a final brown curl into place.

"He is at the mill making final preparations before his departure," she answered crisply as she eyed the taller woman in slight disgust. She was in no mood today to put up with Matilda's verbal abuse.

"Oh dear. How unfortunate. And I did want to see him and ask his advice about some research I am doing," she pouted and fussed with a silky glove.

Christy made no response. She knew Captain Lancer would be returning shortly, for he had a meeting with one of his merchants at 3:00. But she had no desire to relay this information to Matilda. The woman might stay and she would be forced to entertain her. She was curious, however, about what type of research Matilda was doing. Did it have something to do with herself and the lieutenant governor?

"Well I hate to leave without speaking to him. It is rather important," she continued to pout. Suddenly her face lit up. "I know. I shall have Morgan saddle a mount and ride out to meet him. It is such a beautiful day and I would enjoy the ride. Besides, I am sure he would enjoy my company on the trip home after working all day with those timber laborers."

Christy watched her stride confidently away. With no provocation whatsoever the woman had again found it necessary to belittle her. With a shrug of her shoulders, she turned and headed in the opposite direction. She wanted to stay as far away from Matilda as possible. Perhaps she could join the children and Sir Phillip in their new game. She started across the lawn. Suddenly an angry feminine voice broke the stillness of the afternoon. Against her better judgment, she headed for the stables to determine the source of the commotion.

"I told you, madam. Sybil, our gentle mare, is being shoed and cannot be ridden. Alyn is far too spirited today for a lady to handle her. She's not been ridden for some time and is highly unpredictable. You could be hurt," Morgan patiently pointed out to the ill-tempered Matilda.

"Nonsense, Morgan. I am an excellent rider. I can handle this wild one with no difficulty. Now do as I say and saddle her or I will report you to Mr. Lancer for insubordination and disrespect to your betters!" Matilda snapped indignantly.

The large man shrugged his shoulders. She had certainly put him in his place. Under protest, he hoisted the side saddle onto Alyn's back and strapped it into place. The horse pranced skittishly as Matilda slid up into the saddle with the aid of Morgan's strong arm.

"You see, Morgan. I have perfect control of this creature. A mere horse would not dare disobey me," said Matilda confidently as she eased back into the saddle.

Her words proved premature, however. The spirited animal seemed to sense the demanding temperament of her rider. As if on cue, she shook her head and whinnied angrily. Matilda cried out in surprise and pulled the reins tightly. The bit cut the horse's mouth and she reared and pranced about the corral in an effort to dislodge her rider.

"You damn nag!" screeched Matilda as she tried to retain her seat. Despite the strong grip on the reins, the horse continued to buck. Angered and embarrassed, Matilda swung her riding crop down onto the horse's rump. "I'll teach you to disobey me," she cried.

"Whoah! Whoah!" cried Morgan, fearful for the horse and rider both. Vainly he tried to grasp Alyn to still her. But frightened and hurt by Matilda's merciless whipping, she only bucked harder.

"Stop, Matilda. Stop hitting her! You only rile her more!" Christy cried, watching the scene in horror.

But Matilda's anger kept her from seeing the truth for herself. It was now a battle of wills. Her dignity was at stake and she was not about to lose to a horse. But skillful and determined as the woman was, the horse was stronger. With an angry snort, Alyn raised herself high on her hind flanks. Her front hooves pounded the air and her shrill cry pierced the air. Unable to retain her seat, Matilda slid from the saddle and landed in a crumpled, disheveled heap upon the ground. Alyn again raised herself high over the fallen woman in triumph.

Christy leaped for the horse's bridle to keep her from trampling Matilda and led her off to the side.

"My God! Are you all right, madam?" cried Morgan, jumping to Matilda's side to help her up.

But Matilda's eyes were riveted on the horse, who pranced uneasily. The sight of Christy gently stroking her mane only infuriated her more. She pushed Morgan aside and rose clumsily to her feet. She rubbed her backside vigorously, though in fact only her pride had been hurt.

"Are you hurt, Matilda?" asked Christy in concern. But Matilda was consumed by her own anger.

"That horse is a devil. She should be destroyed. No one could ride her!" she screamed. Her eyes flashed dangerously, and the look of hate and revenge flamed in her brown depths. She drew near the horse, riding crop clenched tightly in her hand. Alyn sensed danger and whinnied nervously, backing off. But Matilda closed in. "You'll not get away with making a fool of me, you damn amber devil." Viciously she struck at the horse, adding more welts to those she'd already inflicted on the beautiful brown hide.

"Mrs. Lancer. Please stop!" cried Morgan. He'd never seen such hate in anyone's eyes before.

"Shut up, you fool. This devil needs taught a lesson," she hissed. "Stay out of my way or you'll feel the sting of this whip." Again she renewed her attack.

It was all Christy could do to hold onto the frantic horse. "Stop it, Matilda. Stop this instant!"

Christy's words burned Matilda's ears. It was bad enough this young twit should see her humiliation. But to dare question her disciplinary actions! Her eyes blazed with blind venom. With one quick jerk, she raised the whip in her hand and swung it deliberately at Christy. Christy saw it coming and raised her arm to protect herself. The crop came down with stinging force on her wrist, ripping open the flesh.

The sight of blood seemed to excite Matilda into a raging frenzy. Her pulse raced with an uncontrollable desire to maim and disfigure her adversary. "You miserable little bitch!" she cried as the whip hissed through the air.

Suddenly the whip was ripped from her hand. "By God. Stop this second, Matilda! Have you gone mad?" cried Sir Phillip. "It is plain you overused this whip on the horse. But do not ever dare use it on a guest in my home!" he raved furiously.

"The girl had no right to speak to me as she did. This damn horse nearly killed me. I have every right to discipline this wretched animal. She took it upon herself to interfere. The whip slipped. It was an accident."

"Don't lie to me, Matilda. I saw you viciously attack Miss Patterson. Had I not stopped you, you would have struck her again." For a moment, he turned his attention to Christy. "Are you all right, my dear? Let me have a look at that cut," he said in concern.

"Oh, Sir Phillip. 'Tis a minor cut. There is no cause for concern." Christy assured him, despite the throbbing of her slashed wrist.

"Nonsense. Morgan, find a towel to wrap Miss Patterson's wrist," he ordered the astonished stableman. "I insist you have Bertha take a look at it at once. But first, Matilda, I demand you apologize to Miss Patterson for your inexcusable behavior."

"Apologize? You want me to apologize . . . to her? Never! Never! I told you it was an accident. If she'd kept her nose out of it, she'd not have gotten hurt."

"Matilda, I'm warning you. Apologize this instant or never again darken this house with your presence." Sir Phillip was deadly serious.

Christy was shocked at the dangerous intensity both displayed. Angry as she was with Matilda, she had no desire to be the cause of breaking up the family. "'Tis not necessary, Sir Phillip. Mrs. Lancer need not apologize. It is over and I am fine." She turned her attention to the now calmed Alyn. "It is the horse who has been hurt far more than I. 'Tis not by anger and cruelty you tame a magnificent creature such as Alyn."

Matilda's eyes were like black coals. How dare Sir Phillip threaten her. And how dare this . . . this tramp speak to her in such a belittling manner. "Oh, and I suppose you know just how to tame the beast? You've probably never even ridden a horse, much less a thoroughbred like this one. Imagine, a little nobody like you presuming to tell me how to ride." Since she could no longer inflict pain with her whip, she resorted to stinging words.

Sir Phillip's face grew red in anger. "Matilda, hold your tongue."

But Matilda was not yet finished and certainly not to be intimidated. "You worry so much about little Miss Patterson's tiny cut. What about me? I could have been killed by this horrid horse. I demand she be put away permanently."

It was now Christy's turn to be angry. The attack on herself she could tolerate. But the idea of killing the horse for the sake of Matilda's hurt pride was just too much. Her mouth flew open in shock. "Mrs. Lancer, you can't be serious. The horse has done nothing wrong. It was you who could not control her and only want her destroyed to soothe your injured pride."

Flashing emerald eyes met enraged brown eyes. Suddenly, without warning, Matilda reached up and slapped Christy hard across her face. Christy drew back and held her stinging cheek, too stunned to respond.

Sir Phillip, however, suffered from no such muteness. "Matilda. You have pressed my patience beyond control. If I were Christina, I would definitely wipe that sneer from your face. Since she is too much of a lady to stoop to physical violence, let me tell you something. So help me if you lay another hand on this girl, I will personally take you to task. If you were not the mother of my grandchildren, I would take great pleasure in throttling you."

"You mean to say that you would take this slut's side over your own daughter-in-law's? Why, she is nothing more than some so-called distant relative. No doubt she is an imposter. I cannot fathom how you can even believe her story of being kin to you. She is, no doubt, some whore from London who only wants your money and fabricated this whole story of kinship to get it," cried Matilda indignantly.

"Matilda, you have said far too much. I must ask you to leave at once," thundered Sir Phillip.

Christy could contain her anger no longer, nor would she let Sir Phillip continue to fight her battles for her. She recklessly threw caution to the wind and addressed herself to Sir Phillip. "Your daughter-in-law seems to have missed the point of our argument. We were at odds over her treatment of Alyn, not my reputation. But whatever our disagreement, I will not stand between you and your family. I have no desire to be the cause of hard feelings between you. However, Mrs. Lancer seems to be in need of a riding lesson. I will be more than happy to give her one."

Christy's blood pumped furiously. A torrent of furious rebuttals sprang to her lips. She bit them back and quickly unfastened the side saddle still on Alyn's back. It would be sheer delight to humiliate Matilda. Her actions would hurt far more than any words she could hurl at the spiteful woman. "Morgan, would you please put this saddle away. I will not be needing it," she said and swung the saddle into his arms.

"Will you be wanting one of the other saddles then, Miss?" he asked in bewilderment.

"Oh, little Miss Patterson cannot even ride on a side saddle like a proper lady," interrupted Matilda. "A poor show, riding astride on a man's saddle. I suppose no one ever taught you to ride like a lady," she sneered, mistaking Christy's actions.

Christy did not take Matilda's bait. Instead she kept about her own business. "I may not ride like a lady, Matilda, but at least I can ride. And by the way. You are mistaken about the saddle," she answered as she kicked off her boots. "I need no saddle at all!" With expert sureness, she gripped the horse's mane and swung up onto her back.

"This is madness! You'll be killed!" cried Sir Phillip.

"Good. It would serve you right to break your neck," Matilda cried joyfully as Christy strove to control the spirited animal.

Alyn reared once, and then again, but Christy held on tightly. "Easy, girl, easy," she soothed. Alyn suddenly calmed down and stood quietly, awaiting her rider's wishes. "I regret to inform you, Mrs. Lancer, that I have no intentions of breaking my neck. Unlike you, I know the secret to calming the beast. I may not use all your fancy equipment and airs, but I can ride as you never could."

Sir Phillip was still trying to recover from her sudden, unorthodox actions. "But, Christina. I beg you to get down. It is too dangerous. Alyn has been abused and is greatly riled. You'll have no control without a saddle."

"Do not fear, my lord. I know what I am doing. 'Tis not the acceptable method but 'tis the only way to ride! Have no fear. We ride as one!" Without another word, she secured the reins in her hands and nudged Alyn's sides firmly. The horse took her cue and, in a single bound, leapt the corral fence and was gone, leaving Sir Phillip, Morgan and Matilda in a cloud of dust.

Out in the open and away from the house, Christy let Alyn take the lead. Together they galloped across the gently rolling green valley. Alyn's strong, lightning-quick legs easily cleared a gurgling little brook, flying so quickly the ground beneath was a blur of green. They rode as one wild, free creature, oblivious of the cares and worries they left behind.

A lazy brook barred their path, cutting the valley. But Alyn never slowed her gait. Strength surged through her and she cleared the obstacle with winning sureness. Christy leaned low on the horse's back and landed with the skill and ease she had learned from childhood. No barrier could defeat them. She felt no fear. She had complete confidence in Alyn, and in herself.

Gradually Alyn began to slow, tiring from the strenuous run. Christy stroked her neck and eased her to a slower gait. Both relaxed, pleasantly tired after the ride.

But Christy's contentment was not to last for long. Thundering hooves seemed to shake the earth. She pivoted to discern the cause of the disruption. The captain, astride his magnificent black stallion, bore down on her, rapidly narrowing the distance between them. He wore a dark shirt and trousers, and his tousled brown hair fluttered in the wind. Only the deep, scowling countenance detracted from his strikingly handsome visage. She guessed by the look of determination on his face that she was in for trouble. But whatever the consequences, the run had been worth it.

His words exploded as he reined in sharply beside her. "What the hell do you think you're doing, riding off like a wild woman? You could have been killed!"

Christy smiled coyly into his angry brown eyes. "But I wasn't killed, was I, Captain?" she said sweetly. She shook the hair from her face and slipped to the ground.

Her ploy worked, for he was taken by surprise at her genteel manner. He stared down at her in silence for a moment, and then dismounted himself. The sparkling emerald eyes which regarded him were filled with mischief. Black curls, tangled and in wild disarray, framed her flushed, glowing face. Her round, full breasts rose and fell easily beneath her slightly dusty and wrinkled dress. The picture was completed by tiny toes wiggling in the soft meadow grass. She looked for all the world like some wild young nymph of the meadow.

"Whatever possessed you to do such a thing? I was coming back from the mill when I saw you ride out. I could hardly believe my eyes. Father was frantic with worry and had no time to tell me what happened. He sent me off after you. We were both sure you would kill yourself."

"Well, as you can see I am quite safe and unharmed. Your fears were unfounded, my lord."

Again he felt at a disadvantage. How could he rant on while she replied with such quiet, unruffled calm?

"Will you be so good as to enlighten me on what happened?"

"Oh, nothing really serious happened, sir. It was entirely my fault. I overreacted and behaved childishly. You deserve to be angry with me."

"Come now, Christina. I am sure something drastic must have taken place to provoke you into riding off in such a state. Was it something to do with Matilda?"

The naughty twinkle left her eyes and she grew serious. "Well, Captain, Mrs. Lancer came to see you. When she learned you were at the mill, she decided to ride out to meet you. Morgan told her the only horse available was Alyn, and warned her the horse was rather spirited. But she would not listen to his advice and tried to ride her anyway. When Alyn resisted rather strenuously, Mrs. Lancer tried to calm her with her riding crop."

She paused, trying to read his thoughts, but his face remained expressionless. Taking his silence as a sign of his disapproval, she rushed on. "I could not bear to see her whip the horse. It is cruel and unreasonable. I suppose I spoke rather harshly to her in an effort to stay her beatings. She did not take kindly to my interference. When she insisted Alyn be destroyed because she was possessed of some evil devil, my anger got the better of me. I wanted to show her Alyn needed a firm yet gentle hand to calm her, not whipping. I guess I also wanted to prove to her I could ride Alyn, since she could not." She grew shamefaced at her confession. "I suppose I overdid it."

"Yes, perhaps slightly," he agreed. "But you no doubt did prove your point to her. And to all of us."

Christy looked up to see if he was joking or still cross. Still nervous and unsure of him, she self-consciously brushed back a stray black curl, revealing her bleeding cut.

"It seems Alyn was not the only one to suffer from Matilda's whip."

"'Tis nothing really, Captain. I almost forgot about it," she said, regarding the cut herself.

"Here, let me see that," he said and reached into his pocket to retrieve a fresh linen handkerchief.

"Oh, don't! The blood will stain and ruin it for sure," shrieked Christy, pulling from his grasp.

"Don't be silly. The handkerchief is certainly expendable and I cannot bear to see you bleeding," he grumbled crossly, yet his hands were gentle as he wrapped the cloth about her wrist.

To Christy's thinking he lingered overmuch on the task. The cut was not major enough to warrant such pampering. But she endured his doctoring patiently; touched by his obvious concern.

At last satisfied with his bandaging, he begrudgingly released her hand and broke the silence, putting his thoughts into words. "My dear, you are completely unlike any woman I have ever known, in so many respects. Why, I have never seen a female ride as you do. Wherever did you learn such horsemanship?"

"As I told you once before, my father bred and raced horses," she said, looking away. The intensity of his gaze was slightly unsettling. "Much to my mother's distress, I took an active part in the training and grooming. I spent more time with horses than on the necessary domestic and feminine arts."

"Well, with your sometimes manly attire and your rather unorthodox riding techniques, perhaps her fears were justified," he teased.

Christy swung to face him, hands on her hips and bristling angrily at his statement. "Well let me tell you something, Captain. When the circumstances warrant, I have all the necessary arts and graces to play the coy and helpless damsel." She fluttered her long black eyelashes demurely at him and curtsied low, transformed into the meekest and gentlest of ladies. But when she straightened to once again face him, the fire was back in her eyes. "But, sir, I can also be strong and forceful when the need arises. No one—I say no one—abuses an animal in front of me without feeling the heat of my anger. Alyn is far too magnificent to be cruelly forced to submit to anyone's ill temper. If I did wrong I am willing to pay the consequences. But I would do it again to stop Alyn from being beaten or hurt, or destroyed." She stared boldly at him, openly daring him to dispute her reasoning.

Instead he smiled at her anger. How could he possibly be cross when she looked so beguiling, so defiant, so enticing? Besides, she was absolutely correct. "I do not deny you had just cause for your action. Matilda was definitely out of line. But the next time you go tearing off, please warn me first. You nearly whisked away five years of my life as I watched you fly by."

Christy smiled at his gentle reprimand. "I will not do it again, sir. I promise. I deeply regret causing you to worry. As your humble servant, I only wish to please."

"Is that a fact, my lady," he whispered.

Her eyes flew to his face as strong arms lightly encircled her waist. She had intended her words to be lightly teasing. But the look she saw in his eyes told her he had taken them all too literally. Before she had time to clarify her remark, he pulled her closer and placed his warm, eager lips upon hers.

The heat of his kiss increased, and a new, exciting sensation swept through her body. Her traitorous lips began to respond and she felt herself returning his passionate embrace. At Alyn's insistent nuzzle, Christy quickly pulled away, blushing hotly at her own response. How could her body betray her thus?

"We'd best be getting back, Captain. You will be late for your meeting," she said to cover her embarrassment.

"Yes, of course. My meeting," he mumbled and moved to help her mount.

"No thank you, sir. I can manage fine."

"As you wish," he said, but stood back until she was mounted. Without a word he swung into his saddle and they headed toward Penncrest.

The silence grew heavy between them. Michael turned to regard his companion, and was again bewitched by the sight of her. She sat straight-backed yet relaxed atop

Alyn. Her hair fluttered gently about her face and shoulders. She radiated some inner glow he had never noticed before. She seemed intoxicated with gladness, seated confidently upon her horse, perfectly at home. If only she could be as secure about her own physical attractions and emotions. But perhaps her guard was slipping. It was not his imagination that he felt her response to his kisses. Mayhap there was yet a thread of hope to win her.

"I must apologize for my sudden amorous behavior a moment ago. But I do have some justification for my actions. I was acting partially for scientific reasons. You see, with your rather unorthodox style of riding, your penchant for danger, and your previously masculine wardrobe, I had to reassure myself you were not a tomboy as your mother feared."

"Is that so, my lord? And did I pass the test?" she asked boldly.

He looked directly into her challenging eyes. "You certainly did, my dear. You certainly did."

Christy blushed hotly. She felt the heat of his blunt appraisal as if he had reached out and touched her. To hide her red cheeks, she urged Alyn into a spirited gallop, leaving Michael trailing behind. He laughed softly at her face-saving tactics and picked up the pace to catch up.

Sixteen

The day was warm, bright and sunny, and Christy hurried to finish her work on Michael's accounts. He would probably be home in a week or so and she wanted everything to be in perfect order. Due to her diligent efforts, his records were once again up to date and as they should be. She enjoyed the work. It gave her a sense of purpose and a feeling of reward and fulfillment. It also brought a closeness to him she found both puzzling and exciting. She had missed his presence these past few weeks and found herself looking forward to his return.

With a satisfied sigh, she tallied the last column and quickly locked away the many papers and ledgers. The desk once again in its tidy state, she rose and smoothed her new dress just delivered from the dressmaker. Apparently life here was agreeing with her all too well, for she had gained a few pounds. The new dress was slightly snug in the waistline. Well, a little exercise would correct that problem. And she knew just the type of exercise she needed. It was far too lovely to remain indoors. The late, hazy summer sun beckoned her.

Her mind made up, she headed for the stairs. Alyn needed a run and so did she. Since her rather unsettling episode with Matilda, both Michael and Sir Phillip insisted she ride as often as she wished. She had politely thanked them for their generosity, but it was a treat she allowed herself only seldom. She still had qualms about taking advantage of their kindness.

With an excited step, Christy whisked from the room and headed for the stairs to change into her trousers for the ride. With both Michael and Sir Phillip gone, she had little fear of their disdainful frowns at her masculine attire. Both offered to buy her a riding skirt, but she declined. She rode too seldom to justify such a purchase. As a result, she only rode when both men were gone, and she had only Bertha's scornful lecture about the appropriateness of feminine dressing to contend with. But today not even the housekeeper's displeasure could daunt her happy mood. For some reason she felt gloriously happy. Her spirits were high and she had an insane desire to skip down the hall and up to her room.

Eager to be changed and on her way, she paused in slight irritation at the sound of carriage wheels grinding on the gravel. Curious as to the identity of the visitor, she stepped to the window and groaned aloud as she recognized Matilda's carriage stopping in front of the house.

"Oh fie!" she said aloud. She was seized by a strong desire to rush to her room and hide until the woman had gone. It was far too beautiful a day and she was in too happy a mood to have it ruined by Matilda Lancer's biting tongue. Besides, after their last unpleasant encounter over her treatment of Alyn, she knew Matilda would be out for revenge. Before she had time to flee, however, the door burst open and in rushed Matilda's two children, Michele and Oliver.

"Grandpa! Grandpa! Where are you?" they demanded eagerly and scrambled through the hallway to look for him.

Christy sighed. Escape was now impossible. Chin up, she turned to face Matilda who entered in almost as much of a hustle as her children. "Good day, Mrs. Lancer," she began, making an effort to start out on the right foot.

Matilda glared in her direction but made no effort to return the pleasantry. Instead she fixed on Christy a dark and penetrating stare which said she had neither forgotten nor forgiven the girl for embarrassing her before Sir Phillip and Morgan. Though it had been nearly a month ago, the memory was still a vivid one. "Where is Sir Phillip?" she demanded stiffly.

Before Christy could answer, the disappointed youngsters returned. "We can't find Grandfather anywhere," they pouted, looking completely downtrodden.

"Sir Phillip left quite early this morning on a trip into Charleston. He did not expect to return until late this evening," volunteered Christy.

"Oh dear. How unfortunate. The maid who usually watches the children has the day off. I had counted on them staying with Father while I went into town. They are such a nuisance when I'm shopping. It is quite impossible to select anything while they carry on and prance about. Oh dear, now what shall I do?" she fretted and looked at her two children in open disgust.

Christy turned her attention to the two little children. She had to admit that they were beautiful youngsters.

Though they had inherited the silky blond and curly hair of their mother, the large, round and curious eyes were a mysterious grayish green. Michele, quite petite even for six, had pleasantly chubby cheeks which dimpled charmingly when she smiled. In her lacy pink dress, she looked much like her mother. But the child's features were soft in contrast to Matilda's cold and chiseled ones.

Oliver was slender and had a determined set to his jaw. He was tall for his eight years and would no doubt someday reach Michael's height. With some surprise, she realized he already looked remarkably like Michael. Only the blond hair, instead of Michael's dark brown, took away from the comparison.

Christy felt a twinge of compassion for the two children. It must be difficult to have no father and a mother like Matilda. It was quite obvious they were fully aware of their mother's feeling that they were a bother. No doubt they did not relish the thought of accompanying her on another shopping spree either. The disappointment was clearly visible on their handsome, youthful faces.

"I would be happy to watch Oliver and Michele while you shop, Mrs. Lancer. I am sure they would not mind missing this trip into town," volunteered Christy.

Matilda wrinkled her brow, ready to make a sharp retort, and then suddenly changed her mind. "Well, why not indeed? I usually don't leave them with strangers or unreferred servants, but perhaps this time I will make an exception. I do want to order my gown for the Thanksgiving Ball. I know just what I want but it will take some time to explain my specifications to Kramer. The children are such a nuisance tagging along. Yes, I think I will let you watch them. I am sure you have nothing else to do."

Christy immediately regretted her generosity. Matilda had deliberately insulted her again! Her face grew flushed with anger. But before she could withdraw her offer, Matilda had turned away to speak with her children.

"Now you two be good while I am gone. I will be back as soon as I am finished."

"Mama, we don't want to stay. We want to go with you," insisted Michele, clinging to her skirt in apprehension. She was worried about being left alone with this stranger. She and her brother had heard their mother speak quite unpleasantly about her after their last visit. They imagined her to be some sort of witch. That wasn't quite the word their mother used, but it sounded close.

"Oh nonsense. I don't want you along. You'll stay here with her and that's all there is to it. Now I must be off. Run along now and play," she said and pushed them aside. "See you later, darlings," she called over her shoulder and was gone before anyone could protest further.

With their mother gone, the two young children fixed suspicious eyes upon Christy. Quietly they assessed her, trying to decide just how to handle the situation. Since their mother was away frequently, or alone entertaining various rich suitors, they had often been left to devise their own amusements. Somewhat spoiled, they had learned to act nearly as well as their mother. They could change from charming little darlings into nasty little devils with little provocation. Silently they debated what tactic would work best on this stranger who now lived with their grandfather and uncle.

Christy nearly laughed at the sudden aloof manners they adopted as they relaxed and continued to stare at her. Their mother had taught them well it seemed. "Well, what would you two like to do today? Your mother will probably be gone for some time, so we should have the whole afternoon." Her cheerful inquiry was met by silent stares. "It's a lovely, warm day, isn't it? I had planned on going outdoors for a little walk. Would you care to join me?" she tried again. Again she received no response. They continued to regard her in nonchalant indifference. "Well, if you don't want to take a walk, we could draw, or paint, or whatever you like." Their stony silence continued.

"I see . . . the silent treatment," she said just loud enough for them to hear. Their eyes widened slightly that she had guessed their game so quickly, but they held their tongues.

"Well, let me see. You don't walk. You won't talk. You don't draw or paint. You don't laugh. You don't cry. You don't do much of anything. You certainly are unusual children. Is there anything you do do?"

Michele squirmed under her gentle attack and promptly received a sound rap from her brother.

"Well, it's nearly 11:30. Have you two eaten lunch yet?" Again there was no response, but Christy noticed Michele weaken slightly at the mention of food.

Undaunted by the mute pair, she stroked her chin thoughtfully and glanced toward the kitchen. "Well, all this warm sunshine makes me hungry. Since you two apparently are not interested in anything and would prefer to stand there in silence, I suppose I shall just have to picnic alone. It's too bad, really. Picnics are such fun and I'm sure you would enjoy it," she said and turned to walk away.

"A picnic? What's a picnic?" came a little voice so soft, it was barely audible.

Christy turned in time to see Oliver bestow a warning glare upon his sister for weakening. She had broken their pact and spoken to the stranger. "You mean you've never been on a picnic? You've never packed up a basket full of goodies and lunched out in the sunshine? I can hardly believe it! Why, when I was a little girl, my mother and father and I would go on many picnics out in the countryside. We always had such fun!"

Michele shook her head slowly, her bottom lip protruding slightly as if comprehending the great loss she had suffered. Even Oliver was intrigued by the idea. He forgot the silent routine and ventured to speak. "Mother doesn't like the outdoors much. She says it dirty, with too many insects and horrid animals. She says eating outdoors is for animals."

Not wanting to say anything in front of the children about their mother, Christy bit her lip and chose her words carefully. "Well, perhaps she never had the opportunity to go picnicking to see for herself how much fun it is. Do you two feel adventurous enough to give it a try?" she asked.

There was no denying the new look of enthusiasm gleaming from those gray-green eyes. "Oh yes. Let's do go. I think it would be fun and something new and exciting," said Michele, clapping her hands happily. Her joyful smile revealed two gaping dark holes where new white teeth would hopefully soon appear.

"What about you, Oliver? Would you like to come along?"

"Yes. It does sound like fun. And we needn't tell Mother," he agreed.

"Good. It's settled then. I'll have Bertha pack us a picnic lunch and we'll be off in no time. And I know just the spot. I think you're going to enjoy it. It is too bad you didn't bring some play clothes," she said, eyeing their expensive outfits. "You'd be more comfortable if you didn't have to worry about getting dirty."

"Oh, we're not allowed to get our clothes dirty. Mother gets upset. But we'll be careful. We promise," chorused the children.

Again Christy pitied them and the rigid upbringing they were forced to endure. "Now, while I gather the things we need, suppose you two round up some games for us. We'll definitely need a ball. Is there one in the house? It wouldn't be a picnic without a ball." Without further prodding, the children scampered off in eager anticipation.

Christy smiled after them, feeling all at once young and carefree again. It seemed her own happy childhood had been a lifetime ago. So much had happened that had forced her to grow up all too soon. Life had suddenly become cold and cruel, and she had deliberately tried to forget her happy childhood. It brought too much pain remembering. But now, seeing these children, memories of the happy times she had shared with her family came flooding back.

With enthusiasm to match that of her charges, she headed for the kitchen. After much ado, a large picnic basket was resurrected and soon filled with left-over chicken, biscuits hot from the oven, and a tall container of lemonade. Gretchen, the cook, even snuck in three small cherry pies and a tin of cookies for the three picnickers.

As Bertha supervised the proceedings, she mumbled under her breath about the folly of eating outdoors like a bunch of cannibals. But despite her stern exterior, she thought back to the many family picnics she had gone on with the Lancers when the children were still small. They had been close, happy times before the youngsters had grown up and gone off on their own separate ways.

Final touches complete to the sumptuous feast, the three set off, each with an armful of fun for the picnic. Christy carried the large basket filled with enough food to feed a small army. Oliver carried the blankets and Michele brought up the rear tossing a bright red ball high into the air.

Their half-mile hike eventually brought them to a small pond. The cool, clean water was fed by a winding, gurgling little brook which seemed to appear from deep within the earth. Its leisurely course flowed infinitely across the lush green valley and was surrounded by wild, lacy white flowers and tall, thin green reeds which reached proudly to the sky.

Christy had found the spot on one of her numerous walks and could seldom return home without first visiting the meadow; it was so serene and peaceful.

She spread the blanket beneath the shade of a huge maple tree that stood tall and proud beside the gurgling, babbling brook. Birds flitted back and forth, and an occasional squirrel peered curiously at the three happy intruders.

Christy unpacked the lunch and they ate with great enthusiasm. She was amazed at how friendly and likable the children were after their rather difficult beginning. They responded readily to the smallest amount of attention, and laughed freely and easily. Again she felt their sorrow at being fatherless, and for all practical purposes, motherless. They took to each other immediately, and the meal passed quickly and pleasantly. When the basket was empty, she auctioned off the last cookie, and they sat happily, relaxing and letting their food digest.

A fluttering, multicolored butterfly landed gracefully on a nearby flower and the children marveled at its beautiful coat. A busy hummingbird whisked by in his search for sweet nectar from the many wild flowers around the pond. A furry little rabbit sprinted across the grass and skidded to a stop. He raised himself on his hind legs to regard the trio with mixed anxiety and curiosity. His soft nose twitched continuously and his large pink ears caught the softest of sounds. Oliver moved closer to get a better look, but the little warm ball of fur sprinted off again and disappeared into the tall grass.

"All right, everyone. Who wants to play ball?" asked Christy enthusiastically a short time later. She jumped up and shook out her rumpled skirt.

"Oh me! Me!" both cried happily and Oliver ran to

fetch the ball.

They moved to level ground by the little brook and took turns tossing the ball back and forth, devising new and more challenging games. The sun beat down warm and bright as the afternoon wore on, but no one seemed to notice. They were all caught up in the sunshine, grass and pure, carefree fun. Time ticked away without notice toward evening.

"Throw the ball here!" yelled Oliver to his sister, and then went scrambling after it as she threw it off to his right. "I wish you'd learn how to throw," he grumbled goodnaturedly. "You throw like a girl. I'll show you how a man does it. Now watch," he instructed as he wound up for a thunderous pitch. "Here, catch, Miss Christy," he yelled and tossed the ball with all his might. Christy ran quickly after the flying rubber ball. Up over her head it flew. With a loud splash it landed in the middle of the little pond.

"Oh no! See what you've done. What shall we do?" cried Michele in dismay. They stood at the edge of the brook regarding the floating toy as if it were lost forever.

"Fetch me that long branch lying over there by the tree, Oliver. Perhaps I can fish it out," said Christy. Amid the children's encouraging squeals, she extended the limb over the water toward the bright red ball. Awkwardly she tried to nudge the ball toward the bank. But, each time it drifted within reach, a current would carry it back into the middle of the brook. Before long, the brittle branch became saturated and broke off, sinking into the water.

"Oh, no. What can we do now?" moaned Michele. A

little tear trickled down her cheek. "We were having such fun. We'll never get it back."

Christy could not let their happy day end in disappointment. "Don't worry, honey. I'll get the ball back. But no more tears," she said and wiped away the salty droplet.

"But how will you fetch it?"

"Just you watch now," Christy said mysteriously. She sat down on the ground and began to unfasten her shoes.

"You're not going in after it, are you?" asked Oliver in disbelief.

"Why of course I am. I know of no other way, do you?" she asked, tugging off her stockings.

"But . . . but you'll get all wet!"

"Not if I'm careful, I won't. Don't you worry now. Besides, the water looks so nice."

Oliver thought it over quickly and decided it was a great idea, though he was sure his mother would never approve. "Oh let me go. I'll go. Let me do it!" Flushed with excitement, he sat down to remove his footwear.

"Oliver, I don't know how deep the water is. Can you swim?"

Oliver shook his head dejectedly. "Well then, better let me go," said Christy. She hiked up her skirt to her knees and gingerly dipped one toe into the water to test the temperature. "It's not too cold," she called over her shoulder to the two children watching breathlessly.

Into the water she stepped and slowly made her way toward the ball. "Now don't you two say a word about this," she cautioned them. "If anyone knew I'd gone wading in a pond I'd never hear the end of it." She could just see the look on Matilda's face if she had been here to witness her actions.

"We won't tell. We promise," clapped Oliver and Michele in delight. "It'll be our secret. Just the three of us." It was obvious they were thrilled to share such a secret pact.

The water deepened to her knees, and she held her skirts high up in an attempt to keep them dry. The water was cool, and the bed of the stream was thick with soft, silky mud. She squished her toes in delight and giggled happily as she reached for the ball with one hand, trying to secure her skirts with the other.

Wild giggling came from behind. "Now, don't laugh at me, you two. This is not as easy as it looks," she confessed. Carefully she drew the ball to her and rolled it slowly up her leg until she had a firm grip. "There! Got it!" she cried in triumph.

Suddenly a shower of cold water cascaded down her face and arms. The ball slipped from her grasp as she caught her breath in surprise. Her skirts dipped into the water. Peels of laughter rippled from the edge of the pond, and she pivoted to regard two little demons standing ankle deep in the stream, splashing merrily at her.

"Oh, you little imps. Now I've dropped the ball!" she cried out. They both stopped laughing and looked fearfully at their dripping playmate. She stared back at them, trying to appear upset, but a smile suddenly crept into the corners of her mouth. "Three can play at this game!" she suddenly cried and scooped a handful of water at them.

They squealed in delight as they realized she had only been pretending to be cross with them. Instantly the little brook was a mass of sparkling, splashing water and laughing children as each attempted to soak the others while ducking to avoid being hit with a stream of water. The water felt good, though luckily none of the three had good aim and they usually missed their intended victim.

An angry shriek suddenly penetrated through their laughter. Three sets of eyes turned toward the top of the hill. With a pounding heart, Christy recognized the enraged face of Matilda Lancer. "Oh no," she groaned as the meadow grew deathly quiet. But Christy's glance was pulled past Matilda to another figure approaching from the distance. "Oh, heaven above!" she sucked in her breath. The tall, lean figure was none other than Captain Michael Lancer, home early from his voyage to Boston.

She promptly panicked. With more speed than caution, she lunged for the ball. Her only thought was to reach shore before either he or Matilda. But alas, the slippery silt-covered bottom suddenly turned traitor. In her haste, her feet slid out from under her and she slipped unceremoniously into the cold water. Coughing and splashing, she attempted to rise, but her now heavily water-soaked skirt threw her off balance. Again she slipped into the water. All hope of salvaging even a thread of dignity gone, she finally managed to struggle to her feet and stood motionless and shame-faced in the middle of the pond, ball clutched tightly in her hand and dripping from head to toe.

Matilda's look was thunderous. "My God! What in the world are you doing? Get out of that water this instant," she cried to her children. "This instant!"

A greatly sobered Michele and Oliver stepped uneasily from the water to stand before their enraged mother. Matilda's reprimands rent the stillness of the meadow. She looked first at the children and then to Michael. Finally her gaze fell on Christy, who still stood in the stream, ball in hand and unable to move.

"I let you alone with my children for a few hours and look what happens! You're carrying on like any common peasants; eating on the bare ground and splashing around in this filthy water like beggars. You should be severely punished for this, you little tramp. Just look at the children's clothing. I'll expect you to pay for this. What kind of a woman are you? Why, if they come down with colds and fever, I'll let you sit with them all night," she snarled at Christy.

"We won't get sick, Mama. We were having such a good time. Please don't be cross," spoke up Oliver bravely in the face of her tirade.

"Having a good time, were you? Oh, how could you?" she turned to vent her wrath upon her children. "I taught you to behave as fine, aristocratic young adults. Now the minute my back is turned, you're both behaving like rabble. I'm shamed to tears. Perhaps she knows no better, but you do. Oh, you disgust me. Now march up that hill before I really lose my temper and paddle you right here."

"We're sorry, Mama. We meant no harm." The children quickly retrieved their footwear.

"Don't be cross with the children, Mrs. Lancer. The fault is entirely mine," Christy tried to intercede on their behalf.

"I have nothing more to say to trash like you," hissed Matilda and spun on her heel.

Christy stood in the water watching Matilda and the children scamper away. The day had been so nice. Why had it ended like this? She could handle Matilda's fury, but the children had no defense and would suffer the worst of her tantrums. It was cruel and unfair.

As Matilda's angry shouting died away, she suddenly felt eyes upon her. With acute embarrassment she forced herself to look at the captain. If she could have sunk into the depths of the brook and disappeared forever, she would have done it gladly at this moment. "Welcome home, Captain," she muttered weakly, feeling totally foolish.

She took a deep breath and sloshed her way to the shore. Knees trembling slightly, she tripped on a stone and went sprawling again into the cold water, splashing Michael in the process. With a mumbled curse, she rose and accepted his outstretched hand as she stumbled to the grass. Once on solid ground, Michael dropped her hand and stood back to regard her. The red ball still held tightly in her hands, like a thief caught in the act, she stood dripping before her master.

"You are quite a sight to welcome me home," he mocked, trying to appear stern and suppress the laughter which caught in his throat.

Embarrassed beyond relief, she lowered her eyes to avoid his intense gaze. "I am sorry, sir. I had no idea you were coming home today. Mrs. Lancer asked me to watch the children. They have never been on a picnic and I thought they would enjoy it," she said, indicating the neat little pile of picnic paraphernalia. "We were having such a wonderful time, and were tossing the ball when it fell into the water. I tried to get it out with a stick, but had no luck. So I went in after it. One thing led to another, and I suppose we got carried away, Captain. I am truly sorry." She contemplated her bare toes. "You have every right to be angry with me."

Michael followed her gaze downward. Her wiggling toes and petulant frown were just more than he could bear. He reached for the ball, the instigator of the mess, and took it from her hands. A low, rich laugh started in his chest, and slowly rose to his throat. Tears formed in his eyes as laughter shook his entire body.

Christy looked up at him with fearful eyes, and then became angry. He was laughing at her, and that rankled her deeply. She stepped back, turning from a defendant to prosecutor and was about to bombard him with a cutting remark. But the sodden swish of her skirts wrapped around her legs sent a new stream of water trickling to the ground. She looked down at her wringing wet dress and burst into laughter at herself. "I really do look a sight, don't I?" she conceded.

"Yes, I'm afraid you do. Why, in all my years at sea I never got that wet. It seems you've once again gotten yourself into a real predicament. How do you do it? Matilda's concern at leaving the children in your care may not have been entirely unfounded."

The gaiety suddenly went out of her eyes. "I am really sorry for the children's sake. It is unfortunate about their clothing. I just pray Mrs. Lancer is not too harsh with them. It was really my fault. We were having such fun. They are such delightful youngsters."

"You needn't worry about Matilda. She'll cool off soon enough, and the children will survive. They are used to her tirades by now," he soothed. "I think, however, I had best get you home and out of those wet clothes before you catch cold. I certainly don't intend sitting up with you all night should you catch a cold or fever," he said, imitating Matilda's threat.

"No, I am sure you would not." She laughed merrily and went to retrieve her shoes. With the sun dipping slowly behind the horizon, the day was growing cool and a breeze was beginning to put a chill in the air. She would definitely be glad to get home and into something warm and dry.

Captain Lancer picked up the picnic basket and stood regarding Christy as she attempted to wring out the water from her skirt. The sight of her made his pulse race. Her black hair hung limply about her face and shoulders, and little glistening water droplets clung to her neck and chest. The water-soaked bodice clung tightly to her full, round breasts, revealing taut, tantalizing peaks.

Though Christy shivered from the cold gown clinging to her shapely frame, Michael grew hot from the sight. With great control, he dropped the blanket over her shoulders and clutched the empty basket; glad for something to keep his hand occupied and away from the tempting form beside him.

"Did you have a pleasant voyage, Captain?" she finally asked to break the silence.

"Yes. It was rather uneventful, but we got a good cargo

and a good price for it. I already have numerous offers from various seamen and organizations to buy *The Merrimer*. It should be no problem selling her."

With an abruptness he had wished to hide, he changed the subject. "Has everything been quiet here?"

"Oh yes. I've been working daily on your accounts. They are all posted and in order. Perhaps you would care to look them over when we return?"

He nodded absently, and they walked along in silence for a short while. Suddenly a cry escaped Christy's lips and she reached down to rub her foot.

"What is it?"

"I've stepped on something and cut my foot," she said, trying to examine her toes.

"Sit down and let me take a look at it," he said, putting down the basket and helping her to a rock. Taking her foot into his hands, he examined it closely. "Yes. I see a jagger. I'll see if I can remove it." With extreme care, he pulled the large, ugly thorn from her foot. Her face went white but she uttered no sound. He pulled his handkerchief from his shirt and wrapped her foot tightly to stop the bleeding.

"It seems my blood is forever staining your fine linens. Your large supply will dwindle to nothing should I not exercise more care," she said, trying to cover her embarrassment at having him tend her so earnestly and carefully.

"I think you should stay off that foot until the bleeding stops," he said, ignoring her statement.

"Oh, it's such a small cut. I'm sure it will be fine," she reassured him and stood to prove her point.

"Nonsense. I don't want you putting any weight on it. I'd go for my horse, but I fear there is a storm brewing," he said, indicating the dark, quickly moving storm clouds which seemed to have appeared from nowhere. "I shall have to carry you."

"Oh, Captain. It's only a small cut, really, and you'll get soaked to the skin holding me. Besides, I am far too heavy for you to carry such a long way."

"Too heavy? You're as light as a feather. Why, I've carried sacks of potatoes heavier than you," he declared with a twinkle in his brown eyes.

"Sir, are you comparing me to a sack of potatoes?" she asked, trying to appear indignant, and failing miserably as her emerald eyes danced merrily.

"Here now. If you won't let me carry you, at least lean on me for support."

"Really, Captain. My foot is no doubt healed by this time. I am certainly capable of walking. I'm made of hard stuff, you forget," she said and bounded ahead to prove her point.

A crackle of thunder and a bolt of lightning streaking across the sky made Christy jump. Just as suddenly, and without warning, the sky opened and a torrent of rain came down upon them.

Michael grabbed her hand and together they ran toward the protective cover of a mammoth maple tree. He pressed her back against the huge trunk and shielded her small frame with his body.

Christy shivered from the chill in the cool, wet air, but the look Michael bestowed upon her soon brought a blush to her cheeks. How lovely and enticing she looked, standing wet and vulnerable, and so close beside him as they huddled together in the small area. The air became tense as both were acutely aware of their closeness.

A crack of thunder made her clutch his arm in sudden fear. Despite their many arguments of the past, she had missed him terribly while he had been gone—even more than she cared to admit to herself. Her heart pounded in her chest and she felt an overpowering need to touch him, to feel his strong, protective arms about her.

"I remember well your fear of the storm we had at sea, and the anxiety you caused me when you were nearly swallowed in the raging tempest," he said. His arms closed about her, sensing her need for protection, and at the same time answering his own desire to hold her close. He caressed her cheek and ran his fingers along the side of her face as he held her green eyes captive with his of brown. Another clap of thunder filled the air, and she buried her face into his massive chest, clinging to him in fear. "Don't be afraid, little one. It will not hurt you," he whispered into her ear.

The blanket slipped from her shoulders as she nestled close against him. The heat from his body warmed her. A thrilling tingle spread through her being as he gently stroked her hair.

The captain too felt the spark between them and needed little encouragement. He raised her face and kissed her eyes, her nose, her chin, and finally again tasted the honey sweetness of her slightly parted lips.

"What a marvelous welcome-home present," he whispered into her ear. "Did you miss me while I was gone, my little stowaway?"

She looked at him, her eyes wide and shyly expectant. "Yes. Yes, I missed you very much," she answered.

"Lordy, Master Michael, it's nearly stopped rainin'. You'd best git yerself and Miss Christy in here right away 'fore you both catch yer death," came Bertha's forceful reprimand from the window of the kitchen.

Michael's sigh echoed Christy's, and he grinned down at her, stroking her chin. "Coming, Bertha!" he called over his shoulder. "I guess Bertha is right, love. It seems to have stopped raining. Run into the house and get into something warm and dry while I put this basket away. I'll join you in the study shortly. I think we could both use some hot tea. . . ."

Christy bestowed upon him a breathtaking smile and sprinted for the house. She felt strangely happy and content—a feeling that had been missing in the month he had been away. She was glad to have him home again.

Seventeen

Christy opened the door of the quiet office and stepped outside into the crowded Charleston street. The sudden brilliant sunlight stung her red, puffy eyes, temporarily blinding her from the thriving life about her.

"Watch where you're going, dearie!" came a harsh rebuke as she stumbled against an elderly, parcel-laden woman.

"Excuse me," Christy muttered, clutching a nearby post until her vision cleared. She gazed out into the busy street, but hardly saw the people scurrying about trying to finish their errands and find a cool haven from the oppressive heat. The noon stage thundered by and screeched to a halt in front of the Bay City Hotel, but she was scarcely aware of its existence. Her thoughts were still locked on the events in the quiet little office from which she had just stumbled.

She picked her way across the street to her buggy and set a course for Penncrest. Once away from the humming city life, she settled back to mull over her dilemma.

For the past two months she had been lying to herself about her peculiar early-morning sickness and the disruption of her monthly cycle. However, with the

318

distinct thickening of her waistline, she had finally decided to visit Dr. Littman.

But even though she had finally forced herself to contemplate the real cause of her malady, it had still been a shock to hear the doctor confirm her suspicions. "My dear, you are with child." His words had been calm, but they struck her like a slap in the face. Only after she had sipped on a small glass of brandy the doctor had offered her did color once again return to her thin, pale face.

Dr. Littman had studied her reaction closely, and in his own abrupt and outright manner had asked who the father was. She had reddened with shame, hesitating in her response, but had finaly told him the truth. As for the turbulent details of the conception, she refused to elaborate. What had happened was between Michael and herself, and no one else need know.

"I would guess Michael knows nothing of your condition?" Christy nodded weakly. "Well then, face him. Tell him you carry his child. He is a fair man. He will do what is right for you, I am sure. For the good of yourself and your unborn child, do not take this upon yourself as your own burden. Michael has a right to know the truth, and the duty to take care of you both. Think it over and I am sure you will agree with me. Please promise me, Miss Patterson, that whatever you decide to do, you will come to me if you need help. You need not feel alone. There are those who can and will help you through this."

As she bumped along the dusty road, Christy struggled with mixed emotions. It was wonderful to know that a tiny seed was growing within her; that she would one day hold her baby close and cradle him in her arms. She had always looked forward to the day she herself would become a mother. But in all her wildest dreams she had never guessed she would be in this condition without a husband. . . .

Later that day, her cold fingers brushed against her slightly feverish cheek as she pushed aside a stray curl. The study door stood slightly ajar. Peeking in, she saw Michael seated behind the desk, engrossed in his work. She hesitated to intrude, but the news she had to give him would wait no longer.

She took a deep breath. The whole world seemed hushed—alert and expectant—awaiting her news. Her bold knock sounded loud to her own ears. "Forgive me for interrupting, sir, but I must speak to you," she began with far more confidence than her pounding heart felt.

The room seemed oppressively hot. Michael's shirt was wet with perspiration. "What is it? Can't you see I'm busy? Come back later. I've no time for you now." He picked up a handkerchief and wiped his sweaty brow. The ominous scowl on his face made her reconsider the wisdom of her timing, but her mind was made up. There was no turning back now.

"It is very important, Captain. I do not think it can wait."

Michael threw down his pencil and gave her a withering glare. "I told you not to call me 'Captain' any more. Call me Michael, or Mr. Lancer, or whatever the hell you wish. But desist from the name 'Captain' as I no longer enjoy that occupation. I told you that before. Is your memory so bad you cannot remember such a minor point?"

Christy paled at his cutting insult. His bad humor made her task all the more difficult. Good sense warned her to flee, yet if she backed down now she might never again find the courage to confront him. She must not let him bully her. "I am sorry, sir. I am accustomed to addressing you in that manner and find it awkward to call you otherwise. I will, however, make an effort to call you as you desire."

"Thank you," he muttered. Once again he bent over his work.

Christy frowned at his obvious dismissal. "I would appreciate a moment more of your time. I think you should know . . ." she started and then changed her mind. She had practiced over and over exactly how she would tell him, but now, as she faced his stormy countenance, all her planning and practice vanished. She tried again. "I went into Charleston today. I have . . . I mean . . . I am . . ." she stopped and wrung her hands, frantically searching for the right approach. But the words that had to be spoken stuck in her dry throat.

"Well, girl, what is it? I don't have all day to spend listening to you fumble about trying to decide what you want to tell me. Out with it!" he barked.

Christy jumped at his harsh rebuke. Whatever the cost, she had to break the deadly suspense mounting inside her. The words flowed out in explicit simplicity. "I am with child."

"What did you say?"

Christy took a step back, ready to flee, but he jumped from his chair and strode quickly around the desk toward her. She looked up into his angry brown eyes, but words

321

would not come. Angered further by her muted tongue, he gripped her shoulders and shook them slightly, forcing her to look up at him. "What did you say?" he thundered.

"I am with child. I am pregnant." She stood trembling before him, aching to flee from the room. But her quivering legs would not move. Scalding tears streamed down her face at his sudden speechlessness. His hands dropped from her shoulders as if she were some horrid creature; something loathsome to touch. He stepped away, putting some distance between them, and swung about to confront her.

"So you have gotten yourself pregnant? I am gone less than a month and you are already out walking the streets and flaunting your beauty. You played me the fool, my little cousin. You played well the part of young innocent, and like a fool, I respected your wishes and kept my distance. It seems all the while you were saving yourself for someone else. Tell me, who is this man you find so enthralling? Who is this lucky man you favor so boldly with your love? Tell me—that I may force him to wed you and make a respectable woman of you. Tell me who the father is, that your bastard child may have a name."

"You . . . you are the father." She nearly choked on the words. "The child is yours and no others."

"Mine! Mine you say?" he boomed. In disbelief he backed away and stared dumbly at her, trying to grasp the full measure of her words and control his anger. "How can that be? I touched you only once! You have not let me come near you since that night on the ship!"

"Sir, I believe you are more of an expert on the subject

than I. But am I not correct in assuming that once is all it takes?"

A silence more terrifying than his tirade permeated the room. He turned his back to her and walked to the window. It was some time before he again turned to interrogate her.

"Much could have happened in the month I was gone. How do I know you have not gotten yourself in such a state with some poor beggar, and now plan to lay the blame at my door, thinking to tie me down and live in ease and comfort? Perhaps Matilda was correct. Perhaps you are nothing more than a bloody mercenary!"

His accusations infuriated Christy beyond reason. She flew at him, pounding her fists into his chest. "How dare you question the validity of my words! How dare you!" she screamed. "I was a virgin when you forced yourself upon me. Well, I tell you true, sir. The babe is yours, and yours alone!" Her eyes were black with fury as she marched toward the door. "And if you believe me not, sir, then know that I am due six months hence, which lays the blame without question at your door!"

With that she flew from the room, ignoring the astonished faces of Bertha and Sir Phillip as she brushed quickly past them and up to her room. The silent house echoed with the slamming of her door. But, only the pillow heard the heartrending sobs which tore from her wounded soul.

Christy's words still hung in the air as Sir Phillip strode into the room, shut the door behind him, and turned to question his son. "Michael, am I to believe the words I just heard? Is it true the girl is carrying your child?"

Michael delayed in his response. He crossed the room to pour himself a generous portion of whiskey. After a large swallow, he sat down behind the desk and ran his fingers irritably through his tousled brown hair. "Yes, I suppose it is true," he said quietly and took another gulp of the strong brew.

Sir Phillip regarded his son closely. "I should not be surprised by your part in this. She is a beautiful girl. But, Michael, she is so young; surely she has little experience in these things. Could you not have been more prudent with her? As I say, I have heard of your convincing ways with the ladies, but I am discouraged to see you dote on such a young girl. Are her charms too strong for you to resist?" The disappointment in his tone was blatantly evident. "Must you bring your mistress right into our very home?"

Michael rose and stood before the window. Sweat glistened on his forehead. "I cannot let you wrongly accuse Christina, Father. I must take full blame for her condition. And, God help me, she is not and never was my mistress. One night aboard ship, shortly before we sailed into Charleston, I was drunk and . . ." The words were difficult for him and tasted foul in his own mouth. "I forced myself on her. I've no excuse for my wretched actions. She was entirely blameless. She wanted nothing to do with me then, and still feels the same way now. She won't let me near her. I certainly don't blame her for despising me. I wanted her here under my roof to try to make partial retribution for my actions. I see the damage is far worse than I ever anticipated."

Sir Phillip stood for some time regarding his son's slumped shoulders. "I am beginning to understand why Miss Patterson has, at times, shown such animosity toward you. Your actions were despicable, Michael. I see, however, that you already carry the burden of guilt, so I will not add to your grief. What's done is done. But what is important now is, what do you plan to do about it? I have raised my sons to be honorable gentlemen."

"I will speak to her, Father, but I doubt she will be happy about marrying me. She is none too pleased with me now, or for that matter, ever was."

"I am sure you realize that marriage is the only honorable solution, especially under the circumstances. You are doing the right thing, son. Perhaps this is a blessing in disguise, for you will have a lovely wife and a son of your own. And I will have another grandchild." Sir Phillip gripped his son's shoulder and then walked slowly from the room.

As the heavens grew dark and thunder pierced the air, Michael saddled his great black stallion and hammered recklessly through the rain. He returned hours later, physically spent yet no more at peace with himself.

The seat between Sir Phillip and Michael remained conspicuously empty during the evening meal. Neither of the men had much appetite, and conversation was at a bare minimum. The burden of the situation hung heavily in the air until Michael, not wishing to delay the confrontation further, mounted the stairs and knocked at Christy's bedroom door.

"Come in," came a listless voice.

Michael eased open the door and entered the room.

"Good evening, Christy," he began with an effort. "Your presence was decidedly missed at dinner this evening," he said, trying to make conversation, yet all the time noting her tear-stained face. Her long black hair had recently been brushed, and lay in silky masses on her light dressing gown of pale blue. Though she looked frail and helpless, Michael knew her to be a formidable opponent.

As if reading his mind, she rose from her chair and squared her tiny shoulders. "I had no appetite, sir. Bertha said she would send a tray if I need anything later," she said and looked at him through pale, misty green eyes.

The silence that filled the room was almost painful, but she was determined to force him to take the initiative and speak his mind. Finally, he began. "I've given the matter considerable thought. I suppose the most honorable arrangement, under the circumstances, would be for us to marry as soon as possible. I can make the necessary arrangements and we can be married within a week. Is that agreeable to you?"

His suggestion was so cold and abrupt that, for a moment, Christy could find no response to make. This unfeeling, heartless approach wounded her anew.

"Have you thought of the consequences of marrying a penniless bond servant? Why, how entirely unthinkable!" she said and spun away to the balcony.

"Bond servant, hell. I declared you my servant legally and outrightly. I can, as easily, free you from that bondage. But that bothers me not. You are pregnant with my child and I must pay the price. I will not have my son face the world as an outcast and a bastard. I will not allow him to suffer for my mistakes."

"I suppose I have suffered nothing at your hands since the day we met? You have always been sweet, gentle, generous and kind with me, have you not, sir, while I have done nothing but interfere and cause you grief." The emerald green of her eyes shot heated sparks at him as her tirade continued. "Well, good sir, I would not condemn you to having to live with me. Nay, sir, I will not be that unkind or unreasonable. Send me away to suffer my shame alone, for I cannot and will not marry you."

Again she turned her back to him and gripped the balcony rail for support. She was shocked and dismayed that her anger should have gotten so out of control.

"What the hell is it you want, then? Had I suggested sending you off, you would have just cause to be angry. Lord, it is better for you to become my wife than to raise the child alone. Am I not right? No matter what I say angers you. What do you want from me?"

I need your love and respect, she wanted to scream. Instead, she made a valiant effort to speak calmly and reasonably. "I am sorry for my childish outburst, Mr. Lancer. I had no cause to lash out at you. Please, forgive me. Your offer is indeed a generous one; far kinder than I anticipated. However, marriage is not necessary. In fact, due to certain aspects of my past, it is out of the question."

Michael was taken aback by her sudden change. He stared closely at her pale, tear-streaked face. "I don't understand. What could have happened in your past that would so influence your marrying me?"

"I cannot tell you, but, please, believe me. It is best for both of us this marriage not take place." How could she tell him her parents were branded traitors and marrying her would tarnish the Lancer name throughout all of England.

"Madam, I believe I have the right to forego your objections. Unless you give me solid reasons for stopping the ceremony, we will be married within the week. If you choose to separate after the child is born, that can be arranged. But, until that time, the babe will not be born bastard, and we will both have to suffer this temporary inconvenience of wedlock."

His words had a finality to them. Again he was taking charge of her life without regard to her feelings. "And what about the money I owe you? What about my indenture? Will you free me from this bondage once we are married?"

Her questions, and the impertinence of her tone angered him further. "Aren't you being rather presumptuous, my dear? Why should I? You've done very little in way of repayment. Perhaps once we are married you will find my bed less distasteful, and my method of collecting my due quicker and more agreeable. Under the cover of marriage, you needn't feel the social impact of being my mistress. You may even enjoy it. Besides, if you behave properly as a loving and suitably passionate wife, I may declare you free once the baby is born," he said with false benevolence.

Christy's temper flared again. "Because I am forced to marry you, sir, does not mean I am forced to share your bed."

"By damn, woman. When we are married, it is my legal right to demand some wifely attention. The law does not concern itself with why people marry. It is content with the fact that they indeed have made a legal contract. That legal contract entitles me to your services in the marriage bed."

With that he turned and strode from the room, slamming the door loudly as he left.

Eighteen

The next few days passed in slow agony for Christy. She remained in her room as much as possible, appearing only for the evening meal and then immediately seeking the solitude of her chamber. Sir Phillip and Michael approached her occasionally with requests for her opinion on the wedding details, but she had little interest in it. It was a formality which had to be endured.

On the third morning after their announced engagement, Christy rose early but delayed in dressing. A strange foreboding about the coming day made her reluctant to have it commence. She was sitting at her bureau, still wearing her light chemise and slowly brushing her hair, when Michael knocked and entered her room. She had seen little of him since their heated argument, and their brief encounters were stiff and formal. She regarded his tall, handsome form through her mirror, but did not turn to face him.

"Good morning, my dear. I trust you are feeling well this morning?" he asked.

"Very well, thank you, sir," she responded, but continued her brushing.

Michael watched her for a few moments. The early

morning sunlight put golden highlights on the silky, smoothness on her shoulders. Her skin had the smooth, pale flush of morning. The eyes which regarded him rather passively were a deep, striking green. The prospect of soon waking up to find this tempting beauty at his side was indeed far from displeasing.

"I have sent Morgan into town for Kramer, the dressmaker. You will be needing a wedding gown and countless other items. He should be here shortly, Christina."

He had begun using her Christian name upon her urging. Though she was against this wedding, it would not do for her future husband to continue addressing her as "Miss Patterson." The servants were already highly suspicious about the sudden marriage, and such formality among supposed lovers was quite out of place. With much difficulty, she now addressed him as Michael instead of "Captain" or "Mister Lancer."

She put down her brush and turned to face him. "Michael, it is not necessary to buy me anything. The dresses you purchased for me before are quite sufficient. I need nothing else." She could sense another argument lurking closely, so she kept her tone low and even.

"Don't be ridiculous. You need more than those three plain, common dresses. You will be mistress of Penncrest and must learn to act and dress as such."

His tone was maddening, as if he were speaking to some troublesome child. Christy's face grew flushed in anger, and she rose to her feet to confront him. "If you insist on forcing these costly garments upon me, I will never be able to repay you. My debts are already of tremendous proportions, and I may well spend the rest of my life in servitude, reimbursing you well after the babe is grown."

Michael listened to her words but heard very little of what she said. As she walked, the vague outline of her shapely body was visible through the sheer linen of her chemise. "My dear, should you play the role of gracious, loving and passionate wife well enough, you need not concern yourself with your debts. I will consider your undivided and devout attention payment enough."

Christy's emerald eyes flared as she stepped forward to meet his gaze head on. "You and I know the reason for this marriage is the babe that grows within me. It is strictly for that reason I agreed to wed you. But whether bound by servitude or a marriage license, my feelings remain unchanged."

Behind the thin folds of her chemise, her breasts rose and fell, tantalizing Michael beyond control. Even the anger that flushed her face detracted little from her striking beauty. "By damn, woman, you are stubborn. But I am just as stubborn." He reached out and crushed her to him. Stunned by his sudden action, she looked up into the hungry brown eyes devouring her in a single glance.

"Yes, my sharp-tongued beauty. Your words cut me to the quick, yet your lips cry out to me with their sweet softness. My control grows weak and my desire strong to taste the honey you refuse to offer."

His words and actions left Christy with no delusions as to what was on his mind. She struggled fiercely to free herself but his arms encircled her tightly. Escape was impossible. "Michael, let me go this instant," she insisted, raising her chin defiantly.

Instead of letting her go, however, he took full advantage of her upturned face. His hot, demanding mouth covered hers in fiery passion and he thrust his tongue between her tightly clenched teeth.

Fear and excitement simultaneously raced through her. The hardness of his body pressed tightly against her. She struggled and panted against him as his lips seared her flesh, traveling from her mouth to nibble her ears and neck, and the smooth satin of her shoulders. Her senses tingled; her resolve weakened and she relaxed in his arms. Her body melted against his and her breathing grew quicker. Desire began to burn within her ignited senses.

He slowly raised his lips away from hers and looked deep within the emerald pools gazing questioningly at him. He laughed slowly through smiling lips and he released her with such suddenness that she slipped down onto the couch beneath her. "Do I detect a small dent in my lady's armor? You'd best steel your defenses against me, my love, for when we are married the battle will be fierce, and any weakness will surely mean your defeat."

Christy flushed in anger. "Oh, I despise you!" she seethed. He now loomed above her.

Openly enjoying his advantage over her, he raised her chin with his hand and caressed her neck and smooth, soft cheek. "I care not that you despise me. It is the love of your body I crave."

He spoke softly, yet Christy could feel the devilish gleam in his eyes, and hear the challenge in his tone. "Oh, you rogue. This is one battle you shall not win," she hissed and slapped his hand away angrily. "I'll not be trapped here and forced to submit to your pawing a moment longer."

With surprising agility, she tucked her legs under her, braced herself, and quickly rose to stand on the couch. For once his surprised brown eyes were forced to look up into her emerald ones. She reveled in the minor triumph. But her victory was all too short lived and, in fact, turned swiftly to disaster. Her heaving breasts were now at perfect eye level to her opponent.

"I never knew what advantages could be achieved from having you tower over me." His eyes openly admired her swelling peaks. "But I now see some beguiling possibilities."

"Oh, you impossible wretch!" she cried, mortified by her own stupidity. She lunged for the other end of the couch, determined to jump off and flee. In her haste, her bare foot slipped between the soft cushions. With a frightened cry, she lost her balance and slipped from the couch right into the waiting arms of her future husband. Long, thick lashes fluttered over the wide green eyes staring at him in stunned surprise.

"Really, my pet, you must be more careful. You don't want to lose the baby before we are married. Think how embarrassing it would be to call off the wedding now, and yet explain your continued presence here," he pointed out.

"Oh, you wretch. What a hateful thing to say. You are a cad and an unfeeling ogre to even suggest such a thing. Though I initially regretted the conception of this child, now that it grows in me I want it more than anything. Even if it means being forced to marry you. I will give this child the love and kindness which I have been denied for so long. He will give me happiness and love, as you have not." She squirmed to be free of his grasp.

A black frown clouded his face. He set her upon her feet and headed for the door. "I have offered you a chance for happiness on numerous occasions, but you continually reject my propositions."

"Yes, happiness on your terms," she shot back.

"Well, be that as it may, I see little point in arguing with you further. But, be warned, my little iceberg. A child can fill your time and you can give him love, but you will surely find a void in your happiness without the love and companionship of a man. Now get yourself dressed and presentable, for Kramer will be here shortly. He will be instructed to fit you with a complete wardrobe, and you may be sure I will check to see you have not skimped. Though you choose not to act the part of my wife, at least you will look it. Good day, madam." The slamming of the door behind him only punctuated his final remarks.

Christy's lower lip protruded indignantly at his vicious prophecy. She spun and hurled herself on the bed, fully intending to enjoy a good, self-pitying cry. But, the tears would not come. Michael's words had struck too close to the truth. She knew the love and devotion of a child could never fulfill the craving for masculine attention and affection.

Kramer arrived shortly before lunch. No explanation was given to him for the sudden need for a wedding gown and various other items Michael ordered, yet Christy's swelling stomach left him with few doubts as to the reason for the hasty marriage.

The whole procedure was humiliating, and she was relieved when he finally left with a promise to have her wedding gown completed within the week. The other gowns, bed attire, under garments, cloaks and riding garb would be finished as soon as possible. She cringed at the magnitude of the order. Her debts were ever increasing!

With a weary sigh, she excused herself from lunch, complaining of a piercing headache, and again locked herself in her room. Only sleep could momentarily free her from life's cruel realities. But even sleep would not come. She tossed and turned until she ached from the movement. After nearly an hour, she finally gave up completely. Listlessly she wandered to her dressing table and sat to regard herself in the glass. She felt untidy, and unattractive. Although her waistline had grown almost imperceptibly, she felt heavy.

In an effort to rid herself of these unpleasant feelings, she sat before the mirror and brushed out her long black hair until it shone. With quick and nimble fingers, she swept it up on top of her head, letting a few loose curls dangle mischievously.

She decided on wearing the pale yellow gown Michael had given her after the incident at the well. It had a simple beauty her other three gowns could not match.

Taking a final look at her reflection, she pinched her cheeks for a little color. Though she did not feel much better, at least she would present a more pleasing appearance. She practiced a smile, and made her way down to dinner.

She hardly tasted the delicious fried chicken set before

her, and only Sir Phillip's valiant efforts to break the
awkward uneasiness between herself and Michael kept
the meal from passing in total silence. At length,
however, even he grew weary of supporting the
conversation, and lapsed into contemplating his coffee
cup. When the meal was over, Christy pushed back her
chair, ready to excuse herself. Before she could speak,
however, the doorbell chimed. The butler appeared to
announce the presence of their guest.

"Excuse me. Mrs. Lancer has just arrived. Sally is
taking her coat. Shall I show her in?" he questioned.

"No, Simon. We are finished here. We'll move into
the study. Show her there, will you," answered Sir
Phillip. He waited for the servant's departure, and then
said quietly, "Well, I suppose the time has come to tell
her, if she hasn't already heard."

Christy did not miss the look of dread which passed
between Sir Phillip and Michael. As she preceded them to
the study, she chided herself for delaying in retiring.
Polite escape was now impossible, and a feeling of dread
possessed her at the prospects of being present when
Matilda heard of the upcoming wedding.

Michael and Sir Phillip lit cigars and poured themselves some strong sherry. Christy declined their offer
and chose the least conspicuous seat in the study.

"Good evening, Sir Phillip, Miss . . . Patterson? And
you, Michael, darling," bubbled Matilda in a high falsetto
voice. She flounced into the room, outfitted in a highly
provocative pink evening gown. Without waiting for an
invitation, she chose a goblet and filled it with the sweet
sherry. After taking a dainty sip, she turned her full and

seductive attention on her handsome brother-in-law who stood with one arm leaning carelessly on the mantel.

"Michael dear, how are you? It's been ages since you stopped by to see me. Why, the children and I feel horribly neglected. I just had to stop over and make sure you had not forgotten us," she pouted prettily.

"I must apologize for my absence, Matilda, but we have all been busy of late. Things have been quite hectic," he said, but he volunteered no further explanation, nor did Christy or Sir Phillip.

"Well, my dear, it's not good to devote all your time to work. You need some diversion; especially after spending so much time with those filthy workers. Yes, you definitely need some adult female attention." Her words were honey sweet, yet the glance she threw at Christy held open challenge.

"You needn't concern yourself with my welfare, Matilda. My needs are adequately filled," he replied and shifted uncomfortably.

The uneasiness in the room was punctuated by the heavy silence. Matilda took another sip from her drink. "Good heavens! Whatever is the matter with you all? Why such morbid expressions?"

It was clear the moment for revelations had come. Michael looked about the room for support, yet found none from his father or Christy. He drained his glass, cleared his throat, and addressed himself to Matilda. "I intended stopping by to see you, Matilda, and explain things, but I haven't had the time. I'm surprised you've not already heard the news."

"Why, whatever do you mean? Explain what, darling?" asked Matilda. She leaned closer, fluttering her eyes and giving him the full benefit of her deeply cut bodice.

Michael's glance fell upon her cleavage, but to her obvious dismay, he stepped away to pour himself another drink. After a generous swallow, he resumed his place at the mantel and said, "We've all been busy making wedding preparations, Matilda."

"A wedding? How marvelous. Who is getting married? One of the servants? Don't tell me old Morgan finally popped the question to Melissa?"

"No, Morgan is not getting married." There was a long pause. "I am. It is my wedding, Matilda," he said finally and took another drink.

Matilda's expression was incredulous. "What? Your wedding?" she blurted out, nearly spilling her glass of sherry. "I . . . I don't understand. Is this some sort of joke?" She looked from face to face. No one was smiling.

"No. It is no joke. Miss Patterson and I are to be married next Saturday." Sensing an impending explosion, he moved to stand behind Christy's chair.

Matilda's mouth was agape in disbelief. "You . . . and . . . her? Married?" she said, trying to absorb the impact of the shocking statement. "But why? Surely you do not profess to love her?"

"We are quite fond of one another," volunteered Michael, and reached down to stroke Christy's cheek lovingly with his hand. No need for Matilda to know the real reason for the marriage—at least not yet.

Matilda spun around and placed the half-empty sherry glass on the table. She had lost Michael and his money.

But to have her hopes crushed by this worthless, lying brat was too much to bear. Why? . . .

Suddenly everything became clear. She spun to face Christy. "You're pregnant, aren't you?" she accused, eyes gleaming like a cat's eyes. "You planned the whole thing, didn't you—from the very start! Oh you little slut!" she spat and moved threateningly toward Christy, fists clenched as if to strike.

Christy was alarmed by the hate reflected in Matilda's eyes. She rose hastily and stood beside Michael, hoping for his intercession against this vengeful woman.

"I am right, am I not? Am I not?" she screamed, overcome by rage. She moved to strike, but found her assault blocked by Michael.

"Matilda. Please calm youself," he said sternly.

But, their silence was all the confirmation she needed. "You are a fool for falling for such a ploy, Michael. I thought you had more sense than letting yourself get trapped like this. You don't love her. She's a nothing, a nobody. She has nothing to offer you. No doubt her family is of little repute, or she would not hide her past so diligently."

Sir Phillip came to Christy's rescue. "The truth is, Matilda, they are being married on Saturday. Everything else is of little consequence," he said. The fact was, this match pleased him well. He liked this little orphaned girl Michael had brought home, and he felt if anyone could tame his wild, carefree son, this woman could.

Matilda stood immobile for a time, her eyes taking on a cunning, calculating light. At length, she turned to Michael. "I am convinced you do not want this baby, or this—woman. You must realize there are ways to do away with unwanted pregnancies. I know an old woman who could do the job, neat and clean, and save you the trouble and embarrassment of this ridiculous marriage. I can arrange the whole thing." She placed a well manicured hand upon his arm.

Christy nearly fainted from Matilda's suggestion. How could anyone, especially a woman and mother herself, even think of something so abominable? "Mrs. Lancer. You may call me anything you wish, and you may treat me as you like. But hear this. Do not ever again dare suggest killing my baby. Though there are those who do not want him, let no one dare try taking him from me, for I will kill to save him."

The threat in her voice was unmistakable, and Matilda backed away in some trepidation. Even Michael and Sir Phillip were surprised by the intensity of her retort.

"I agree completely with Christina. The child is mine and I will not see it killed, nor will I take the chance that Christina might be injured. I am disgusted you would even suggest such a thing," came Michael's equally hot reply. He lightly rested his arm about Christy's waist to punctuate his position.

"Well don't snap at me. I'm only thinking of your welfare. Yes, you may as well keep the child. He is yours and as such has the rights of a Lancer. But, you need not be saddled with this bitch. After the child is born, send her away and raise the babe yourself. You certainly need not marry her. No one would expect it of you. Why ruin your life over the likes of her. Get rid of her!"

Michael felt Christy shudder at Matilda's words.

"Matilda, that's quite enough. Christina and I will be married. I will not have my son raised as a bastard child. The wedding will be within the week. Now, if you wish to attend, you are welcome. If not, the wedding will go on without you. It is of no concern of yours." Unconsciously his grip tightened on Christy's waist.

"Let me show you to the door, Matilda," said Sir Phillip as he quickly rose and rather roughly caught the woman's shoulder, ushering her unceremoniously from the room. She attempted to protest, but Sir Phillip's grip was strong and determined, and she had little choice but to follow.

With Matilda gone, Michael turned his attention to Christy. At Matilda's open threat, her face had turned ashen pale, and she shook uncontrollably. "Are you all right, Christina? Let me pour you some brandy. It will calm you," he said in concern.

"No, thank you. I will be fine. Just give me a moment," she said, making a valiant effort to still her quivering lips.

"Please calm yourself, Christina. You mustn't become so overwrought. Of course I would not separate you and the baby. You are to be my wife, and have my child. Nothing will change that. What frightens you so?"

"I'm sorry, Michael. You are right. I'm sure my fears are unfounded. It's just I feared you would take Matilda's advice and send me away once the baby comes," she said weakly, trying to hide her true feelings.

"Don't be silly, Christina. I put very little stock in Matilda's musings, and I would certainly not send you away on her whim or anyone else's. Please trust me, little one," he said a trifle more gently.

Christy nodded and gave him a half-hearted smile. She suddenly felt incredibly weary. She turned to make her way to the stairs, but was still shaking and somewhat unsteady. The long, unpleasant day had taken a definite toll.

"Here, let me help you. You look terribly pale. Shall I summon Dr. Littman?" he asked in concern.

"No. I will be fine. I just need to lie down for a time. Really," she insisted, but gratefully accepted the support of his strong arm about her waist.

As they entered the hall, Bertha passed by. One look at the young girl's pale complexion told her she was distraught and feeling poorly, and needed some tender ministrations. With her usual air of authority, she took charge. "You let me take care of this child, Master Michael. She needs some womanly attentions," she said and led the exhausted Christy to her room.

In no time Christy was undressed and nestled comfortably in her warm bed. Blessed sleep came almost instantly.

Nineteen

The next few days passed in an eternity of slowly ticking minutes, yet Saturday morning arrived all too quickly. With the rising of the sun, Christy found herself seated in a closed carriage on her way to Charleston. She and Michael were to be married in the little church she had gone to some three months ago looking for refuge from the night, and her fear of Michael. Since that time she had often accompanied Michael and Sir Phillip to Sunday services, yet this trip to the church would change her life.

When they arrived at the church, Morgan helped her from the carriage. She felt incredibly alone, yet at the same time suffocated as an older woman and two young girls quickly escorted her to the little room outside the entranceway and began the lengthy process of preparing her for the fast-approaching ceremony.

As they fussed about, brushing and coifing her silky black curls, she thought of her parents. Surely they would have been pleased she was marrying so well—into a respected and wealthy family, despite the fact that the marriage was more out of necessity than love. She whispered a silent prayer to them, asking that they give their blessings to her this day.

Her hair arranged impeccably, the ladies coaxed her to her feet and positioned her in the middle of the room. An exquisite gown of delicate white silk brocade was lowered over her head and shoulders and settled into place. The gown fit superbly, thanks to Kramer, and gave full credit to her full, swelling breasts and still tiny waistline. The delicate whiteness of the gown contrasted strikingly with her shining black hair, and made the deep emerald of her eyes even more captivating. The long, full sleeves of the gown were tightly cuffed at the wrists by tiny pearl buttons edged with lace trim. A gift from the groom, a single, flawless pearl offset by two tiny diamonds, hung delicately about her slender neck. To complete the picture, matching earrings peeked from behind the long, flowing lace veil which nestled decorously in the black curls about her head.

The fitting at last complete, Kramer and the three ladies stepped back to survey the final product of their efforts. "Oh, mademoiselle looks breathtaking," complimented Kramer. "Truly there has never been a more beautiful bride than this, nor one more serene."

Finally all was ready, and the signal was given. Her long, flowing gown and veil were straightened behind her. The music began. Slowly she propelled herself down the long aisle. Her surprisingly steady fingers clutched a bouquet of perfect red roses. Closer and closer she moved toward the lean, handsome man who would soon be her husband.

Michael Lancer stood tall and erect at the altar. With composed ease, he waited patiently for his bride. Christy wondered what he felt at this moment. She realized that she cared deeply about this strange, complex man. He would soon be hers and she his. Though she knew he held no feelings of warmth for her, when she finally stepped to his side and gazed up into his eyes, she whispered a vow to herself that someday she would make him love her.

With delicate care, he lifted the veil from her face and stared in renewed awe at her loveliness. Full red lips held the touch of a smile, and long, lush black lashes lowered demurely over eyes of a deep emerald green. He could barely take his eyes from her, and only the minister clearing his throat reproachfully, forced him to drag his gaze from the beauty at his side.

Ancient, traditional words of love and promise passed between them, heedless of the true cause for the union. In no time their vows were complete and Michael swept his new bride down the aisle and into the small throng of friends and family waiting to congratulate the handsome couple. Everyone expressed their happiness and best wishes, and only Matilda spoiled the reserve with her caustically whispered remark that pregnancy agreed with the bride in that she looked quite lovely.

Amid a sea of people and well-intended instructions, they were whisked from the church and crowded into the large carriage. Morgan wasted no time in returning them safely to Penncrest where a gala dinner had been planned. Christy drifted through the evening, smiling when required to and playing the happy bride. Yet she felt apart from the world, as if it were all a fantasy or an illusion, and she would soon awake to find herself in the cold, dark house of Henry Slate. Only the strangely comforting presence of Michael at her side kept her on the brink of reality.

Finally the last guest departed and the sleepy servants set about the chore of cleaning up. Exhausted from the emotional and physical demands of the day, Christy excused herself and went to her room. Because of the sudden and hasty demands of wedding preparations, the sleeping arrangements of the master and new mistress had not been discussed, and she was glad she still had the solitude of her own room. She doubted Michael would insist she move in with him, especially once she grew large with child.

She walked to the balcony and gazed out into the dark, starry night. Moonlight touched the golden band on her finger, exquisite in its simplicity, and sent spirals of light across the room. She was now mistress of this house, Mrs. Michael Lancer. But had her position really changed? She was still tied to a man who did not love her. Had she exchanged the chains of one form of bondage for another? Only time would tell, but for the present, marriage would mean little until she won the love and respect of her husband.

A short time later, two new servant girls hired especially for the new mistress, entered to help her disrobe and prepare for bed. It still embarrassed her to be treated thus. She was prefectly able to care for herself. But Michael had insisted.

When the servants finally finished their fussing about her and departed, she was adorned in a pale white gown of cloudy, milky sheerness. Her long hair had been brushed until it shone, and lay loosely about her shoulders. She blew out the candle and again stood in the darkness by the balcony; the room illuminated only by the glow of the silvery moon.

She rested her hands on the balcony as a soft summer breeze touched her hair and set her gown swaying gently about her. Her mind drifted out to the dark night, breathing in the solitude and peace which it offered.

The symphony of the evening stillness muffled the opening of the door and the quiet tread of boots upon the floor. The gentle light from the moon penetrated through her gown, revealing in minute detail the slender, shapely form beneath. The intruder eagerly drank in the loveliness before him.

"You are lovely beyond words, my dear. I greatly envy that moon, for he casts his light down upon you, touching you everywhere, while I must be content to stand alone in the shadows."

Christy was not surprised to find him materialized from the darkness. She could feel him moving closer. A terrible sadness poured over her as she relinquished the peace of the night and turned to face her husband.

"I thank you for your compliment, my lord, but at this moment I despise this body you praise. This beauty you see is naught but a curse. Were I less attractive and appealing, and you came to me as you do now, I would know you truly loved me for myself. As it is, I fear your heart is barred against me, while your body longs to take me." Her eyes searched for his in the darkness. If he would admit only some small, tender feelings toward her, she would be his. But as he moved closer and stroked her face gently, his words crushed her hopes.

"You speak in solemn riddles, my dear. I only know

that I want you now more than anything else in the world."

A tear trickled unheeded down her cheek, and the feeling of deep despair nearly overcame her. "My lord, if you come to take what is rightfully yours as my husband, I can do little to stop you. But know, sir, that my feelings are unchanged. I do not give myself freely in retribution for my debts."

The stillness of the evening suddenly snapped with his anger at her words of quiet resignation. "I come to you openly now, as your rightful husband, and yet you once again turn me away on this of all nights. You are right. I could take by force what is legally mine, but it would only add more fuel to your fire against me. So, woman, live in my house. Play the part of mistress and loving wife so that the world may view us as happy man and wife. But my dear, know this: the days and nights here in Charleston can get long and cold alone. And remember, by your own choice, that is how you will endure them. Alone!"

With that he turned and stormed from the room. . . .

Christy rose with the early morning sun the next day. She had slept very little and the daylight seemed a blessed relief to the tossing and turning, and cold, harsh thoughts which had haunted her in the darkness.

More than once she awoke in cold fear, plagued once again by her old nightmare. She had stood for nearly an hour out on the balcony, looking out into the darkness of night, searching for some small fragment of peace.

Finding none, she had finally crawled back to bed and to fitful slumber. Now, with the light of dawn, the ghostly shadows had vanished and her surroundings once again took on their natural perspective.

She dressed very slowly. She knew she was expected to summon her maids, yet was reluctant to do so. How could she meet their questioning eyes when they found her alone in her room. No, she was not up to that yet—not this morning. Best she enjoy her solitude now. It would vanish all too soon.

After a final glance in the mirror at herself, she slowly descended the stairs and entered the breakfast room. No one was about, but a fresh, steaming pot of coffee sat on the server. She poured herself a cup and sat alone at the huge dining room table, sipping on the rich, hot brew, letting it warm and relax her tense body.

"Lordy, Mistress Lancer. Why didn't you tell me you were waiting? I'll fix you something right away." Bertha bustled in all aflutter at finding her new mistress unattended.

"No thank you, Bertha. I'm really not hungry. Coffee is fine," she said.

"You really should eat, Mistress. If not for yourself, then at least for the babe," Bertha mothered, and then stood aghast at her own audacity. "Oh please forgive me, madam," she breathed fearfully and waited for her due reprimand.

No one had announced Christy's condition to the servants. It was supposed to remain a secret until they had been married a respectable amount of time. The fact that all the servants already knew the truth seemed inconsequential. Christy guessed the house was already in a flutter due to the fact that she kept her own room and did not move in with her husband. She also expected it to be whispered about that they had not even spent their honeymoon night together, but in fact had had an argument and retired to their own separate chambers. She knew it was impossible to stifle such gossip, especially when the rumors were all too true.

"Perhaps I'll have something later, Bertha. For now I am content with coffee."

Recovering slightly from her wagging tongue, Bertha turned in a businesslike manner to her mistress. "Would you like to go over today's menu, madam?" she asked somewhat stiffly.

Christy was hurt by Bertha's sudden change in attitude. After the incident at the well, the housekeeper had warmed considerably toward her. Now suddenly, and seemingly overnight, she had withdrawn back into her shell of aloofness. It seemed clear that, though Bertha had liked her in her previous capacity as "cousin" in the house, yesterday's marriage vows had changed all that. She was no longer a guest, but now mistress and had to be treated as such, with all due respect and formality, whether she earned it or not.

This role as mistress of a household was all too new, and Christy was anxious to assume her responsibilities in the proper manner. The only way she knew of to do this was to resecure the trust and aid of this priceless housekeeper.

"Bertha, I know very little about the many complex requirements of running a house. It is a very new and rather frightening undertaking for me. Therefore, I would very much appreciate your teaching me all that I need to know, and helping me cope with my new responsibilities. In the meantime, however, you have run things so well and smoothly these past years, I see no reason to interfere. I trust your skill and judgment completely."

Bertha was obviously pleased and relieved by Christy's words. "Very well, Mistress Lancer. As you wish. But I'll be sure to ask you on important household matters."

"That will be fine, Bertha. I have much to learn about being mistress of a grand house, and as much to learn about being a wife and mother. It is a great deal to undertake all at one time," she commented and fingered the beautiful gold band on her finger. "I will count on your help in many things," she said, looking into the black woman's face.

"Yes, ma'am. I'll be more than happy to give you a hand," answered Bertha with a smile. "Oh, by the way, Mistress, Master Michael has asked me to hire a personal maid for you. I got rid o' the two young girls who tended you last night. They were too flighty and disrespectful to suit me. I hired on a young girl from just down the road a piece. She'll tend to yer personal needs. I think you'll like her. She comes from good, hard workin' folks."

Christy grimaced. "Oh, Bertha. I need no personal maid. I am perfectly capable of caring for myself. I need no one fussing over me," she resisted.

"No matter, ma'am. Master Michael done told me to hire a maid for you. It's only right as mistress of this here house you have someone do yer hair and help with yer other needs," argued Bertha.

"Oh, very well, Bertha. If my husband insists, I shall have to submit. But it will take some time getting used to being fussed over," she said, somewhat dejectedly. Being mistress certainly did not mean always getting your own way.

"Indeed, my dear. I do insist. And as my wife, are you not entitled to be 'fussed over' as you put it?" interrupted Michael who had slipped quietly into the room.

Christy looked up, startled by his silent entrance, and blushed at his words. Of course he was right, and she was again made to feel a silly little fool.

"Will you be wanting breakfast, sir?" asked Bertha, anxious to leave them alone.

"No, Bertha. Coffee will be enough," he said.

Bertha poured him a steaming cup and made a quick departure. After a few sips, he turned to regard his new bride. "You look lovely this morning, Mrs. Lancer, despite your insomnia of last night."

Christy had ignored his gaze, toying with her coffee cup, yet looked up in surprise at his statement. "Thank you, sir, and you are correct. I slept very little. But how could you know?"

"You forget, my dear. Your room adjoins mine. Several times I heard you cry out from some fiendish nightmare. The quiet house amplified your troubled pacing. Perhaps the doctor could prescribe something to help you sleep," he said, not unkindly, but neither was his tone overly friendly.

"I am sorry if I kept you awake. I will strive to be more

quiet in the future when I suffer from insomnia," she said, trying to avoid another argument.

"Actually, I had trouble sleeping myself. It passed the time listening to you pace the floor. I found myself pondering my new state as spouse. Somehow I had always imagined my life as a married man would not be quite so celibate and filled with solitude. I suppose I have been misinformed on this matter," he said in a slightly mocking tone.

She blinked back tears. "I do not think you were misinformed, my lord. Marriage is a sharing and loving experience. But since ours is not one of love, but rather of 'honor,' shall we say, the rules are somewhat different." Her voice was toneless and she hastily rose to leave. She did not want him to see her cry, to see the hurt and pain that filled her heart. She felt too weak and vulnerable to fight him today. "If you will excuse me, sir, I have work to do on your accounts. I have fallen behind these past few days."

Irritated she had not taken his bait, he shoved his coffee cup aside. "You needn't bother with them any longer. I shall hire a secretary to handle my affairs."

"Are you not pleased with my work, then?" she asked, somewhat hurt that he should take the task from her.

"Your work was adequate. But I can hardly expect my wife to be bothered with my accounting."

"But I thought we agreed that in that way I would pay off my debts to you," she said, growing more bewildered by the moment.

"Damn it, woman. I'm sick to death hearing your incessant moaning about your debts. If you worried half as much about pleasing me as you do about balancing those confounded ledgers, I'd forget your debts."

"But I enjoy the work. We agreed I'd do it . . . that I'd be your secretary. I thought that pleased you," she said, close to tears. "I see no need to stop now, just because we are married."

Michael sprang from his chair in rage. "I said *no,* woman! The money is of little consequence to me now. It's only led to an eternal noose about my neck. I'll pay for your debts the rest of my life!"

Christy choked back sobs, devastated by his words. Tears streamed down her face and she fled toward the door.

"I did not tell you to go. Come back here and sit down," he ordered. "Come back here!"

Christy's heart skipped a beat at the ferocity of his barked command. She gripped the doorframe for support, breathing heavily. A gasp sounded in the hallway and she looked up to see Bertha's aghast expression. She and surely everyone in the house had heard his shouting.

Her tears ceased. She squared her shoulders and slowly turned to face him. "Sir, by your own choice you have made me your wife. As such I have every right to expect that you speak to me with civility. Do not bark at me as if I were your dog. If nothing else, I demand common courtesy from you. I am going to my room. If there is something else you have to discuss with me, you will find me there." Her eyes flashed at him in contempt and with supreme control she forced herself to leave the room with a dignified, unhurried step.

"Bravo, my dear girl. 'Tis time this son of mine learned to speak properly to a young lady," came the voice of Sir Phillip who had walked in on the end of the discussion.

Christy nodded mutely in his direction, but did not reply. She did not trust her voice. When the door closed behind her, she grabbed her skirts and dashed up the stairs. Once alone in her room, the stifled tears spilled unheeded.

It was late afternoon when a knock finally came at her door.

"Christina, it's Michael. May I come in?"

"The door is open," she answered and glanced up as he entered her small, sunny room. The stiff set of his jaw made her uneasy. She looked down, concentrating on the tiny robe she stitched for the baby. She refused to look up at him, though she felt him watching her closely. At length, he spoke.

"I am sorry I raised my voice to you, Christina. Please accept my apology. I must indeed learn to curb my sharp tongue," he managed to say, though with considerable effort.

She knew apologies did not come easy to him. This particular one surprised her. She stopped her sewing and gave him her attention. "I accept your apology," she said quietly. "And, I, in turn, wish to apologize for upsetting you. But, Michael," she hurried on, "please remember that since the very moment we met long ago on board your ship, things have been highly confusing for me. Quite without intent, I found myself on your ship bound for Charleston. A short time later I found myself growing heavy with your child, and now I find myself your wife and mistress of this large household. It is all new and rather frightening to me. I only ask you to be patient with me."

"Your request is a legitimate one, and I will try to be more understanding. It is not in my nature to be patient, however, so you may have to remind me from time to time." His tone remained gruff, yet his scowling countenance grew less severe.

Christy did not respond, but instead sat quietly regarding her husband; hating him and loving him at the same time. At length he spoke again.

"The Middletons, our neighbors in Charleston, are hosting a Thanksgiving Ball in three weeks. They invited me to attend some time ago. I had declined the offer, but now I believe it would be a good way to let you meet some of the families in Charleston. I understand gossip has already begun as to my sudden marriage to a stranger from London. I would like to bring you out and stifle such talk. I will tell them we accept the invitation and will be present. Wear something nice—that green velvet you have. I want you to look your best in front of these people. If they are going to talk, we may as well give them something to talk about," he said.

Christy bit her tongue to stifle a retort. She'd always dreamed of going to a ball, yet could he not have asked her in a more amiable fashion? "Very well, Michael, I shall make the necessary preparations," she answered and picked up her sewing.

Seeing his wife little inclined toward further conversation, he bowed stiffly and left the room.

Twenty

Christy spent most of her days working on blankets and little outfits for her new baby. The sewing helped occupy her time, and she began to look forward with great expectation to her baby's birth.

Bertha showed her little things about the house and explained how everything fit together to run smoothly. She learned quickly and began to enjoy the aspects of being mistress of the house. Perhaps she imagined it, but she felt she had matured greatly in these past few days, and noticed that even the servants had begun to treat her with more respect. Her confidence in herself was growing, and it was a rewarding experience.

Her new life still had certain aspects, however, that were greatly lacking. She saw little of her husband after their wedding day. He had threatened to stay away from her, giving her a full dose of loneliness, and his steadfast adherence to that threat was beginning to wear.

Despite the fact that they nearly always fought when together, she dearly missed his presence. It hurt her deeply that he could so easily ignore her and cast her from his mind. Though he made it painfully clear just what a burden she had placed on his previously free life, she still hoped for some sign of affection. When he was near, usually only at dinner, she tried to please him in little things she did or said. But time after time he chose to ignore her until finally, completely discouraged, she did not seek out his presence as before. It was a wretched existence, but she had Milly, her sweet personal maid, Sir Phillip, and her ever growing baby to boost her spirits.

This late summer day was little different from the others of the past few days. She watched Michael ride out early in the morning with Hoffman, the overseer. After inquiring, in what she hoped was a normal, steady voice, when Master Michael planned on returning, she was informed there was little likelihood of his arriving back until quite late. She tried to hide her disappointment from the watching servants, yet she knew they must think it odd that newlyweds should see one another so little, and argue so often. It was embarrassing, degrading, and disappointing.

With a sigh, she returned to her room and spent most of the day sewing. After a quiet dinner, Sir Phillip excused himself on some errands, and again she found time ticking by at a painfully slow pace. Tired of sewing and feeling restless, she wandered into the study.

Michael's desk was piled high with unposted accounts and bills. As yet he had not found a secretary to suit his needs, and had badly neglected the paperwork. Christy had not mentioned helping him again, since he had been so outraged when she had offered to continue her services after they had been married. If and when he ever did hire someone to settle his affairs, the man would surely have his work cut out for him in straightening out this mess.

She leafed through the bills, shaking her head in disgust. It upset her to think how hard she had worked to put his accounts in order, only to have them again fall into chaos because of Michael's stubbornness.

She pulled his chair close and sat down to get a better idea of how far behind he was. She made a pencil notation here, a tabulation there, and before she knew it, out came the ledgers and accounts, and she was engrossed in straightening out the mess and putting it in order.

Milly came in to rekindle the fire some time later, but Christy sent her off to bed. Soon the fire died down again, and the room grew cold, but Christy worked steadily on, losing all track of time. Her long efforts were finally beginning to take on a semblance of order, and she had no desire to quit until the job was done. Perhaps Michael would not notice she had tampered with his books until some days later, and hopefully by then they would be getting on better.

With a tired yawn, she totalled the last column. Suddenly a door slammed and from out in the hallway came the voice of her husband, loud and rowdy. Another voice, sounding low and patient, droned in contrast.

An angry shout arose and Christy heard the sounds of a slight scuffle. She glanced at the huge mahogany clock on the wall and gasped at the lateness of the hour—past midnight! There was little doubt in her mind that Michael was drunk, but where had he been for so long—and to come home in such a state?

The skin began to prickle beneath her simple gown. No doubt he would be terribly angry if he found her here, working on his books after he had strictly forbidden her to touch them. His temper was difficult enough to cope with when he was thinking rationally; but the prospects of facing his drunken anger made her blood turn cold. The memory of his last drunken escapade still burned vividly in her mind.

She squeezed her eyes closed, willing him to pass the study and go directly to bed. She breathed easier at the following silence in the hallway, counting her blessings. But Lady Luck was not so kind as she appeared.

"Sir, where are you going?" came Morgan's agitated question.

"I'm going to the study to have a nightcap," Michael slurred.

"Oh, no!" Christy caught her breath and sat tense and uneasy. She could hear his heavy boots thundering across the marble floor toward the study.

"Sir, I think you have had enough for one night. Come along now to the kitchen and I will make you some good, strong coffee," said Morgan.

"I don't want coffee, damnit, man. I tell you I want another drink!" he boomed back. "Get your hands off of me!"

Again there were sounds of a scuffle, and suddenly the study door burst open with such force, Christy nearly crumpled to the floor in shock.

"Well, well. What have we here?" questioned Michael as he stood leaning heavily against the door frame for support. "Has my new little bride been so generous as to wait up for my return? My gratitude is overwhelming for this small display of kindness," he said sarcastically. "Or perhaps you were anticipating I would not return at all. I am sorry to disappoint you, my love."

Christy sat stock still behind the desk and watched as he belched loudly and staggered toward the table of liquor. At his approach, she rose slowly from her seat. His unsteady fingers grasped the liquor flask.

"I think you have had enough, Michael. Let Morgan get you some hot coffee," she suggested.

Michael glared openly at her. "I don't want coffee, wife. I want a drink!"

"But, Michael . . ." she began.

"Damnit, I told you I want another drink. I am master here. Do you dare cross me?" he challenged belligerently.

When Christy and Morgan maintained a stony silence, he grinned snidely and poured himself a brimming glass of the hearty brew. After a few generous gulps, he turned his gaze to Christy. "Join me in a drink, my sweet," he cajoled. "Perhaps it will melt some of the ice which runs in your veins."

His wicked laugh bounced about the painfully quiet room. "You see, Morgan, since we've been married, my wife finds my presence distasteful and my company unworthy of her. Imagine that! My life is more the role of a celibate monk than a newly wedded and never-bedded husband. Why, that voluptuous little bar maid in the tavern was a far more willing bed mate than my glass-encased wife. But she is not satisfied with keeping me in a constant state of excitement and then forbidding me to come near. Nay, she is not satisfied with that. I think she is a witch, for now she has cast a spell over me. I cannot even look at another without seeing her face before me; teasing and tormenting me, then leaving my loins with a hard, unfulfilled hunger. Damnit, even this whiskey does not wash her image from my mind," he cursed and gulped down another swig of the liquor.

Christy wanted to die from humiliation. "Michael, please. There is no need to speak like this. Please go to bed. You will feel better tomorrow."

"All right. I'll go to bed. But only if you join me in a little romp," he laughed.

Christy blushed scarlet in horrified embarrassment. She cast a sidewards glance at Morgan and noted the high color on his equally embarrassed face.

"That's enough, Michael. I will not remain here and be insulted any longer. If you wish to drink yourself into oblivion, I will not stand in your way. But do not expect me to remain and be subjected to your insults."

His eyes moved quickly to the paper-littered desk and then back to her. As she stormed past him toward the door, her arm was seized in a steely grip. She was jerked to a halt.

"Take your hands off of me!" she ordered and shook his arm, her eyes blazing.

To her surprise, he complied, but silence hung stiffly in the air. He looked at the desk and back to his wife, his mind slow in comprehending what he saw. "What the hell have you been doing here?"

"Really, sir, your language . . . in front of a lady . . ." Morgan coughed nervously in reprimand.

"Morgan, I have no further need of you. I have a matter to discuss with my wife—alone. It seems she has once again gone against my wishes. Leave us," he ordered without taking his flaming eyes from Christy.

"Will you be all right, ma'am?" asked Morgan.

"It is quite all right, Morgan. I will be fine. Thank you for your help," said Christy, sparing him the embarrassment of her husband's rude behavior.

"Very well, madam. If you are sure . . ."

Christy nodded and he quickly made his exit. When the door once again closed them in together, she squared her shoulders and faced her husband boldly. "Michael, your behavior before Morgan was disgraceful. You are wretchedly drunk and inexcusably vulgar. I insist you put that brandy down and seek the privacy of your room until you can behave in a more mature manner."

The bravery in her command quickly vanished as he looked at her in pure rage. "What the hell right do you have ordering me around? Do you forget who you are? Your memory is far too short for your own good, my dear. And you have the audacity to give me commands!"

With an angry swipe of his hand, he scattered the papers and ledgers about the room. "And what the hell are you doing here? I commanded you to stay away from my accounts, and here I find you deliberately ignoring my orders. What do you have to say?" he bellowed.

"Since you have been unable to find an accountant, your bills and paperwork have piled high. I only sought to put them in some order to keep your accounts balanced and the creditors from your door," she explained.

"I don't need or want your help. For that matter, I never did. I only told you to work on my ledgers to keep you from nagging me to death. When I really want your help, I will ask for it." He glared back at her.

Tears welled up in her eyes at his drunken outburst. "If you are quite through with your insults, I shall retire, sir."

"No! I'm not through with you yet. Stay and have a drink with me," he ordered and attempted to fill another glass.

"No, Michael. I do not care for the whiskey, and I am tired and cold after working so long on your accounts," she replied and headed for the door.

An alarming growl from behind filled her with fear. "Would you pay half as much attention to me as you do to those damn accounts, I would be a happy man," he screamed angrily, and with a swipe of his arm, sent the few remaining papers sailing to the floor.

Christy's patience was at an end. She would no longer tolerate her husband's drunken temper. With determination she squared her shoulders. Eyes ablaze with emerald fire, she spoke with slow, seething sureness.

"If you recall, my husband, 'twas you who bade me settle your accounts. Whatever the reason you had me tackle the job, you must admit I made order out of chaos. I worked hard and long on those books and I will not sit back and see my efforts destroyed by your stubbornness. So do not chastise me when I look out for your best interests."

With that, she turned and headed for the door. If he insisted on behaving irrationally, let him bear the full impact of his actions. A glass fell to the floor and shattered. She did not pause to turn and look, but kept walking toward the door and pulled it open.

Suddenly the door was ripped from her grasp. A resounding crash shook the house as it was slammed closed. She did not move. She did not breathe. Her back still to Michael, she stared at the cold, white knuckles pressed against the door just above her head. His intoxicated breath upon her neck prickled her skin in fear.

Slowly the clenched fists relaxed and color returned to his fingers. But Christy knew his anger had not subsided. She watched his hand move from the door with steadfast sureness. She scarcely breathed as his fingers curled about her neck. Surprisingly he did not hurt her, but instead manipulated his hands in such a way that forced her to turn and face him. The look of unmasked anger clearly showed in his eyes. She had pushed him too far. Her legs turned to putty, but she fought to hide the fear which filled her.

"So, you find my books more agreeable than you do me? Well, perhaps I have been too lenient with you, and you need to be reminded of your duties as my wife. After all, you claim you have my best interests at heart, do you not? And it is not healthy for a man to remain unfulfilled for long."

"Take your filthy hands off of me, Michael Lancer," she rallied bravely.

"Ah, my pet, it won't work this time. There is no escape for you now. You will be mine tonight," he muttered.

His lustful gaze scorched her flesh and he pulled her close, despite her earnest struggles. Hot, searing kisses covering her lips. Boldly he ran his hand down the neck of her dress—down to her heaving breasts. His clumsy, drunken fingers clutched at her gown which obstructed his efforts.

Purple with rage at his drunken manhandling, Christy jerked free of his grip. She stumbled back against the wall, leaving him holding the torn cloth of her gown in his sweaty fingers. He stared down in momentary confusion, then turned and hungrily eyed the bare white skin of her heaving breasts. Undaunted by his slow reflexes, he began to slowly push her fighting body to the couch at the far side of the room.

"No! Stop it! Leave me alone, Michael!" she gasped as she struggled against him, kicking and punching at the air.

Though his mind was set, his body proved slow and sluggish from the excessive amount of alcohol he had consumed. It took all his concentration to control her as she struggled wildly to be free. Yet, despite his drunkenness, he was winning the battle. He continued to drag her across the room, but, his clouded vision failed to alert him to the chair which stood as an obstacle in his way. His leg banged squarely against the chair. Dull-witted, he lost his balance and toppled to the floor, dragging her with him.

She hit the floor hard, the breath knocked out of her as his weight fell on top of her. She groaned in pain, unable to move his dead weight from her.

Stunned, he remained still for a moment, trying to regain his senses. The fall sobered him slightly, and he clumsily sought to regain his footing. Once up, he extended his hand to her, but she rolled away and rose slowly to her feet. Fear was gone and she was consumed by an overpowering rage.

"I called you an animal once before. I see the title still fits. You took me once against my will, and I now carry the seed of that act in my womb. Is it now your wish to kill me and the tiny life which grows within me with your force and clumsiness, and thus rid yourself of two burdens at once?"

Something in the deadly seriousness of her voice and her blazing, determined eyes sobered Michael further. He rubbed his hands through his hair and gazed rather cautiously at her. He had again acted like a fool. But how could he make her understand that she so possessed his mind, he could do little but think of her? More than once today he had nearly missed an accident at the mill because his mind had been dwelling on her and not on the task at hand. He had eventually fled to a tavern in hopes of relieving the tension in his mind and body. Unfortunately both had proven futile and had, in fact, only made him even more desperate. Her beautiful, sensuous face came to mind all too often.

He looked again at her torn, rumpled dress and silky hair in disarray, feeling suddenly wretched, both mentally and physically. "I am sorry, Christy. God, I didn't mean to hurt you. I don't know what came over me," he offered in apology, ashamed beyond words. "It won't happen again. I promise. Please, forgive me," he pleaded, leaning heavily on the back of the chair.

Christy eyed him warily. She knew it was the alcohol that made him act as he had, yet she could not excuse him. She was ready to tell him so when suddenly his pallor increased and he clutched the desk to support himself. Without hesitation, she fetched a waste can and placed it before him. She had often witnessed the same reaction from Henry Slate after one of his drunken escapades, and knew only too well what was to follow.

When his sickness was over, she sat him in a chair and cleaned up the mess. All again in order, she stood before him, hands on hips, and shook her head in disgust.

"I think it is time you went to your room. I will help you," she said, pulling him up with great effort and taking his massive body under her shoulder.

At length they staggered to his room. She kicked open the door and sat him in a chair. Quickly she turned down the blankets of the bed and then returned to her semi-conscious husband.

He stared rather sheepishly at her through his sick, drunken haze as she struggled with great difficulty to remove his boots. He was powerless to assist her in undressing himself; a fact which only increased his shame. With firm yet gentle fingers, she removed his shirt and then regarded his tight trousers. He would have to bear the discomfort of his pants, for she dared not venture to remove them and again stir his more passionate senses.

Seeing she had done as much as she could to make him comfortable, she again tugged at his arm and dragged him to his feet. "Come, Michael. Get into bed. You will feel better in the morning," she said and hoisted him off the chair.

He was in too much of a stupor to argue, and was asleep before she could cover him with the blankets.

Christy stood over her sleeping husband, illuminated by the moonlight which filtered in through the balcony. He looked so serene and harmless, lying there, oblivious to the world. She wished he could be thus without the affects of drink. How could liquor evoke such contrary reactions in a man? One moment he was violent and vulgar, the next docile and childlike.

She shook her head in consternation. On impulse she bent down and brushed a kiss on his forehead, stroking his face with her hand. Perhaps this would be her only opportunity to ever have the upper hand on her wild and passionate husband. She took a final look at her sleeping prince and hurried from the room to seek her own bed.

Twenty-One

The bright morning sun filtered through the window balcony and awoke Christy early the next morning. She stretched luxuriously and then nestled back onto the pillow. She listened as Michael, in the adjacent room, rose and sluggishly prepared for his daily trip to the mill. No doubt he felt a bit under the weather from his large liquor consumption. She wondered just how much of the previous night he remembered. She had no intention of letting him forget his abhorrent behavior, yet she predicted that if he remembered anything of his sickness and her helping him to bed, his injured pride would be punishment in itself.

His door finally banged shut and she listened to the unusually heavy tread of his boots down the hall. Yes, he must certainly be paying for his drinking spree.

She rose, stretched and walked to the window. Michael and Hoffman were heading toward the stables. She watched the two men cross the yard. As if feeling her eyes upon him, Michael turned and looked up to her window. For a moment their eyes met. Christy hastily retreated behind the drapes, but not before seeing the scowl on his face deepen at the sight of her.

She shrugged listlessly. Apparently he was still very angry with her and would no doubt resume his charade of distant aloofness. "Damn him for a stubborn fool," she said aloud as she dressed for the coming day.

She descended the stairs slowly, wondering what new rumors the servants had spread after last night's noisy scene. She listlessly munched on some toast, at Bertha's insistence, but her appetite was minimal.

"Well, good morning, my dear. You're up early, as usual. May I join you?" asked Sir Phillip enthusiastically.

"Please do," she invited. "The sun shone in my window so brightly, I simply couldn't stay in bed and waste a moment of it," she said to her kind father-in-law. He seemed to be her only friend of late.

"I quite understand. It does promise to be a beautiful day. What busy schedule have you planned for today?" he asked as he commenced polishing off the steaming hot breakfast the maid placed before him.

"Oh, I have no special plans. I suppose I shall do a little reading or sewing—perhaps take a walk down to the pond," she said, trying to sound enthusiastic.

"Well, I must say that doesn't sound too exciting. Why, I have an idea! Unless you object, perhaps I can tear you away from your tasks. I am going to Charleston to check on some business at the shipyard. I do not relish the long trip alone and am in need of some charming feminine company. Would you do this old man the great honor of accompanying me?" he asked.

Christy's face lit up. She enjoyed being with her father-in-law, and the thought of an outing was terribly pleasing. "Oh, Father. The honor would be entirely mine. You spoil me with your kindness," she said with a bright genuinely happy smile.

"Nonsense, you brighten my day, little lady. Besides, I'm sure you are ready for a change of scenery after being closed in for so long. Even if my son chooses to ignore his lovely wife, you can be sure I will not follow his rude example," he said as he pushed his empty plate away.

"Oh, Michael is very busy, Father. He has many things on his mind. It would be selfish of me to expect too much of his precious time."

"Don't excuse him, Christina. You are far too liberal with him. You must be forceful and demand the time and attention you warrant as his wife. I fear if you don't take him to task now, he may come home more often as he did last night."

"Oh, you heard him then?" she asked with intentional innocence.

"I fear the entire community heard him, my dear."

"Yes, I was afraid of that. But he was not himself. I am sure he did not mean it and will not come home like that again," she said, again apologizing for him, yet all the while remembering too clearly his many cruel and cutting remarks.

"At the risk of interfering, Christina, may I say that I know my son only too well. I must stress the necessity of confronting him and discussing your differences. Get them out in the open. It is not good to allow these things to drag on indefinitely. Solutions become insurmountable."

"You are right, Father. But no matter what I say only

seems to upset him of late. My very presence is distressing to him. I . . . I just don't know what else to do but stay out of his way." A sparkling tear managed to spill down her cheek before she could wisk it away without being detected.

Sir Phillip reached across the table and patted her hand gently. "Take heart, my dear. Though my son has given you little cause to believe he cares for you, his heart is not nearly as cold as you might think. He feels a great deal for you. It is just difficult for him to express his emotions. Be patient and give him time. I am confident all will be resolved in due course," he said gently.

"I pray you are right, sir," she answered. "Oh, how I pray you are right."

Her glum appearance disturbed Sir Phillip, and he longed to bring back the sunshine to her smile. "Well now, enough of that. Run along and get your cloak, or your purse, or whatever other paraphernalia you ladies carry about. I shall meet you in the foyer in fifteen minutes and we will be off," he said with enthusiasm as he gulped the last of his black coffee and placed the cup noisily on the table.

Christy threw him a grateful smile and hurried to her room to collect her cloak and purse. Milly fetched her things and bade her mistress have an enjoyable day. Fifteen minutes later, and without a moment wasted, they were off in an open buggy heading for Charleston and chatting happily.

The exceptionally pleasant morning and afternoon passed all too quickly for Christy. They stopped at the busy harbor where Sir Phillip took her to his offices on the waterfront and showed her around, explaining different procedures and details of the shipping business.

His office, a small room set in the rear of a large warehouse, was piled high with papers, crates and assorted boxes. He cleared a paper-laden wooden chair for her to sit on, and then excused himself to take care of a few important matters. When he returned shortly, they resumed their tour of the shipyard.

Christy was fascinated by the complexity of the business and the many facets that went together to keep things running smoothly and profitably. Sir Phillip introduced her to a few of his foremen, and although she guessed they were a hard lot of men, they treated both of them with great respect.

Their tour finally at an end, they lunched at a quaint little cafe and then strolled leisurely past stores and shops, stopping now and again to admire some impressive item, or debate over something unusual.

It was truly a pleasant day and did much to improve Christy's sagging spirits. Tired but happy, they retraced their steps to the buggy. As they turned the corner, they suddenly found their path blocked by Matilda and the Lt. Governor Joanace heavily engrossed in conversation with a man Christy had never seen before. He was a short, stocky fellow of rather flabby proportions for his young years. He was dressed in a sea captain's uniform and Christy felt an uncanny warning that he was not a man to be crossed.

Sir Phillip groaned when he spied them, but could do little else but smile and extend a polite greeting.

On seeing Christy and Sir Phillip so unexpectedly,

Matilda's face burned hot. Christy wondered if the woman was suffering from the heat, but noted that even Joanace looked caught somewhat off guard and uneasy. She wondered if it was her imagnation, yet had the distinct feeling they had been discussing something to do with her.

The sea captain regarded Christy with open, unmasked interest. Again, was it her imagination, or did Matilda's hurried "Hello, dears, how are you?" seem a trifle off key and nervous? Was her laugh all too shrill and unnatural? And before either she or Sir Phillip could respond, all three excused themselves on pressing business and hurried off without another word, not even having the courtesy of introducing the sea captain.

"Peculiar woman, she is," muttered Sir Phillip as they stood watching the vanishing trio. "When I saw her I feared she would rush over and ruin our day, as she usually does. Instead, she turns and runs off like she'd been caught in some plot. Very peculiar, I must say. And, what business could she have with those sort of men?"

"Yes, their behavior was odd. But, Father, as you once told me, one must never be surprised at anything Matilda says or does. I am beginning to realize the wisdom of those words."

The strange encounter kept her pondering for days thereafter. . . .

Later in the week Christy sat at the dinner table facing her husband as he spoke with vigor and enthusiasm to his father about a new device he had installed at the mill. He is so handsome when he smiles, she thought, allowing her mind to wander slightly from the men's technical conversation.

With a glad smile, she remembered two days ago when they had returned from town. Michael had already arrived home from the mill and had been waiting patiently for them. She had watched closely to determine what sort of mood her husband was in and was simultaneously astonished and delighted at the change which had taken place. At dinner he had made a concerted effort to be completely charming, and showed great interest in their day's excursion. He complimented her warmly on her beautiful appearance and insisted on her presence after dinner in the study.

Since then, Christy still remained amazed at his change into a truly loving husband. He was constantly attentive to her every wish, and never failed to display some interest in her daily activities. This evening he was even more charming than usual, and she found herself responding warmly to her husband's sudden change of character. Perhaps when he had finally realized the consequences of his drunken escapade, he had reconsidered and decided to change his tactics. Whatever the reason for his unexpectedly congenial behavior, she was extremely happy with it. Even Sir Phillip noted with pleasure the change in them both. Had his son finally come to the realization that the way to win a lady's heart was not with force and anger, but with kindness and love?

A smile touched Christy's lips as she returned her attention to her husband.

"And, my dear, since you have persisted so diligently

in keeping the creditors from beating down my doorstep with your work on my accounts, I believe it is time you visited the mill to see for yourself how it works. Does the idea please you?"

"Oh, I would like that very much, Michael," replied Christy, eyes sparkling with excitement. "I am anxious to see just what occupies such a great deal of your time and interest."

Plans were made for an early departure, and shortly after the table was cleared, Christy summoned Milly and sought her bed. She wanted to be fresh and full of energy tomorrow for her husband. She knew she would not be faced with the melancholy she'd suffered of late in trying to sleep. She had something truly encouraging to look forward to.

Twenty-Two

The sky was a brilliant blue, and big, fluffy white clouds dotted the brightening eastern horizon as Michael and Christy set off on the chill October morning toward the mill. The trees were still a lusty green, but it would not be long before their colors would change to brilliant reds, rustic oranges and bright golds.

Christy enjoyed the beautiful countryside, and the feeling of her husband close beside her on the carriage brought her much contentment. His presence warmed her, and for the first time since their marriage, she felt very close to him. He had changed so quickly and completely, she wanted desperately to forget that vulgar, brutal man who had attacked her, and think only of the gentle, charming one who now sat at her side, tall and strong.

"Are you warm enough? Perhaps I should have brought along a blanket for you. The morning air is chilly this time of year," he said, eyeing her beside him.

Christy's spirits were high, and she was in a very playful mood. "Oh, no. I am fine, really. The day promises to be warm, and I am not yet old and decrepit that I need to be covered with a heavy blanket," she teased him.

"Indeed, madam, if you are old and decrepit, I envy those gentlemen of your generation for you certainly hold your age well," he said with a smile.

"And you, sir, may also boast of agility and good fortune, for even in my advanced age, you exceed my years and yet remain unaging," she bantered back, smiling mischievously.

"Oh, a deep blow, little wife. A deep blow indeed. Though I snatched you from the cradle, I am not so old and so senile as to overlook the charms and beauty of my young wife, or to take advantage of her generosities," he shot back and then threw his head back and laughed heartily at the surprised look which touched her face.

When she realized he only jested, she blushed at her own reaction and laughed with him.

They reached the mill in good time, and Michael ceremoniously swung his wife from the buggy and onto solid ground. Offering her his arm, they walked together through the thriving mill. Michael explained in some detail how the plant worked, and Christy marveled at the intricacies of the process.

He explained that some years ago he had conceived the idea of a mill to process the vast amounts of available lumber in the area. It had taken a considerable amount of time, labor and capital to get the mill constructed, and locate the necessary manpower. Less than two years ago the job had finally been completed. Now that he had the time and could devote his full attention to the mill, he was constantly designing newer, quicker and more efficient methods of operation.

As they walked around the mill, she noted with pleasure that his men treated him with admiration and great respect. Milly's father worked for Michael here at the mill, and the girl had often repeated her father's words of praise toward his employer as a fair and just man who often worked right alongside his people.

As they toured the mill, Michael was aware of the curiosity his wife generated among the mill workers. A few approached him on some trivial matter just to get a closer look at his new bride. He beamed with pride at the envious looks his men displayed, and thoroughly enjoyed his role as loving husband. Christy seemed to warm preceptibly to him also, and no one would have guessed their marriage was anything but ideal.

One of the men made a humorous statement, and her musical laughter filtered through the humming mill. As always, she looked beautiful today in a new gray tweed suit which had been purchased shortly before their wedding. Until two days ago, she had refused to wear any of the fine, beautiful things he had purchased especially for her. But since he had adjusted his attitude toward her in a positive direction, she had begun to dress in a more fashionable and becoming manner, hoping to please him.

This particular suit had a straight skirt, and a short, tight fitting jacket which came to her waist. A white lace blouse buttoned high on her neck, and ruffles spilled from the cuffs of the jacket and lapel. Her hair was tucked neatly beneath a small gray hat dipped stylishly to one side, and a large colored feather fluttered in the breeze as she moved her head from side to side. She was the perfect picture of a grand and gracious lady, and he was undeniably proud to have her by his side.

With a final look about to make sure all was as it should be, Michael ushered Christy back out into the sunshine. "Well, my dear, now that you have finally seen my little hobby, what do you think of it?" he asked as they headed back to the carriage.

"Oh, Michael, 'tis hardly a 'little hobby.' It far exceeds what I had imagined it to be like. It is simply marvelous, and so complex. I am very impressed. You are truly a genius to have designed such a complicated system. I see now that you were not simply a roving, carefree bachelor after all, but actually did have responsibility and other interests," she said and scooted away in a fit of giggling as he attempted to wack her unceremoniously on her bottom.

"Into the carriage, impertinent wife, lest I take you over my knee and teach you to have a little respect for your husband," he said as he helped her into the carriage. His eyes lingered on her swaying hips and his longings grew intense. He breathed heavily and jumped up in the seat beside her. Though she had warmed considerably toward him, he sensed she needed more time before she could accept his love.

"I hope you don't mind, but while we are out I would like to stop at the Anderson place for a few moments. Pete has some thoroughbreds I am anxious to take a look at. Perhaps you will enjoy it since you told me your father owned and trained horses," he said as they rambled down the road, leaving a trail of dust behind them.

"I would indeed enjoy it, Michael," she said enthusiastically.

"You must promise, however, dear wife, not to go galloping off astride one of his horses, for he is a conservative man and you might shock him," he teased and touched her leg with his own.

Christy blushed, remembering all too clearly the incident he referred to. "Oh, Michael, you needn't worry. I promised not to do that again. I realize how rash my actions were. Besides, I would not embarrass you in front of your neighbors. I promise to behave myself, as a good little wife should. Have I acted properly thus far?" she asked in innocent jest.

"You have far exceeded all expectations with your charm and beauty. You had my mill workers gawking enviously at you. And with the way you look today, my love, I find my own energies taxed to the hilt to refrain from continually staring at your radiance," he complimented. "Yes, you have made me a very proud husband," he said earnestly.

They continued on in comfortable silence for a short time, until Michael stopped the carriage in front of a large old house. A brown collie barked savagely at them, all the while his tail wagged vigorously in greeting.

Christy looked up to see a man, about thirty-five, with a mop of curly red hair and a matching beard approaching them at an easy gait. "That's enough, Turner," he called to quiet the dog, and then turned to his visitors. "Well, well, Michael. What a pleasant surprise to see you. It's been nearly a year, I believe, with you traveling and all.

What brings you here? You've no doubt heard of my new shipment of horses and come to take a look. They're a fine lot. I'll say so myself," he said. "You'll be glad you came."

Michael jumped down from the carriage and the two men shook hands vigorously. Their friendship went back many years.

"You're looking fit as ever, Pete. And just as sharp. And you're right about why I dropped by. I heard great things about your new line from Morgan, my stableman. He's a fine judge of horse flesh, but I had to come and see for myself," responded Michael.

He noted with amusement that his companion's eyes looked past him to the woman who waited patiently in the carriage. Taking his cue, he turned to Christina. "Forgive me, my love, for keeping you waiting," he said and offered her his arm. When she was down, he made the introductions. "May I present my young bride, Christina," he said. "My dear, this is an old friend of mine, Pete Anderson."

"I am very pleased to meet you, Mr. Anderson."

"Likewise, I'm sure, ma'am. I was surprised to hear Michael had finally gotten married. But now that I see you for myself, I can understand why," he complimented.

Christy dimpled prettily. It seemed her husband's roving bachelorhood had been common, widely circulated knowledge.

Michael laughed at his friend's straightforward remark. "You give away too many of my secrets, Pete." He turned to Christy. "You see, Christina, our families both moved here about the same time and we went to school together. We were and still are, for that matter, great friends, though we don't always see eye to eye on certain things. This red-haired leprechaun taught me just about everything I know about horses. He's the best horse expert in the territory. I often suspect he now regrets teaching me so much, for I was a good learner and it's not easy to fool me now," he laughed in ribbing jest.

Anderson's red hair seemed to redden further at Michael's good-natured insinuation. "Why, Michael, the way you talk, you'd think I tried to cheat you. I've been nothing but honest with you," he defended himself and turned to her. "He's exaggerating, of course, Mrs. Lancer, for I am an honest businessman." It was apparent he was slightly miffed at his friend's teasing remarks in front of his new wife.

"Ah, good friend, you've caught me there, for as I live and breathe you are the only honest horse trader I've ever known," he said and Pete Anderson lost his defensive look and beamed with pride.

"But be that as it may, I've brought another expert along with me, Pete. Christina tells me her father used to sell horses in London. I believe I can rely on her good judgment as well as yours," said Michael and placed a possessive arm about her tiny waist.

It was Christy's turn to be on the defensive and offer explanations. "Mr. Anderson, my husband greatly exaggerates my knowledge of horses. Though my father was indeed an expert in the field, my interests were mainly in riding and grooming. I paid little attention to line and breeding," she explained as they walked toward the corrals.

Four long rows of stables made up the Anderson ranch. Though not each stall was presently filled, it had a capacity of holding up to 100 horses. Behind the stables were large, divided corrals where the animals grazed leisurely in the autumn sunshine. The three walked along the fence toward the stables. Christy openly admired the number of fine horses Pete owned.

"I take great pride in my line of animals. I always have had a deep love for the beasts," he said, beaming slightly. "Yes, 'tis my first love—fine horses."

"Your first love, Mr. Anderson? But I thought you were married?" asked Christy, deliberately teasing him.

"Besides Becky, my wife, that is," he hastily clarified his remark. "Naturally I love my wife more, though at times she has accused me of putting the horses before her," he said, his face turning as red as his beard.

Michael could not but help Christy in her role as devil's advocate. "I must say, Pete, at times I believe Becky's accusations ring true. If she weren't such an excellent cook, you'd no doubt have sold her off long ago for a quality stallion," teased Michael.

Glad for the diversion onto safer grounds, Anderson was quick to extrapolate on the virtues of the fine animal before them. "This is my prize stallion, shipped all the way from France. As you can see, he's from fine stock. Got good teeth and straight lines, and his legs are firm," said Anderson proudly.

"Yes, he is indeed a fine-looking animal. But I'd still match my own stallion easily over this one," said Michael.

"Well, Michael, I must admit that black of yours was the best horse I ever had. His value would surely even now be doubled."

"Yes. I paid dearly for him, but would gladly do it again, for he serves me well," agreed Michael.

"He is an exquisite animal. I wholeheartedly agree with you both. His power and strength are a good match for my husband's. They ride perfectly together," commented Christy as she turned to regard the horses in the next stall.

They moved down the line, regarding each horse and its good and weak points. Christy soon became bored with their highly critical arguments and wandered away to explore on her own.

When she came to the end of the stable, one look at the horse inside brought out an involuntary exclamation of delight. The two men looked up, startled by her outburst, and hurried to her side.

"What is it, Christy? Are you all right?" Michael asked in concern, and then relaxed as he saw her gently stroking the nose of a docile, beautiful young filly.

"Oh, Mr. Anderson. What a beautiful little filly you have here. How young she is, but how strong and steady she stands, and has no fear of me," admired Christy openly.

"Oh, this mare and filly are indeed my pride and joy. I had my misgivings about her birth, for the mare did not fare well on the ship. But all went splendidly and both are healthy and strong. I am surprised, however, the filly and the mother even let you near them. They are quite protective of one another and even I have trouble at times getting their cooperation. And now here you are, standing there petting them both, easy as you please. 'Tis amazing, indeed," commented Anderson in real astonishment.

"I must admit, Mr. Anderson. I have a great love of Arabians. They are a graceful, intelligent and spirited breed," said Christy and continued to stroke the long, silky mane of the mare, while her filly nuzzled close. "I've not seen one since I left England. They are rare, indeed, even here."

"I am again astonished you know this breed, Mrs. Lancer. It is quite new to our fair land, and even to England. How is it you are so well acquainted with Arabians?" Anderson was impressed by her knowledge.

"My father traveled abroad frequently in search of new and fine breeds of animals. When he first saw this strain, he immediately realized their exquisite quality and had a few shipped to England. They became quite popular and my father was always thankful for his foresight. I took a special liking to these swift yet graceful horses, and when one of the mares gave birth, my father gave me her foal. I have never treasured a gift so highly. We grew up together and were practically inseparable," said Christy and gave the Arabian a final pat on her long nose.

"You brought her with you, then, to Charleston? I'd like to have a look at her," said Anderson.

Christy paused. The memory was still a painful one. "No. Two years ago . . . I was forced . . ." she stopped and began again. "Due to extenuating circumstances, she had to be sold. It was a sad experience for me, and I miss her still," said Christy, trying to avoid Michael's sympathetic brown eyes. She was a trifle too close to tears as it was.

Some of the gaiety had gone out of Christy's mood, and the two men strove to remedy the situation. It was not long before they succeeded and had her smiling and laughing once again.

After inspecting Anderson's remaining horses, they left the stables and stood in the hot afternoon sun bickering over the price of a few horses which had caught Michael's liking. Christy had no desire to take part in their business and meandered slowly across the yard, enjoying the warm sunshine and the soft breeze on her face. The men walked slowly behind, taking a step, then stopping to haggle, then walking and stopping again.

As she passed a small barn, she heard a rather peculiar yapping sound from within. Slightly curious, she pushed open the door and stepped inside, allowing her eyes to adjust to the darkness within. Once accustomed to the light, she followed the noises.

"Oh, you dear little things!" she cried as nine little puppies scrambled and jumped about their rather tired but content mother.

Keeping an eye on the mother dog, she bent slowly and reached out a hand to the little puppies, all struggling and demanding their noonday milk. "Oh, you are all so tiny and cute," she cooed as a fuzzy little head nudged against her leg.

"Christina, are you in here?" came Michael's voice from the doorway.

"Yes, Michael. I'm over here. Come and see what I've found," she called softly.

The two men approached and she rose with one whimpering little pup. "Look, Michael. Aren't they sweet?" she asked and cuddled the pup close.

"Oh, I see you've come across Babe and her pups, Mrs. Lancer," said Pete as he patted the Labrador on her head.

"I heard their crying and had to investigate. I hope you don't mind. They are just adorable," she said, eyes sparkling.

Michael had to agree the pups were cute, but his wife was far more adorable. She looked like a happy little girl who had stumbled across some hidden treasure. Her lips were curved in a soft smile, and her eyes sparkled merrily as she gently stroked the puppy nestled in the palm of her hand.

With a tiny sigh, she relinquished her little bundle of fur. "Well, little fellow, you'd better go back to your mother or you'll miss dinner," she said softly, putting him down and nudging him away. He paid no heed, but again nuzzled his way to her hands. "Go along now or there won't be any milk left after your brothers and sisters get done," she tried again, but to no avail.

"He's stubborn, that one," said Pete. "I'd say he's taken a liking to you, Mrs. Lancer. Unfortunately the litter is too big. The mother can only take care of eight pups, so one gets left hungry. I'm afraid I'll have to drown one—most likely that little one," he said, indicating the puppy she held in her hands. "He seems to be the runt and is getting no nourishment."

"Oh, no! You can't kill him!" cried Christy in horror and held the little brown puppy close to her face. "Oh, you just can't!" she said again, tears forming in her eyes.

"Well, Mrs. Lancer, I don't see what else I can do. It's better he not suffer than letting him starve to death," he said, feeling like a brute yet knowing there was little else he could do. "I've no time to be hand feeding a puppy, especially a runt like this one."

"Oh, there must be something else that can be done," she pouted as the puppy whimpered in her hands. "Oh, Michael, please, can I have him? I promise I will take care of him myself and he will be no trouble to anyone. He is so tiny and defenseless," she pleaded like a little child. "I could not bear to see him killed or starve to death."

"Christina, a puppy is a lot of work, and especially one that has to be hand fed. Besides, he's so small he will probably never amount to anything," said Michael. "If you really want a pup, take one of the larger, stronger ones that has a better chance."

"How can you judge like that? Because this particular puppy is small and defenseless does not mean he is worthless. Why, if you judge an animal by its size, do you also use the same criterion for people? I am small, too, even for a woman. Do you then consider me worthless as well?" she shot back in her own defense as well as the pup's.

Michael and Pete were stunned by her plausible argument.

"I dare say she's got you on that one," chuckled Anderson, glad he was not on the receiving end of her flashing green eyes.

"I certainly had no intention of comparing you to a runt, my dear. Stature has no bearing on a person's worth; animals are different sometimes, that's all. But, if it's all right with Pete, you can have the puppy. I know when I'm licked." Michael laughed and reached out to pat the puppy's fuzzy head.

"Oh, thank you, Michael. Thank you, Mr. Anderson." Christy's eyes sparkled once again. She forgot herself and stood on tiptoes to plant a kiss on Michael's cheek. Her action took him by surprise, leaving him delighted and momentarily speechless.

Anderson, again ready to retreat to safer ground, spoke up. "Well, now that that's settled, why not come and sit a spell? I'll get us something cool to drink. Becky should be home soon. She's out shopping. I'm sure she would like to meet you, Mrs. Lancer," he offered and indicated a pleasantly shady portion of the porch.

"No, thank you, Pete. We'd best be getting home. I've not fed my wife all day and she will be accusing me of being a poor provider. Besides, we've come from the mill and I'm sure she is tired," he said and looked at Christy for confirmation.

"Yes, Michael, I am tired and hungry. Perhaps some other time, Mr. Anderson. I would enjoy meeting your wife."

They headed for the carriage, and Michael helped Christy in. Once she and her little brown bundle were comfortably settled, he turned to bid his friend goodbye.

"Well, I'll be over sometime within the next two weeks to pick up my horses and settle with you, Pete, and tie up some loose ends. Give my regards to Becky, will you?" said Michael.

They shook hands and Michael stepped into the carriage beside Christy.

"It was nice meeting you, Mr. Anderson," she called.

"The pleasure was mine, Mrs. Lancer."

Michael slapped the reins over the horse's back. With a jerk the carriage set off, and Christy waved to Pete until he was a tiny speck in the distance.

"Thank you for letting me have the puppy, Michael. I'll take good care of him. He'll be no bother to anyone, I promise," she said and stroked the warm little puppy and purred softly to him.

"If that's all it takes to make you happy, I'll bring you ten puppies," Michael said, a little more huskily than intended.

"Oh, Michael, one is more than enough," she laughed and then paused at the peculiar, almost loving expression he had on his face. Their eyes met and held for a moment.

Unable to understand his look, she turned away in embarrassment. "Don't you think he's cute?" she said to break the silence.

Michael turned his attention to the little puppy who was sleeping soundly in his wife's lap. "Well, I suppose you could call him cute," he said rather begrudgingly. "I believe I might be just as content if you held me as close and gently as you hold him. Would you purr as nicely for me if I held you in my lap?" he laughed, but there was a note of seriousness in his tone.

"Well, dear sir, I am not a little puppy, nor do I purr like a kitten. And though the idea of sitting on your lap is not totally displeasing, I do believe it may be frowned upon as highly improper." She laughed a little nervously.

"I doubt it improper should a husband and wife enjoy such closeness in the privacy of their room, my love."

The conversation was becoming far too dangerous for Christy's liking. She changed the subject. "Don't the Andersons have any children?"

"No. It's very unfortunate. They want children very badly, but for some reason have had no success. Their house is big and empty without little ones. I think that's why Becky sometimes finds the need to go on shopping tours. At least Pete has his horses to keep his mind occupied. But they are still young enough and perhaps will yet have children."

"Fortunately we will not suffer from such uncertainty or fear, will we, my husband? We will have a son, and he and this little puppy will grow up together and have each other to play with, won't they?" she said, holding up the puppy and looking into his sad black eyes.

"Are you sure it will be a boy, then?" he asked, somewhat amused by her certainty.

"Oh, I have no doubt of it. And I'm sure he will be as stubborn and bullheaded as his father, too," she replied.

Michael turned in his seat, ready to retort, when he saw the mischievous look on her slightly upturned lips. "Oh, you little vixen. You should talk about my stubbornness. Why, I've a strong desire to stop this buggy and put you over my knee. 'Tis high time you learned who the boss of this family is," he said.

"Sir, you would not dare?" It was half a question, half a statement.

"My dear, I imagined you knew me well enough by now to realize I do not often speak in idle threats. Why, I could accomplish the deed quite easily here in the open, with no interference from the servants," he said, and to emphasize his words, he stopped the buggy, placed the reins on his knee, and turned to his wife.

"Michael . . . I . . . I was only teasing. I did not think you would take me seriously," she stuttered, contemplating her chances of escape.

"Yes, the more I think of it, the more merit the idea has. You dealt me quite a few blows this afternoon with your quick tongue. Perhaps a little spanking would be my only means of retribution."

"Oh, gentle, understanding husband. I implore you reconsider. My pride as well as my bottom are easily injured. Think of the grave damage you could render to my tender person," she argued, displaying to him the most innocent and meekest of expressions.

Michael looked at his wife steadily. He knew her game, yet when she looked at him thus, his defenses crumbled and he could no longer let her believe him serious. Though he never had any intention of carrying out his threat, the prospects had some beguiling possibilities.

"Though you use your look of sweet and tender innocence to flay the enemy, it could well prove to be your downfall, for it makes me eager to forget the battle and move directly to collect the prize."

His words, as he could see by the slightly worried expression on her face, had only increased her concern. "However, I believe I shall forego both the battle and the spoils and head directly home. I fear I would make a poor warrior, for my stomach cries out for appeasement so that I must forget all else until it is satisfied. So, dear wife, we will call it a draw and begin with a clean slate. Are these terms agreeable to you?"

"Indeed, kind opponent. As usual, your wisdom has saved the day. Now, I bid you make haste for home lest my puppy, my baby, and myself die from lack of nourishment," she bid regally.

"Your wish is my command, my lady," he replied and urged the horse homeward.

When they were within sight of Penncrest, Christy lightly touched his knee. "Michael, I had a wonderful day today. Thank you so much," she said quietly.

"The pleasure was mine, Christy. I promise it will be only the first of many happy days to come," he answered and gently squeezed her fingers.

Twenty-Three

Christy rose, put on a warm robe and stepped out onto the balcony into the crisp morning air. In the week since her trip to the mill with Michael, the weather had changed drastically. The days were cold, and frost nipped the grounds at night. Nature had also turned the area into a mass of brilliant colors. Leaves that would soon fall to the ground and die put forth their last mighty effort and carpeted the landscape with brilliant autumn shades.

Such was the scene that greeted her on this cool sunny dawn that would all too quickly develop into a day of lengthy preparation and nervous excitement. In only a few hours hence, she would be seated beside her new husband heading for her very first ball.

But dancing was the least of her worries this night. Would she measure up to the wealthy and influential people she would meet? She desperately wanted to make Michael proud of her. Their marriage had caused considerable commotion in the community, and no doubt everyone there would be exceptionally critical of her as an unknown outsider.

Feeling somewhat more at ease, she summoned Milly, who entered cheerful and smiling with her mistress's breakfast. Christy was genuinely fond of the sweet girl who was not much younger than herself. They got along splendidly, and Christy was grateful for Bertha's wisdom in choosing the girl. They had become close friends, and at times it might have been difficult for a stranger to distinguish maid from mistress. They learned much from one another, also. Milly taught her some of the little tricks and airs of acting the grand lady, and in turn Christy began to teach the maid how to read and write.

They spent most of the morning adjusting the velvet gown to accommodate her swelling waistline, talking and exchanging information on the ball and who might be there with whom. After lunch, they took a short walk about the grounds, as much for fresh air as for a diversion, and then returned to begin the lengthy dressing.

Milly was especially good at fixing Christy's hair, and after a leisurely toilette, Christy sat before the mirror while Milly combed her long, clean, silky tresses until they shone. With deft fingers, she then arranged her mistress's beautiful long hair in dangling curls upon her head. It was a time consuming and involved process, but one both women enjoyed. After nearly an hour, Milly tucked in place the last curl and stood back to survey her handiwork.

"It looks lovely, Milly. You've far outdone yourself again," complimented Christy as she tilted her head from side to side, sending the dark curls in a merry dance about her head. A sudden loud knock from the door startled them both.

"Christina, are you nearly ready? I wish to speak with

you a moment," came Michael's voice from behind the door.

"Oh no, my lord. Mistress Christy is not dressed. You cannot come in," cried Milly in a tither. It would not do for him to see her until she was ready and looked her best.

"I fail to understand why I cannot see my own wife, with or without clothing," he said a trifle angrily. "Now will you open the door, or shall I?" he demanded, reaching for the doorknob.

Christy flew to the door and turned the lock to bar his entrance. "I am sorry, Michael, but you must wait until I am ready. I shan't be much longer," said Christy, winking at Milly.

"That's ridiculous, Christina. Now open this door," he boomed and pulled impatiently on the knob.

A torrent of giggling sounded through the door, but its occupants refused to admit him.

"Whatever you wish to speak to me about will simply have to wait, sir. Now please be patient and I will be down shortly," replied Christy. She did not wish to make him angry, but she would not give in this time.

"Damn fool women," he muttered under his breath, but they heard his heavy footsteps pounding down the hall and eventually fade away.

Christy and Milly breathed a sigh of relief and giggled merrily at one another. Christy wanted to look her best for Michael tonight. It was important he be proud of her. He was angry now, but she would contend with that later.

Powder on her nose and a blush to her cheeks, Christy

slipped into her emerald green velvet dress. She had fallen in love with this dress when she had first seen it at the dressmaker's shop. It seemed like such a long time ago; so much had happened since then. It had appeared a waste of money to purchase such an expensive and elegant gown then, since she was only a bond servant. But now she could truly enjoy the elegance it brought as Mrs. Michael Lancer.

Milly hurriedly fastened the many tiny pearl buttons in the back of the gown, and turned to give her mistress a thorough inspection. "Oh, Mistress Christy. You look beautiful, just beautiful. Without a doubt you will be the loveliest lady at the ball. The others will surely die of jealousy," she breathed and clasped her hands together in pride at her young mistress.

Slowly Christy moved to scrutinize her image in the mirror. Yes, she had to admit she did look nice. She could feel it. The emerald of the dress matched her eyes perfectly, and her dark hair shone in lustrous contrast. Long, wide sleeves hung in huge billowing folds, delicately edged in fine white lace. The neckline plunged deeply to reveal her full, swelling breasts in a most provocative manner. She blushed at her own bold display, but Milly reassured her the cleavage was most fashionable and quite becoming. The waistline gathered tightly, due to her slightly growing stomach, but unless distinctly pointed out, no one would notice.

A soft smile touched her lips as she turned to face Milly. She was pleased with her appearance and hoped her husband would find no fault.

"Well, Milly, I guess I am ready at last, and cannot

improve further on what I have. Besides, I dare not keep Master Michael waiting much longer for I do not want him to be too impatient with me."

Her ruby red lips trembled slightly in fear and excitement at prospects of the coming ball. She had always dreamed of going to such a party in a beautiful gown, escorted on the arm of a handsome man. Now her dream was becoming reality.

"Have a wonderful time, my lady. And remember, hold your head high and proud, for you have naught to be ashamed of," were Milly's last minute words of advice as she opened the door and Christy slowly stepped out.

"Thank you, Milly. I will try to remember that," she said and the two women hugged one another tightly.

Taking a deep breath to calm her fast-beating heart, she curved her slightly parted lips into a soft smile and glided down the dark hallway. She stopped in the shadows and glanced down below to where Michael paced impatiently, venting his wrath upon a patient Bertha.

"What can be keeping her so long, Bertha? She and Milly have been locked up in that room all day. Why does it take women an eternity to get dressed? We'll end up being late," he ranted.

Bertha offered no comment. How could a man ever understand the careful, and unhurried preparations that went into making a woman beautiful?

"Humph!" he grumbled again, becoming more agitated by the moment. "Run up and tell her to hurry, will you? My patience is about gone," he stormed back and forth across the shining waxed floor.

Christy watched in silent amusement as he paced.

Despite his irate temper, he looked dashing in a dark suit and tightly fitting trousers and waistcoat which accentuated his lean, strong torso. A white ruffled shirt completed the picture as he pounded back and forth in finely polished high black boots.

His dark brown hair was carefully groomed and tied with a black ribbon, and his face was smooth and clean shaven. His appearance was impeccable, and Christy could not have asked for a more handsome escort. She would have to keep her eye on him lest some pretty lady snatch him away.

She decided it best to make her entrance before he tore up the house, so she glided slowly and gracefully down the stairs. As she silently moved, she spoke in a quiet, reserved voice, just loud enough to catch his ear. "I am sorry to have kept you waiting, my lord. I am ready now."

He was halfway across the room when he heard her voice. "It's about time," he began, spinning about and striding toward the stairs, ready to scold her severely. "Why the devil did it take you so long? I . . ." his reprimand died on his lips as he gazed up at the vision of loveliness above him. "I . . . I . . ." he stuttered rather breathlessly as he stood rooted to the spot below her.

She could not have asked for a more enjoyable reaction, and smiled prettily. Hand on the railing, she glided the rest of the way down the stairs and stopped to stand before him. She was totally enjoying his speechlessness, though she sought to hide it from him.

"I really am sorry to have kept you waiting. Please, forgive me, my husband," she said with deliberate meekness. He still did not speak, so she fluttered her long eyelashes in a flirtatious fashion. "Does my appearance please you?" she asked coyly, spinning about to give him a complete picture.

Michael took a deep breath and finally regained his voice. Yet when he spoke, it sounded quite noticeably deeper than it had only a moment before. "My dear, to behold such loveliness I would have waited for all eternity."

"You are too kind in your praises, dear sir. But I strive only to please you. Your wish is my command." She continued on with the game, smiling meekly at him and again fluttering her long thick lashes provocatively at him. When he again remained silent, she stepped away from him, letting her skirts sway in a tantalizing fashion.

"You speak little, my lord, which is unlike you. Perhaps the dress does not please you. I can always change to my shirt and trousers and play the tomboy. I believe you considered me less trouble then. But you need only tell me what is your desire, and I will too gladly comply," she flirted and again turned to face him.

With deliberate slowness, Michael regarded his wife. From her gleaming curls, sparking emerald eyes and invitingly parted lips, to the tips of her small slippered feet, she looked ravishing.

Rallying to the cause, he called her bluff. "You look far too enchanting to share with anyone else this night, my love. I believe we shall forego the ball, for I want you all to myself. I should be insanely jealous should any other man even glance your way. And since I cannot take my eyes from you myself, I am sure every other man will have the same difficulty. No doubt I shall be fighting off your admirers all night. Since that will surely be the case, I shall spare myself the torment and enjoy your loveliness in solitude."

His eyes sparkled with the joy of the blow well struck as he watched her coy smile turn to a somewhat nervous frown.

Again she had played her game too well, and had unwittingly incited his passionate desires. She did not want to fight him off tonight, nor did she want to miss the ball. "Oh, Michael, you would not deny me the opportunity of going to such a grand party, wearing a beautiful gown, and on the arm of a handsome escort?"

He stepped beside her, feeling the victor and grinning devilishly. "You would reject an offer of my undying devotion this night to attend a mere party? Ah, my love, you cut me to the core, inflicting upon me a mortal wound," he said, striking his chest above his heart. "But fear not, fair maiden. You will go to your fine ball, and acquire the envy of every woman, while I am forced to fight off the advances of every man. But first you must suffer another gift from your devoted husband. Come along to the study for a moment. I have something to give you," he said and took her hand in his, drawing her along reluctantly behind him.

When the door to the study was closed behind them, he opened a safe which stood concealed behind the desk and drew out a small box. Christy watched in silence, wondering what he was about.

"This was my mother's, and her mother's before her. It is of great sentimental value. Before she died, she bade me carry on the tradition and give it to the woman I chose as wife. I give it to you now, Christina," he said and placed the satin-covered box in her hands.

She looked questioningly at him. Whatever lay inside the box was very important to him, for he had loved his mother deeply. She felt an incredibly overpowering happiness inside that he should give her so dear a gift. Surely he must care something for her to part with such a token.

With trembling fingers, she slowly slid open the lid. "Oh, Michael!" she gasped in surprise and delight, hardly believing her eyes. "It's . . . exquisite!" she exclaimed, touching the necklace almost reverently.

Five large, dark, teardrop-shaped emeralds were set in a delicate spray pattern with dozens of tiny intermingled sparkling diamonds, all connected on a delicate gold chain. It was beautiful and positively priceless.

"I would be greatly honored if you would wear it tonight, my love. It will look lovely with your eyes and your dress."

Christy nodded, too overcome with happiness to speak.

"Allow me," he whispered, taking the jewel from the box.

With great care he fastened it about her neck, deliberately allowing his fingertips to linger on her long white neck and creamy shoulders. The path of his fingers left trails of fire wherever he touched, and she closed her eyes, reluctant to break the spell. He placed a soft kiss upon her bare shoulder and turned her to face him.

"You look magnificent, Christina," he whispered, almost reverently as he gazed down at her. "I am indeed the most fortunate of men to have a wife as lovely as you."

She felt a fire within herself near bursting. The dark, firelit room, the exquisite gift, and her husband's tender words were weaving a spell she found difficult and unwilling to break. Her eyes danced with happiness, and she fingered the priceless jewels lovingly. All too aware of her own racing pulses, she sped to the mirror across the room to see the jewels for herself.

"Oh, Michael, I don't know what to say. I've never had anything so beautiful. I will cherish it always," she breathed.

The crackling fire and their heavy breathing were the only audible sounds in the firelit room. Michael moved up behind her, watching her glowing reflection in the mirror. Her beauty was intoxicating, and in another moment he would be powerless to stop himself from kissing that slender neck and traveling slowly down to find the treasures which lay just out of sight beneath her gown.

Suddenly a sharp knock on the door intruded upon the silence of the room. They pulled apart suddenly.

"I'm sorry to interrupt, sir, but the carriage is ready and the horses grow restless," apologized Morgan, the coachman, in some embarrassment. His eyes traveled from the slight frown on his master's face at the interruption to the glowing countenance of the young mistress.

"Yes, yes of course, Morgan. My wife has bewitched me and I lost track of the time. We will be along directly," said Michael.

"Very good, sir," Morgan said and turned to go. "If I may be so bold, my lady. You look beautiful tonight."

"Why, thank you, Morgan. You are very kind," she said sweetly and moved away from her husband to a safer distance.

"I cannot but agree, Morgan. She will certainly be the most beautiful woman at the ball. But as you say, we'd better be on our way. Ask Milly to fetch Mrs. Lancer's cloak," he said.

He extended his arm to Christy as they left the room. "It seems even my coachman is anxious to have you close so he may gaze upon your loveliness. I must beg you not to leave my side this night, for someone will surely snatch you from me, and I would die from a broken heart," he declared sincerely.

Christy smiled in genuine happiness as he helped her with her cloak. Once settled in the cold carriage, she sat close beside him, grasping at the heat his body radiated. She shivered slightly. How close she had come to meeting his desires. It was frightening and exciting both. As the blush on her cheeks cooled from his tender advances in the study, she shivered again with a new nervousness at the prospects of meeting his friends and neighbors.

Michael had explained earlier that Molly and Henry Middleton owned an extremely prosperous rice plantation. Each year, for the past five years, they held an extravagant ball. The wealthiest and most influential families in the area would be in attendance. For that reason, an invitation to attend was considered mandatory to retaining social prestige in the community.

These facts' only intensified the knot forming in Christy's stomach.

Twenty-Four

It was a relatively long trip to the Middleton's who lived just outside of Charleston, but Michael kept up an unusually lively level of conversation. He was in high spirits and anxious to show off his new bride to those who had not as yet met her. His interesting stories about some of the guests made her feel a little less nervous and more equal to the task ahead.

The huge, white-pillared and well-lit house was visible from quite a distance away, and as they approached the sound of laughter greeted their moving carriage. Before Morgan could descend, a well-dressed footman opened the carriage door, handed Christy out, and held the door for Michael. Morgan noted with pride how the man's gaze lingered long after his mistress had climbed the stairs and disappeared into the house. His young master had done well to bide his time until now in choosing a wife.

A formal, erect butler opened the door before they could knock. Once inside, Michael and Christy were met by a middle-aged, rather stiff-laced maid who promptly took their cloaks and pointed the way to the noisy ballroom.

High-pitched female laughter drifted down the hall,

along with the sounds of the orchestra tuning up. The heavily perfumed air was mixed with tobacco smoke, which cast a hazy, cloudy look upon the gaily lit and lively ballroom.

Michael took Christy's hand and tucked it securely under his arm. Her fingers were cold and trembled slightly, and he squeezed them reassuringly. "Ready, love?" he whispered.

Christy gripped his arm firmly. His strength and confidence, plus his one tiny yet so precious word of endearment were all the support she needed. She took a deep breath and up went her chin, eyes flashing with confidence. "Yes, Michael. I am ready," she answered in a cool, steady voice.

Michael raised an eyebrow in wonder at the quick change from shy, unsure girl, to a woman with poise and elegance. She was truly a marvel, and he looked forward to showing her off as his prized possession.

They strolled arm in arm into the crowded, gaily lit ballroom, and waited patiently in the reception line for their host and hostess. They stood in the entranceway, in plain view of all, but neither was aware of the sudden hush in the room, followed almost immediately by quickly wagging tongues.

In only a moment Mr. and Mrs. Middleton disengaged themselves from the crowd and moved quickly to greet the new arrivals. "Oh, I'm so glad you decided to come, Michael. The ball would certainly not be complete without a representative from the Lancer family. I do regret your father was called out of town and could not attend," bubbled Mrs. Middleton.

She was dressed in a wine-colored gown of expensive satin which complemented her rather plump figure. Her husband wore a dark brown suit, carefully tailored to fit his heavy frame in a becoming manner. It was easy to surmise that the Middletons had a fondness for living life fully and completely.

"And this must be your beautiful new bride. It is so nice to have you come. Please accept our heartfelt congratulations and best wishes on your marriage. We really had our doubts of ever seeing Michael wed, but I see he has done wisely in waiting," complimented Mrs. Middleton with a friendly warmth Christy immediately appreciated.

"Thank you, Molly," replied Michael on behalf of his wife. "I had not realized my bachelorhood caused such a stir until I finally gave it up. I feared married life entailed too great a sacrifice, but I now find it quite pleasant. My only regret is not having met Christina sooner," he said and squeezed her hand lightly.

"Yes, I can certainly understand that, Michael my boy. You definitely have chosen yourself a beauty. If I were only thirty years younger . . ." agreed Mr. Middleton with a twinkle in his eyes.

Christy's cheeks pinkened at their unmasked appraisal, but Michael was ready with a quick reply. "Thank you both. I consider myself extremely lucky to have found such a rare flower." He smiled down at her in a most endearing manner, and Christy's heart swelled with hope. Dare she believe his words held some small note of truth and tenderness?

"Oh, Henry. Look. Here are the Eldermans. I'm so

glad they could come, especially so soon after little Carrie's illness," said Mrs. Middleton as a handsome couple walked through the door. "Would you please excuse us while we say hello to Doris and Matthew?" asked Mrs. Middleton as she drew her husband away. "Please make yourselves at home and have something to eat and drink. The dancing will begin shortly."

"Thank you. It is a pleasure to meet you," answered Christy as Michael drew her into the thriving party.

As they moved slowly around the room, Michael introduced her to friends and acquaintances. Most of the people she met were genuinely friendly and congratulated them on their recent marriage. Though there were a few awkward questions raised about how and when they met, Christy answered smoothly and in generalities, which seemed to satisfy the inquisitive. They portrayed the ideally content newlyweds, and she felt a strange happiness growing within which radiated from her whole being. Her striking beauty brought admiring stares wherever she went, but she was oblivious to all but the handsome man who remained devotedly at her side.

After a few more introductions, they sought the privacy of a quiet corner and sipped contentedly on champagne punch.

"Michael, I fear this strong drink will go to my head if I am not careful," began Christy, but was suddenly interrupted by a rather loud and boisterous voice.

"Well, well, Mike. Who is this ravishing beauty you've not let out of your sight?" the man began.

Michael grimaced and Christy felt him stiffen as the heavy-set young man approached. No one called him

Mike, and he obviously held no friendly feelings for this man.

"Hello, Gregory. I am surprised to see you here. I'd thought you were still off pirating around the coast, despite the recent tax on imported slaves. It seems you and your kind, like Henry Lauren's, feel no remorse at the pain and suffering you inflict. Your pockets must be suffering, though, for I notice your 'cargo' is shorter these last trips due to the tax," said Michael with a contempt he did not even try to hide.

"Why, Michael, my line of work is just as respectable as yours. We are all in business to make money. My business just happens to be in the transfer of population from one area to another. We are all well aware of your views on slavery. It's easy enough for you to condemn the practice since you don't need massive labor forces in your shipping and timber mill businesses. But, I warrant if sailing gets any more hazardous and less profitable, you'll change your views quick enough," he said in a condescending tone.

"Now see here, Piper . . ." began Michael, his temper flaring.

"Oh calm down, Mike. No need to get all riled up. We can battle out the issue some other time. Right now I'm interested in meeting this ravishing young creature beside you," he said, cutting Michael off rather rudely.

"Gregory, may I present my wife, Christina," he said rather gravely. "Christina, this is Captain Gregory Piper."

Something in the sarcastic grin the man bestowed on her tickled Christy's memory, but she could not quite place where she had seen this man before.

"Your husband does not approve of my work, but it pays well," he said smoothly, and before either could anticipate his movements, he seized her hand and held it tightly in his sweating fingers. "But, enough of that unpleasant business. I would much prefer to concentrate on you. You are indeed an enchanting little creature," he drolled on. "I've been anxious to meet you ever since I saw you and the elderly Lancer in Charleston."

Suddenly Christy realized he had been the sea captain she had seen conspiring with Matilda and Lt. Governor Joanace. Meeting him face to face was even more unsettling than at a distance. She simply could not shake the feeling that somehow her fate would be determined by some act of this man.

His very touch made her skin crawl in repulsion, yet she could not pull her hand away without appearing rude. His eyes lingered overlong on her swelling breasts until she felt naked before him. He was totally disgusting, and she was overjoyed when Michael whisked her away on an excuse to meet another friend. "Oh, Christina, there are Pete and Becky Anderson. I do want you to meet Becky. Please excuse us, Gregory."

"Of course, dear boy. Of course. It has been a real pleasure, madam. I look forward to seeing you again," he said eloquently, releasing her hand begrudgingly. His gaze lingered on her long after they had moved away, and his eyes glinted in a wicked manner.

"I am truly sorry you had to endure Piper's attentions, Christina. I had no idea the Middletons would invite scum like that to their party," he said angrily as he maneuvered her through the crowd.

"Perhaps he has come as someone else's guest," offered Christy. Though she did not know the man, she could easily share Michael's dislike of him.

"No one in their right mind would associate with someone of such low character. He is a detestable human being, as is his business. I will make every effort to keep him away from you, my dear," assured Michael as they approached a young couple standing alone.

When Pete spied Michael and Christy moving in his direction, he tugged on his wife's arm and rushed over to meet them. "Well, Michael, Mrs. Lancer. It's good to see you again. I had heard you were not coming. I'm glad you changed your mind. No doubt you've come to show off your beautiful bride," he winked at Michael.

By now a large-framed young woman, easily matching the height of her husband, came to join the group. Though Becky Anderson was an exceptionally large woman, she was dressed impeccably in a dark blue gown and was quite attractive.

The two women, so physically different, surveyed one another for a moment in silence. Simultaneously smiles appeared. They knew instantly that they would be friends.

"You must be Christina. Pete spoke of little else the day you stopped. He certainly did not exaggerate your beauty," she said in a straightforward, complimentary manner. "I've been simply dying to meet you since he told me in minute detail how you stood up for me and my shopping. I knew right then we'd be friends."

"Well, Mrs. Anderson . . ." began Christy.

"None of this 'Mrs. Anderson' stuff. Since we're to be friends, the name is Becky."

"You are right, of course, Becky. As soon as I heard your husband mention your name, I knew we would get along well together. It's all very strange yet exciting, as though we've known one another for years," said Christy.

The two women stood off, chatting happily together, and their husbands, seeing themselves excluded from the conversation, took to discussing their favorite topic—horses.

After a few moments, Peter Anderson intervened on their conversation. "And how is that little puppy of yours?"

"Oh, Mr. Anderson. He is doing just fine. Why, I can hardly feed him enough he is that hungry. I fear he will grow so big he will eat us out of house and home. I have named him Brutus, for I have great expectations for him," answered Christy. They all laughed and continued their light banter for a few more minutes.

"Well, I can see the orchestra is just about ready to begin playing, and before I start dancing I simply must quiet my ravishing appetite with some of that delicious food over there. Would you excuse us? We'll see you later," apologized Becky as she and Pete headed for the large table of food.

They both laughed, and Christy was about to make a comment to Michael when she felt her arm being forcefully pulled from his. She turned in surprise at the rough handling, and to her dismay, saw Matilda Lancer seize her husband possessively and greet him in an overly affectionate manner.

"Why, Michael dear, how marvelous to see you here. You told me you were not coming. You look as dashing as always. I cannot keep my eyes off you. 'Tis truly mine and all the other single ladies' misfortunes that you've gone and gotten married," she said, a trifle too loudly so that those standing nearby could not help but hear.

She waited expectantly for him to return the compliment, but to her embarrassment, he remained silent. She was dressed in an exquisite gown of navy satin that gave full credit to her substantial bosom and slim waistline. Her hair was piled high on her head, and her heavily darkened eyes and lips spoke their own message to Michael.

Christy was acutely embarrassed by Matilda's outward show of affection toward Michael. She had deliberately snubbed her, not only by completely ignoring her, but by her insulting comment. Christy sensed those around were waiting for her reaction, and she knew she would be judged by her behavior. She ached to turn and scratch Matilda's eyes out. Instead she smiled sweetly at the two.

"Yes, Mrs. Lancer. I quite agree. Michael presents a most handsome picture, does he not? I am indeed quite lucky to have him as my husband," she paused innocently as those about grinned behind their drinks. "You look charming tonight, also, Mrs. Lancer. I am sure you have all the gentlemen's admiring gazes," she added as a finishing touch. Matilda was certainly not prepared for such an open compliment from the woman she had just insulted. She noted with some dismay the hidden grins of those standing nearby. How dare this little tart make a fool of her! It would serve them both right if she announced to the whole crowd the true reason for the sudden marriage. Feeling trapped into returning the compliment, Matilda begrudgingly muttered, "Why thank you, my dear. You look lovely, also." It was obvious the words were spoken with great difficulty.

Christy smiled prettily, playing the perfect lady, and made a slight curtsey. Was Matilda's face green with envy, or was her green pallor simply a reflection off her own emerald dress? Regardless, the thought was comforting to Christy.

Matilda sniffed and smiled stiffly. This girl was again turning things to her own favor. She decided she needed help in dealing with her. She turned and waved vigorously to a male reinforcement heading toward the small group.

Michael groaned at Gregory Piper's approach.

"There you are, darling," she said, relieving him of one of the glasses of punch he carried. "How terribly sweet of you to treat me with such devotion," she oozed sweetness and put a polished hand upon the sea captain's arm. "I believe you know Greg Piper, Michael dear," Matilda said, again ignoring Christy. "He docked just three days ago after a short trip to Barbados and was gallant enough to escort me to this grand ball," she said smugly, hoping for some jealous reaction from Michael. Instead he only looked in disgust at the two. Who else but Matilda would associate with such a cad?

"The pleasure is mine alone, madam," said Gregory. She fluttered her eyelashes and bestowed upon him a wide, inviting smile.

His eyes, however, did not remain long on Matilda. He looked past her to the small beauty at Michael's side. "I have already had the pleasure of seeing Mike and meeting his delightful young bride," he said and again devoured Christy with his eyes.

Michael's arm went possessively about Christy's waist. In another second he would throttle the wretch for openly looking at Christina in such a lustful manner. To his relief and Christy's, however, the orchestra leader asked for silence and Mrs. Middleton addressed the gathering.

"On behalf of Henry and myself, we welcome all of our distinguished guests. It is truly our pleasure to have you all here, for we do so look forward to having you come to our annual Thanksgiving Ball. Please, enjoy yourselves. There is plenty to eat and drink, and should you crave something you don't see, you need only ask. But, enough of that. You all know you are free to help yourselves. Besides, you came here to dance, not listen to me prattle on," she laughed and everyone clapped. "Thank you. Thank you all. Now, Henry and I usually ask two of our distinguished guests to open the ball. This year, in honor of our newly married couple, I would ask Mr. and Mrs. Michael Lancer to open the floor to dancing. Would you two do us the honor of leading the ball?" she asked.

Everyone turned to the startled couple and clapped. Michael bowed graciously to his hostess. "Christina and I would be honored," he said and offered Christy his arm.

Immediately her knees began to shake, and she was glad for his support as he led her to the center of the floor. "Michael, it's been years since I last danced. I was only a little girl then," she whispered. The confident smile which lit up her face completely belied the fear pulsing through her.

"Fear not, my lovely lady. Relax and enjoy it. I will take great care with you," he smiled back as the orchestra jumped into a lively waltz.

In only a few short steps, she found herself swaying and gliding easily across the spacious, highly polished floor. She followed his every movement as he spun her into graceful turn after turn. She became oblivious to all about them; aware only of his hand, sure and strong about her waist, and his handsome face smiling reassuringly at her as they swirled on a cloud around the marble floor in perfect time to the music. Her cheeks were delicately pink as their eyes locked together. Love gripped them both and held them in its bewitching web.

Their magnetic happiness penetrated the room, and people stopped talking to form a circle about them as they danced slowly and smoothly about the floor. They made a stunning couple, with him so tall and lean, and her so radiant and petite.

The waltz ended and another began. The floor soon became crowded and Michael and Christy had to make room for the others. But the moment was forever etched in her mind. Her greatest expectation had become reality, and had far exceeded itself. She was gloriously happy.

The evening passed all too quickly for her. Christy found herself constantly besieged by eager men who pleaded for an opportunity to whirl her once about the floor. Not wanting to be impolite, she graciously accepted, and suffered with a smile as some of her less agile partners stepped heavily on her lightly slippered feet.

Finally, in almost desperate exhaustion, she searched frantically in the crowd for that one handsome face that meant so much to her. When at last she spied him, the anxious expression on her face clearly urged him to rescue his bride in all due haste. He eased his way through the dancers and tapped her current admirer on the shoulder. "Please, excuse me, Mr. Dartman. Would you mind if I reclaimed my wife for this dance?" he asked politely.

"Course not, old man. Course not. You're a lucky fellow," said the heavy-set man as he begrudgingly relinquished his stunning partner.

"Oh, thank you, Michael. I did not think I could stand one more person tramping on my feet. I am exhausted," she breathed in relief as he spun her around the floor.

"Oh, my dear wife. Did I not warn you that you would be besieged with ardent admirers? 'Tis the price you must pay for being the bell of the ball," he teased lovingly and whirled her off the floor and offered her a brimming glass of hearty punch. "Drink this. It will relax you a little."

In a few moments the punch eased the aches in her body, and she and Michael watched the dancers floating about the room.

"Well, my love, most of the guests are beginning to leave. If you are not too tired, may I request the honor of one last dance before we depart?"

"I would dance the night away gladly and without fatigue if you were my partner," she said and placed her hand upon his arm.

The orchestra was playing a slow waltz, and Christy and Michael whirled about the floor, once again lost to all but one another. His eyes held her bewitching emerald orbs in a trancelike manner, and a slow smile crept to his lips. She was suddenly possessed of an overpowering desire to feel those warm lips upon hers, and she blushed at her own boldness. It must be the effects of the champagne which caused her to react thus, she rationalized.

So absorbed were they in one another, they were hardly aware the music had finally ended. Slightly embarrassed, they quickly left the floor and retrieved their cloaks, bidding the Middletons farewell and expressing their thanks for the marvelous evening.

Morgan was waiting with the carriage, and helped his two tired charges get settled.

"Cold?" asked Michael as the carriage jolted along the road toward Penncrest a few minutes later.

"I had such a marvelous time, Michael. I shall forever look back upon this evening as one of my happiest. But, for the moment, I fear I am too tired even to shiver," she laughed.

"Come closer then, my sweet, and we shall keep one another warm," he offered and drew her close, pulling the heavy blanket Morgan had secured about them both.

Michael looked down at his young wife whom he held tenderly in his arms. She looked so serene and content, and completely trusting—like a small child. He had never felt so intensely about any woman before. She had completely stolen his heart, and he felt near bursting with love for her. He watched as Christy drifted into slumber.

The carriage at last pulled up in front of the darkened house. He felt reluctant to wake her, she was so content. He brushed a kiss on her soft cheek and shook her shoulder gently. "Wake up, little one. We are home."

With a sigh, she awoke and sat content for a moment, till leaning against his shoulder and making no move to alight.

"Come, my sleeping beauty. It is far too cold to sit in this carriage all night," he teased.

His words finally penetrated through her sleepy mind and she sat up quickly, suddenly aware of her whereabouts. "Oh, I had forgotten where we were," she apologized, rubbing her tired eyes and still feeling slightly groggy. "I felt so warm and secure, I thought myself asleep in my room. I am so sorry for falling asleep on you. I am not sure if it was the champagne or the dancing that made me so tired. You must think me terribly rude and very poor company."

"Nonsense. I am honored you were content enough to sleep in my arms. Can I not convince you there is as much, if not more, contentment and warmth in my bed?" This night he would surely be content to just hold her beside him and feel and smell the honey sweetness of her being.

She could not read his thoughts, however, and guessed he was back to his hopeful and passionate proddings. "I am sorely weary, my husband, and I doubt I would find much rest in your bed. I fear you have things other than sleep on your mind," she teased back as he helped her from the carriage and stepped aside as Morgan led the weary horses to their warm stable.

They walked up the cold marble stairs, shivering again from the cold.

"I suppose, as usual, my dear, you are correct. I bow to your wisdom. You seem to know me far better than I know myself. I must admit I am only a mortal man, and to have you close beside me without touching you would be more than I could endure," he said with a sigh as they entered the dark, silent house.

A single lamp, lit in anticipation of their late arrival, sent ghostly flickering images about the quiet foyer.

"The house is like a tomb. I suppose everyone is asleep. Shall I summon Milly to help you?" he asked as he picked up the lamp to shed light on the stairs as they slowly climbed to their rooms.

"No. It is late and there is no need to waken her. I can certainly manage on my own," she assured him as they groped their way up the dark stairway.

"Ah, I'm glad to see a warm fire still smoldering in your hearth. It would not do for you to catch a chill while undressing, my love."

Still feeling dizzy from the champagne and the magic of the past few hours, she removed her cloak and tossed it on the bed. Then she turned to face Michael, still standing in the doorway.

"I had a wonderful time, Michael. As long as I live I shall never forget this magical night," she whispered. "And I shall forever cherish this necklace as my most prized possession. It means much to you, and truly is a gift from the heart. For that reason, I will never part with it," she said, fingering the jewels and bringing his eyes to her tempting neckline.

When she again looked up into his eyes, she was stunned by her sudden desire to throw herself into his arms and feel his touch upon her. She shook her head, blaming her peculiar urges upon too much punch. When she spoke, she did her best to inflict a note of cool and final determination in her tone, though her actual resolve as far from firm. "Good night, Michael. We should both sleep well after such an exciting evening."

A look of disappointment flickered quickly across his face at being turned away again, but he covered it immediately. "Good night, Christina. Pleasant dreams." He took her hand in his and placed a warm kiss on her palm.

She quickly looked away, fearful he would see the weakness in her eyes. Misinterpreting her action as a sign of rejection, he dropped her hand, bowed gallantly and disappeared into the dark hallway.

She closed the door with a sigh and sat before the mirror to regard her image. Slowly and reverently she removed the sparkling necklace, recounting the pleasant events of the evening just passed. It had been perfect . . . well, almost perfect. There was something lacking; something that kept the evening from being completely wonderful and fulfilling. What was it?

As she brushed out her silky curls, her thoughts focused on Michael and the strange longing she felt to be with him. She loved him and wanted him, but her stubborn pride stood in the way. She would not willingly go to him until she was sure of his love for her.

The chilliness of the room caused her to shiver, and almost reluctantly she rose to remove her gown. With her stomach growing, it would no doubt be some time before she could again fit into the slender waistline. It was a wonder that no one had noticed and made a comment. Perhaps they had just been too polite. What was even more puzzling was that Matilda had apparently held her tongue. She simply could not figure out that woman.

She reached for the many tiny pearl buttons which fastened at the back of her gown. To her dismay, she found it impossible to unfasten them herself. She frowned in consternation. Should she go to the servants' quarters and wake Milly to help her? No, that would be unkind. The girl worked hard and needed her sleep. Yet she could not sleep in the delicate gown without ruining it.

That left her only one resource—to knock on Michael's door and ask him for his assistance. Perhaps he would already be in bed. Or what if he misinterpreted her presence at his door as a sign of submittal?

After careful debate, she made up her mind. She would just have to take her chances and disturb him. It was unthinkable to ruin her gown simply because she was afraid of Michael. She sighed quietly and picked up a candle. The hall was dark and strangely quiet, as if waiting for something or someone. But who? What? She shook her shining black curls and moved toward Michael's room.

Christy shivered in the drafty hallway and hurried to his door, fearful she would change her mind if she delayed longer. With a knock almost deliberately too soft to be heard, she waited patiently, trembling slightly yet refusing to admit the real reason for her shivering. She almost hoped he was asleep and would not respond to her knock.

A moment passed and then the door opened slowly. A look of surprise registered on Michael's face as he recognized his night visitor. The soft light from the candle in her hand played tricks on his eyes, and he beheld a Greek goddess of bewitching beauty. He wondered if he were indeed dreaming. Surely it was too much to hope that she had reconsidered and come to him of her own free will.

Pulses quickening, he opened the door wide. "Come in, Christina," he said softly and stood aside as she seemed to float past him.

Once inside, Christy found the room quite dark, except for the light from the fire which cast eerie reflections upon the ceiling and floor. At the sound of the door closing, she turned her full attention to him. He stood tall and lean in an exquisite silk smoking jacket. The room smelled heavily of tobacco, but it was not an unpleasant aroma. It seemed to suit him, as he stood holding the still-smoking cheroot in his hand.

She could see the unmasked desire in his eyes, blazing hotter than any fire. To her dismay, her own emotions seemed to heighten in response. Her muteness disappeared and she stepped back quickly just out of his reach. "I'm sorry to trouble you, Michael. I had hoped you were not yet asleep. It seems I cannot unfasten my gown. The buttons are just out of my grasp. Would you be so kind as to help me?" she asked nervously, already regretting her decision to seek out his assistance. The strange yet delightful pulsations of her blood were beginning to bubble with desire.

Michael quickly masked his disappointment. "For a moment I had hoped you'd come for another reason," he murmured as he moved behind her.

She deliberately ignored the implication of his tone. "It is so late I did not want to waken Milly. Yet I find myself in a helpless predicament in unfastening my gown. I am glad I did not awaken you."

"I seldom retire immediately. I prefer to relax with a good smoke. I am pleased you came to me for help. But then, is that not one of a husband's more pleasing duties? To help his wife with her dressing . . . and undressing?"

Christy squirmed uncomfortably under his long, labored progress. His hands were surprisingly slow and clumsy. No doubt he was out of practice with women of late. She remembered he had not been plagued by such awkwardness that night on the ship. How peculiar just a few short months could change a man so quickly.

"Are you having trouble?" she questioned at his delay, becoming somewhat impatient with him for his slowness, and with herself at the effect his nearness was having on her.

"Yes, I am," he said. The trouble is not with the dress, but with the fire you stir in me, he thought to himself.

He lightly fingered the pearl buttons and pressed his hands beneath the cloth to touch, ever so gently, the smoothness of her flesh. A voice inside her beckoned her to flee at once. But the warning came too late. In her moment of hesitation, he brushed her hair aside and let one finger float along the outline of her neck and down to her shoulder. Warm lips pressed against the nape of her neck. She drew in her breath. Surely he felt the wild thumping of her heart!

She was powerless to control the shiver of excitement that made her whole body tremble. He sensed the battle that raged within her, but he was now determined to overpower her with sweetness. Perhaps this new tactic would work better than violence. Whatever, he could see her defenses rapidly weakening, and would not give up until she fled in anger, or succumbed to his gentle petting. Whatever the outcome, this time it would be by her own choosing. He would do everything in his power to convince her to his way of thinking, but the ultimate decision would be hers.

"Michael, please don't," she begged in a half-hearted effort to stay his advance.

"My love . . ." he whispered and turned her to face him. As she moved, her gown slowly slipped to the floor.

She stared down in mute astonishment at the crumpled velvet. How naive of her to think this wily Don Juan had lost his touch. His skillful fingers had released her from her gown, leaving her glowing body clothed only in a thin, filmy chemise. His gaze was filled with admiration, as he drank in her loveliness. She shivered as the flame in his eyes singed her senses.

He approached her slowly, almost reverently, to stand before her. "You are cold, Christina. Let me warm you, my love. Let me bring you to a joy you have never known. Let me teach you the love a man can give a woman," he murmured in her ear and ran his fingers along her neck and down her back.

She stood before him in the soft firelight, wanting to run, yet powerless to do so. The subtle yet sensual mood of the room, combined with his hypnotic words, put her in a trancelike state. She shook her head slowly from side to side, her eyes wide and troubled. Yet she made no effort to move. He kissed her long dark lashes and teased her ear with his tongue. As he stroked her back gently, she wondered if she imagined his touch. He pulled her close and his lips took control of her rosebud mouth in a searing kiss. His hands traveled slowly over her back and down to her shapely hips in an unbearably teasing manner. He leaned away slightly and his hand moved between them, up her stomach, and to her soft, ivory mounds.

A surprised whimper sounded in her throat as her chemise slipped open. Her breasts lay bare before him, glowing provocatively in the firelight. How foolish of her to think him slow and clumsy. His hands moved so expertly. She felt marvelously giddy and weak in his passionate embrace.

His lips again sought her in a hungry, eager kiss that made her head spin. His practiced fingers left flames of desire in their wake as they traveled slowly down her back to stroke the smooth softness of her buttocks. She could feel his hardness against her, teasing and frightening her in a confusion of heady sensuality.

"No. No, please," she breathed, yet her senses cried for more. He smothered her protests with his commanding lips, and his hands moved relentlessly up and down her derrier, cupping, squeezing, demanding.

Her quiet moan sounded in his ear, and as her legs buckled beneath her, he scooped her up into his arms. His eyes bespoke the fire of his passion, and he wasted no time in laying her gently on the soft down quilt.

Her silky hair fanned out across the pillow as she lay before him, only the white chemise separating him from her intoxicating charms. Brown eyes touched her in a passionate caress as he shed his clothes in a moment, impatient at each second he was denied the feel of her silken flesh. His naked form slipped beside her, and Christy was wrapped in his massive embrace. His strong, furry chest tickled her breasts, and she suddenly felt unsure and afraid.

"No, Michael. Please. I shouldn't be here. I only came because I could not unfasten my gown. Michael, I am afraid. Please do not hurt me," she whimpered, remembering the pain he had caused her aboard the ship. A single tear trickled down her cheek and disappeared beneath her chin.

"Do not be afraid, my love. It will be different this time. I promise I will not hurt you. I want you to feel the pleasures your body is capable of experiencing. I want you to know the heat of my love," he reassured her.

She felt giddy with desire. It would be different this time. Her pulsing senses assured her of that. How could she deny longer the love she craved from him? The need to feel him touch her, tease her, possess her? Surely he felt some measure of fondness for her? She would make him love her and want her as much as she did him. This was a start—a new beginning.

Her emotions raged as his hands stroked her stomach. Fire leapt through her body as he urged her legs apart and touched the warm tangle of her waiting cavern. She groaned beneath his petting, feeling an overpowering excitement and intensity never before experienced.

"Oh, Michael. I cannot endure it!" she begged, abandoning herself to him. Her arms entwined around his neck and she pulled him fiercely to her.

"Yes, my love. Yes," he breathed into her ear. "Come soar with me!"

Her groan of delight sounded in his ear as he gently joined himself to her. She arched beneath him, accepting his pulsing manhood, and soon they were lost in the violence of their passions.

"Michael!" breathed Christy as the tide of passion carried her up and up, finally breaking in a wave of blinding, triumphant ecstasy.

Twenty-Five

Christy awoke very early the next morning. She yawned, stretched, and again nestled back upon the pillows as she looked about the room which was illuminated by the first shades of dawn. She found it quite pleasing to the eye.

The room was very large, dominated by a massive wooden dressing table and chest. A large desk stood against the wall near the balcony door, and two overstuffed chairs complemented the mammoth bed on either side. With the heavy, rugged furniture, and few delicate furnishings, the room was unmistakably masculine—unmistakably Michael's. She decided that it suited him quite well, though, if she had her choice she would add a touch more color to keep it from being too overbearing, just as its occupant could be at times.

Her inspection of his room complete, she raised herself on her elbow to give her perusal to her husband. He was lying on his back, with one arm stretched out across the bed beside her. The sheet was pushed down to his waist, baring his massive hairy chest. She could not resist the urge to run her fingers over his broad shoulders, and did so with unconcealed delight. She knew only too well the immense strength in those powerful limbs, yet as he lay quiet and sleeping, she could appreciate his power.

Her sleeping prince was so handsome! A lock of dark brown hair lay across one eye, and she tenderly brushed it away. Ever so lightly she ran her fingers over his nose, down to his stubborn chin, and then again across his lips. What a fine man he was, and how proud she was to have him as her own.

She rested her head on one hand, and again outlined his face with her fingertips. "Michael Lancer," she whispered to the sleeping form beside her. "Though I am unsure if you truly love me, hear me well. I swear, if it takes to my dying breath, one day you will take me in your arms and whisper the words I long to hear, the words that will bind you to me as surely as I am now bound to you. Some day you will love me with the fierce intensity with which I love you, for I will give you no rest until you do. You may have won the skirmish last night, but the main battle is yet to be fought."

With her pledge made, she smiled down at his sleeping countenance and placed a quick kiss upon his lips. The morning air was chilly on her bare shoulders, and shivering slightly, she moved closer to him and pulled the blankets securely about them both. She snuggled next to him and closed her eyes contentedly.

"Battles are indeed challenging. But when one's opponent is as lovely and appealing as you, I much prefer foregoing the fight and settling a peace treaty immediately," said Michael softly as he kissed her on the ear and folded her in his arms.

Christy's eyes flew open and she blushed in embarrassment. "Oh, your tactics are surely sneaky and unfair, my husband. You played the part of sound sleeper too convincingly and now you know my deepest secrets," she said as she turned to face him.

"I have a confession to make, Christina. Last night you made me the happiest man in the world by freely giving me your love. But I must regretfully admit that in all reality, your cause is a hopeless one. You cannot force me to love you."

His words cut like a knife stabbed fatally to her heart. Her limbs drained of strength and she felt like a lifeless rag doll. "Michael, though it was never my intention for you to actually hear my words, your answer has struck me a fatal blow. I hoped, I prayed, that after last night, after giving me your mother's jewels, after the magic of the ball, and after the passion we shared—after all those things—I dared to hope you held some measure of love for me, and I was not just some trollop to satisfy your desires. But now, by your own admission, you find loving me impossible."

"Christina. Dry those emerald eyes which I love so much. Dry them quickly, for they are shed without just cause. The words I spoke were true enough, indeed. You cannot force me to love you. In the affairs of the heart, force has no power. But, my love, my words were meant to comfort, not to bring pain. I spoke without realizing how they would sound to your ears. What I meant to say was that you cannot force me to give of something I already give freely, and with fierce intensity. Something I give liberally, and receive with even more joy. Do you understand what I'm trying to say?" he asked and forced her chin up to look into his eyes.

"No," she whispered weakly, but with a tiny ray of hope beginning to appear.

"What I am trying to say, and obviously doing quite poorly, is that I love you, my wife. I love you more than I ever dreamed I could love anyone. I have for some time—I think since the first time I saw you laying limply in my arms aboard *The Merrimer*. I was afraid to admit to myself how deeply I cared for you, for I believed love brought only heartache and sorrow. But you, my love, have brought me more happiness than I have ever known, and I will never let you go." He pulled her close and stroked the smooth, creamy flesh of her shoulders.

The full impact of his words was slow to register. "Oh, Michael, you mean I never was your bond servant? All this time you loved me, yet did not tell me? But why? I thought you hated and despised me all these months," she said, still fearing to let herself be completely happy lest something else come between them.

The pathetic humor of the situation hit him. He laughed lightly. "I never told you my true feelings because I thought you hated and despised *me* for what I had done—for the way I treated you. I felt it beyond hope that after my wretched behavior, you could care for me."

"Oh, Michael! I love you so much," she said with great intensity as she clutched him tightly. Her eyes filled with tears that spilled down her cheeks unheeded. "It feels wonderful to at last be freely able to tell you how I feel. I have held it in so long," she murmured. "I love you. I love you. I love you."

"And I too love you, my sweet. To say the words out loud at last is like a great weight being lifted from me.

How sweet and honest they sound, even to my own ears," he whispered.

Christy laughed despite her tears as he gently brushed the damp hair from her face and ran his fingers along her long, slender neck. He was acutely aware of her smooth, soft warm flesh against him, and his pulses began to quicken. He lifted her tear-stained face and brushed away a few remaining tears. "Oh, my love . . . my only love," he whispered and lowered his warm, hungry lips to hers.

His arms pulled her closer to him, and his hairy chest tickled her naked breasts. Her lips returned his eagerness with a new, completely giving response and soon they were carried away together in a rippling sea of passion. . . .

Milly knocked softly on the door to her mistress's room. She had not wanted to disturb Miss Christy early, for she would no doubt be tired after the ball and arriving home late. But she was truly surprised when the clock struck eleven and her mistress had as yet not summoned her. When her knock received no reply, she slowly opened the door and entered, yet was even more surprised to find the bed still made and obviously not slept in, and her mistress nowhere to be seen.

She checked the dressing bureau and noted the absence of the velvet gown. Surely something was amiss that her Lady Christy had not returned from the ball last night. In alarm she headed for the stairs to question Bertha, and in her haste, ran headlong into Christy, wrapped securely in the folds of one of Master Michael's dressing gowns.

"Oh, Mistress Christy, I beg your pardon. You had me

terribly worried when I found your room empty. I was going to ask Bertha if you had been delayed at the Middletons'. Are you all right?" she asked anxiously, noting Christy's hair in wild disarray about her shoulders. And why was she wearing Master Michael's robe when she had many of her own? Where had she been all night?

Before Christy could answer Milly's questions, Michael appeared and stood behind her, putting his hands lovingly on her shoulders in a possessive, tender fashion. He was dressed in a casual shirt and trousers, and Milly could not remember ever seeing him so docile. Christy tilted her head back and smiled up at him, and then turned her attention to her puzzled maid. "Milly, everything is just fine. You needn't have worried. As a matter of fact, things could not be better," she said and squeezed Michael's hand.

It was then that Milly understood the intensely happy look on both of them, and all was clear at last.

It didn't take long for the word to spread about the house that the newlyweds had at last made peace. Whatever the reason for the reconciliation, everyone benefitted, for their newfound happiness was contagious and spread throughout the house like wildfire. Everyone smiled approvingly when their mistress moved to her rightful place in the master's bedchamber. It was heartening indeed to see them so happy and so much in love.

Sir Phillip was most pleased of all to return from his trip to find the happy state of affairs. They all relaxed for some time in the warm study, and Sir Phillip, though tired from his journey, listened as they told of the ball and their reconciliation. The happy mood was set, and he joined in telling them story after story about when he and Eleanor had first been married, and their happiness together. The evening ended happily, and Christy and Michael climbed the stairs together to seek the peace and solitude of their room.

Twenty-Six

Christmas came and the New Year found Michael and Christy still reveling in their new happiness. Life had taken on a new, rosy outlook. They spent much time together, and her musical laughter, which filtered through the house, lightened everyone's spirits.

The baby growing in Christy's womb unquestionably made his presence seen and felt. Her stomach was swelled largely, and at times his incessant kicking gave her little rest. Though she felt awkward and unattractive in her lumbering state, she immensely enjoyed the intimacy she shared with her child. It was a new and exciting experience for her, and she was eager to share it with Michael.

Upon Michael's urging, she began completely remodeling and refurbishing the nursery. It was indeed a pleasant task to choose the colors and furnishings in anticipation of the arrival of their first child. His coming was no longer viewed as a tragic accident, but was looked forward to with joy and great expectation. She worked closely with the painters, carpenters and designers in the hope that everything would be completed when the baby arrived in a little over two months. She often came to

Michael with her ideas, but he offered little in the way of suggestions, saying he trusted her judgment completely.

So it was that when she was not checking on the progress of the carpenters, Christy could be found curled up in a chair in the study, either under the spell of a good book, or working diligently on some small garment for Baby Lancer. She enjoyed the tasks and they kept her occupied during the cold January days.

For the most part the inclement weather kept the residents of Penncrest housebound. Heavy rains, high winds, biting cold, and great gullies of mud made roads impassable, confining Michael and Sir Phillip to the house, a fact which greatly disturbed them. Work at the mill and shipyards had been curtailed due to the weather, and the two idle men did much to disrupt the normal, routine household functions for they did not endure their confinement well. Used to a life of constant activity, their forced boredom was a hard cross to bear, and they drove the servants to near madness with their constant watchful presence.

"Mistress Christy!" came Bertha's distraught voice. The heavy housekeeper pounded down the stairs and into the study. "Is there naught you can do with Master Michael and Master Phillip?" she asked in exasperation.

"Why, Bertha, what is it?" asked Christy in concern, setting aside her sewing to regard the agitated black woman.

"I do hate to come to you complaining, ma'am. But they've got my servants near crazy with their questions, and are constantly underfoot. It's pretty near impossible to get any work done with them loitering about at every turn," she said in a huff.

"I know what you mean, Bertha. Both Michael and Sir Phillip are used to a regimented daily routine, and to be confined to the house for so long is driving them, and everyone else, to disaster. Let me see if I can get them out of your way for a time," she answered and rose from her warm seat by the fire. "Where are they now?"

"In the nursery trying to tell the carpenters how to do their work," she answered in exasperation and fled to the kitchen, muttering under her breath.

Christy slowly mounted the steps, holding her protruding midriff and puffing slightly. Sure enough, she found both men in deep discussion about the best and safest method to fasten the balcony door against the curious fingers of a little one. Christy smiled to herself. "Well, gentlemen, have you solved all the world's problems?" she asked cheerily. "Surely you must be discussing serious business to be so preoccupied."

Sir Phillip and Michael looked up to see the source of the interruption. "Why, there you are, my dear. We were just discussing the window latches. What do you think would be the best way to handle the matter? They must be simple enough to open easily, yet too difficult for a child to maneuver. What is your suggestion?" asked Sir Phillip in all seriousness as he and Michael rubbed their chins in deliberation. The two carpenters, diligently trying to work despite the interference, cast a discouraged look in his direction.

"Hmmm," began Christy, imitating her two favorite gentlemen by rubbing her chin and prancing sternly, brows drawn, about the room. After an appropriate lapse of time, she turned to answer. "Well, gentlemen, after careful observation, I believe the best course of action would be for us to leave these men to their work. I am sure they are entirely capable of solving such a dilemma in a satisfactory manner."

The two workers bestowed upon her a relieved nod, thankful they would soon be allowed to continue without further interference.

"But, Christina, this is a serious matter. The health and well being of our child is at stake," argued Michael, sure the matter could not be solved without his expertise.

"I am well aware of that fact, dear husband. But you and your two brothers and sister somehow managed to sprout to adulthood without so much as a single latch on the window. Surely our son will do as well after these men have installed a safety device. Now come along you two. I do sorely desire the company of you two handsome gentlemen. The rain has let up at last and I've need of a little fresh air," she said, leading them out in an effort to divert their attention.

"Oh, it's far too cold and damp for you to be outdoors," said Michael, suddenly an authority on pregnant women.

"Nonsense, darling. We've been cooped up so long. A little exercise and change of scenery will do us all good. I believe we are all becoming quite housebound," she argued. "Now, shall I go alone, or will you two gentlemen join me?" she asked in an intentionally inviting yet decisive manner.

"I certainly would not even consider letting you go outside alone. If you insist on going, I shall go with you," said Michael in a paternal manner as if addressing a pouting child.

Christy ignored his condescending tone and smiled sweetly up at him. "Splendid. And you, Father? Will you join us?" she asked.

"Not today, my dear. Not today. My old bones are far too frail for such conditions. I believe I shall settle down by the fire with my accounts. I have a few items which need posting. Thank you for the invitation, but you two run along without me," he answered, waving them off and heading down the stairs toward the study.

In a short time Milly had Christy bundled up snugly against the cold, and she and Michael set off in the crisp air at a healthy pace. He held her arm securely lest she slip and fall. Though such a precaution was slightly unwarranted, Christy enjoyed the feeling of his strong arm about her, and his pampering attentions.

A sliver of sunshine dared to poke its head through the dense clouds. The air, though cold, had a clean smell to it. Their breath began to come as little frosty clouds in the cold air as they breathed heavily of the peace and tranquility. Christy laughed aloud as Brutus, the ever-growing pup, romped in the mud, his tongue lolling happily from the corner of his mouth.

"Oh, it's really quite pretty, isn't it, Michael?"

"Oh, exceptionally beautiful," he answered as he turned to regard her rosy cheeks and sparkling emerald eyes. Though he had thought it inconceivable, she looked even more beautiful than before. Whether it was from anticipation of the coming baby, or their newfound love for one another, or both, he did not know for sure. But whatever the reason, he was again reminded of just how fortunate he was in having her love.

Seeing the devilish look in his eyes, she punched his arm playfully and laughed. "Oh, Michael! I mean the sun glistening on the land. Despite all the rain and mud, there is a quiet tranquility about the air," she said, shutting her eyes and drawing a deep, cleansing breath.

"Oh, yes, the scenery is beautiful too," he agreed, smiling wickedly down at his lovely wife.

"You are incorrigible," she accused. "With my large and steadily growing midriff, I feel far from enticing."

"Oh my dear, even in your rather overbearing state, you have the bewitching power to set my blood rushing madly. Oh but that I could spirit you off to the stables and prove my point to you," he said roguishly.

"Oh, so it's your horses you miss all this time. I'd thought you content inside the house with me," she said with a playful glint in her eyes.

"Why you little imp!" cried Michael as he realized her playful charade. With little effort he caught her breathless and giggling form in his arms. "You shall pay for your impertinence, wife," he said and scooped her into his arms, holding her precariously over a large mound of slimy brown mud. "Why, the very idea of such talk to your lord and master is sheer folly on your part," he continued. "Cease your attack and surrender immediately else I shall drop you in this mound of muck," he threatened.

"Oh, strong and monstrous adversary. On behalf of our son, I surrender unconditionally. But were I not in such a family way, you might not reign long," she countered bravely as he drew her close, hugging her to him. She folded her arms tightly about his neck, returning his hug, and nestled in his embrace.

"Now that I have surrendered, what punishment will the conquering lord inflict upon his poor, defeated foe?" she asked in a meek voice.

"Well, 'tis the victor's prerogative to bind and chain his slave and cast him into the dungeon. Since we have no dungeon here at Penncrest, I am forced to settle for locking you away in my room forever, that you may not escape from me."

"My kind lord, with you at my side to guard me, 'twould be no punishment at all, but a reward instead," she answered in all honesty.

"Oh, I love you, Christy. God, how I love you," Michael whispered, his voice suddenly low and husky. "In all reality, I am your prisoner, for you have put your chains about my heart, making me powerless and unwilling to escape. Oh, happy, happy prisoner, I," he said in her ear.

"Michael, for so long I ached to hear such words from your lips and thought I never would. Now they fall like silken threads upon my ears, soft and tender, that I cannot hear them enough. I love you, Michael Lancer. I love you with all my heart," she whispered and reached up to meet his heated lips with her own.

They stood in the quiet, gently falling rain, locked in an embrace which warmed the very ground about them. They felt no cold. They saw no rain. They heard no sound. They only felt their arms about one another, and their love touching and soaring together.

Approaching hoofbeats in the mud shattered their private world, and Michael reluctantly set her upon her feet. He heaved a disgusted sigh and, arms locked together securely, they approached the carriage as their uninvited guest alighted.

"Hello, darling. How are you? Such frightful weather we've been having. Whatever are you doing out in this wretched mess?" asked Matilda Lancer as she stumbled from the carriage.

She used an obviously planned slip of the foot as an excuse to place a well gloved hand upon Michael's free arm. He was forced to release Christy to steady his sister-in-law. Once her balance was restored, however, he quickly withdrew and again placed his arm about Christy.

"Christina wanted to get some fresh air, so we were just taking a little walk," he answered. "It's really quite lovely out. Especially after all the rain we've had."

Determined to be disagreeable, Matilda brushed a few raindrops from her cloak. "No one in their right mind would want to come out into this mess without just cause," answered Matilda snidely. "And I see nothing lovely about this cold, wet weather." Her meaning was quite clear. "I do believe, my dear, the cold has mesmerized you," she said to Christy as she stood rubbing her hands together and stomping her feet to keep warm.

"Actually I think it was a splendid idea. The sun is quite warm and the air refreshing," he answered, smiling down at his wife. "We were having a very enjoyable walk, that is until you came upon us," he said, coming to Christy's defense. His meaning, too, was quite clear.

Matilda noticed his coolness and preoccupation with Christy. Her eyes flashed. "Well, I've not seen you since the holidays. I just wanted to see for myself that you were well and happy," she answered, shivering again in the cold, yet trying not to look as uncomfortable as she felt.

"Why how nice of you to be concerned, Matilda. But we could not be better. Christina has been taking very good care of me," he said and bestowed a quick kiss on Christy's cheek.

Matilda was hard-pressed to hide her displeasure. "I see. How very nice," she answered sharply. "Well, I'm going into the house before I positively freeze to the spot. Coming, Michael, dear?" she threw over her shoulder. "If your wife feels the need to continue her walk, there is no need for you, too, to freeze to death."

"We'll be along directly," called Michael, but to Christy, he whispered, "The old barracuda. Ice runs in her veins. I'd think she'd be right at home in the cold. It suits her temperament."

Once inside, Milly took their heavy cloaks and promised to bring tea. They settled comfortably around a blazing fire in the study, where Sir Phillip sat reading. Matilda made certain she positioned herself beside Michael on the couch, snuggling close on the pretext of being cold.

Christy smiled to herself at Matilda's obvious tactics. It was amusing to see the lengths she would go to capture Michael's attentions. When Milly arrived, Christy helped her with the tea and then took a place in a chair by the fire to observe the group quietly.

"Well, dears, what's new? It's been ages since I've

seen anyone. This wretched weather has kept me locked up until I thought I'd go mad," Matilda started in a bubbling manner.

"We are all quite fit and happy, Matilda," answered Sir Phillip. "The house once again has a charming mistress, and soon will be filled with the laughter of children."

Matilda turned slightly green at his implications. "Well, when you have a screaming brat giving you no rest day or night, you may not be so happy and content," she answered. "Babies are a nuisance and only grow into bigger problems. Believe me, I know. I have two of the little beggars," she said resentfully.

Christy cringed that she could speak so meanly about her own lovely children. She missed the youngsters, for Matilda rarely brought them with her these days. They were sweet children, despite their mother's influence. "How are Michele and Oliver?" asked Christy. "They must be out enjoying today's sunshine."

"Oh, they are driving me crazy. They are so bad these days. A constant drain on my patience, they are, I'll tell you," she said and turned to Christy. "And I certainly do not permit them to play outdoors in this weather."

Christy bristled at Matilda's scathing tone. A retort was hot on her lips when Sir Phillip, seeing the impending disaster, interjected.

"Too bad you didn't bring them with you, Matilda. They would certainly have brightened my day. I miss the little imps," he said.

"Oh, 'tis too much trouble getting them dressed and undressed in this weather. First they are too cold, then they are too hot. It's impossible to please them," she sniffed as if the burden were too heavy to bear. "Besides, I thought my presence alone would brighten your day," she said.

Michael rose from the couch without responding, forcing Sir Phillip to answer. "Yes, yes, of course," he mumbled without conviction. "We are glad to see you."

Christy hid a grin behind her hand as she watched Matilda's balloon deflate.

Obviously piqued by their lack of enthusiasm, she changed the subject. "Father, you should be happy you were out of town and missed the ball. Why, it was simply wretched this year. It lacked the color and vitality of other years, and even the orchestra was inferior. No one could dance to their music. Besides that, the Middletons invited no one of any high, social importance. Why, they even excluded Lt. Governor Joanace. How terribly rude. I am sure he felt snubbed. I would have invited him myself had I known he was not included. He really is a marvelous man. Don't you agree, Christina?" she asked pointedly.

Christy had no time to hide her surprise at Matilda's direct inquiry about the governor. "I . . . really don't know," she tried to sound noncommittal and looked down to contemplate her tea.

"Really, how strange. He still insists you remind him of someone he knew in England. He has an extraordinary memory, he tells me. Peculiar he should be so mistaken about you," Matilda said. "Yes, as I was saying, the ball was really a disappointment this year. Had it not been for dear, devoted Gregory, the entire evening would have been totally boring," she concluded and sipped on her drink.

Michael helped himself to more tea. "Why, on the contrary, Matilda. I felt the Middletons outdid themselves. It was one of their best efforts. And as far as not inviting Joanace, I was told he and Governor Glen are not on good terms. Glen was there and it would have been awkward to also invite Joanace. Besides, it is certainly the prerogative of the host and hostess to invite who they choose. Yes, I thought the ball was simply grand. And honoring Christy and me by asking us to open the ball was a great compliment. The orchestra too was superb— quite a well-known group of players. Christina and I had no difficulty dancing. Christina and I had a marvelous time, didn't we, love?" he asked, directing his attention to Christy. He was shocked by her sudden pallor. Perhaps the walk in the cold had been too much for her.

"Yes, we had a very nice time," she agreed with him, but would make no further comment. Matilda's pointed yet subtle remarks about Joanace had upset her greatly, and she wished to rile the woman no further.

Seeing Christy on edge and noncommittal, Matilda pressed her advantage. "Well, I am sure it was your first such affair, and anything would have impressed you," she answered, deliberately baiting her remark to cause some reaction from Christy.

"Perhaps you are right," answered Christy, still trying to remain as cool and aloof as possible. She had no way of knowing, however, that her continued silence only added fuel to Matilda's growing anger.

Michael was puzzled by Christy's lack of fight. He

knew her definitely capable of taking her own part against Matilda, yet today she sat quietly and let Matilda batter her. Why? "Nonsense, Matilda. As I said before, I have been to many such functions, and I found this one especially enjoyable. I believe it all comes down to the company you were with. Christina and I had a marvelous time because we had one another. Perhaps if you had chosen someone else besides that wretched slave trader to escort you, the evening may have been more enjoyable."

"How can you say such a thing about that wonderful man? He's making large amounts of money in his business, and there is nothing illegal about it." She was defending herself and her choice more than the sea captain. She liked him little enough herself, but was using him for her own purposes.

"You mean to say you let yourself be seen in public with a lowlife like Piper? Really, Matilda, how low can you stoop? Besides, is money all that important to you that it does not matter how one comes by it? His business may not be illegal as yet, but it is highly immoral," answered Sir Phillip indignantly.

"Why, how can you say such things about Gregory? Or your own daughter-in-law?" shot back Matilda in anger at Sir Phillip's sharp rebuff.

Sir Phillip made no answer, and Matilda stumbled on. The time was right to begin her second attack. "And who is to say what is illegal or immoral? Why, I heard a story not long ago about a girl who sailed all the way from England as a stowaway with a ship full of men! Can you imagine that! Now that's what I call illegal and immoral.

Undoubtedly a 'lowlife' as you put it," Matilda let her bombshell drop, and sat back to watch their reactions.

Christy nearly spilled the tea she held in her lap. Panic registered on her face, but Michael's cool, reassuring glance told her he would deal with the situation. "Why, Matilda. That sounds like a highly unlikely story to me. I would not trust anyone telling such an obvious tale," he replied, calling her bluff.

Christy's expression still held a worried look, and even Sir Phillip had been shocked by Matilda's comment.

Matilda's smile broadened. Michael was playing perfectly into her hands. "Oh, I believe my source is quite reliable, dear," she answered, casually buffing her painted nails.

"And just who is it that told you such a story, Matilda? I am anxious to know," questioned Michael, suddenly becoming wary. Had one of the men on his ship betrayed his trust? If so, who and why?

"Oh, I've forgotten his name right now," she hedged. "You know how bad I am at remembering such things. But he was an acquaintance of a friend of mine. I trust him completely."

Matilda smiled. Her whole scheme was based on the premise that Christy had told Michael nothing of her past. If that were the case in actuality, then her next question would surely reveal the truth. "Don't you believe that mutual trust is important between people, Christina, dear?"

Christy swallowed hard and smiled nervously at Matilda. Her hands shook as she placed her tea cup upon the table. "Of course, Matilda. Trust is quite important," she said, trying to hide her trembling fingers.

But Matilda's watchful eyes caught her agitated state. She had scored a point and hit her target point-blank. Her guess had been correct. Now she planned to put icing on the cake. "And you, Michael, do you not believe trust is necessary in a relationship?" she asked sweetly, taking the final swallow of her tea.

"Of course, Matilda. It is the most important aspect of any relationship. If you cannot trust someone, it is far better to be done with them," he said.

"I quite agree, darling. A lasting relationship is based on mutual trust. For example, I am sure you trust your little wife would never lie to you, or deliberately hold back information. That would be a total lack of trust, would it not?" asked Matilda smoothly.

The room spun as Christy watched Michael's brow grow dark. What was Matilda leading up to?

"Of course I trust Christina. She is my wife, and mother of my child. Why would she lie to me? What makes you suggest otherwise?" he questioned irritably, trying to discover just what she knew.

"Oh, no reason at all. You needn't get so upset. It was just an innocent question," she said and smiled again at Christy who sat stock still and was deadly white.

Christy's grip eased slightly on the chair. It appeared Matilda, for some unknown reason, was going to hold her tongue. Christy had no doubt now that she knew a great part, if not all, of her past. How she had found out, and what she planned to do about it were questions Christy found both frightening and disturbing.

Michael's agitated voice broke into her musings.

"Really, Matilda, I fail to see any point in this discussion. We were talking about the ball," he said in annoyance.

"You are quite right, of course, darling. I don't know why I brought it up. The cold and rain must be getting to me," she said in feigned apology. She took a final look at the distressed and anxious faces around the room, and rose ceremoniously, straightening her skirt. "Well, I'd best be getting back home before this wretched rain strands me here," she said cheerily.

Her sudden movement brought Sir Phillip from his reverie. "Here, let me help you with your cloak," he offered, a trifle too quickly. The thought of her being stranded with them was positively too abhorrent to contemplate.

"Thank you, Father dear," she said sweetly and turned to Michael who was still scowling and petulant. "Goodbye, Michael, darling. Stop by and see us soon, will you? It's so lonely without a man about the house." She fluttered her eyes seductively.

As she walked through the doorway, she stopped and turned to address Christy, somewhat as an afterthought. "Oh, do take care of yourself, Christina dear. I see you've grown quite heavy with child. It's quite a cumbersome, unattractive time when one is swollen and unshapely. 'Twould be a shame if you could not get your figure back after the baby is born. I've seen many women just never lose all that extra fat," she said and smiled cuttingly at Christy, very well pleased with herself. She had more than accomplished her purpose in coming. The girl would have a lot to think about now.

"Bye, all. And don't forget to drop by, Michael. I'm

sure you would enjoy the visit, now that your wife is preoccupied with the child," she called over her shoulder.

As soon as Sir Phillip and Matilda left the room, Christy rose, none too steady. Michael crossed the room quickly, seeing her so pale and upset. "Are you feeling all right? The walk must have been too much for you. Shall I send for the doctor?" he asked in concern as he touched her feverish forehead.

"No, Michael. Thank you. There is no need to summon Dr. Littman. I just have a headache. I will be fine. If you will excuse me, though, I think I will lie down for a time."

"Very well, if you think you don't need the doctor. Here, let me help you," he offered, still concerned.

"No. I'm really fine, Michael," she insisted, refusing his assistance, and sought the quiet of her room.

Once alone, she lay down on the bed and let her mind tackle the questions Matilda's visit had fostered. Why had she deliberately questioned her on Joanace's character? How had Matilda found out about her being a stowaway? Had someone on the ship told her? But who? Surely it was not just coincidence she had told them her little story.

And what about her pointed question about trust and holding back information? If she knew more than she was letting on, was her question meant to feel out Michael to see how much he knew? If Matilda actually knew the truth, why had she not revealed it? What devious plot was she devising? Christy certainly did not fool herself that it was Matilda's kind and gentle nature that had caused her to hold her tongue. What was the real reason? What was the purpose behind it all?

She forced herself to make an appearance at dinner, looking and feeling drained. She ate little, as did Sir Phillip and Michael. They too seemed to be lost to their own thoughts. Matilda's visit had put the whole house in a state of depression.

During the course of the meal, Christy noticed that Sir Phillip looked extremely tired of a sudden, and most definitely had something of grave importance on his mind. He fidgeted nervously, and Christy had the distinct impression he wanted to conclude the meal and discuss his business alone with his son.

Still suffering from her own tormented thoughts, and a wretched headache, she took the cue and left the men alone. The look of relief was apparent on Sir Phillip's face when she excused herself. As she climbed the stairs, she was curious about her father-in-law's peculiar behavior. Something was most decidedly perturbing him. Was she the cause of his anxiety? Had Matilda put some doubts into his mind about her? Did he suddenly regret his son marrying her?

That night in bed Christy's tormented musings gave her little rest, and for the first time since the ball, her old nightmare returned to plague her sleep. More than once she awoke, trembling and frightened, to find Michael patiently stroking her face and holding her tightly. His presence beside her was a tremendous comfort, yet a constant reminder that a decision soon had to be made.

She must have finally fallen asleep sometime very late, for when she awoke the next morning, she reached for

Michael beside her, but to her dismay, found the bed empty. Apparently he had been unable to sleep and had slipped out quite early, not wanting to awaken her.

She nestled back under the warm blankets, feeling tired from the ordeal of the previous day and her fitful night. She found herself again going over her alternative courses of action. The light of day cast a different outlook on her problems, and with a new determination, she resolved to go to Michael today and tell him the truth— everything. The risk was too great that Matilda would tell him what she knew, and if Michael were to discover the truth, it was better it came from her own lips. Perhaps he would take the news more calmly, hearing it from her rather than a third party.

With her decision at last made, she felt as if a great burden had been lifted from her. She closed her eyes to rest, confident her final decision was a wise one.

The baby kicked suddenly, asserting his presence, and she laughed softly. Yes, there was no doubt he would be strong and forceful, as was his father. They had not as yet discussed the question of a name for the baby. She decided that if all went well with revealing her traumatic past to him, she would bring up the matter of names with Michael very soon. After all, they only had two months left.

Feeling somewhat better, she rose a few minutes later, stretched and summoned Milly. It was becoming increasingly impossible to dress herself without great difficulty, and she appreciated the help and company of Milly more than ever.

"Good morning, ma'am. How are you feeling today?"

asked Bertha as Christy slid into a chair at the breakfast table some time later.

"I'm fine, Bertha. Michael has the patience of a saint. I fear my nightmares last night gave him little sleep," she said and sipped on a tall glass of juice. "Where is he, Bertha? I didn't hear him rise. Has he gone to the mill? He mentioned he might go if the weather cleared."

"Why, no, Mistress Christy. Both he and Sir Phillip left very early this morning for Charleston," she explained. "Oh Lordy me, ma'am. I plum forgot. The young master said he did not wish to waken you, after your fitful night, so he left this note for you," she said and handed her a sealed envelope.

Christy ripped open the note with some concern. What could have been so important to send them off without even waiting until daybreak? She read the bold writing of her husband quickly, and then reread it more slowly.

Dearest Christina,

Please forgive this hasty and untimely departure. Only the most serious of matters could drag me away from you, my beloved. Hopefully when Father and I return, we will have good news for you. I am sorry I cannot explain further at this time, but please trust me, and know that I love you deeply. I will count the minutes until my return to your side.

Your devoted husband,
Michael

Christy quickly wiped away a tear which had escaped down her cheek. She did not understand his sudden urgency in going to Charleston, but whatever the cause, it was surely important. His few short lines explained nothing of his business, yet his words of endearment and assurance of his love for her did much to boost her sagging spirits.

She was somewhat dismayed that their talk would be delayed, for now that she had at last made her decision, she was anxious to have their confrontation at an end. But, she comforted herself, perhaps it was well she had more time to choose her approach and its possible effects more carefully.

Finishing her breakfast, she tucked the note inside her gown and sought the warmth of the fire. The day was cold but sunny, and she spent most of it sewing. The carpenters had finished the nursery, and she and Bertha spent some time choosing colors and furnishings for the tiny room.

It was a long but relatively pleasant, uneventful day; much an improvement over the previous one.

It was very cold when she went to bed, and she missed Michael's presence terribly. She hoped he would soon be home and done with whatever was troubling him. The agony of waiting to learn her fate was somewhat lessened by the loving note he had left. Surely his love for her would override whatever obstacles her past placed in their path.

With those thoughts in mind, she curled up in the huge bed and drifted off to sleep.

Twenty-Seven

Christy awoke the next morning and shivered from the cold. The wind howled fiercely outside, and she had a strange foreboding about the day ahead. She shivered again, trying to dispel the eerie feelings that had come over her. It was silly to be so superstitious. No doubt her low spirits were due to Michael's absence and the mental anguish of her impending confession.

When Milly arrived to help her dress, she informed Christy that Bertha had been called away very early to tend an ailing servant in a neighbor's home. It was unlikely that she would return until the following day. Milly assured her that Bertha had made all necessary arrangements to keep the household running smoothly during her absence.

Christy had no appetite and only nibbled on her breakfast. Listlessly she wandered into the study and huddled beneath a blanket, idly stitching a wrap for the baby. But even this normally pleasant task did little to improve her lethargic mood. The wind continued to howl outside, and the dismal sky threatened to blanket the earth with snow any time.

Disgusted by her own ill temper, she headed for the

stairs to check on the progress of the painters in the nursery. As she reached the landing, a blast of cold air assaulted her. Confused that the front door should have been left ajar, she moved to close it. Suddenly a heavily cloaked figure emerged from the shadows. Christy gasped in surprise. "Matilda, you startled me. I didn't hear the bell. No one announced your arrival," she said, wondering at Matilda's peculiar behavior. She shivered and drew her shawl tighter about herself. The chill was as much from the cold as from the prospect of facing Matilda alone.

Matilda cast a glance about the hallway. No one was in sight. "Where is Michael?" she demanded coldly, ignoring Christy's surprise.

"He and Sir Phillip have gone into Charleston on some pressing business," she replied, eyeing the woman leerily.

"When will they return?" barked Matilda as if she were conducting an inquisition. The cold, calculating look in her eyes, and the demanding tone of her voice frightened Christy.

"I have no idea, Matilda. They may return today, or not for a few days. Is there something I can help you with?" she asked, wondering if something urgent had come up.

"You've got it wrong, dear. You can't possibly help me. But I can definitely help you. I knew Michael and Sir Phillip were gone. I just wanted to make certain. You see, I specifically planned my visit during their absence so we would have no disturbances. It's you I came to see. Come into the study where we will not be overheard."

Christy hesitated. She had no desire to be alone with Matilda.

"Come along. I've not all day and I want this business finished up with. You've wasted far too much of my time and efforts already," snarled Matilda in a low voice.

Again Christy did not move. What right had Matilda to order her about in such a manner?

"I said, come along!" cried Matilda. The woman grabbed Christy viciously by the wrist, pulling her into the study.

Once inside, Matilda quickly closed and bolted the door. When she turned to face Christy, a look of triumph outlined her hard face. Christy's heart pounded wildly. "It is not necessary to bolt the door, Matilda. No one will disturb us. I'll send for some tea. You must be cold," she said and picked up the little bell on the table.

"No! Put the bell down. No one knows I'm here. I want to keep it that way. Besides, you needn't play the mistress of Penncrest for me. I know who you are and what you are, and unless you do as I say, everyone else will know too," seethed Matilda.

Christy turned pale and shivered again. Never before had she seen such hate in Matilda's eyes. "What . . . what do you mean?" she stuttered, trying to sidestep the issue.

"You know exactly what I mean. You needn't play the innocent little lady to me. I know all about you. You may have fooled Michael, but you tangled with the wrong person when you interfered with me and my plans," she glared.

"I don't know what you mean. I never intended to

interfere with you in any way, Matilda."

"You really think I'm fool enough to believe that? You had a taste of the fine life as a child, and the moment you saw Michael, you set out to get him and his money, despite all my warnings to you. Yes, I know all about your clever plans, my dear," she sneered.

"Just what is it you profess to know?" asked Christy with as much beligerance as she could muster.

"You lived in a nice, luxurious house in London with your parents, being pampered and catered to like any rich brat. Suddenly they were killed in an accident and the truth about their cheating emerged. They were branded as traitors, and all their possessions sold off. That forced you to live with your uncle, one Henry Slate, who treated you so badly, you ran away and hid yourself aboard Michael's ship to escape him. Too bad you had to pick his ship to stow away upon, instead of one run by some miserable old captain who would have punished you properly."

"How . . . how did you find out?" Christy choked, suddenly ready to collapse. With unsteady hands she clutched the back of a chair for support. She would not give Matilda the satisfaction of seeing her crumple into the chair.

"I'll only too gladly tell you, dear. It really wasn't all that difficult to discover the truth once all the pieces started falling into place. You see, I despised you from the first time I laid eyes on you. I did not believe a word of this 'distant cousin' story you and Michael fabricated for decency's sake, yet I had no proof to the contrary. That is, not until the day we met Lt. Governor Joanace. You tried quite well to hide your initial shock at seeing him. But despite your denials, I got the distinct impression you knew exactly who he was. You may have fooled the others with your theory of many Pattersons, but I thought the whole thing rather curious. I made an appointment with him, and after a little coaxing and explaining, he was quite helpful in detailing the rather shocking story of the deceitful and traitorous Pattersons. No wonder you deliberately keep your past a secret. I'm sure you're afraid you'd be outcast here as you were in England if the truth were known," she hissed.

"'Tis not true! My parents never cheated anyone!" cried Christy in defiance. "It was all a plot devised by Joanace. My parents stood in his way, and he killed them and then fabricated the story of their guilt. None of it is true. My parents were honest, upstanding citizens," she declared heatedly.

"I care little of your sad tale, my dear. What matters is that they were legally condemned. Mr. Joanace admitted confiscating all their possessions. Then he lost track of your whereabouts. You see, even after fitting some of the pieces together, we still were not completely sure you actually were the daughter of these outcasts. He said your age was about right, but he couldn't be completely certain. With my persuasion, he agreed to look into the matter immediately. When I left him, there were still a few things which did not fit in. For instance, why and how did you get on *The Merrimer?* What connection did you really have with Michael?"

She paused for effect and then continued. "I was passing by Kramer's shop when I recalled something he had mentioned once about seeing you the day the ship docked. After a little coaxing and threatening to take my business elsewhere, he told me a rather interesting story of his first meeting with you. Really, my dear, I'd have thought after spending all those months with a ship full of eager men, you would have been far more qualified for the life of a whore instead of sewing, or sweeping," she laughed wickedly.

"Michael's men never touched me, Matilda. Michael saw to that," cried Christy in defense of her honor.

"Oh really dear? That's not what I was told. Kramer's story definitely piqued my curiosity, and I went so far as to contact a man who sailed on *The Merrimer*. He too had an interesting story to tell me. He said you were quite a saucy little bitch. I believe you may remember him. He was a disgusting little man by the name of John." Matilda's voice shook with laughter as Christy paled and shivered at the very mention of the man's name.

"Yes, I thought you might remember him," she laughed, encouraged by Christy's horrified reaction. "He filled me in on the details of your appearance aboard the ship as a stowaway. He also admitted having a rather enjoyable little tussle with you, though unfortunately Michael cut it rather short." Again she laughed wickedly. "How truly gallant of Michael to save you for himself. I'm surprised though that he would stoop so low. He is surely accustomed to a much better class of woman than you. I suppose, however, that you served sufficiently to satisfy his more basic, primitive needs."

Christy felt sick with fury, but Matilda went on with vengeance. "I'd love to know how you lured him to your bed and spread your legs for him. I'm sure that after looking over your possibilities as a fugitive and a branded traitor, you decided that being his little whore was the only way to assure yourself of an easy life, at least until he tired of you. But becoming pregnant and demanding he marry you, thus ensuring yourself a permanent life of wealth and ease—that was a stroke of genius. I'd not have thought you bright enough for such a plan, my dear. How he fell for such a ploy is still beyond me."

"That's not how it happened. I did not lure him to my bed. You have it all wrong, Matilda."

"Oh, do not take me for a fool, you little bitch. Michael always loved me, even when I married that half-wit brother of his. He would not willingly turn to another woman except for a few moments of pleasure. I am all he needs. You seduced him with your childish charms and ways, as you do now to keep him from me," Matilda hissed menacingly.

"You are mistaken, Matilda. Michael doesn't love you. And I have not tricked him. He returns my love freely and happily. He may have cared for you at one time, but it is me he loves now," Christy defended herself. Too late she saw the error in making her statement.

In sudden outraged anger, Matilda slapped her hard across the face, sending her staggering across the room. Christy whimpered at the sudden pain and rubbed her cheek.

"Don't you ever, ever say that again. Michael loves me. I've made him a happy man on many occasions. We were going to be married until you came along. All his money and his strong social title were to be mine. Mine, do you hear? Until you came along with your lies and witches charms. Yes, it is me he loves, not you. In fact, he truly loathes you for getting in our way. He has told me so." Matilda's face was blood red as she stood over the cowering girl.

"No. No! I don't believe you. Michael never professed to care for you. Why would he have wed me if he loved you?" asked Christy, sure the woman was mad, yet unwilling to listen to such lies.

"If you recall, I tried to make him see reason. But, he is too damn noble for his own good. He hadn't a chance to escape, with you and his miserable father badgering him into seeing things your way. Remember now that I tried to warn him about you then, but I had no solid proof against you to give him at the time, and was therefore powerless to stop the marriage. It ate at me to know I was so close to discovering the truth, yet too late to stop that farce of a wedding. Time was against me, for shortly after your marriage I received news from Joanace. He said without a doubt that you were daughter to the notorious Pattersons. His sources informed him that you had apparently run off from this Henry Slate and had not been seen since.

"The pieces at last all fit together. You stowed away on the ship to escape from him. I know the whole truth about you now. And, to think, you would have gone on happily forever, deceiving us all, had it not been for that chance meeting with dear Mr. Joanace."

"You . . . you have no proof, Matilda. No one will believe you."

"On the contrary, dear. I have all the proof I need. I

have the men on board *The Merrimer* who will back me. And people will surely enjoy that story. And what better witness do I need than Lt. Governor Joanace? Surely no one will question his testimony," she laughed. "But, should all these witnesses fail, I still have one who will unquestionably seal your guilt beyond a doubt." Matilda paused to heighten the effect of her next words.

"Who . . . who is this infallible witness you claim against me?" asked Christy, sure she could produce no such person.

"Perhaps no one will believe me, or the others," Matilda said, clearly enjoying her advantage, "but they will surely believe Henry Slate."

"Henry Slate!" cried Christy in horror.

"Yes, dear, your sweet Uncle Henry Slate," she affirmed.

"But he is in London."

"Oh, my dear, how careless of me. I must have forgotten to tell you. Your uncle is on his way here this very moment," said Matilda, savoring the words in ultimate joy.

"Slate, coming here? Why? It isn't possible!" cried Christy, slowly slipping into the chair. She was now trembling uncontrollably, and could do nothing to stop herself. Waves of nausea gripped her and she clutched her stomach tightly.

Matilda was pleased beyond hope with Christy's reaction. She closed in for the kill. "When I finally learned the truth about you, I decided the only way to put my facts to true advantage was to have Slate here in person. I immediately sent for him, offering him a substantial sum of money for his immediate departure. If all has gone as planned, he will be arriving on the next ship from London. It should be a touching reunion," she said, her voice honey-smooth and delighted.

"Why? Why would you do such a thing?" muttered Christy, not wanting to believe what Matilda had revealed so gleefully.

Matilda's mood suddenly changed. "Because I despise you. I want you as far away from Michael and his money as you can get, for I want them both for myself. I have no intentions of you or your brat standing in my way any longer," she spat, her face ugly with hate.

"Michael will not let Henry Slate take me away. He loves me and I love him. I will go to him and tell him the truth. He will find a way to stop you both," argued Christy.

Again Matilda's mood changed to one of cunning. Christy was now vulnerable and defenseless, and obviously in love with her husband. All these factors would now serve her well as she spun her web.

"You are right. I've already thought of that. I am quite sure Michael will not stand by and let Slate take you. He is too proud and noble for that. But even if you succeed in again bewitching him with your evil charms, you cannot stop me. I will tell the whole world of your shame. And think of what news of your reputation will do to him, and Sir Phillip, and your baby. What do you think the Lancer name will be worth once it is linked with that of traitors? They will be banned from society, outcasts like yourself. Is that what you want?" she demanded.

Christy's head spun from Matilda's attack. "No. I can't

let that happen to them. They are too good and kind. They do not deserve to suffer because of me." Christy sobbed into her hands. "Is there nothing I can do to make you hold your tongue? What price do you want to keep your silence?" asked Christy in despair, setting swollen, glassy eyes upon her tormentor.

Matilda smiled. The girl had played right into her hands. Moving slowly up beside Christy, she stood towering over the girl, staring down with unmasked hate. "I will tell you exactly what to do to ensure that Slate and I keep our peace. I can pay him to keep silent. From what I hear of his character, money will more than appease his needs. As for me, the only way I will hold my tongue is if you promise to leave this place tonight, and never come back. You must leave here quietly, and never again in any way communicate with the Lancers. You must leave and permanently sever all ties with them. If the Lancers mean anything to you, you must do as I say. Do you understand?"

Her words tore at Christy like daggers. "Yes, I understand only too well. You offer me no choice at all, Matilda. I love Michael and his family deeply and it will cause me unbearable pain to leave without so much as a farewell. Yet, if I choose to remain, you will bring shame and heartache upon those I hold so dear. Yes, Matilda, it is a bitter choice you ask me to make. A bitter choice indeed."

"Oh, your suffering softens my heart not. You brought about your own heartache with your cunning and deceiving ways. But think of this, too. Weak as you are, you may decide to stay and drag the Lancers down with you. But are you also willing to sacrifice the fate of your child for your own happiness? If you go now, your secret goes with you, and you and your baby will have a chance to find some peace and live normally. But if you stay, your child will forever carry the burden of your shame and your selfishness. Are you willing to make so many others suffer in order to spare your own insignificant feelings?" reasoned Matilda, knowing Christy was not thinking clearly, and making the most of it.

"You have thought this out well, have you not, Matilda? You have trapped me in a corner with no chance of escape. You know very well I will do as you say. You give me no choice to do otherwise. So rejoice in your cunning victory. I will leave this place and these people I love, as you deem necessary, never to return. I will go to spare them the humiliation I know only too well.

"But you must promise that I carry my secret shame with me. You must promise never to reveal the truth to anyone. If you grant me no such guaranty, I will not go."

"You needn't worry, my dear. Once you are gone, you can take your damn secret to your grave. I'll have what I want and it will no longer be necessary for me to trouble myself with your sordid past."

Matilda's concession gave Christy little reassurance. But she was in no position to argue. She had to take Matilda at her word. "Very well, Matilda. I will do as you bid, but know I do so unwillingly and with much malice toward you. Only a cruel and wicked human being would plot so deviously to destroy another. Someday you will answer for your hatefulness."

Matilda only laughed at her warning. "Save your idle prophesies. They frighten me not. Had you not been so deceitful and devious yourself, you'd not now be in this position. I'm only doing my duty. Michael deserves better than the likes of you. He needs me and will be mine soon. But enough of that. You must forget him now. He is lost forever to you and you've only yourself to blame. Now listen well to the arrangements I've made. I have a place for you to stay until after the child is born. Even I am not so cruel as to force you to travel a great distance in your 'fragile' condition," she granted benevolently. "When the baby is born and you are again ready to travel, you will go to New Orleans. You will be taken care of, one way or another. Do you understand?"

"Yes," said Christy, but something about the evil glint in Matilda's voice rang deeper in her ear. Just how did Matilda plan to take care of her? She was suspicious, but it really did not matter. Whatever Matilda's plan, she had little choice but to concede. She vowed to keep her eyes open to any danger that might be lurking. Her tears had ceased to flow and she sat in mute silence listening as Matilda further outlined her plan.

"You will leave late tonight, when everyone is asleep. There will be a carriage waiting for you at the head of the lane. It will take you to a little town outside of Charleston where you will meet another coach. This second coach will take you to your destination. All you need concern yourself with is waiting for that first coach. Do you understand? And dear, do travel light. You will have little need for all your costly gowns."

"Of course, Matilda," said Christy lifelessly. Her

whole world was crumbling around about her and she could do nothing to prevent it.

"Good. But let me warn you. No one must know you are going. You must slip out quietly and without detection. The separation must be total and complete, for if anyone learns of your purpose, know this. I will have Slate and Joanace tell your story to all, and everything will be lost to you—everything!" she warned. "Do you understand? Do not delude yourself that I am incapable of carrying out my threats to the fullest, my dear."

"I understand, Matilda. I will do all that you ask. But what if Michael comes looking for me? Surely he will wonder that I have disappeared so suddenly and without apparent cause," she asked, still hoping to find some dent in Matilda's plan.

"He won't come looking for you, my dear. I will take care of that," said Matilda confidently. "He will be upset and angry when he finds you gone, and he will come to me for solace and comfort. I will make him forget you in a very short time," she puffed.

"Though you force me to flee because I love him and wish to protect him, pride yourself not that he will run to you for comfort. 'Twould be ironic indeed, Matilda, though you accomplish your purpose in disposing of me, that Michael does not comply with your scheme and fall willingly into your clutches."

"Oh, you little bitch!" cried Matilda in anger and lunged to strike. Christy ducked and stealed herself for another blow, but Matilda's anger had already vanished. "Well, don't worry yourself about that, my dear. If something should go amiss—and nothing will—at least I will have the consolation of knowing that, though I do not have Michael, neither will you. At any rate, I usually get what I want, and I want Michael," she said with sure determination. "All is settled then. Will you be ready and waiting tonight?" asked Matilda as she stepped to the window to regard the blistering weather.

"Yes, I will do as you say, Matilda, for you give me no other recourse," answered Christy, despondent beyond words.

"Good. If you hold true to your part of the bargain, no one will be hurt. And I trust you do not wish to see a respected family like the Lancers suffer for your sins?"

"No, they must be spared. But someday, Matilda, you, Joanace and Slate will be repaid for your wickedness. To that I give my solemn vow."

"You frighten me little, my dear. Now go and prepare for your departure, but do it quietly. I trust I will never see you again. It has been anything but a pleasure knowing you. I will not regret your absence in the least." With that, Matilda bestowed a triumphant smile upon the hapless girl, well pleased she had shattered the life of her enemy and remained the conqueror.

Quietly she opened the study door and, satisfying herself that no one was about, stepped from the room and out the door. Her patience and perserverance would at last be rewarded. The girl would be gone tonight, never to be seen or heard from again. Penncrest, Michael and all their wealth would be hers.

Twenty-Eight

The silence of the house thundered in Christy's head. She slumped in the chair, transfixed by the deafening quiet. The room spun about in a nauseating whirl. Her trembling hands felt cold and clammy. Her body and mind were numb. Time ticked by with heedless abandon.

Again the arguments danced through her mind at a dizzying clip. She could go to Michael, as she had planned, and tell him the whole wretched story, and together they could battle Matilda. But could they succeed in negotiating her silence? Would Michael's anger at her long silence turn him to Matilda's way of thinking? No, she would not believe that. He loved her and would stand by her. But what if Matilda could not be bribed? Then they would all suffer. No, she must flee with her unborn child, as Matilda had ordained, in order to spare those she loved.

Tears welled up in her eyes and dropped slowly upon her icy hands. The clock in the hall chimed and still she sat, feeling empty, drained and too exhausted to move.

"Oh, my lady, here you are," said Milly as she bustled into the room to tidy up. "I've not seen you all day."

Christy made no response.

"Why, Miss Christy. It's frightfully cold in here, and you've no candle burning. I would gladly have lit the fire for you," said Milly, coming closer. It was peculiar indeed for her usually boisterous mistress to be so sullen and silent.

Again Christy made no response. Was Milly's voice real, or part of her dreamlike musings?

"Are you all right? Why, my lady, you are cold as ice!" cried Milly as she touched Christy's shoulder lightly in an effort to rouse her.

With supreme effort Christy focused dazed, distant eyes upon the girl. "I hadn't realized the fire had gone out. It is rather cool in here," she said. She had surmised the coldness she felt had come from within, rather than from the frigid room.

"Here, let me light a candle and bring you a blanket, mistress. And some hot tea to warm you," said Milly as she hurried to light the lamp.

"Thank you, Milly, but I think I shall lie down. What is the hour?" she asked in a toneless voice.

"Why, it's after seven, ma'am. Nearly time for dinner," said Milly, still perplexed by her peculiar mood. "Oh, mistress, you look terrible! Are you ill? I shall send Morgan for the doctor at once," she cried as she brought the candle close and gazed with concern at Christy's chalk-white face.

"No. I am fine. Just tired, Milly. If you will help me to my room, I believe I shall rest for a time. And tell Nellie not to bother with dinner. I have no appetite," she said and rose stiffly.

Milly was surprised when Christy led the way to her

old room instead of Master Michael's. She explained that it was too lonely in the big bed without her husband. But the truth was, the heartache of seeing his possessions and feeling his presence all about was just too much to bear. She could not look upon his things, knowing she would never see him again.

Milly helped her to bed and started a blazing fire. A short time later she returned with some hot tea, which helped somewhat in warming Christy's chilled frame. The hot liquid, however, did little to relieve the intensity of her heartache.

"Will there be anything else you'd like or need, ma'am?" asked Milly after Christy had finished her tea and settled onto the pillows.

"No, Milly. Thank you. I need nothing more. You may have the rest of the evening off for I think I shall stay in bed."

"Very well, Mistress. Should you need anything, just ring the bell. I will look in on you a little later to see if you are all right," volunteered the girl.

"That won't be necessary. I wish to be alone. I will not need you," said Christy, a trifle more harshly than she had intended. It would not do for Milly to walk in as she was preparing to depart.

"As you wish, ma'am," said Milly, slightly hurt and puzzled by Christy's sharp attitude.

"Milly, I didn't mean to speak so harshly. I really do appreciate your concern, but I am fine. You have been a tremendous help to me. I could not have managed without you. I will never forget your kindness. You are a true friend," said Christy, trying to control her trembling lips.

"Oh, you're quite welcome, Miss Christy. I truly enjoy my work here," said Milly, confused even more by her peculiar mood.

"Good night, Milly," said Christy in an effort to cut the one-sided goodbye short. She could not long control the tears which threatened to spill at any moment.

"Good night, ma'am," answered Milly softly, still shaking her head in confusion as she closed the door and set about her household tasks.

A few hours later, after relentless tossing and turning, Christy rose and gathered together a few of her belongings. She folded two warm dresses into her small case and various undergarments. Matilda had stressed traveling light, and Christy realized the prudence in carrying as little as possible.

She fingered the beautiful emerald necklace Michael had given her. The sweet happy memories it brought back caused tears of pain and sorrow at her impending flight. She must leave it behind. She was not fit to keep such a gift. Perhaps he would marry again and pass the jewels on to a woman more worthy of his love and devotion. Hurriedly she closed the velvet-lined box and huddled in a chair beside the fire, waiting for the designated hour of departure.

The fire crackled and the wind howled outside in the cold, windy night. Within the hour she would be forced out into the night as a fugitive once more. The thought tore her heart asunder, for never again would she see

Michael, or feel his arms about her, or hear his words, soft and tender, whispered in her ear.

"Oh, Michael, my darling Michael," she whispered into the fire. "Please do not let Matilda's evil lies cause you to hate me. I implore you now, wherever you are, to forever hold a small measure of love and tenderness in your heart for me. I love you deeply, and only flee to protect you from the pain I myself know only too well. Think not too ill of me, dear husband, for the memory of our happiness together will sustain me through all that lies ahead."

She placed her head on her arms, again fighting off tears, but the longer she thought of Michael hating her, the more distressed she became. With a small degree of rebellion, she rose from the warmth of the fire and sat at her desk. Picking up a quill and writing paper, she wrote with trembling, unsteady fingers:

Dearest Michael,

I could not leave without some small word of fare-well. Though I cannot explain my reasons for depart-ing, please know that I do so to spare you much shame at my hands, for I love you more than life itself. You and your family have been far too good to me that I could knowingly cause you disgrace and pain.

Know that I cannot keep these precious jewels from your mother, for you gave them to me in love and trust, and I have failed you in both. I hope that someday you will find someone worthy of your love who will bring you happiness and honor.

Know, too, that I will always love and cherish our

child, for in him, I will always have a part of you.
Goodbye, my dearest husband. I pray you will find it
in your heart to hold some small fondness for me.
Your loving wife,
Christina

Christy reread her words. A stray tear trickled down her cheek and dropped on the paper. She hastily brushed it away, but not before it left a small smudge.

With a sigh, she folded the letter, picked up the lamp, and headed for Michael's room which had only this morning been her room also. She pushed the door open hesitantly, fearful that perhaps Matilda would pop out and snatch the note from her hand. She quickly scanned the room, hoping that, by some miracle, Michael would appear. The room, however, looked dark and uninhabited, and she stepped inside and closed the door.

Slowly she looked around, wanting to remember every detail just as it was. She touched the dressing table and ran her fingers over the smooth posts of the huge bed. This large, soft, wonderful bed had brought her whole world together. Though their reconciliation had been all too short, this bed had taken her on a new and fantastic experience in the world of love and passion. And it was in this bed that Michael had first professed his love for her.

In her haste to leave, she nearly knocked over the chamber maid as she passed with an armful of fresh linen. Not wishing to stop and explain her tearful condition, she mumbled an apology and hurried on to the solitude of her room.

She sat in the chair, but the warmth of the fire could

not penetrate her despondent mood, and she sat shivering miserably. Time seemed to drag with deliberate slowness, yet at the same time it ticked on with deadly determination. Finally the huge clock in the hallway below struck fifteen minutes before the hour. Her body seemed to be laden with heavy weights as she rose.

She wrapped her cloak tightly about herself and reached for her valise. The wind howled outside; nature's turmoil seemingly matched her own. She took a slow, final look about, extinguished the candle, and turned with a heavy heart to slip quietly down the stairs and out into the cold, dark night.

The wind made eerie noises as it rustled the tree limbs before the dark, sleeping house. Looming shadows seemed to take on demonic forms, and she shivered, ready to quit her vigil and take to flight. Just as her nerves reached a point of breaking, out of the gloom came the black form of a carriage. The sound of slowly plodding horses' hooves whipped nearer, and she felt again a twinge of fear. The carriage lurched huge and ominous, closer and closer, until she was convinced that a dozen ghouls would spring from the coach and set themselves upon her.

The monstrous vehicle slid to a slow, almost stealthy halt. She squinted through the darkness. She held her breath in terror. A huge black man, well-camouflaged in the darkness, jumped from his seat on the coach and approached. Without a word, he stopped a few feet away. The whites of his eyes seemed to bore through her heavy veil. She shivered in terror at being at the mercy of this unfeeling stranger.

The horses pranced nervously in the windy darkness, seeming to sense the presence of evil. The wind howled again and he reached for her case. Opening the door, he motioned her to enter. As she brushed past, she stole a look in his direction. His eyes were fixed steadily upon her. Even the darkness could not hide his cold, ruthless expression. Her skin crawled in fear.

She quickly moved to the far corner of the carriage and peered nervously at him. Seeing her seated, he placed the valise on the floor and closed the door, yet he did not immediately move away. Instead he stared at her in calculated silence.

Christy tugged at the veil which hid her face and stared down at her lap. Her heart pounded wildly. Would he kill her here and now? She felt near ready to die of fright. Suddenly he disappeared from the doorway, and she felt him swing up onto the seat above her. The carriage started with a jerk, and the long ride began.

She huddled in the corner of the coach, staring listlessly out at the passing darkness. The going was extremely slow due to the fierce wind which rocked the carriage about. It was all she could do at times to keep her seat and not be thrown to the floor. Numerous times she attempted to get some sleep, but the bumping carriage, and the terrible, biting cold made even resting impossible.

They traveled for hours without stopping. With the light of day came also heavy downpours of rain. Even the sun denied her its warmth and cheer. The dreary morning wore on. Her stomach growled and the baby kicked fiercely within her. She felt hungry and totally bruised and exhausted from the long journey and wondered how she could endure more. Matilda had said she would be taken somewhere outside of Charleston, and there to meet another coach. Surely, even with the slow, treacherous going, they must have traveled a considerable distance from Charleston.

Just as she was about to bolster her courage and summon the driver to plead for a brief respite, the carriage came to a slow, grinding halt. She peered outside. Thick, ominous wilderness surrounded them.

Wearily she straightened her hat and skirts as she waited for the driver to open the door. He descended slowly and she held her breath as he peered in at her. He was a huge man, with arms that looked like tree trunks. A long, ugly scar divided his cheek. His thick lips were set in a hard, cruel line. The cloudy daylight revealed no kindness reflected in the large dark eyes which seemed to mock her helplessness. She swallowed hard and stumbled hurriedly from the carriage.

Her long cramped legs were stiff and unwilling to accept her weight. She tottered unsteadily, trying to gain her balance. The driver made no move to help her. Instead he watched in withdrawn contempt.

She cast a quick look about, hoping to see an inn or tavern. Instead, off to her right stood an abandoned, dilapidated shack nestled in the heavy trees. "Where are we? Why have we stopped here?" she wanted to know, her pulses quickening in sudden fear. "Are we only stopping here to stretch?"

He merely shook his head.

"I . . . I don't understand. Mrs. Lancer told me we

would be stopping at a public tavern to rest and eat, and I was to meet another coach that would take me to my final destination. This place is obviously deserted, and has never accommodated lodgers. There must be some mistake," she said, panic edging her frail voice. Had this man brought her here, out in the middle of nowhere, to kill her?

"There's no mistake. This is the place," he muttered, seeming to enjoy her panic.

Christy stared again at the shack, incredulous as to how and why she had been brought here. She took a few steps closer, still unwilling to believe her eyes. A sound behind her made her whirl about in time to see the black man pull himself up onto the carriage. He tossed a small bundle to the ground near her feet and cracked the whip smartly over the horses' backs.

She watched in utter disbelief. It was not possible that she was to be deserted here, in the middle of nowhere, alone and fightened! "Oh, please do not leave me alone here! Please don't go!" she cried and ran in desperation after the departing coach.

White teeth glistened as the man sneered down at her. The whip whizzed through the air and cracked on the horses' rumps. They whinnied loudly and set off at a fast gallop.

Though she knew it was hopeless, Christy continued to run after the disappearing carriage, calling out to the driver to stop. He paid no attention to her pleadings. Finally he disappeared completely from sight.

Christy stumbled to a stop, panting heavily. Warm tears stung her cold cheeks and she crumpled to the ground, gasping sobs racking her shivering body. Was she to be left alone and deserted here to die? Had that been Matilda's plan all along? Was that what she had meant when she had assured her that she would be taken care of, one way or another? Oh, what a fool she had been to fall for Matilda's scheme. The woman must surely be laughing merrily at her own cleverness and at Christy's ignorance.

The tears stopped at last, and she picked herself up from the damp ground. Slowly Christy retraced her steps back to the clearing. She picked up the bundle the black man had tossed and, with no small amount of trepidation, pushed open the door to the cabin.

The one room shack was even more disgusting inside than it appeared from outside. Light seeping in from numerous cracks in the ceiling and walls revealed cobwebs that filled the corners and hung from the ceiling. She shivered yet forced herself to step inside and get a better look at the dirty interior.

The place looked as if it had been uninhabited for years. A small stove stood at one end of the room. At the other was a cot covered with dirty blankets. Squeaking and scurrying feet sounded in the darkness and slowly died away as her furry visitors rushed to their hiding places. She closed her eyes and breathed deeply, fighting the faintness which threatened to render her unconscious.

When the spell passed, she felt somewhat calmer, and stepped to the dusty table and placed the small parcel upon it. It wobbled unsteadily as she tore off the wrappings. Inside the package were a few small morsels of food and water. No doubt Matilda had bestowed this small sustenance to keep her alive for a few days in order to let her suffer for her sins.

Christy shivered again as the wind howled outside. Wearily she closed the door. It did little to stop the draft. With fingers numb from the cold, she stuffed the stove with a few stray pieces of wood which lay about the room. In a short time she had a fire going and the cabin was considerably warmer. The comforting fire eased her weariness somewhat, and she looked about the room again, wondering where to begin. If this wretched hole was to be her residence, she would have to make it somewhat more habitable.

She began with the cot, dragging the assorted rank and dirty blankets outside to shake out the dust and let the air freshen them. Movement was slow and difficult with her large stomach, and she often had to stop and rest.

After she had the cot outside, she tackled the cobwebs and dirt about the room. When darkness at last fell, she was forced to cease her cleaning, but when she sat down at the clean table to nibble on some biscuits, she was a little more at rest with her surroundings.

Exhausted from the previous sleepless night and strenuous cleaning, she lay uneasily down on the somewhat fresher cot. The wind howled through the many cracks in the cabin and her imagination ran rampant. She forced herself to relax, thinking of Michael.

All during the day as she worked busily at cleaning her lodgings, she had continuously reassured herself that her sentence here was only temporary and she would not be

left to die. She convinced herself that Michael loved her
and would not listen to Matilda's lies. Surely he would
come riding up at any time and rescue her from this
dreary, lonely exile. With those thoughts of reassurance
firmly planted in her mind, she was able to relax and
ignore the fearful, howling wind. Finally she drifted off
to a restless slumber. . . .

Christy awoke early the next morning to a very cold
and profoundly quiet cabin. She shivered violently.
Surely today Michael would come for her.

She rose and quickly rekindled the stove with the last
of the wood in an effort to bring a little heat back into the
drafty cabin. Putting on her cloak with the idea of
searching for more wood, she opened the door, wondering what tempests the night had brought. She gasped in
surprise at the blanket of white covering the ground.
Nature itself seemed to be revolting. Her shock slowly
diminished and she gazed at the snow-covered world in
wonder. It was remarkably beautiful, yet the quiet,
unblemished whiteness made her realize just how very
much alone she really was.

It was nearly imposssible finding dry firewood under
the snow, for going was difficult and she had to take
much care lest she fall. Finally, after much time and few
results, she returned to the cabin to make do with what
she had. Perhaps tomorrow the snow would melt and her
search would be less difficult.

Closing the door against the cold, Christy busied
herself with a little cooking and further cleaning her
temporary home. By nightfall she felt a little less sure of

her imminent rescue, but still did not doubt Michael's perserverance.

And so passed the next few days. She would rise and bring warmth back to her abode, then venture out to gather wood for heating and cooking. It was a dreary, lonely existence, and slowly, as each passing day brought no sign of Michael, or anyone else, her spirits began to wain.

A week passed, and her meals became smaller and smaller as her supply of food slowly diminished. If it was Matilda's wish that she starve to death, the end would certainly not be long in coming. Her daily efforts to uncover firewood cost her much strength, and the wet sticks did little to warm the cabin. And now with her food dwindling, so was her strength. The babe growing within cried for nourishment, and her anguish at being helpless to save herself and the baby added to her distress and ever-deepening hopelessness.

It was too much of a struggle to go on, and, as she lay in bed, too exhausted and distressed to sleep, she ceased to reassure herself of Michael's undoubted appearance. If he truly loved her, he would have come for her long before this. Even the snow and mud would not have kept him back for long. With a tear of self-pity, she gave up. Matilda had surely won and would have her way. She would die, alone, in this wretched hole, unloved and unwanted.

Christy now had to face the facts. Matilda had been right, after all. Michael had never loved her, but had always loved Matilda. She and her unwanted child had just been in the way all this time. With her gone, they would once again be free to marry. It had all been a charade, and she the hapless pawn.

In her weak and despondent state, these realities were as harsh and cold as the elements outside the cabin. After the seventh day, she made no effort to venture out, though the snow was slowly melting. She remained huddled beneath the flimsy blankets, too despondent even to rise from the bed, and with no desire to go on.

Twenty-Nine

Michael and Sir Phillip, unavoidably delayed in Charleston by the bad weather, finally returned to Penncrest late in the afternoon five days after their departure. Tired and cold from the long journey, they removed their heavy traveling overcoats and went immediately into the study to relax and enjoy a strong drink before the evening meal.

"I wonder where Christina is. I hope she's not upset with us for being away so long, especially after leaving on such short notice," commented Michael when she did not appear. A new thought suddenly struck him and he stood in the doorway. "Bertha? Come here. Bertha, where is Mrs. Lancer? Has she been informed of our arrival? She's not ill, is she? It's not the baby . . . ?" his concern was growing by the minute.

"No, sir . . . no . . ." she moaned, wringing her hands in open despair.

"What is it? What's happened?" cried Michael as he gripped her by the shoulders.

Suddenly from around the corner appeared Matilda, exquisitely attired in a mauve gown with plunging neckline and short, fluffy sleeves. She was more than aware of the sleek, sensual appearance she exuded. Her hour of triumph was at hand, and she was dressed for the part.

"Really, Michael. Calm yourself. You mustn't become so upset. Come into the study," she invited and brushed past him. "Oh, Bertha, I'll handle this. You may go," she dismissed the distraught servant with a wave of her hand.

Michael nodded to Bertha and then followed Matilda back into the study.

"How are you, darlings? Did you have a good trip?" she cooed, standing enticingly before Michael. She fluttered her eyes seductively, setting the scene. With Christy gone, her beauty would have no competition.

"The trip was satisfactory, though the weather was abominable," Michael answered stiffly, ignoring her obvious flirtation. He was in no mood to come home and find her here. Obviously she had again verbally abused Christina. No doubt it was the reason for her absence now. He turned and poured himself another drink, and handed one to his father. "Where is Christina? Is she not feeling well? I thought she would be eager for our return."

Matilda sighed loudly and turned dramatically toward the door, smiling to herself. When she again turned to face the two men, her face was a study in concern and worry, and she wrung her hands nervously. "Oh, Michael, darling, I just don't know how to break this to you. I've been just sick with worry and compassion for you. As soon as I heard the news, I came straight here and have been waiting four days now so I could be here when you returned, to comfort you. Oh, it's all so terrible," she went on, playing her part expertly.

"What are you talking about, Matilda? What is wrong that has you so upset?" he demanded with little interest. He was well accustomed to her over dramatic renditions of minor catastrophies. But suddenly, Christina's peculiar absence and Matilda's uninvited presence smelled of trouble. "Is something wrong with Christy? Is it the baby?" he demanded, setting his drink down hurriedly and striding toward the door to rush upstairs.

Matilda grabbed his arm as he passed, noticing the troubled look clouding his handsome face. What a fool he was to have fallen into the girl's clever trap. "No, wait, Michael. Don't go," she said, clinging to his sleeve. "I just don't know how to tell you," she deliberately dragged out the suspense.

"Damnit, woman, what is going on here? Tell me!" he demanded, grabbing her roughly.

"Michael, please, you're hurting me," she pouted at his none too gentle handling. "I only came to comfort you in your hour of loss and to offer my sympathy that your new wife has up and left you. Don't be angry with me. Save your fury for she who deserves it," she whimpered with feigned hurt.

Michael released her abruptly, unable to comprehend her words. "Christy—gone? What the hell are you talking about?"

"Oh, darling, your temper is misdirected. I'm so sorry to have to be the one to tell you. I stopped by four days ago to pay my respects, and the servants told me she had disappeared sometime during the night. No one has seen or heard from her since."

"God, no! I don't believe it! Why would she run away? Where would she go?" he ranted, pacing nervously and running his fingers through his hair as he always did when he was upset.

Sir Phillip jumped to his feet, nearly choking on his drink. He was visibly as shaken as his agitated son. "Tell us exactly what you know," he demanded sharply, staring at her with keen, mistrusting eyes.

Matilda took a deep breath. "I don't understand why you are both so angry with me. I only sought to help you through this terrible ordeal. I can see I am not appreciated," she said, again playing the sufferer.

"We are not angry with you, Matilda. We are shocked by the news and seek to discover exactly what happened more quickly than you seem able to tell us," he explained as if to a small, ignorant child.

"Well, as I said, I just stopped by to pay a friendly visit. I was shocked to find her gone. Apparently she snuck out during the night, leaving no word with anyone. What a dreadful girl to do such a thing, after all you've done for her," she concluded.

Dissatisfied with her lack of information, Michael strode to the door. "Bertha! Where the devil are you?" he bellowed into the hall. "Come in here."

A moment later the distraught housekeeper appeared in the doorway.

"Come in, Bertha. What do you know about my wife's disappearance?" he demanded. "When and how did you discover her gone?"

Bertha took a gulp of air, swallowing hard. She wiped her hands on her apron and looked first at Michael, then to Sir Phillip. Her attention lingered for a moment on Matilda before she turned back to address Michael.

"Well, sir, I was called away last Monday to tend to a sick servant. Didn't get back 'til late the next mornin'. Mistress Christy didn't come for breakfast as usual, so I fetched Milly. The girl said her mistress had seemed rather quiet and real tearful the night before. She figured Mistress Christy had decided to sleep late so didn't figure to bother her. Well, it didn't set well with me, being so unlike the young mistress. So I went to check on her myself. I found her room empty, her bed not even slept in. Your room was empty too," said Bertha, trying to speak evenly.

"She hardly took nothing with her, sir. And her so close with the baby and all. I been near crazy with worry ever since, it being well over a week and all. I tried to find you, but had no way of getting a message to you," Bertha stuttered, tears threatening to spill down her shiny cheeks. She twisted her apron around and around in her hands.

Michael let her words sink in. "Did she take the carriage?" he asked, trying to fit the pieces together.

"Well, sir, that's the strange part of it all. Morgan said all the horses and carriages are here. She must have gone on foot, or else had someone meet her."

"Oh my God!" exclaimed Michael, beginning to pace again. "Have you questioned the other servants? Did no one see her go? How far could she go in her condition, and in this wretched weather?"

"No one saw nothin', sir. Milly said she found her sitting alone in the study late the evenin' before, without so much as a light or fire. Milly put her to bed, as she wanted nothing to eat for supper. But she insisted on going to her own room. Milly said she'd look in on her comfort later, but the young mistress protested harshly. No sooner had she scolded Milly than she thanked her for all her help. The girl was right confused, but just put it to her condition," commented Bertha. "Later that night, one of the maids was carrying linen to the spare room and ran right into Mistress Christy coming from your room, lookin' all tearful and upset. That was the last anyone saw her," finished Bertha, a little breathless and teary-eyed herself.

Again Michael tried to make sense from her story, and again he came up blank. "I just don't understand. My God, why would she go? And who came for her? She knows no on here," he asked, becoming more agitated by the minute.

Suddenly a new thought struck him and sweat broke out on his forehead. "My God, do you think someone may have kidnapped her? But who? Why?" He paused and then rushed on. "Did anyone come to call during the day? Did she receive any messages?" he demanded urgently. "Did you receive a ransom note?"

"No, sir. We heard nothin' like that," said Bertha, also alarmed by this new prospect.

"Of course you've not heard anything about a ransom, Michael," interrupted Matilda. "There was no kidnapper involved."

Michael spun to face her. "What makes you so sure?"

"It's all quite clear, really. If you'd only have let me explain, I could have spared you the embarrassment in front of this servant," she sniffed.

"Matilda, get to the point. What makes you so sure she was not abducted?" interjected Sir Phillip.

"Well, if you check your safe you will find all your jewels missing. The theft was discovered shortly after your wife's disappearance. Ask the servants if you don't believe me, or check for yourself," she suggested.

Michael could not believe what he had heard. He raced to the safe behind the desk. It was empty, except for a few odd papers. "I just can't believe she would take the jewels. If she really wanted to leave, if she was not happy here, all she had to do was ask me for money. I would have given her all she wanted. But why would she go? I thought she was happy here. I thought she loved me," he muttered half to himself. "I just can't believe she would steal them and run off."

"Well, it seems far too great a coincidence to be brushed aside lightly, if you ask me—everything disappearing at once," sneered Matilda.

"Bertha, when were the jewels discovered missing?" asked Sir Phillip, still unconvinced of Christy's guilt.

"Let me think, sir. Oh yes. You see, I didn't get back 'til late Monday mornin'. When I found the young mistress gone, I set the servants to searching the house. It was them found the safe open and papers lyin' all about. I just can't believe she would do such a thing,

Master," cried Bertha, speaking her piece.

"I can't believe it either. But, I intend to get to the bottom of this." He paced nervously, his mind a whirl of unanswered questions. "Did anyone hear any noises or disturbances during that night? Like someone breaking in?"

"No, sir. Everyone said the place was quiet, like always, 'cept for the howling o' the wind."

Again Matilda interrupted. "Oh come now, Michael. Everyone can see the truth but you. Quit making excuses for her. As you can see, the safe was not broken into, but neatly opened. You filed your bookkeeping accounts there, didn't you? Your wife worked on your books and knew the jewels were there, right? Who else would have the combination of the safe except you and Sir Phillip, and Christina? Since both of you were gone, that only leaves your little wife—caught red-handed. Face it, the little thief robbed you blind and got out while she still could."

"Though the facts point to her guilt, I am still unwilling to believe she did such a thing without some provocation. Did no one notice a stranger about, or see her speaking to anyone in secret?" Michael directed his questions to Bertha.

"Morgan said he saw Miss Matilda's carriage early the morning before she disappeared. Said it was parked away from the house," informed Bertha, giving Matilda a wary glance. "He said it was gone in a very short time."

"Thank you, Bertha. That will be all for now. Please keep what you have heard in strictest confidence until we discover the truth. If we need you again we will call," said Michael in forced control. Bertha's statement had put a new light on things.

When the servant had gone, Michael spun to regard his sister-in-law. "Were you here the morning before Christina disappeared? What do you know about this that you have not said?"

Matilda's regal, secure look suddenly changed to that of one on guard. She had not counted on any of the servants spotting her carriage. She had deliberately parked it out of sight of the house and walked to the entrance. "I don't know what you mean, Michael dear. You needn't be so upset with me. I just dropped by to pay a friendly visit. When I found you gone, I stopped for a time to chat with your wife. It would have been rude not to say hello," she said, again playing the misunderstood victim.

"Your story does not sit well with me, Matilda. Why would you go out of your way to visit Christina? It's clear you've disliked her from the start. I'm sure your visit was not out of friendliness or courtesy. Did you say something to upset her?" snapped Michael.

"Yes, and why did you park your carriage down the lane, away from the house? The weather was certainly not conducive to walking," questioned Sir Phillip, picking up something different in her exchange than Michael had.

Matilda was quickly becoming upset at the turn of events. Instead of setting them against Christy, she found herself on the defensive. She ignored Sir Phillip's questions, for which she could give no plausible explanation, and turned to Michael, her temper flaring. "Michael Lancer, don't talk to me about belittling people, after you have the nerve to bring that slut to this house and then pass her off as your cousin. Do you really think I fell for such a story? I would have thought you'd have better taste in a mistress, my dear."

"The girl was never my mistress, Matilda. I admit we are no kin, but I also admit that she is with child because of my doing alone. She is a respectable woman and she is my wife. Nothing will convince me otherwise except solid, conclusive proof to the contrary," Michael spat at her.

Matilda had certainly not counted on him taking Christy's defense. She had assumed that once he found she'd fled with his jewels, he would be filled with anger. Things were beginning to get out of hand, and drastic measures were in order. It was time to play her trump card.

"I am well aware of the fact that she is no relation to you. You must take me for a fool to think I'd believe such a story. But the undeniable fact is that she is a liar and a thief," she seethed back at him.

"What the hell gives you the right to call my wife a thief? Though the evidence points strongly to her guilt, nothing has been proven yet," flared Michael. His eyes narrowed to tiny slits as they pierced into hers. "Perhaps some accomplice forced her to behave this way," he allowed.

"I have every right to call her a thief and a liar,

Michael," she snarled back at him. His glib tone infuriated her, and without thinking, she went on. "Stop defending her and open your eyes. You will discover, no doubt, that this whole thing, from the very start, was nothing but a plot to get your name and your money. As far as trying to figure out who her accomplice is, I can save you the trouble. I already know she is in cahoots with her uncle, Henry Slate. Does it all fit in now, Michael?" she questioned acidly.

"Henry Slate? You must be crazy, Matilda. He is in London," Michael said with irritation. "How could he have anything to do with this?"

"London? Don't be so sure, my dear. I myself saw him get off a ship right here in Charleston not five days ago! He sailed on Greg Piper's ship. That's how I know. Again, my dear Michael, can you pin that on coincidence? It's too much of a coincidence to believe that it was not all planned from the very start, right after she left London."

Part of what she said struck a nerve in Michael's mind. For a moment he remained silent. "It is rather peculiar that her uncle should suddenly show up at the same time as her disappearance, it's true," he admitted. "But I still cannot believe she planned this whole thing and has run off with him. She feared and despised him for the way he mistreated her. I myself saw the scars on her back where he had whipped her," he said, recalling the pain she had suffered at his hands.

Matilda sensed his weakening and seized upon the opportunity. "Are you certain it was Slate who beat her? Can you be certain that wasn't just another lie she told?

Perhaps it was some other unfortunate soul they had tricked and robbed who took his vengeance out on her," argued Matilda strongly.

"Forget that slut, Michael," she breathed earnestly, looking deeply into his eyes with the most provocative of expressions. "She's nothing to you, and she has used you sorely. It is I who loves you. She never has. Take me. Let me make you a happy man," she cooed and ran her fingers lightly through his hair, ignoring the fact that Sir Phillip was present and watching the whole display with open disgust.

Michael's skin crawled at her touch. He quickly disengaged himself from her and walked away. "Do you forget so quickly that despite her actions, we are still married? I cannot so easily abandon my vows."

"Oh, Michael. Nothing would stand in your way from divorcing her, not after what she has done. It would be a simple thing for you to divorce her and marry me," she pleaded.

Michael stared at her with a mixture of hatred, pity and resignation. "Don't hold your breath waiting for me to crawl to you. That will never happen, even if what you say about Christy is true. I fully intend to get to the bottom of this. I will go after her and Slate and I will find them if it takes the rest of my life. But I will know the truth, and she will be punished for her deeds if she is found guilty."

"No! You mustn't try to find her. She will only fill your head with more lies," cautioned Matilda. She knew only too well that once he made up his mind to find her, find her he would. Then the whole scheme would be lost and she would be implicated. "You will be sorry if you go after her. I swear you will live to regret it," cried Matilda in unmasked panic.

"I already regret this whole sordid mess," Michael replied and strode quickly from the room. He sought the solitude of his bedchamber to mull over all that he had learned.

Thirty

Once in his room, Michael shrugged off his heavy boots and slumped on the chair beside his bed. He toyed with a cigar, forgetting to light it. He could not believe that Christy had truly stolen the jewelry out of maliciousness and then fled in fear—yet the safe was indeed empty of its contents, and she was gone without so much as one word of explanation. All the facts seemed to fall so neatly into place, completely indicting her. It was almost too neat.

He pulled off his heavy shirt and threw it irritably on the bed. Something slipped to the floor. He stooped to pick up the note. A familiar velvet-lined box lay on his pillow. He opened it up and stared at the dainty necklace he had given to Christy the night of the ball. His pulse racing, he held the note close to the candle and read his wife's words.

According to the missive, and by her own admission, she had fled, refusing to give him a reason. Yet as he read, he realized it was not the note of a spiteful woman running off with her husband's possessions. It seemed more of an apology, and as if she had truly been frightened away against her will. Did the truth of the matter lie in the fact that she had found out about Slate's

504

arrival, and fled to avoid his finding her? But no, that seemed unlikely. And she had left behind the priceless emerald necklace!

The more he mulled over these new developments, the more his mind fostered the notion that Christy's sudden disappearance warranted investigation. He could not rest until he knew the truth, one way or another. He would begin his search immediately, for anything was better than the torture of sitting and debating over the endless possibilities.

With renewed determination, he rose and again pulled on his heavy boots and warmest shirt. Throwing a few necessary articles in a small sack, he strode from the room and down the stairs to the study.

Sir Phillip, sitting alone and staring dejectedly into the fire, looked up as his son entered.

"Where is Matilda?" asked Michael in a gruff voice.

"She has gone to her room to pack, Michael. I believe you hurt her pride immeasurably by defending Christina and putting her in her place. She said she will not spend another night under this roof if she is not welcome." He paused and chuckled without humor. "I did nothing to discourage her departure."

Michael ignored his father's humorless joke, and poured himself a hefty drink to prepare himself for the cold journey.

His father eyed him in concern. "Do you believe Matilda's theories about Christina? I just can't comprehend the girl running off like this. We've been so good to her, and she seemed very happy here. I can't understand it. It makes no sense at all."

"I don't understand it either, Father. But all the evidence points to the truth in what Matilda said. Her disappearance in the night without a clue, her uncle's sudden arrival in Charleston, the missing contents from the safe. Everything points to her guilt," he said and then reached into his pocket. "That is, everything but this letter." He handed his father the now-crumpled missive.

As his father read, he paced the floor nervously.

"Hmmm," said Sir Phillip as he removed his spectacles. "This note does seem to cast an even more mysterious light on the situation. She professes her deep love for you, but gives no reason for fleeing other than her desire to spare us shame. It must have something to do with her past, Michael."

"Yes, I am sure it has everything to do with what happened in London," agreed Michael.

"This bit about the jewels has me baffled, though," continued Sir Phillip as he rose and joined Michael in pacing the floor. "It seems peculiar she would have left the most precious of jewels behind and confiscate the other less costly ones. It strikes me odd she would mention the jewels at all if she decided to steal them. I find it very unlike her to steal anything at all. I would have trusted her with my very life."

"God help me, I just don't know what to think," Michael sighed and ran his fingers through his tousled hair. Pain and exhaustion dulled the usual brightness of his brown eyes.

He took a final swallow of the strong brew and set the glass on the table. "I'm going to look for her," he said. "I must know the truth. Even if Matilda was right, and this whole thing was a plot against us from the start, even if she did run off with the jewels to meet Slate, I still must find her and hear it from her own lips. I am still not convinced of Matilda's conjecture that she joined up with Slate in this plot against me. She hated and despised him. I intend to go to Piper and find out for myself if this Slate arrived on his ship."

Suddenly he struck his fist against his palm in anger. "If only she'd told me about her past, none of this would have happened. It could all have been avoided," he said heatedly.

"Yes, all this secrecy has led only to hardship and pain. But take heart, Michael. She will be found and the truth uncovered," comforted Sir Phillip, placing a hand upon his son's sagging shoulder.

"I must know why she left, and I must know it now," said Michael with determination.

"But, Michael, 'tis folly for you to set off now to find her. The night is cold and dark and you are tired from our journey. Besides, she has been gone five days now. There will be no clue, and anyone who may have seen her will surely be abed. Wait until morning, at least, when it is light and we will organize a search party," he pleaded, fearful of his son's hasty decision.

"I cannot wait, Father. I must find her. I'll not rest until I know the truth."

His eyes traveled up the stairway as he heard Matilda bellowing orders to the servants to speed up her departure. "Though I hesitate in asking this even of you, Father, please see if you can get more explicit details from Matilda. I have a hunch, from all her subtle revelations, that she knows far more about this whole thing than she is admitting. She greatly disliked Christina, and would, I am sure, feel no remorse at her disappearance. See what you can do," he concluded.

"Well, Michael, I see I cannot stop you. You have made up your mind. But please, be careful," cautioned Sir Phillip in an anxious voice. "You are upset and I would hate to see you remorseful at some irrational, hasty action."

"I will stay calm, Father, and level-headed. No matter what the truth," he promised as he walked down the hall and donned his heavy coat and gloves.

"I will find out what I can here. If anything turns up, I will send someone to our lawyer in Charleston. Keep him apprised of your whereabouts," said Sir Phillip.

Michael nodded his appreciation, clapped his father on the shoulder for reassurance, and disappeared into the darkness of the night.

Thirty-One

The sun shone in through the cracks and holes in the little cabin on Christy's eighth morning of confinement. She had slept very little. Again and again she'd awakened in terror from her old nightmare. In the darkness, images of Matilda laughing wickedly and triumphantly as Michael held her close in his arms plagued her sleep.

She lay shivering and exhausted under the blankets, but a new determination was growing within her. The more she deliberated over the past events and her present predicament, the more angry she became. Why should she succumb to the trials imposed upon her through no fault of her own? She would not let Matilda and the others render her to mortal defeat. She would rise up and live to see them punished for their wicked actions.

With renewed determination, Christy dragged herself from the cot, washed her face and combed her hair. Since her supply of food had run out, and her intense hunger had subsided somewhat, she satisfied herself with the last swallow of water.

Wrapping her cloak tightly about herself, she took a deep breath and opened the door. The sun was just beginning to rise. The cold nipped at her hands and cheeks, and her breath made clouds in the frosty air. Her legs felt weak and unsteady, but her mind was made up and she would walk until she found help, or collapsed.

She could not stay any longer and starve or freeze to death in the wretched cabin. She would not give up without a fight. There was only one road out of the forest, and she stayed as close to it as possible. She had no desire to become hopelessly lost in the vast wilderness.

Going was painfully slow because of the snow and mud and her additional growing burden, but she kept on, undaunted and trying to ignore the cold and pain which seeped into her toes and fingers. She drew her hood as close about her as possible to shield her face from the wind, and plodded along. The morning sun rose high in the sky, and she began to despair of ever reaching civilization. Her legs and back ached almost unbearably from the long and unaccustomed walk, and she was frequently forced to stop and rest.

After covering little more than a mile, her determination and her strength were quickly ebbing and, as she continued walking on guts alone, she debated if indeed she might be forced to return to the shelter of the cabin. But turning back meant utter defeat. Without food to replenish her strength, she would have little chance of setting off again on a long walk.

With her determination quickly ebbing, she stopped and leaned heavily against a tree for support. The tears she had stayed so valiantly again began to flow, slowly wetting the cherry red of her frostbitten cheeks. She was again forced to face defeat, and this time it seemed unequivocably to point to final defeat. It was over, and she had lost.

Somewhere from the deep recesses of her consciousness she heard the faint sound of horse's hooves. She pulled herself from her despondent reverie and listened more closely, fearful she was only imagining the sound. Her ears strained. Yes, it was the gallop of a horse. She was saved!

From deep within herself she called upon the last reserve of strength and hurried down the road toward what she prayed would be her salvation. Far down the road she spied the lone horseman. She waved her arms frantically and called out in desperation. He approached very slowly, and only when he was within a few feet of her did she stop waving, satisfied that he had seen her and would stop. Breathless and excited, she waited as the heavily cloaked horseman drew up beside her.

"Oh, good sir. I am so happy to see you. I am lost and do sorely need your help," she said through chattering teeth. "I was beginning to fear I would never again see another person. You are truly a welcome sight," she said breathlessly.

The hooded rider looked down at her in mute silence. He shifted in his saddle but did not dismount. Instead he continued his silent perusal of her.

Blind fear coursed through Christy. Perhaps she was in more danger now from this unknown stranger than when she was alone. She tried to banish such thoughts from her mind. "I was separated from my coachman in the storm. He has not returned and I felt I must seek out help on my own," she pleaded. Still he remained seated on his horse, uncommunicative and noncommittal. Her skin crawled in fear. What was wrong with this man that he refused to speak?

"Please, sir, could you help me to the nearest town?" she was finally forced to plead.

At last he shifted heavily in his saddle. After taking a deep, prolonged breath, he spoke. "Why, 'tis a good thing I came along, then, with you all alone. I would have been terribly upset to have missed you," he muttered through his hood. "The town is some distance away and it is doubtful you could make it without me," he said in an unmistakably smug tone.

Something about his voice sounded profoundly evil to Christy, and she drew back, even more fearful than before. "Perhaps I'll just go on alone anyway. I don't wish to detain you from your business." Despite the fact that he had informed her the town was some distance off, she decided she would prefer facing the cold and darkness to remaining another moment with this strange man.

"Why, you look exhausted. It's clear you'd never make it to town. Besides, it would definitely be ungallant of me to allow a fair and obviously well-bred lady like yourself to die of cold and exhaustion. I have better plans for you. You are of no use to me dead," he said and laughed wickedly as she drew back.

"Sir, I do not know what you mean. Of what use could I be to you?" she asked, taking a few more steps back. His voice was beginning to sound familiar to her ears.

"Of course you know exactly what I mean, my dear little Christina," said the rider. He clutched the soiled hood and pulled it from his face.

Christy's hand clutched her throat in paralyzing fear.

A low, deep, piercing scream escaped her lips and echoed through the silence about her. Every fiber in her body was on end as she stared in horror at the ugly, malicious form of Henry Slate.

"Why, my girl, you don't seem at all happy to see me, after I came all this way. Show your long-lost uncle a little respect," he sneered.

The sight of her most hated enemy seared her eyes. "No! No!" she screamed. She grabbed her skirts and began to run wildly toward the woods, hoping against hope she could lose him. Slate cursed in anger and kicked his horse. She turned to dash in another direction, but again found her path blocked by the horse's body.

"'Tis no use, my girl. You got away from me once. I'll not let it happen again," he growled as he maneuvered the horse about her darting figure.

Exhausted and seeing escape was hopeless, she ceased her flight and stood before him shivering. Tears spilled down her cheeks and her breath came in heavy, gasping sobs. She held her stomach tightly, trying to control the heavy spasms which shook her entire body.

"That's better now," he mumbled, for he was having no small degree of difficulty controlling the spirited horse in his drunken state. "Now, I believe there is a small cabin you stayed in not far from here. I'm damn near frozen to death and hungry as well. Get moving, now," he ordered roughly.

"No! I'm not going with you," muttered Christy in defiance.

"Oh yes you are, my girl. This here piece of metal tells me you'll cooperate," he said in a wicked and determined voice as he pulled a heavy black gun from his cloak and poked her roughly on the shoulder. "Do you want me to blow you to kingdom come? You know I will, too, dearie, for I've no great fondness for scum like you. Traitorous, lying and cheating just like them skunks of parents you had. Now, hurry along. I'm losing my patience," he grumbled cruelly and again poked her roughly on the back.

"Leave me alone," she snapped, but turned and began walking very slowly in the direction he indicated.

Christy stumbled along ahead of the horse and rider. She was bruised from his poking, and cold and completely exhausted from the long walk, but fear kept her going.

The walk back seemed infinite, but finally the cabin came into sight. Henry Slate fell heavily from his horse and tied it to a nearby tree. As he did so, Christy stood outside the door of the cabin, hesitant. It was dangerous enough to be alone outside with this demented maniac, but the prospect of being shut inside was even more terrifying.

Irritated by her hesitation, he shoved her through the door with decided roughness. "Well, it ain't no palace, but I guess it'll do till we get our business straightened out," he smirked.

Christy stood in the shadows, making no comment. Her heart still pounded from the long walk and the shock of his presence.

"Well, don't jist stand there, useless and wringing yer hands like of old. Get a fire going. It's cold as hell in here. And I'm hungry. Brought some food with me. Cook it up," he ordered, tossing a small bundle on the table.

"There is no wood for a fire," murmured Christy, and she remained standing fearfully in the darkness of the corner.

"Well, damnit, get some," he bellowed in anger.

Slowly Christy moved toward the door. The possibility was remote, yet perhaps, just perhaps there was a chance she could get to his horse, or even hide in the thick forest until nightfall. If only she could get out of the range of that gun for a few seconds.

"Where the hell are you going?" he screamed as she moved past him to the door.

"I'm going outside to find some firewood," she murmured, keeping her eyes lowered.

"To hell with that. I'll not let you out of my sight for a second. Use some of the garbage lying around here. Toss in this chair," he instructed and shoved an old, unsteady chair at her.

Her hope of escape crushed, she complied without a word. In a short time the cabin was warm and she set about preparing the bacon, beans and biscuits he had brought, almost glad for the task to keep her mind and fingers occupied. As she worked, Slate watched her closely, gulping huge amounts of cheap whiskey which dripped down his stubbled chin and onto his dirty shirt. It had been nearly nine months since he had seen her, but his hate and dislike for her had abated little.

The sizzling meat at last ready, she set it before him and he ate hungrily, slurping his food with his grubby fingers, yet never taking his eyes from her. Repulsed anew by his presence and wretched manners, she could not bring herself to sit and eat with the man. Instead, she stood nervously by the stove, chewing on her lip and trying to determine just what he expected of her.

In a very short time, he finished his meal. He washed it down with whiskey and tossed the empty bottle against the wall. It shattered in a hundred pieces. Laughing wickedly, he pulled a full bottle from under his heavy coat. Belching loudly and wiping his face with the back of his hand, he pushed the chair away from the table, crossed his arms over his fat stomach, and regarded Christy.

"Now that my hunger is satisfied, we can get on with business," he began. "You've grown up these past few months, I see. It seems you've been busy, too, since you left me so suddenly. Got yourself with child by some wealthy nobleman, didn't you? I thought we taught you better'n that. I always knew you'd come to no good, you slut," he insulted. "But at least you went for class and money 'stead o' some poor slob like me. I've got to give you that much credit," he said and took a huge swallow from his bottle. He wiped his wet mouth with the sleeve of his shirt and belched again. "Guess you hankered again for the rich life."

"Why did you come here? How did you find me?" she blurted out, choosing to ignore his vicious insults. He was drunk and was deliberately toying with her, and she would not stand by and listen to his rantings. She would give him no chance to begin again his litany of insults against her beloved parents.

"Well, that's a rather interesting story, girl," he

began, rubbing the black stubble on his grimy face, only too willing to change the subject.

Smiling openly at her look of digust, he went on. "'Bout three months ago a man approached me, came right to the house, he did. Asked me all kinds of questions about you and your stinking parents. I gladly told him all I knew. He came back a few days later and offered me three hundred pounds if I'd leave London and sail here on his master's ship—passage paid. I couldn't turn down three hundred pounds plus passage, so I left that hole I lived in without a backward glance. The ship weren't no pleasure boat, I'll tell you. It stank of bile and sweat, and the moaning and shrieking of darkies kept me up all night. I almost regretted leaving London, not knowing exactly what I was getting into. But when I arrived a few days ago, a lady approached me and offered me one hundred pounds more to come out here and 'dispose of' a little problem, as she put it. Told me a touching story and then said there'd be more to come if I did the job well." Slate smirked at his niece.

"Who . . . who was this woman?" stuttered Christy. Before he spoke, she knew the answer.

"'Twas a pretty, tall lady with shiny golden hair. Told me all about how you'd snagged her rich brother-in-law right from under her nose. Seems you've been a burden to her, too. You cost me even more trouble and heartache than her, so I was more than happy to oblige the lady, and here I am," he said, enjoying her look of terror.

Though she had these many days suspected Matilda of some devious plot, to hear Slate's words sent a new chill through her. She leaned heavily against the wall for support. It was all painfully clear now. Matilda had planned the whole thing from the very beginning. She had convinced her to flee on the pretext of keeping her secret, only to send Slate here to kill her, in case she had not already died from hunger or exposure.

"Henry, if it is your intent to kill me, I pray you reconsider. Matilda Lancer is a demented woman and will surely double-cross you before this is over. Let me go. Take the money you already have and buy some property, or start a business. There is great opportunity here. You will gain little in killing me but getting the law after you. Please leave me be," she pleaded.

"Why should I spare your stinking hide? Is there something in it for me? This Lancer woman's offered me plenty. What can you give me to change my mind?"

"Henry, I have nothing to offer you now. I have no money or valuables. But believe me, after the baby is born, I will work and repay you every cent Matilda promises," she vowed.

"Bah! Why should I wait for you to trickle money to me, copper by copper, when I can have it all now, I ask you?"

"Because . . . I . . ." began Christy.

"Hold your tongue, girl. I'll tell you what's in it for me. I thought his out real careful. You're worth far more to me alive than dead. This Lancer woman offered me only a small pittance of what great sums I can get from you," he smiled, and took another huge swallow of whiskey. "I plan to double-cross her before she can do it to me, and end up a rich man in the process."

"But I have no money of my own. I told you that. My only possessions are the clothes on my back."

"Your husband suffers from no similar lack of funds and can make me a rich man just with his overflow. I know all about the Lancers, thanks to a certain Captain Piper. You see, I checked them out before I came out here. They will pay a pretty sum to ransom you back," he said, toasting the air as he drank, well pleased with himself.

"So, that is your plan," said Christy, finally seeing what he was driving at. "Well, I do hate to disappoint you, but I doubt they will pay one cent for me. You see, I ran off and left them. Why should they pay to bring me back?" she asked, hoping to call his bluff.

"Yes, now that you mention it, I do recall something that Lancer woman said to the effect that you had disappeared in the night, taking with you all the Lancer jewels," he spat, knowing full well she knew nothing of it.

"What jewels? I don't know what she was talking about. I took nothing with me but two dresses!" she exclaimed.

"Well, she said she had to make your escape seem believable," sneered Henry, thoroughly enjoying it all.

"Oh, so that is how she poisoned their minds against me," she said. "How cleverly she figured out the whole thing. She is a thoroughly deceitful and wicked woman. What a fool I was to ever trust her," seethed Christy.

"Yes, it seems we deceitful and wicked people stick together, don't we?" said Henry with a vicious laugh.

"But, I don't plan on letting her get ahead of me. My only interest lies in the money I can get from this husband of yours. So, since you're probably right about yer husband not being willing to pay yer ransom, I have another little idea, which may just be better than my first," he said, leaning back in his chair and rubbing his stubby beard thoughtfully, all the while drinking heavily.

Christy could see he was becoming intoxicated and knew his good humor would soon change and his fearful temper would follow. She would have to weigh her words very carefully.

"What I want you to do is go back to yer husband on yer knees. Promise him that you will be his loving wife, and are sorry fer yer folly in running off. Tell him you will do anything if he will just forgive you and take you back. Use yer charms and his bastard child to change his mind about whatever feelings he has for this Lancer bitch. Tell him it was all a mistake. You can manage that, can't you, girl?"

Christy's head spun dizzily. She felt near suffocating despite the chill of the room. "You don't know Michael Lancer, Henry. He is a stubborn, strong-willed man. He is not so easily manipulated. How will I manage to get him to forget Matilda if they have both been plotting against me all along?"

"Oh, you are a smart girl. I'm sure you'll come up with something," he answered snidely.

"Even if I could think of something, and he would take me back, surely you are not suggesting this out of the goodness of your heart," said Christy suspiciously.

"Why, of course not. I don't have a heart, remember?" he laughed cruelly and continued on with his plan. "What I plan is to help yer husband spend some of that money of his. After you've gotten back into his good graces, you'll begin filtering his money from his bank account to me. It's all quite simple, really. You'll be alive to have yer brat, and I will be a rich man. No one need know the truth 'cept you and me. It's time I got what I truly deserve, 'stead of having to scrounge for every last shilling. You owe this to me, girl, for all I did for you," he finished.

"I owe you nothing, Henry Slate. I worked my fingers to the bone to support you and your loathesome habits. I more than paid my dues to you. As far as the Lancers, I will not cheat them for you or anyone else. Get your money elsewhere," she spat angrily at him, jumping to her feet, fists tightly clenched in rage.

Christy watched as his self-assured mood degenerated to one of anger. "If you do not do as I say, then I'll blackmail you. I'll use the same ploy Matilda Lancer used. I'll expose you and tell everyone about yer cheating parents. Then what will people think of the new mistress of Penncrest?" he sneered. "Listen good, my girl—"

"No I will not, Henry. If I cheat the Lancers then what is to stop Matilda from carrying out her part of the threat and exposing me?"

"You will do as I say, without question. You owe this to me," he snarled in his drunken, demented voice and rose from the chair, knocking it over roughly.

"Never. I will not run away from my past any longer.

521

Neither you, nor Matilda nor Michael will profit further at my expense," she screamed, shaking in anger, her eyes a sea of raging green.

"Perhaps then this will persuade you to my way of thinking." His grimy hand disappeared into his coat. When it emerged, his fist clutched an ugly black whip.

Christy gasped in horror. All color drained from her face.

"Ah, so you have not forgotten my little friend here," he said in a deranged voice.

"My God no, Henry!" she screamed and rushed for the door in a frantic effort to escape the deadly whip.

Slate anticipated her attempt to escape. Even in his drunken state he was faster. He grabbed her roughly by the arm as she passed and struck her hard across the face. "You'll do as I say or I'll beat you until there is nothing left of you or your baby," he cried, his anger completely out of control.

"No. Never," she whimpered as she held her smarting cheek.

Anger consumed him and he slammed her against the wall with all his strength. Her head swam dizzily from the impact and she gazed in utter terror as he uncoiled the whip and raised it to strike.

With a sob she spun to face the wall as the edge of the whip dug into her flesh. There would be no stopping him now. He was beyond reason, beyond feeling. He would whip her until he collapsed from drunken exhaustion.

"Please, don't! Stop!" she pleaded. It was useless. He could not even hear her, so caught up was he in his rage.

Her fists beat against the wall as the lash ripped her dress and cut into the soft skin of her shoulders. "Henry, stop!" she cried, near hysteria. Again and again the cutting tip split her tender flesh, driving her back against the wall and down to her knees.

She clenched her teeth and her nails dug into the flesh of her palms as she fought to repell the pain. Her fingers scraped at the wall as she clawed her way to her feet. "You'll not . . . get . . . away with . . . this," she cried between clenched teeth. His response was another crack of the snake, biting into her slender neck.

"It's my duty to punish you. You must pay for your sins and those of your parents!" he screamed, taking the role as God's vengeful servant.

Christy heard the whip whistle through the air, and stiffened for the blow. A dizzy, buzzing sounded in her ears as she struggled to remain conscious.

Henry laughed wickedly and raised the whip to strike again. Suddenly it was ripped from his hand with savage force. Taken completely by surprise, he whirled around in drunken rage. "What the hell do you think yer doing, man?" he cried. "This bitch is mine. She is a scourge to mankind and must be punished. Git out of my way," he screamed and reached for the whip.

Too late he read the look of intense fury reflected in the brown eyes searing down at him. Had he had the time or the good sense, he would have cowered fearfully. But he never had a chance to flee, or utter another word. A huge, deadly aimed fist solidly blocked his vision. Pain crashed in his head and he felt himself flying through the air. In blinding darkness he crashed to the floor in an unconscious heap.

Without waiting to see if his crippling blow had rendered the man totally senseless, he raced to Christy's side, the ghastly whip all but forgotten in his left hand. Momentarily helpless by his own emotional fury, he stood gazing down at the tiny, crumpled woman whimpering softly at his feet. He was speechless with rage. Livid fury distorted his features as he bent and slowly turned her to face him.

The lull in her beating confused Christy. Had Slate collapsed in drunken exhaustion? She turned eyes glazed with pain toward her persecutor. But no, his huge form towered over her. She blinked her eyes, frantically trying to clear her vision.

"Henry . . . stop. Henry . . . My God! . . . Michael?" she choked as the menacing figure transformed into the face and form of her husband. His rigid features were a mask of fury and his eyes glowed hot as coals. She blinked again. The whip was coiled in his hand. He was poised and ready to strike. "No—no! Don't hit me, please," she cried. He'd come to punish her for running off, for interfering with his life. He hated her. He was going to kill her!

Driven by blind compulsion to escape, she scrambled to her feet. He reached out to grab her. She gasped in terror and jerked away, staggering toward the door.

"Come back. Where are you going?" cried Michael as she stumbled out of the shack.

Christy ignored his order to stop. Driven by an inner force, she staggered from the cabin and raced recklessly toward the dark forest. A patch of ice tripped her and she fell to her knees. Overpowering panic consumed her when she turned and saw him quickly approaching. Ignoring the waves of pain and the frightful cold biting at her uncloaked form, she dragged herself to her feet and drove herself on.

"Stop!" cried the voice behind her. "Come back!" But she ignored his commands and plunged ahead.

Tree branches ripped at her face and hair. She thrust them aside. Nothing would stop her until she was safe. She gasped for air, her lungs burning unbearably. She was tired and cold, so terribly cold, but he was after her. If he caught her, he would kill her. Tears stung her cheeks and blocked her vision, but she raced on blindly. Too late she saw the steep downhill grade cutting off her escape. Too late she tried to stop. Her foot slipped on an ice-covered rock.

A cry escaped her lips as she frantically tried to regain her balance. Footing was impossible. She was falling. Trees blurred into a sickening whirl as she plunged down the steep grade, tossed over and over like a lifeless rag doll. . . .

She felt strong hands lifting her bleeding, tortured body. "Help me. Please help me," she whispered, her words barely audible. "Don't let my baby die. Please help me," she moaned desperately, struggling to see him— hoping her pleas would penetrate through his anger.

Michael's face was partially indistinguishable in the haze through which she looked, and his shadow blocked out the light from the sun. She was unable to see his eyes or to discern his feelings. She did not know if he was still angry with her, but in her helpless state, she was forced to rely on him for aid.

Before she could focus her eyes, a sharp pain struck her stomach. She doubled over in pain as a thick, heavy blackness encircled her and carried her off into blessed oblivion.

Thirty-Two

"How is she? Will she . . . will she make it, Doctor?" demanded Michael anxiously as Littman closed the door of Christy's room and limped slowly down the hall.

The elderly man turned exhausted eyes on Michael. "Calm down, son. You will be of no use to anyone if you work yourself into a frenzy," he admonished gently.

"But you've been in there with her nearly four hours! How is she?"

The doctor turned in the darkened hallway to regard him. "I'll give it to you straight, Michael. The girl is in serious condition. She has hemorrhaged greatly from the miscarriage and is extremely weak. It is hard enough for a woman to lose a child before it is born, but she has been through much shock, and her other injuries only add to the seriousness of her condition. I honestly don't know if she will make it or not. We must wait and see," he said with a heavy heart. "She has been through so much, let us pray she has the will to live through this."

"Is she awake? Does she know about losing the baby?" Michael wanted to know.

"She was unconscious for most of the ordeal and has not come 'round as yet. It is doubtful she will immediately remember anything that happened after the fall," he said, bone-weary.

"Is there anything I can do?" asked Michael, frantic with worry and not yet ready to let the doctor leave.

"Have someone with her at all times. As I said, if she does not know about the baby, it will be a tremendous blow and she will need comforting. Don't be upset if she is terribly depressed for some time," he warned. "Someone should be with her constantly to bathe her with cool water. We must get her fever down. Her continued high temperature is what concerns me now. Other than that, there is nothing more that can be done. The rest is up to her, and God. I'll be back tomorrow. If she gets any worse, send for me immediately," he said wearily and headed toward the door.

"I will, Doctor. And thank you. I . . . I just couldn't bear to lose her," he admitted as Dr. Littman turned to go.

"Well, son, that is a possibility you may well have to face. Her condition is quite serious. But tell her how you feel. Even though she is unconscious, she may be able to hear something of what you say. It may give her some added fight," he prescribed. He paused, as if debating his next words. "May I give you a little non-medical advice, son?"

"Why of course," replied Michael.

"I sense the two of you care deeply about one another. It is high time you openly admitted it. You are both too proud for your own good, and it has brought disaster to all. I only hope it is not too late for you to remedy the situation," he advised.

"You're right, Doctor. If—when—Christy gets well, I

fully intend to get this whole thing straightened out and tell her just how very much she means to me. I intend to get to the bottom of why she ran away, and do all I can to remedy the problem," he vowed solemnly.

Michael waited until the doctor's carriage had vanished, and then quickly retraced his steps to Christy's room. Anxiously he scanned her feverish face for himself. It hurt him deeply to see her thus. If only he'd been able to get to her sooner and explain everything, all this could have been avoided.

Bertha sat quietly sponging off Christy's forehead. She looked up at his anxious, worried face. "'Tis a terrible thing to have happened to the child. Her so sweet and gentle. But don't you worry none, Master. She is young and will have many more babies. Don't you worry now. She'll be just fine. You'll see," she said, but her gentle black hand quickly swiped away a tear which straggled down her cheek.

"I hope and pray you are right, Bertha," he said. "Here, let me take over for a time. You've been in here with the doctor and I'm sure you must be tired."

"Nonsense, Master. You been up all these many days and would be no use to Mistress Christy. You go get cleaned up and rested. I'll have Milly take over 'til you're up to it. Won't do Mistress Christy no good to have you sick, too. Now go on. Listen to old Bertha," she persuaded gently and opened the door to see him out.

She was right. The past few hectic days were finally catching up with him. His haggard, unshaven face exemplified his state of near exhaustion. Though he preferred sitting at Christy's side, he knew the wisdom of

Bertha's words and realized his wife would be in competent hands. With no further protest, he dragged himself down the hall and fell heavily into bed, too tired even for a smoke. He was asleep almost before his eyes closed.

Milly, Bertha and Michael all took turns the next few days tending to Christy. She was never left alone for more than a few minutes. Cool compresses were periodically applied to her forehead in an effort to make her comfortable and break the fever.

Michael preferred to stay and keep watch during the long nights. It seemed that when darkness fell, she was plagued by her past hellish nightmares. Often she would cry out in pain and delirium, thrashing about in bed so that he had difficulty restraining her. The tiring episodes, however, served to enlighten him as to the horrors to which she had been subjected. Continuously she cried out—to her parents, to her cruel uncle, and to Michael himself.

Through the many sleepless nights her ranting continued, and at times made little sense to him. Some of her fears, however, brought a frown to his brow. He felt the full impact of all she had suffered. Her feverish terror made him realize just how cold and miserable he had treated her in the past. Was it her past fear which had caused her to run from him in terror? Perhaps so. Well, all that would change, if only she would pull through. But each day her fever seemed to grow worse, and she became weaker and weaker. Even her delirious tantrums became less frequent as she had less and less energy to expend.

Finally, after another episode of tossing and turning

and whimpering softly, she quieted, and exhausted from the ordeal himself, Michael slipped into a nearby chair and was soon fast asleep.

Sometime during that night, Christy's fever broke. It was not until the next morning, four days after she had been returned to Penncrest, that she awoke to find herself in a dark, stuffy room. With dazed eyes, she quickly scanned her surroundings. On first glance it was unfamiliar. Panic churned in her stomach. Slowly her mind began to focus on the familiar and she recognized her room at Penncrest.

Her mind refused to focus, no matter how hard she tried. Why did she hurt so much? She tried to raise herself up, and in doing so felt a sharp pain in her stomach. She glanced down at the smooth, flat blankets covering her. Something was wrong. Something was terribly wrong.

With a cry of anguish, she gripped her stomach. "My baby! My baby! Where is my baby?" she wailed. "Somebody tell me where my baby is. You've taken him from me. I want to see him. You cannot keep my baby from me!" she screamed hysterically. Ignoring the pain and dizziness, she rolled to the edge of the bed, trying to stand and look for her infant.

Her frantic cries penetrated the silent house. Roused from sleep, Michael raced down the hall and burst into her room. His joy at seeing her awake and rational after her long sickness was quickly replaced with concern as he caught her just as she slipped to the floor, too weak to stand. She gazed up at him with initial relief, but the sight of him looming above brought painful, frightening memories flooding back.

"You tried to kill me! I saw you with the whip," she accused breathlessly. "Where is my baby? You took him from me, didn't you? Let me go!" she seethed, well aware, however, that without his aid she had not the strength to rise.

At last she was forced to cease her protests and permit him to help her. The effort of standing alone was just too great. But once back in bed, she again took up the assault. "Where is my baby, Michael? I want to see him," she demanded. "You've no right to take him from me. You promised you would never separate us."

Michael was shaken by her unwarranted venom. Did she honestly believe he had deliberately spirited the baby away to keep them apart? How ridiculous. But then, how could he bring himself to tell her that the baby was dead? Could she handle such news in her weakened, over-wrought condition? "Christy, please get ahold of yourself. I did not take the baby from you. I swear I didn't," he said, trying to regain her trust.

"Where . . . where is he, then?" she asked suspiciously.

"The doctor tried, but . . . you were so upset and frightened. When you fell . . ." he began again, trying to break the news to her as gently as possible.

"What is it, Michael? Tell me," she began rather irritably. "Oh my God! My baby . . . dead?" she shrieked.

"I'm sorry, Christy. The doctor said the combination of your exposure, shock, your uncle's beating, and the fall all added together to bring the baby too soon. He was born dead," he said sadly. "There was nothing he could do."

Christy lay limply on her pillow, refusing to believe what she had just heard. It was too painful, too horrible to comprehend. She needed to lash out, to hurt, to relieve the tremendous pain in her heart. Her eyes filled with anger, and slowly she turned her wrath upon Michael.

"You killed my baby! You killed him!" she said in a low, venomous voice.

Michael was dazed and confused by her accusations. He bent to touch her shoulders in an effort to comfort her and repudiate her remarks. "Christy, calm down. It's not true. I love you. I would never hurt you or the baby. You've got to believe that."

"Don't touch me. Get away! Get your hands off me," she screamed and pushed him away. "Get out! Leave me alone. Have you not done enough already?" Her face was livid and she was quickly becoming hysterical. "I saw you standing over me with the whip in your hand, ready to strike out, just like in my dream. I saw the fury in your eyes. Matilda told you the truth about me, didn't she? She told you about my parents, and you came after me to punish me for keeping my past from you. You no longer trust me but really hate and despise me, as you have all along. I was such a fool to believe you cared about me or the baby. Oh, I wish that I had died with my baby, for now I have nothing," she cried in anguish.

The door burst open suddenly and in rushed Bertha, an anxious look on her face. "What is it? Child, you must settle down. What has upset you so?" she questioned.

Michael was at wits end and was greatly relieved at Bertha's support. "Bertha, she won't listen to reason. She blames me for losing the baby and is talking nonsense about me trying to kill her," he explained hurriedly as Christy struggled and screamed on.

"I want my baby. You killed him," she sobbed.

"There, there, Mistress Christy. You're far too weak and sick to be thinking clearly. Try to calm yourself," said Bertha as she attempted to soothe the frantic girl.

"Christy, please understand . . ." began Michael, ready to go to her again.

"No, sir. You leave her be. She'll be needing a woman's shoulder to cry on just now. She's overcome with grief. Now you just leave us be," said Bertha.

Despite his protests, she led him to the door, trying to give him a few words of explanation and encouragement. His face suddenly went white and she turned in time to see Christy rising shakily from the bed.

"I'm going to find my baby. He's not dead. He can't be," she moaned. Too weak to stand, she again crumpled to the floor.

Michael moved to help, but Bertha waved him away and bent to the now silent, whimpering girl. "There, there, child. We was worried 'bout you, being sick for so long. There, there now. Don't you worry," she soothed and rocked Christy back and forth on the floor, cradling her in her arms.

Bertha raised her arm slightly, indicating to Michael that she had things under control. With a heavy sigh, he turned, hurt and confused, and closed the door softly behind him as Christy's sobs floated down the hall after him.

"I don't understand why she thinks I wanted to hurt her. I never laid a hand on her except to help her. For some reason, though, she thinks I was hell-bent on taking up where Slate left off in his beating her," Michael was saying to his father a short time later as he paced restlessly in the study.

Michael himself looked tired from the long and trying ordeal. His usually neatly combed hair lay in mass disarray about his head as he ran his fingers nervously through it. Heavy, dark stubble from his unshaven beard covered his drawn face, and deep circles appeared under his tired, dulled eyes. His clothes were limp and wrinkled, and as he took a large swallow of liquor, a new stain joined the others spotting his white shirt.

"Well, son," began Sir Phillip, watching from across the room with unspoken sympathy. "From all that you have told me, she was frightened and confused. Why she ran away in the first place is still a mystery. But according to the facts we do have, this Slate only appeared on the scene shortly before you arrived. I still find it difficult to believe she knew of his coming and had planned everything from the start," he conjectured. "It is difficult to say, indeed. I'm afraid all we can do is wait until she is stronger to find out these answers."

There was silence for a time as both men mulled over their own thoughts, trying to sort out the puzzling events. At length, Sir Phillip broke the silence. "What was that you mentioned about a dream she had?"

Michael rose and again began pacing. "Well, it seems that ever since I met her, she's been plagued with this recurring nightmare about someone beating her. I've seen her struggle and cry out in her sleep many times in utter terror. Lately though, her sleep has been restful. She seemed at ease and content. I assumed whatever it was troubling her had rectified itself," he explained.

"Quite peculiar, I must admit," puzzled Sir Phillip. "You say she has not had this nightmare for some time now?"

"No, not since before the ball," began Michael. "No, wait a minute," he remembered, stopping in his tracks. "The night before we left for Charleston, right after Matilda's visit, she woke up crying and afraid. It took me some time to quiet her that night. She seemed even more disturbed than usual. I think she really wanted to tell me about it that night, but for some reason was still hesitant. Anyway, I thought it odd she should be again plagued by this cursed dream. But who is to explain such things?" he said, resuming his pacing.

"You've no clue as to just what this nightmare is about?" asked Sir Phillip. "I'm grasping at anything that might help us resolve this mess," he explained.

Michael stopped suddenly and turned to face his father, his features nakedly revealing the deep extent of his emotions. "Father, I love her deeply. More deeply than anything else in the world. Even if she did run away with her uncle, and even if she did steal the jewelry, I still love her. I would never intentionally hurt her. I've been a cad and cruel in the past, I must confess. But all that has changed forever. Nothing can destroy the deep feelings I have for her. Why can't she see that? Why doesn't she understand?" his heart cried out in unmasked despair.

"Well, son, it's hard to say what she thinks right now. She's been through a great deal in too short a time. No doubt it has all caught up with her at last. I felt, as I know you did too, that these past few weeks had been happy ones for her, and her life was beginning to settle down. But perhaps this newfound joy and love were too new and too unfamiliar for her just yet. This ordeal with her uncle may have temporarily confused her thinking. Be patient, Michael, and give her time. Once she is well, I am sure all will come out as it should."

Sir Phillip clapped his son on the shoulder and looked directly into his eyes with all the confidence he could generate. Michael's eyes reflected no such confidence. "I hope you are right, Father. I could not bear to lose her now," he said softly.

A knock sounded at the door and broke up the close moment between father and son. Michael stepped to the window and gazed out as Sir Phillip went to open the door.

"Excuse me for interrupting," began Bertha, looking tired as she stood a little ill at ease in the hallway. "I thought you might want to know how Mistress Christy is faring."

"Yes, of course, Bertha. Come in," said Sir Phillip and stood aside as she entered. "How is Christina?"

"She's sleeping comfortably now, sir. Though she still has a slight fever, I think she'll be fine. She be real weak and thin, but with rest and proper eatin', she'll be just fine," she said and waited for some response.

"Thank you, Bertha. That is truly a relief," said Sir Phillip and glanced at his son who stood at the window regarding the blackness of the night.

"I wish her mind could be so easily cured," Michael muttered partially under his breath.

Bertha regarded him with a mixture of pity and understanding. No husband could have attended his wife so dearly as he, and no husband could have been more hurt by her outburst. "If I may be so bold, Master Michael. I tended many women who lost their babies at birth, though none so frightful like. I reckon I kin understand her feelings now," she began hesitantly.

"Please go ahead, Bertha. Feel free to say what you think, for she surely has me befuddled," said Michael, still despondent.

"Well, sir, Mistress Christy was out o' her head with fever. She couldn't have known she'd lost the child. Her being weak and confused as to what happened, she just shot out at the first person she seen. I'm sure she don't blame you none. But the hurt of losin' the babe is deep, and she plum had to let out the pain. It's natural, 'specially after carryin' a child so long."

Michael made no immediate comment, but continued to stare outside. Sir Phillip too seemed lost in thought. Bertha again felt uneasy, fearing she had taken too much upon herself, making excuses for her mistress. She turned to go, but stopped in the doorway as Michael turned to address her.

"Thank you, Bertha. I think I understand a little better now," he said. "In the meantime, I will stay out of her way. The weather should be clearing and I can involve myself at the mill. Though this separation will be difficult, I can see the wisdom behind it," he sighed heavily.

"Yes, sir," the woman answered and walked slowly from the room. They were all like family to her, and she needed no reward but to see them happy once again.

Thirty-Three

Slowly, Christy's physical strength began to return, thanks to the diligent efforts of Milly and Bertha. They were constantly urging her to eat and take moderate exercise. As a result, in a few days she was able to walk about her room, or sit in the warm sun at the balcony window.

The doctor continued to check on her progress, but after his fourth visit, he realized she was coming along adequately and was in good hands with the watchful Bertha. Though he was deeply concerned about her desperately low mental state, there was little he could do to remedy the situation. He had seen many women go through similar depression after losing a child, and he hoped that time would heal the sorrow.

During her recuperation, Christy refused to see anyone except the doctor and the women tending to her needs. She spoke little to anyone, and would sit for hours staring into the brightly decorated nursery. She felt a complete and devastating emptiness at her loss. The man she had loved with all her being had deliberately sought to destroy her. And in so doing, he had taken from her the only part of him she had ever possessed, his son. It was a double loss, crippling, demoralizing and unbearable. Her initial shock and anger at him had dissolved into this deep, intense sorrow which refused to be dispelled.

During the weeks that followed the accident, Michael and Sir Phillip stayed away from Christy at the suggestion of Bertha and the doctor. It was a disheartening banishment for Michael. Her harsh, bitter accusations still rang clearly in his mind.

The daily meals were the worst time for everyone, including Sir Phillip. The empty place at the table was a silent yet tormenting reminder of the recent tragedy. Without Christy's gay, lively banter, the meals passed quickly, and for the most part in silence. The strained efforts at conversation between the two men soon dwindled to listless silence.

Finally one morning Michael could take no more of the restrained, heavy atmosphere. "Damnit, Father. It's been nearly three weeks since the accident. Christy has not asked to see me even once in all that time. I can't stand it any longer. It's time the air was cleared and all the issues laid out in the open." With that he rose from the table and mounted the stairs. He stared at the heavy door for some time before he knocked. "Christina, it's Michael. May I come in? I'd like to speak to you," he called hesitantly.

Christy heard his voice as if through a tunnel. A warning sounded in her head that her self-imposed solitude would soon be shattered and she would be again forced into the rushing, swirling waters of life. She steeled herself for the confrontation with him. "Come in. The door is open," she answered apathetically.

He entered quickly. Silence settled in the room. She did not leave her seat by the balcony, nor did she turn to face him. At last he was forced to come and stand before her.

In the early morning glow of the sun, Michael was shocked by how thin and pale she looked. Her emerald eyes lacked the customary sparkle he had grown to know and love so well. Even her hair seemed to have a dull, lackluster film instead of its usual shine. Looking at her blank, impenetrable expression, his determination was renewed to break this spell of depression which surrounded her. "How are you feeling?"

"Fine, thank you," she answered in a faraway tone.

"I'm glad to see you're getting your strength back. You've lost a considerable amount of weight. Is there something special you have a taste for? I'd be glad to ask the cook to make you something, or send to Charleston if we do not have it. You must eat to regain your strength."

"No, thank you. I need nothing. I have no appetite," she replied in a lifeless tone.

Safe within the walls of her own little world, she wanted no part of him. He had taken her love and crushed it beneath his foot without a care. She hated him for it. But oh, how desperately at the same time she fought to snuff the embers of her emotions which threatened to rekindle into the flame of love. How could she love and hate him at the same time? These feelings threatened to tear her asunder. In confusion, she withdrew deeper behind the safety of the wall she had built around herself.

"I've reopened the mill. The weather has finally cleared. It's still quite cold, but we've been spared any more snow. The men seemed quite happy to get back to work." His attempt at small talk met with her continued silence.

"Brutus has been puzzled by your absence in the study. He had grown accustomed to sitting beside you at the fire, and he looks for you now. If you'd like a change of scenery, I'll help you downstairs," he offered.

"No, thank you. Perhaps in a few days," she answered noncommittably, still refusing to meet his gaze.

"Damn it, Christy. Let's call a truce. It's time we talked about what happened. There's nothing we can do to bring the baby back, but it's time this whole bloody mess gets straightened out," he said in a slight agitation. "It's gone on for too long. I stayed away from you like everyone suggested, to give you time to get over the . . . accident. But it's been nearly three weeks now. We can't go on like this."

"There is nothing to straighten out. Everything is perfectly clear," she answered.

"You're wrong. Nothing is clear. Nothing. Look at me. At least tell me why you ran away in the first place. You owe me that much."

At last, with an almost painful slowness, Christy raised her eyes to meet his. "I had to go away," she said simply.

"But why? Why did you have to go?"

"You know very well why I went. Considering the circumstances, I had no other choice."

"You're wrong, Christy. I don't know why you went. Was it because you stole the jewels—because you needed money and were afraid I wouldn't give you any? Did you steal them with a plan to meet up with your uncle and split the profits?" he asked.

The sudden mention of Slate flooded Christy's memory with thoughts she had deliberately suppressed since the accident. His name sent a shiver through her. "Where is Henry? What has happened to him?" The faraway look disappeared from her eyes and her voice took on a new sense of urgency.

"I don't know what happened to him, Christy. When you ran out of the cabin, I completely forgot about him. He must have taken off after you fell, for when I returned he was gone. I've sent people out trying to track him down, but have had no luck thus far." He paused, still unsure of where she stood in this matter of her uncle. "Did you send for him? Why did he beat you? I simply don't understand any of this. I thought you were happy here with me. Why did you run away? Why?" he asked in desperation.

Christy's mind whirled in confusion. If he had plotted with Matilda, then why was he questioning her about Slate and playing the ignorant victim? Hadn't he and Matilda sent for Henry? Wasn't the whole thing a plot to get her out of the way so they could be together?

Yet his questions seemed so sincere, as if he were genuinely confused. Dare she allow herself a glimmer of hope that he was ignorant of the whole devious scheme? Did he still love her? She had to know the truth, and it had to be now. "Michael, do you love Matilda?" she asked point-blank. His simple, honest answer could clarify everything.

"What? What kind of a question is that? You know

how I feel about Matilda," he exclaimed in genuine surprise.

"Answer me, Michael. Yes or no. Do you love Matilda?" Again her voice was coated with urgency.

"No, I don't love her. I never have. She means nothing to me," he answered, still bewildered. "Why do you ask? What does she have to do with you and me?"

Fool that she was, she wanted to believe him. But his answer only confused her more. "Then, Michael, why did you come after me with the whip in your hand?" she answered his questions with one of her own. "From the very first night on your ship I've been plagued by a nightmare. It was always the same, yet grew more ghastly as time passed. Henry Slate had me trapped against a wall and was whipping me. When I pleaded for mercy and looked up to stay his hand, it was you I saw standing above me. It was you who towered over me with vengeful hate in your eyes. Why did you want to hurt me, Michael? Why?"

"Oh my God, Christy. When you accused me of wanting to hurt you, I thought that it was just a reaction from the shock of learning the baby was dead. I had no idea you really believed it. Have you been harboring this notion that I appeared at the cabin to punish you? My God, no wonder you refused to see me. I could not fathom why you ran from me in terror," he reasoned aloud, finally beginning to understand.

Christy too was beginning to see how wrong she'd been in her assessment of the situation. "You . . . you mean you did not come after me . . . to . . . punish me?"

she stuttered.

"Oh, Christy, my anger was not at you. I swear it. When I returned from Charleston, Matilda told me you were gone. I was angry and my pride hurt at being taken for a fool. But when I found your note, I was not convinced you were guilty of theft and treachery. I became crazy with worry and left immediately to search for you. It took me two days of riding. By sheer chance I came across the cabin in the woods. I saw smoke coming from the chimney and then heard you cry out. When I burst through the door I found that man—Slate—whipping you unmercifully. I admit, when I saw you lying in the corner, whimpering softly while he ripped your skin to shreds with that lash, I went crazy with rage. I tore the whip from his hand, and before he could explain or protest, I smashed his face into the wall. It was my consuming anger at him you saw. I never had any intention of hurting you."

"I didn't see anything, Michael. I only know that one minute Henry was whipping me, and when I looked up, you had materialized in his place and had the look of deadly revenge on your face." Tears began to form in her eyes as she stared up at him in confusion.

He knelt down before her and took her hands in his. "My dear Christy. God forgive me for frightening you so. But please believe me. I would never, never hurt you. I would never deliberately seek to cause you pain, no matter what you did or said."

"Oh, Michael, I just don't understand. This is all so confusing. When I saw you looming threateningly over me with the whip, I thought you'd come to punish me for not revealing the morbid truth to you. I just assumed Matilda had told you all about my wretched bygone heritage and you had come for revenge. How else could you have found me?"

"No, no, Christy. You must not blame yourself. It was all a misunderstanding," he tried to comfort her as she rocked back and forth in overwhelming remorse, fearing she would again revert back to her withdrawn depression. "Christy," his voice took on a new urgency, "why would Matilda know where you were? What should she have told me about you? How was she involved in your decision to run away?"

"Oh, Michael. It doesn't matter now. Nothing matters," she sobbed. Her mind was far removed from Matilda and her connivings. For some unknown reason, the woman had not revealed the truth to Michael. He still knew nothing about her past. If that was the case then . . . then she had killed her baby by running away in pure ignorance and misunderstanding. *She* was responsible for the death of her own child, and no one else. Tears streamed down her white face and she rocked herself back and forth in anguish. "I killed my baby. I should have told you the truth long ago. It's all my fault. Because I did not, my baby is dead. Oh, I am not fit to live," she moaned.

"Christy, it was an accident. It was not your fault. You cannot blame yourself. There will be other babies. You'll see," he said, trying to comfort her.

He encircled her small, quivering body in his arms, but she would not be consoled and cried even harder. In her weakened condition, Michael feared for her health. His words were even and smooth as he sought to soothe her, but his anger mounted as he churned over the information she had revealed about Matilda. He wanted to press Christy for more details, but her extremely agitated state prevented further discussion.

"Here, let me help you to bed, Christy. You will feel better when you get some rest. You must calm down or you will be sick again," he said gently and lifted her to her feet. She was trembling violently and he led her like a small child to the bed.

Eventually her sobbing quieted and she lay exhausted and numb; her face was as white as the pillow. As he watched the pain play across the delicate features of her face, he grew more and more perturbed. Somehow Matilda was responsible for a great deal of the pain and heartache they had been put through. Christy was too distraught with grief to elaborate. It was time he confronted Matilda directly.

He looked down again at Christy. Tears glistened on her pale cheeks. Fearful of leaving her alone, yet anxious to be off to Matilda's, he rang the bell for her maid. "Milly! Milly. Where the devil are you?" he called out the door.

The sound of scurrying footsteps preceded the concerned maid hurrying down the hall. "What is it, sir?" she asked breathlessly. She looked past him to the white, still form of her young mistress.

"Stay with her until she is asleep. She has had a bad shock and I don't want her left alone," he ordered.

"Shall I send for the doctor?" she asked anxiously as she moved to the bed and took Christy's limp hand in her own.

"No. I will be gone for only a short time. There is some urgent business I must attend to," he said gruffly as a terrible scowl darkened his face.

"Yes, sir. I'll take good care of her," she said and turned to stroke Christy's forehead. "There, there. It's all right, Mistress Christy. You just rest," she soothed, all the time wondering what had happened to cause her mistress's distress and put Master Michael in such a foul temper.

Michael stormed from the room. "Tell Morgan to saddle my horse!" he yelled to anyone within earshot. His angry tone vibrated through the house. When the servants heard that tone from him, they were immediately prepared to jump to his orders.

He hurried to his room and quickly shrugged on his coat and boots. The scowl still darkened his features as he stalked down the hall at a thunderous pace, nearly colliding with his father.

"What the devil is going on, Michael? I heard you screaming for the maid and then Morgan. What has happened?" he asked in concern.

Michael stopped abruptly, yet his manner indicated he would not be detained long from his purpose. "I think I am on the verge of uncovering the true cause of Christy's flight, Father. The details are still sketchy, but I intend to get to the bottom of it once and for all. It seems Christy was convinced I'd come to punish her that day in the cabin. That's why she ran from me in fright. But this time she distinctly implicated Matilda. Unfortunately I could not get her to elaborate, for she became hysterical, blaming herself for losing the baby. Milly is with her now," he said and then went on. "Father, I am certain Matilda was directly involved with Christy's running off. I don't know exactly how, but I intend to get to the bottom of this," he said with determination.

"Please, Michael. Calm down. You mustn't do anything rash. Let me go with you," pleaded Sir Phillip.

But Michael's mind was made up and he paid no attention to his father's admonitions. He brushed past him quickly and raced down the hall and out to the stables. With reckless urgency, he swung himself onto his stallion's back and galloped off toward Matilda's house.

Thirty-Four

The late January air whipped at Michael's face and hands as he thundered down the road. If his assumptions proved accurate, Matilda had been directly involved in causing the unbearable heartaches of the past few weeks. He knew he would be sorely pressed to restrain himself from throttling her.

The hearty gallop succeeded in easing his tension, and when he reached Matilda's, his anger had cooled somewhat and he was thinking a little more rationally. A grumpy stable hand, roused from a mid-morning nap, led Michael's horse to a warm stable as he strode with quick, strong strides up the stairs. Without knocking, he entered the large, ornately furnished house. The door slammed loudly behind him, and he stomped impatiently back and forth, slapping his gloves in his hands as he waited for someone to appear.

"Good morning, Mr. Lancer," came the cheery voice of Nadine, the maid. "May I take your coat?" she asked politely as she noted his coat thrown carelessly over a chair.

"No. Leave it," he said gruffly. Impatiently he searched the dark hallways. "Where is Mrs. Lancer? I

551

wish to see her immediately," he ordered.

The little maid was startled by the abruptness of his manner. He usually had a friendly word for everyone. Today his mood was dark indeed. "I believe she has not risen as yet, sir," she answered.

"Not up yet! It's close to noon. Does she sleep the whole day?" he cried impatiently. "Go awaken her. My business cannot wait."

"Sir, Mrs. Lancer does not like to be roused before she is ready," explained Nadine cautiously. She knew her mistress's temper at any disturbance of her sleep. She could also see, however, that Master Michael's temper was red hot and explosive.

"Damnit! If you're afraid to get her up, I'll do it myself," he thundered and headed for the stairs, his anger once again beginning to boil.

"But, Mr. Lancer . . ." called the flustered little maid after him.

"Michael, what on earth are you doing here? What a pleasant surprise," exclaimed Matilda who suddenly appeared at the top of the stairs. With practiced ease, she glided slowly down the stairs toward him. Despite the lateness of the hour, she still wore a lacy dressing gown, attesting to the fact that she had indeed just risen.

"I have a matter of some urgency to discuss with you, Matilda," he said sternly, retracing his steps back down to the lobby.

"Well, darling, as you can see, I am not dressed," she said with feigned modesty, deliberately calling attention to the sheer gown and her obvious physical attributes.

"To hell with that. I care not what you wear. If you'd

rise at a respectable hour, you'd not be caught in your sleepwear," he criticized.

"But, Michael, dear. Sleeping late is one of the few luxuries I allow myself," she replied sweetly.

"Come now, Matilda. You surely jest. I know of no one who bathes herself in more luxury," he argued.

She pouted prettily and was about to defend herself, but such pointless banter made him all the more edgy and anxious to commence with the business at hand. "Come into the parlor. It's best what we have to discuss be done in private," he ordered sharply.

"Of course, darling," Matilda cooed. She glided ahead of him into the bright little room.

He quickly shut the door behind him, but did not immediately speak. He wanted to lead into the issue as cautiously as possible. Perhaps he could get her to make an admission on her own.

With his desire for privacy and his calculated silence, Matilda mistook the look of anger on his face for one of frustrated passion. "What brings you to my humble abode? I suppose it must be because your wife—is she recovering?—won't let you near her. It's been ages since you've come to call. I was afraid you'd completely forgotten me," she purred like a kitten.

Michael's pulse began to race, but not from any passionate urgings. Did Matilda actually believe he had come to her for compassion and sexual fulfillment? He almost laughed in her face at the repugnant thought. Instead, he buried his hands in his pockets and turned away, hiding his contempt. "You seem to know quite a lot about what happens at Penncrest, Matilda. Who is this informant of yours?" he asked.

"Oh, dear, I have my ways of finding out these things," she answered in a light tone, plucking an imaginary thread from his jacket. "Besides, you mean so very much to me, darling. I want to know all about you so that I can make you happy."

Michael was repulsed by her flirtatious manner. He pulled away abruptly. "Since you claim to know so much about what goes on at Penncrest, and avow to look out solely for my well being, perhaps you can tell me how it is you know so much about my wife's disappearance and her uncle's arrival."

Matilda backed away in sudden trepidation. The intensity of his gaze frightened her. "Why, whatever do you mean, my dear? How would I know your wife planned to run off? I was as shocked as you were," she evaded, avoiding his gaze and smoothing an imaginary wrinkle in her dressing gown.

"Were you really? That's odd. I got the distinct impression you knew all about it well before anyone else did," he said.

Matilda kept her eyes lowered and moved away lest he see the truth in them. "Shall I ring for coffee, dear? I only awoke a short time ago and simply must have my morning cup of coffee." She moved to ring the servant's bell.

"I want no coffee, Matilda, and you will have to suffer without it also for a time. What I want from you are straight answers." His voice was low and had a deadly calm to it now.

Ignoring his increasingly hostile tone, she went on.

"Why, of course my dear," she answered, still trying to retain her coolness. She reclined on the satin-covered sofa. "Do sit down here beside me and make yourself comfortable."

"No, thank you, Matilda. I prefer to stand," he said, leaving her no room to argue.

"As you wish, dear," she replied. She could feel his turbulent mood and sensed there was no way to forestall the unpleasant confrontation.

"How were you involved in Christy's running off, Matilda?" he asked, point-blank.

Matilda dropped her eyes and plucked carelessly at her robe. "I told you all I knew before. Must I go through it again?"

"As a matter of fact, I talked to Christy just this morning. So don't lie to me, Matilda. I am fully aware that you are a great deal more involved than you let on. For your own good, I suggest you tell the truth."

Matilda could feel herself being backed against the wall, and didn't like it one bit. "I'm sure I don't know what you're talking about, dear," she claimed innocently.

"You know perfectly well what I mean, Matilda," cried Michael in mounting disgust. His anger at her games was growing. "By your own past words and actions you have implicated yourself."

She swung her legs to the floor and raised herself to stand imploringly before him. "Oh, Michael, forget that worthless wife of yours. She means nothing to you and has caused you tremendous grief. And now that the baby is dead, you have no further commitments to her. Send her away. Forget her. You don't need her," she beseeched, gripping his arm with intensity. "Oh Michael, it's me who loves you, not her. I can give you everything you could possibly want—wealth, social status, passionate fulfillment. What can she possibly offer you but poverty and a disgraced background?" pleaded Matilda.

Michael looked down at Matilda in shock and disgust. Did the woman truly believe her own words? Did she actually think he would fall for her scheme? He shook off her touch as if she were possessed of a wretched disease. "Matilda, I do believe you actually have yourself convinced of what you are saying," he said coldly. "The truth is, though, that you have it all wrong. Wealth, social status and dignity are what I have to offer you, not the other way around. And you speak of love and passion. I can get more warmth from an interested trollop for far less a price than my name and entire fortune." He paused to glare at her.

Matilda's initial shock and hurt were quickly replaced by an all-consuming rage. "So you find me so repulsive and unworthy of your high and mighty standards, do you? Well let me tell you, if I do not measure up, then you will surely be surprised and humbled when I reveal what I know of Christy. You think so much of your charming little wife. Would you be so devoted if you knew that in reality she is nothing but a traitor and a fugitive from London?" she spat.

Michael's eyes opened wide. "What are you talking about? How do you know this?" he demanded.

His shocked expression encouraged her to go on, and she did so in unmasked delight. "Yes, it's true, my dear.

Her parents were involved in some illegal and disrupting business. They were killed on their way to some unauthorized rally. Investigations were conducted after their untimely deaths and their illicit activities brought out in the open. Mr. Joanace, then the commissioner of London, uncovered their deceitful practices of cheating and defrauding the government. That, sir, is treason, and he rightfully confiscated their possessions in retribution for their debts, and then made an example of them by disgracing their name through all of England."

After the initial shock of her revelation, Michael turned and regarded her closely, his eyes slowly narrowing to tiny brown slits. But instead of the dazed reaction she expected, his tone was cold and low. "Spare me your wretched revelations, Matilda. If you seek to unnerve me with your knowledge, you'd best resign yourself for a disappointment, for I already know all about Christy, her parents, and the accusations leveled against them. I have known for some time already. As a matter of fact, I had my lawyer check into it long before we were married. He is still uncovering details of their death and disgrace. There is more to the story than what the public was told, and I intend to find out the truth. But all that matters little to me at the present moment, Matilda. It is your involvement which concerns me."

If Matilda's revelation did little to unsettle Michael, his words had a stunning affect on her. She gaped at him in pure amazement, her mind racing frantically trying to make sense of it all. "I . . . I don't understand. If you've known about her past all along, if she told you the truth, then why did she agree to run away?"

She turned away, unable to face the blazing gaze focused on her. But he would not let her hide her face from him. He grabbed her shoulders and spun her about. "So, you now admit it was your plan to spirit my wife away?"

"I didn't mean what I said. You had me confused. You put the words in my mouth!" She tried to pull away, but he held her tightly.

"Damnit, woman. I put no words in your mouth. You've lost at your own game. You are a vile, deceitful woman, Matilda, and my only feeling for you is contempt," he said and abruptly let her go.

Matilda's eyes narrowed to tiny slits matching his. Her voice was raspy and she looked wild, almost satanical. Recovering from her cowardice, her mind worked once again in an effort to twist the facts to her advantage. "Well, if you love your precious little wife so, and she loves you, then tell me why she never told you about her parents—if she trusted you and loved you so?" she went on before he could reply, her mind working rapidly.

"I'll tell you why she held her tongue. Because from the very beginning, she and her uncle planned the whole thing, every last detail. They schemed to find a rich, unknowing sucker. You came along and fit the part perfectly, playing right into their hands. She seduced you and then no doubt played upon your honor as a gentleman to make restitution. It was truly a stroke of fortune the bitch got pregnant. That made it even easier. Oh yes, Michael. Open your eyes. Instead of accusing me, you should put the blame at the appropriate doorstep, and thank me for my intervention. As it was, when I confronted her with the truth and threatened to expose her to you, she got scared and ran off with what she could get her hands on—namely your jewels. You thought you had this all figured out, didn't you? Well, did you even consider that possibility, my dear, trusting fool?"

Again, to her vexation, Michael's reasoning matched her own. "Matilda, your lying and preposterous conclusions insult me beyond endurance. If you were a man, I would beat you to a pulp," he said as his eyes burned into her and his hands flexed in and out of tight fists.

Matilda, however, would not be silenced or put down. "Before you totally discount my theories, tell me this. Have you found the jewels? Can you prove me wrong, then?" she shouted back.

Michael had to admit that though he knew Matilda was drawing at straws, she had a valid point. His faith in Christy, however, would not be shaken. "You argue well for one professing to know so little on the subject, Matilda. But your arguments are not convincing enough. I admit you nearly had me convinced of Christy's guilt that day I returned from Charleston. The facts you laid out were neat. But irrefutable as the evidence seemed, I still loved Christy and found it difficult to believe she would plan such a deliberate act of treachery against me. Perhaps it was my pride which refused to let me surrender to your musings. At any rate, when I found the jewels she left behind in my room, the ones I gave her the night of the ball, my confusion was even more acute. Someone else did it to frame her."

"Michael, that's ridiculous. You're making excuses

for her. Why would anyone go to such great lengths to frame her? She's a useless little nobody."

"Well then, tell me why would she leave behind the priceless emerald setting I gave her and take those jewels of far less worth? Besides, the note I found in my room along with the emeralds belied her guilt," Michael continued.

"What note?" cried Matilda, unable to hide her surprise.

"The note explained she was leaving to spare my shame," he answered.

"She could have written the note to throw you off—to soften your heart—to confuse you," she shot back.

"I think not. The words were indeed sincere. Besides that, the jewels were not in her possession when I found her at that wretched cabin. What happened to them is still unknown," he said, though he had his suspicions.

"Well, who else could have taken them then, if not your wife? Perhaps Slate has them. He needs the money badly enough," she said, pulling at her last chance and knowing it useless.

Michael's control was nearly drained. He'd played Matilda's cat and mouse game long enough. "What do you know about Slate, Matilda? How do you know he needs the money? Tell me, woman, before I forget myself and strike you down!" he said, grabbing her roughly. "Somehow you found out about Christy and sent for her uncle, planning to blackmail her, didn't you? You both planned to blackmail her, did you not?"

Michael was amazed at the wicked look which came into Matilda's eyes. She appeared possessed of some evil spirit, and when she spoke, her voice hissed like a snake's. Her hatred flared and she at last gave up all pretext of innocence in her consuming rage.

"Well, I see you are not as stupid as I thought. You have guessed quite a bit, haven't you, my dear? But you're not as smart as you think, for the plan was far more complex than that." She pulled from his grasp with surprising strength.

Matilda now told him everything. "From the moment you introduced her as your 'cousin,' I despised her and suspected there was more to it than you were telling. I kept my eyes and ears open, and that day we quite unexpectedly ran into Governor Joanace my patience paid off. I had a little chat with Joanace. We discussed many things, and he mentioned the Pattersons of London. He could not be certain, however, that Christina actually was their daughter. So I began checking about. I heard Kramer's rather touching rendition of how she came into his shop, penniless and looking for work when you first docked. I also talked to a few men who sailed with you on that voyage. They told me how she got there. It all began to fit together, and I went back to see Joanace.

"The rest was quite easy after that. I enlisted the help of Gregory Piper, who was more than willing to find this uncle of Christy's when he stopped in London. I had to pay him handsomely, of course, but it was well worth the price. People will do anything for money, you know," she sneered. "I advised Piper that if he discovered this uncle was a poor, wretched slob of low character, and I had no doubt he was from the stories of his beating his niece, to offer him a substantial amount to induce him to sail here and play havoc with her life. The plan suited him well, as did my promise to increase his purse should he do the job well," she explained.

"When her uncle arrived, it was my plan to have him abduct her and get her out of the way. However, her 'love' for you and her desire to protect your reputation from her disastrous past improved my plans tremendously. I gave her a choice to either leave without a word to anyone, or suffer from public knowledge about her past which I threatened to divulge. She jumped at my suggestion to flee rather than subject you to the embarrassment and ridicule of the whole town finding out about her. Such a devoted little fool she is," commented Matilda.

"But anyway, the rest you know. I sent her off to the cabin to await the arrival of Slate. If she was not already dead from hunger or exposure, I had no doubt his appearance alone would kill her. Unfortunately you came across them too soon, before he could finish the task of disposing of her."

"My God, Matilda. I can't believe how devious you are," said Michael in undisguised shock. "Why would you do such a low, horrendous thing? What did Christy ever do to you that you should want to cause her such suffering?" he asked, for the moment too stunned to be angry.

"I'll tell you why, Michael, dear. Because I've had my eye on you and your money. That small pittance your wretched brother left me will soon be gone and I could not think of a better way to replenish my assets than cashing in on your share. You were available, and I was still somewhat in the family, so why should I sit back and let some other bitch enjoy your wealth? I laid my plans very carefully to get you, and all was going nicely. That is until you brought that meddling bitch back from London. Oh, it came so close I could almost taste the victory," she cried.

"My God, woman. You are truly demented. Even had Christy never entered my life, I never would have married you. Never! You mean nothing to me. But know this, Matilda. You'll not get away without paying for the damage you have caused. You will pay!" he cried angrily and took a step toward her.

Matilda regarded his ravaged face and listened to his threats with wicked mirth. "You scare me little with your vows of punishment. You have no proof, absolutely none, that I had anything to do with this. Your idle threats frighten me little," she snapped.

"By your own words you have admitted the whole story to me. Do you expect me to remain silent and let this go as if it never happened?" he asked incredulously.

"Oh, you can say what you wish, but it will be your word against mine. And with Lt. Governor Joanace on my side, you will have no chance of winning. You may as well resign yourself to defeat, dear boy, for when I get finished with you, you'll regret you ever met Christina. I'll show you who has power and influence. Once I get done, everyone in Charleston and the entire region will know that the illustrious Lancer bachelor picked himself a traitor and a fugitive for a wife."

"I won't let you get away with this, Matilda. I won't let you!" cried Michael, his fury almost completely out of control. He grabbed her by the shoulders in a death grip and shook her roughly. Her eyes gleamed all the brighter, like a fiendish viper. Her manicured nails dug into the flesh of his arms as she laughed demonically into his dark eyes. "You can't stop me now. I'll get my revenge. I'll make you suffer in disgrace and humiliation, and once you are beaten down and weakened, I'll send that bastard from London to visit your little wife. He'll make her pay. You'll all pay for belittling me. You'll all suffer!" she cried insanely.

Michael felt nearly blinded by his own wrath. His entire being ached to take her skull and crush it savagely in his hands. But the lunacy shining from her eyes sobered him somewhat, and he forced himself to breathe deeply and try to think clearly and rationally. He could not hope to conquer her insanity with his own rash words and actions.

His mind raced quickly, searching for some wedge to use against her. He knew only too well of his slim chances of implicating her with Joanace on her side. His only hope was to find this uncle of Christy's and try to secure his cooperation in testifying. It was a long shot, but at this point anything was worth a try. "Where is this man Slate now?" he asked her.

Matilda's face molded to a grotesque sneer. "You must find him first, and I'll never tell you where he is. Never! You'll not use him against me," she cried, her madness incited all the more. "I'd kill him first before I'd let him turn on me."

"No you won't, Matilda. I'm going to find him. I'm determined to see you punished for your wickedness," he promised, equally as determined as she.

"Oh, I'll kill *you* myself before I let you put me in prison!" she shrieked in sudden fury.

She lunged at a large vase of flowers and heaved them with deadly precision right at Michael's head. He dived aside as the glass missed his head by only fractions, shattering across the room.

"Oh, I hate you! I hate you!" she screamed. With a piercing screech she lunged at him. Like a wild beast, she clawed and kicked savagely at him with murderous intent.

She fought with the strength of a madman, and Michael struggled with difficulty to protect himself from her flailing limbs. One rocketing arm jerked free of his grasp, and he sucked in his breath as her claws raked his face. Blood trickled down his cheek. In mounting fury, he heaved her across the room away from him. She smashed into a table and crashed heavily to the floor.

Dazed by the fall, Matilda lay still for only a moment. Again lunacy shone through her brown eyes. She crouched on the floor and gazed upon his scarlet, infuriated expression.

"Lordy, is you all right in there?" cried a horrified maid who threw open the door in alarm at the sounds coming from the parlor. She gazed in disbelief from her laughing mistress, rocking back and forth in a heap on the floor, to Michael Lancer, livid with fury.

"You've not heard the last from me, Matilda!" cried Michael as he dabbed at his bleeding cuts.

His threat was answered by another peel of laughter as Matilda continued to rock back and forth on her knees, lost in her own private, deranged world.

Ignoring the frightened and confused servants milling about, he thundered from the house. In moments he was astride his huge stallion and racing toward Charleston. He would find Slate and the proof he needed to convict them both of their wicked schemes.

Thirty-Five

It was nearly two weeks later when Michael once again saw the familiar silhouette of Penncrest, illuminated by the full, bright moon. Stars twinkled like diamonds in the clear heavens above, and he hoped the good weather was an omen of better days ahead.

The hour was very late as he reined in the weary stallion, and he took care to keep his movements quiet. He had no intention of disrupting the whole house at this late hour. Besides, his explanations had better wait until morning when he was well rested and fresh. He filled his loyal horse's stall with fresh grain and water, and made his way with a weary step to the silent house. As he mounted the stairs he noticed a light shining in Sir Phillip's room. Rapping softly, he pushed open the door and went to stand before his father, who sat by the fire reading.

"Michael, you are safely home at last. I trust this nasty business is all cleared up and taken care of?" the older man asked, snapping the all-but-forgotten book shut and motioning his son to take a seat on the bed.

Michael acquiesced, rubbing his fingers wearily through his thick brown hair as he sank down onto the mattress. "Yes, most everything is at last settled. There are only a few loose ends left, but they will be tied up in short order. I will explain it all to you at length tomorrow. For now, I desire nothing more than the comfort of my own bed," he said wearily.

"I can understand that, and I will have to be content to wait till morning to appease my curiosity," responded Sir Phillip.

Michael rose stiffly and headed for the door. "How is Christina?" he asked hesitantly. All his good news could help him not if she was still at odds with herself and everyone else.

Sir Phillip sensed his son's anxiety and quickly sought to ease his doubts. "Michael, you would be surprised at the change that has come over Christina. She is doing remarkably well. Though she still blames herself for the death of the child, she has accepted the fact and is steadily improving both her mental and physical state. She will soon regain her former strength. Needless to say, I am quite delighted."

This was indeed good news to Michael's ears. But one question still burned in his mind. "How does she feel about me, Father? Will she see me?" he asked, worry creasing his brow.

"You needn't worry, son. I believe you will find her most eager to see you," said Sir Phillip with a twinkle in his eyes.

Again Michael was relieved to hear such promising news. There was still much to be settled between them, and the sooner it was done the better.

"Well, the news I bring should definitely make her

happy. I only hope she is not upset we launched into the investigation behind her back. This whole thing has been blown out of proportion," he said.

"Yes, you're right, but don't be too surprised if she beats you to the revelations. She has repeatedly expressed a strong desire to speak to you on a matter of extreme importance, which, she confessed, has been plaguing her for some time," replied Sir Phillip.

"Well, tomorrow should certainly be a day of truth and honesty. I only pray all turns out well," said Michael wearily.

"I am sure it will," answered Sir Phillip.

Michael nodded agreement and headed for his room. As he passed the door to Christy's room, he stopped for a moment, ready to knock. How he longed to hold her in his arms and soothe away her fears and worries; to explain his many hasty excursions to Charleston. He was ready to knock, and then, on impulse, moved on to his own room. He hated to disturb her sleep, and he felt too tired to go into a lengthy discussion at this late hour. . . .

Despite the many pressing issues he had on his mind, Michael slept soundly and awoke early the next morning feeling rested and equal to the day ahead. He dressed quickly and headed for the dining room to join his father for breakfast. The day seemed unusually bright and warm, and he hoped it would stay that way. As he entered the breakfast room, Sir Phillip glanced up from his coffee.

"Well, good morning, Michael. I must say you definitely look more rested than when I saw you last night. I trust you slept well?" he asked and without waiting for an answer, continued on. "Come sit, have some coffee and a good breakfast while you tell me all that happened," he invited.

Michael sat down just as Bertha entered. She murmured a few words of greeting as she poured him a steaming cup of black coffee. A few moments later a serving girl returned with two heaping plates of hot cakes and biscuits. Both men dug into the meal with relish and neither spoke again until their plates were empty and appetites more than satisfied. At length, Michael launched into his recitation, beginning with his encounter with Matilda.

"As determined as Matilda was to keep the whereabouts of Slate a secret," he said, "I was equally if not more determined to find him. My fury at them both drove me until I discovered the facts I needed. You see, once I arrived in Charleston, I went directly to Blake, our lawyer, and asked him to check with his informants on the whereabouts of Slate. I had a strong hunch that he had not as yet sailed back to England, and was waiting to hear from Matilda, or else was devising his own scheme to swindle us.

"It didn't take long for this Henry Slate to be spotted. It seems in the short time he had been in Charleston, he already acquired a reputation as a loud, violent-tempered man with an insatiable thirst for spirits. He had a room at a cheap waterfront inn, and frequented one tavern in particular. After a few shillings to loosen his tongue, the proprietor told me this Slate had to be physically evicted on numerous occasions after becoming drunk and picking fights with the other customers. He said he carried a big black whip, and even when sober seemed itchy to prove his skill in its use. It also seems, interestingly enough, that he boasted of having a great store of wealth at his disposal, but the owner told me his cash reserves seemed quite limited. Apparently Matilda had not paid him adequately, or else he had already squandered his money on drink," calculated Michael.

"At any rate, I didn't have long to wait to meet him for myself. He came in looking drunk before he touched a drop, and proceeded to polish off three quick shots without a pause. I watched him for some time at a distance. He looked my way more than once, yet gave no sign that he recognized me. So after a while, I deliberately sidled up to him, bought him a few drinks, and got him talking. The free drinks really went over with him and he acted as if we were long lost friends.

"After he got sufficiently drunk, I casually asked him about his origins, and he more than willingly relayed his story of having to raise a no-account niece of his late wife's who eventually ran off. He launched into his many hardships, glad for a sympathetic ear. In fact, I was afraid he'd drown me with his innumerable woes. Finally I got him back on track of Christy by asking him what brought him to the Colonies. At this point, he was so drunk, he could hardly keep his seat, but his tongue wagged on freely." Michael paused briefly to catch his breath.

"Go on! Go on! You've got me totally enthralled. Just what did he confess to?" urged Sir Phillip.

"Well, he said that a little over two months ago a man appeared at his door, offering him a large sum of money if he would answer some questions about his niece and her family. He decided he had nothing to hide and related every detail with relish. This messenger, Piper from Matilda's story, returned a few days later and offered him more money if he would consent to sail with him here. He was told that a friend had found his niece, and if he was interested, would line his pockets quite well if he would come and get her out of the way—take her secretly back to England, or devise some other means of disposing of her. He was told that she was creating a nuisance to a local influential family and her disappearance would be a great favor to the community." Again he paused, causing Sir Phillip to stir impatiently.

"Yes. Yes. Do go on."

"Well, needless to say, he set sail immediately on Piper's slave ship. He went on to say that upon arriving, he was met by a pretty but pushy woman who took him aside and laid out her plan to him to get rid of Christy. Timing was critical, she stressed to him, but he dallied a day longer than planned and did some quick investigating on his own. He discovered from the tavern owner that Christy had married and was quite well off.

"He seemed nervous all of a sudden that he had perhaps revealed too much to me. But after another reinforcing drink and some gentle prodding on my part, he finally went on. He volunteered that after finding his niece was worth a substantial sum, he decided to ignore Matilda's plan to 'dispose of' her. He told me he owed this Lancer woman nothing, and could accumulate far more money for himself by blackmailing Christy into stealing my money for him. He insisted that since she had caused him so much grief and hardship, it was only right she now share her good fortune with him. But he said the girl would not cooperate in his little scheme and he was forced to use some convincing measures. He snorted beligerently when he told of some big bastard barging in and laying him out cold.

"I was hard pressed to control myself at this point, and figured it was about time I laid my cards on the table. 'You've been informative, my dear friend,' I said to him. Then I made a tight fist and slowly put it right under his dripping nose. 'Does this look at all familiar to you?' I asked him. 'Take a good look at it, and at me,' I said. It was a real treat to watch the color drain slowly from his face. I've never seen anyone sober up so quickly. 'It's . . . it's you,' he stammered and jumped unsteadily to his feet, knocking over his chair in the process. 'Why yes, I'm that big bastard, as you put it,' I said.

"I was prepared for his attempt at a quick exit, and gripped him by the collar as he dashed out. He squirmed pathetically the entire way to the jail.

"Between the sheriff and me, we explained his choices if he cooperated with us, and the stinking coward willingly retold the entire story. In his effort to vindicate himself, he even gave us some additional information about Matilda. He admitted to having seen certain jewels she had stolen, jewels which she told him he was to receive in payment for disposing of Christy. He cried like a baby when the sheriff locked him up, claiming all along he had been framed and it was all the doing of Matilda Lancer," concluded Michael.

Sir Phillip sat in silence for some time trying to grasp the facts. "Then Matilda was definitely behind the theft all along? But why would she break into our house to steal them? She certainly is not destitute enough to risk being caught in the act," remarked Sir Phillip in bewilderment.

"Yes, that bothered me too, until Slate elaborated. It seems her idea was to steal the jewels and give them to Slate in payment. He was to wait and sell them later. That way they would serve a double purpose. They would be used as booty for a job well done and also their disappearance would be used as evidence against Christy."

Sir Phillip nodded his head silently, pondering these new findings for a moment. "But, I am still not sure why Matilda would go to such great lengths to frame Christina. What could she have hoped to gain from it all?" he asked.

"Father, if you would have seen the demented look on Matilda's face, you would realize she has been consumed by her own hatred and greed. She admitted to having schemed for many years to marry me, since her own funds are badly depleted. When Christy came along and ruined her plans, she simply could not cope with it and devised this plot. She has been eaten up with her sickness," he said in disgust.

"Yes, it's all a rather ugly story, isn't it?" agreed Sir Phillip.

Both men meditated in silence for a time, sipping absently on their coffee and puffing on cigars. It was a great deal to absorb at one time.

Christy rose later than usual that morning. Though the sun seemed bright and cheerful, she lay in bed daydreaming and hoping that perhaps today would be the day Michael returned. The past two weeks had been a struggle to fight the weakness of her body. But at last she had won the battle and felt stronger and more like herself. Now an even more pressing battle had yet to be fought. Her resolution to confront Michael with the truth about her past was a constant drain on her. She would be relieved when he returned and she had at last cleared the air. She had much to discuss with him, much to explain, and many apologies to make. She had behaved poorly toward him when she was sick, accusing him wrongly and vengefully. Would he ever forgive her?

How long ago it seemed since he had held her lovingly in his arms and smothered her with spicy, passionate kisses. A tingle swept through her at the memory of his strong, hard body pressed tightly to hers. Oh, to only have those days of peace and happiness back once again!

Sir Phillip had given her no clue as to why Michael had suddenly disappeared to Charleston, but she told herself that his absence was due to her accusations and his need to find peace away from her for a time. She could not blame him, after all, for not wanting to be exposed to such a wretched, ungrateful wife. He said he loved her when she had last seen him, but had her bitter insinuations caused him to reconsider?

She refused to consider this new, frightening conjecture and rose immediately. Milly arrived shortly to help her dress and brought the glad tidings that the young master had returned.

Christy was both elated and withdrawn at the prospects of facing him. Anxiously she fretted before the mirror, wanting to look her best for him, yet too jittery to sit still for the process. Finally, with a nervous sigh, she sent Milly off and with a controlled, unhurried step, slowly descended the stairs. The heated voices of Michael and Sir Phillip coming from the breakfast room made her pause momentarily before entering. Perhaps this was not the time to interrupt. She was ready to turn and walk away when part of what she overheard made her blood turn cold.

"Yes, I agree, Michael." It was Sir Phillip she heard speaking. "She should never have been permitted to marry into the family. The marriage was a farce from its very inception. There was no love or respect involved. It was merely a matter of social convenience. And considering her temperament and background, the marriage was ordained to be a disaster from the start and certainly lived up to all results thereafter. She has caused nothing but strife, friction and havoc within our family since the day she came to Charleston. And now look at the heartache she has caused us all," he said vehemently.

"I can only agree with you, Father. We both should have seen her for what she is long ago," agreed Michael. "And now, because of her cunning and deceitful actions, I have lost my son. That indeed is a hard, cold reality to swallow."

Again there was a heavy silence. Christy remained rooted to the spot, too shocked to breathe, too crushed to even run.

"What I don't understand is how she ever could have conspired with such a low-life as Slate. She knew only too well of his greedy, violent character, yet she willingly bound herself to him. Though it may seem harsh to say, I'm glad he's turned the tables on her. Soon she will be locked safely away in a jail. The sheriff is on his way to arrest her. She undoubtedly deserves whatever fate befalls her," uttered Sir Phillip.

There was a slight pause, and then Christy heard Michael's heavy, disheartened sigh. "I don't know how I could have been such a fool. After all her talk about loving and caring for me—and her little skits of affection. All she ever really wanted was my money and the Lancer name to cover her own sinking reputation. After our last confrontation, and all the facts I now know, it would be best I never see her again, for I would surely throttle her with my bare hands," he said with sincere conviction.

Silence followed, but Christy's ears rang with a deafening, humming roar. Their words stumbled over and over in her mind, growing louder and more hateful by the second. The horrible, accusing words vibrated through her entire being. She wanted to silence the ringing in her ears; to run from those who despised her so. But her legs were rooted to the floor. She could not move a step.

"Miss Christy? Are you all right?" asked Bertha as she spied the girl standing motionless in the doorway. "Miss Christina, you are pale as snow. Are you ill?" she questioned and moved closer when the girl did not answer.

Startled by Bertha's outcry, Michael and Sir Phillip turned in their chairs to discern the cause of the commotion. They were surprised to see Christy standing in the doorway, shockingly pale and trembling violently.

"Child, are you all right?" cried Bertha again as she quickly made her way to Christy's side.

The dizzy, roaring in Christy's head continued, but at last she heard Bertha's concerned outcry. With considerable effort, she pulled herself from her stupor and turned to gaze at the three with dazed, unbelieving emerald eyes.

"I . . . I didn't mean to eavesdrop. It was an accident. I had no idea you hated me so all this time. I had no idea. I really believed you cared for me. You . . . you should have told me the truth. My own blindness has played me the fool. Will you ever forgive me?" she cried, wringing her hands.

"Christy, whatever do you mean?" asked Michael in confusion as he rose from the chair to move to her side.

"I will be gone from your sight. You need never look upon this wretched form again. But please, please don't let them take me away. I won't go with them. I'll be gone before they get here. I could not bear to be locked away," she cried in anguish. Fear of being sent to prison suddenly broke the spell of her paralysis. Her legs sprang to life and she began to run as fast as they would carry her.

Michael looked in absolute confusion at his father who

sat shaking his head, equally as dazed as his son. "I don't understand what that was all about. What did she mean?" he began. "Is her mind playing tricks on her? I . . . Oh my God!" he cried suddenly. "She must have overheard our comments about Matilda. She thinks we were talking about her," his mind exploded with a new understanding. "I must find her at once and explain." He burst from the room and raced up the stairs toward her room, four at a time.

"No, master. No!" cried Bertha who stood in the hallway franticall wringing her hands and pointing. "She's gone outside, and without even her cloak. She'll die from the cold, and her still weak from losing the babe. You must stop her before she gets hurt!"

Michael's face was creased with concern as he bounded back down the stairs toward the door. Quickly he grabbed an old coat hanging in the foyer and raced through the door after Christy. He looked quickly about, but saw no trace of her. Where could she have disappeared so quickly?

Without hesitation, he raced for the rose trellis, a place he knew she found comforting. It was vacant. Dodging Brutus, who thought he played some new sort of chase game, he raced back to the front of the house just as Christy rushed past, mounted bareback on Alyn and riding at a reckless pace.

"Christy! No! Let me explain! Come back!" he called frantically after her fleeing figure.

In record time Michael reached the stables to find a stunned and trembling Morgan gawking at the fleeing form of his mistress. "Fetch my saddle quickly," ordered Michael as he tugged his stallion from his stall.

"Sir, she came racing in with no warning and jumped atop Alyn—no saddle or nothing—and took off. She'll be killed, sir, if you don't stop her!" he cried anxiously. He had a tremendous fondness for his new mistress and feared greatly for her safety.

Michael ripped the saddle from the stableman's unsteady grasp and deftly put it on the horse. "I'll stop her, Morgan. Don't worry," he called over his shoulder as his weight came crashing down on the horse's back. Taken by surprise at his reckless force, the stallion reared in protest. But Michael's strong hand put him quickly under control. A moment later a cloud of dust was all that remained of horse and rider as they thundered down the road in furious pursuit.

Blinding tears scalded her flushed cheeks as Christy recklessly urged Alyn ahead, racing at full speed in a course as far from Penncrest as possible. Horse and rider thundered over streams, fences and fallen trees. The ground was nothing but a blur beneath them. Christy had no idea where she was going, but cared little. Her head thumped wildly and the pain in her heart ached almost unbearably. The bitter cold air assaulting her face and limbs brought a thankful respite. A distant voice from behind called her name, frantically begging her to stop, but she blocked out the sound from her mind and only urged Alyn on the more.

But Alyn's strength soon began to wane under her rider's merciless demands. Her strides grew shorter and her pace began to slow. The distance between pursued and pursuer lessened as Michael took full advantage of his horse's superior strength. Within a minute he was riding abreast of Christy.

Side by side they thundered down the meadow. Mud and stones spewed the air in their wake. Slowly, carefully, Michael extended his hand and grasped Alyn's reins. With controlled pressure, he gradually forced the speeding horse to a slower gallop.

Emerald eyes wild with fear peered at him as he jerked Alyn to a halt. Christy's chest struggled up and down as she strove to catch her breath. Without waiting for an explanation, she heaved herself from the horse, propelling herself up the embankment with all her strength. But still weak from her sickness and exhausted from the strenuous ride, she was no match for Michael's long legs and superior speed. His hands reached out and firmly grasped her shoulders. They grappled together in the tall grass. Ferociously she pitted her meager strength against him. The one-sided battle caused her to slip and, with a frightened cry, she tumbled to the ground, pulling him down with her.

"Michael . . . Michael . . . I know you hate me, but please let me go. Don't let them take me away. I am sorry for the pain . . . the heartache I caused. I never wanted to hurt you. You must believe me," she sobbed.

"Christy, listen to me, please . . ." began Michael, but she would not be silenced.

"My name is cursed in all of England, and I can only bring you shame and disgrace. 'Tis why I protested so violently to marrying you, and 'tis why I ran when Matilda threatened to expose me if I did not leave. I could not bring shame to you who have been so good and kind to me. I could not." Scalding tears of shame and regret spilled down her cheeks. She no longer struggled against him, but lay still and rigid as the truth tore from her very soul. "Now the heartache is only worse."

"Christy, oh my Christy . . ." said Michael, but she was determined to finish and make her peace.

"Michael, I tell you now. You married me solely out of a sense of obligation to the babe you fostered. Your son is dead now. He no longer grows within me because of my reckless and selfish actions. And if that is not enough, you also know now of my shame and disgrace." She stumbled on her words, yet forced herself to continue. "I grant you free choice to dissolve this marriage and divorce me. You fulfilled your part of the contract. You have just cause to be done with me, and no one will blame you for severing all ties. You are free, and I will disappear from your life and cause you no further pain and disgrace," she said and rolled on her side, unable to face him. "Only please, please do not send me away to prison. I will pay for my wretchedness with my own guilt for the rest of my days. Have mercy, Michael. Please be kind."

She clenched her hands into fists and pounded them agonizingly against her temples. Though her eyes were squeezed shut, tears streamed down her face and dropped gently upon the grassy meadow. Life and death seemed to totter in the tempest raging within her.

"Oh Christy, you have nothing to apologize for. I do

not hate you, little one, and the only pain you have caused me is worry about you," he soothed. "Come. Stand up. The ground is cold and you are shivering," he said and gently lifted her to her feet, confident she would not try to run again.

Again she blinked back tears and stared at him with compounding confusion. "But I overheard you tell your father that you never wanted to see me again. I heard you both say you hated and despised me for the sorrow I've caused, and for the death of my—our son. I heard you say those things with my own ears."

He brushed a stray lock of hair from her damp face and wrapped her shivering body in the folds of his heavy coat, glad he had grabbed it on the way out.

"Oh Christy, my love. Why must we be forever separated by a sea of misunderstanding? Had you not run off so quickly, I could have explained. It was Matilda we were discussing, not you, my love. She has been a thorn in our sides since she married Henry. Yes, love, it was Matilda we were berating, not you. Never you, my sweet," he soothed.

But as much as she ached to believe him, doubts still stood in the way. "But Michael, the words I overheard could have applied to me as well as to Matilda. Have I not caused you consternation since the moment we met? And what of my past? Matilda and Henry Slate plan to reveal the whole story to everyone. If people discover who I am, it will bring disgrace to you and your family," she argued, again looking away.

With gentle firmness, he turned her face to his

and held it between his hands. "Look at me, Christy," he ordered gently. "Listen carefully to what I have to say. I care not what skeletons lie in your past. It is the present and the future with you that interests me. I love you very much, and nothing can stand in our way," he said. "You are what is best for me. If I have you and your love, my life is complete. I need nothing more," he said and touched her shoulder gently.

Her eyes met his, searching deeply for the truth in his words. "Then you do not care about the false accusations leveled against my family? You do not care that I lied to you with my silence? That I never told you the truth?"

"Oh, my dear one, what must I say? What must I do to convince you?" He smiled down at her and hugged her close. "Christina, you need not fear the intensity of my love is any less because of what you just told me. I swear it makes no difference to me. In fact, since we are being so frank, I too have a confession to make. I must admit to withholding information from you, too. You see, I have known since before we were married all about your parents and their sad fate. It hindered me not then, and will certainly not stand in the way of my love for you now," he said.

Christy's eyes opened wide. "But how did you know? I don't understand. Why did you not tell me?" she asked, incredulous at his revelation.

"I thought it best to keep my investigations secret until I had the whole story. Also, I must admit, I had hoped all along that you would love and trust me enough to confide in me. I had no idea my silence, and your desire to spare me shame, would cost us both so dearly," he said solemnly and wiped a stray tear from her cheek.

"Oh, Michael. What a fool I was to hold so tightly to my secrets. I debated many times, wanting to tell you, yet afraid to," she said in remorse.

"Well, it is over now, and we must look forward—never back. At last we have each other, and can plan for a happy future. But no more secrets between us, eh, my love?" decreed Michael with a smile.

"No more secrets, Michael," she breathed and threw her arms about his neck, tilting her face up to his. "But Michael, I want you to know that my parents were innocent of tax evasion and treason. It was a plot against them from the start, initiated by Joanace. He had them murdered, confiscated their possessions, and called them traitors. I tried to clear their name, but I was only a child then and had no strength or support to fight him," she explained. "But someday I will force him to admit the truth and clear their name," she vowed vehemently.

"You need not suffer any longer in shame. This very day a subpoena has been issued to Lt. Governor Joanace on suspicion of blackmailing and murdering your parents. I am confident that in a short time their names will be cleared and your confiscated possessions returned," he said and watched as her eyes grew wide in wonder.

"But how, Michael? I don't understand."

"Well, when my lawyer was searching for certain aspects of your past, he discovered a few facts which did not add up. I authorized him to delve further into it, and he came up with some evidence against Joanace. When I left my lawyer yesterday, the papers for the arrest of our lieutenant governor were already drawn up and ready to be served. Slate is already in jail, and by now Joanace should be behind bars and ready to be sent back to England for trial, for it seems your parents were not the only innocents to suffer at his hands. Once he is brought to trial, it is only a matter of time before he is convicted and the name of your parents cleared," he concluded.

Christy's face glowed with breathtaking beauty. "Oh, Michael, I am totally speechless. I am indeed the most fortunate of women to have you for my husband," she cried.

Christy relished in the feel of his strong arms about her. His fiery lips set her pulse racing, awakening her long suppressed desires. He too experienced intense longing after their needless separation. His fingers ached to once again feel the smooth, silky softness of her quivering flesh pressed tightly against him. Their closely kept secrets at last bared to the wind, he felt they could at last glory in the love which flowed between them. Together they could fight whatever Matilda or the others threw at them; together they could explore and discover the great reservoirs of love and passion.

Flushed and breathless, Christy at last pulled away. "Michael, we should be getting back. Since we left in a bit of a flurry, I fear your father may send out the servants in search of us," she said.

He pulled her close again and stroked her hair. "Yes, my love. I suppose we really must get back for my reserve grows weak. Just having you near sets my blood to boiling, and I may be unable to control my desire to lay you down right here in the meadow," he said huskily.

Christy nodded dreamily and they walked arm in arm to the horses. Nestled securely together atop the beautiful black stallion, she leaned her head against his shoulder as he cradled her in his arms. Slowly and in blissful silence they rode back to the house, Alyn following contentedly behind.

Thirty-Six

Sir Phillip anxiously greeted Michael and Christy as they approached the huge white house. But one look at their radiantly happy faces satisfied him that they had, at long last, reached a state of understanding. It pleased him immensely to see them so much in love. As Morgan took the two horses to the stables, he sauntered down the steps and clapped his son on the back. "I hope those radiant faces mean all is settled? Come into the house and we shall toast the occasion," he offered, leading the trio up the steps.

"Yes, Father. We must drink to a new beginning, and a future full of joyful promise," agreed Michael and squeezed Christy's arm.

She smiled up at him, returning the pressure on his arm. "A toast my be in order, gentlemen, but it is not yet ten o'clock. We would surely scandalize the servants. Perhaps we should postpone our celebration to a more appropriate hour." She laughed merrily. A tremendous burden had been lifted from her, and she felt almost giddy with joy.

They all laughed and had just reached the top of the

stairs when Morgan heralded the arrival of two mounted men. As they drew nearer, Michael recognized them as officers of the law.

"Christy, my love, these men have no doubt come with news of Matilda's arrest. The details may be rather unpleasant, I fear. Perhaps you would care to wait in the house until they have gone. I will fill you in later," offered Michael, hoping to spare her any bad tidings.

"Your concern is touching, Michael, but I would prefer to hear what they have to say," she said, somewhat stubbornly.

The trio retraced their steps to the pavement below and confronted the two officers.

"My name is Lieutenant Baker. This is Officer Tanner," said the smaller of the two uniformed men in way of introduction. "Is one of you gentlemen Michael Lancer?"

"I am Michael Lancer. How can I be of assistance?" he asked, stepping forward.

"I've some unpleasant news to relate to you, so I'll get right to the point. Do you know anything about the whereabouts of a woman named Matilda Lancer?" he asked, all the while watching Michael's face for possible clues.

"Matilda? Why do you ask? Were you not sent to arrest her this morning?" questioned Michael cautiously. "Has something gone awry?"

The officer shifted uneasily and spat into the dust. "Mr. Lancer, as you are aware from your signed warrant, Tanner here and I were commissioned to arrest Mrs.

Lancer this morning for the attempted murder of your wife," he said. Both men eyed Christy with anything but official interest. "You are Mrs. Lancer, I presume?" he questioned arrogantly.

"Yes," whispered Christy, blushing hotly at their unmasked perusal of her.

Pulling his gaze from her back to Michael, the officer continued. "When we arrived this morning to make the arrest, we found Mrs. Lancer missing and the man, Henry Slate, her co-conspirator, shot. We have reason to believe she may be heading in this direction. She is armed and dangerous," he finished and stood back to watch their reactions.

Christy nearly collapsed in Michael's arms at the shocking news. "Slate . . . shot? By Matilda?" she cried. All color drained from her face and her hands began to shake.

"My God!" exclaimed Michael in disbelief, unwilling to believe what he heard. "Slate must have escaped jail. Is he hurt badly?"

The officer looked at Christy, wondering how she would react to his answer. He directed his attention back to Michael. "I'm afraid he's dead. Shot in the back."

"Oh, how terrible," murmured Christy. Though she despised Slate, the news of his gruesome death sent a chill through her. Her knees grew suddenly weak and she clutched at Michael for support.

He put a reassuring arm about her, holding her close and trying to absorb the hurt and pain she was experiencing. "Are you all right, my dear? Let me take you inside," he suggested in concern.

"No, Michael. I will be fine in just a moment. Really, I will. It's just the shock," she explained in an effort to regain her composure. "Go on, Lieutenant."

Michael nodded to the short man. "It's all right, Lieutenant. Go on. Tell us exactly what happened."

"Yes. I was getting to that," replied the officer somewhat irritably. "It seems Slate stole the jailer's horse, then headed directly for Matilda Lancer's residence. According to the servants, he arrived quite early and woke the entire house, demanding to see Mrs. Lancer. According to the housemaid, your sister-in-law tried to get rid of him but he insisted she owed him some sort of payment. She took him into the parlor and shut the door to keep their discussion private, but according to the housemaid, the two of them argued so viciously, the servants could hear nearly every word.

"It seems Slate accused her of sending you, Mr. Lancer, after him to frame him and send him to jail. She denied knowing anything about his arrest, and finally succeeded in getting him calmed down. It seems the fighting started all over again when he demanded some jewels as payment for his part of the deal. He claimed she owed them to him. The servants, who had gathered in the hall, said their mistress held her own and called him a fool, refusing to give him one shilling since he had bungled the whole episode. Apparently her words angered him greatly, for the maid heard Slate threaten to shoot her if she did not come up with the jewels."

"Go on, Lieutenant. Go on," urged Michael impatiently.

"Apparently Mrs. Lancer was little frightened by the threats, for she laughed all the more at his demands. She said she had no wish to turn over the precious jewels to a hunted and escaped convict and had every intention of selling them and using the money to establish herself in a respectable home far from Charleston. She had Joanace on her side, and felt safe from any accusations he could level against her. But then Slate told her Joanace had been arrested on various charges, including murder, and that a warrant for her arrest had been filed. He also informed her the authorities were probably on their way to arrest her. He ended by admitting he had willingly implicated her in the whole scheme.

"The news was her undoing, it seems. Nadine said she hardly recognized her mistress's voice, it sounded so hateful. Matilda accused Slate of being a coward and using her name to make things go easier for himself. He admitted it was true, that he owed her nothing and again demanded the jewels. A scuffle ensued and they heard furniture crashing about.

"Suddenly a gunshot pierced the air, followed by a deafening silence. The servants summoned their courage and rushed in to find Matilda standing over the bleeding Slate, a wicked gleam on her face. When she saw them gawking at her, she began ranting like a mad woman, all the while brandishing the gun threateningly at them."

The full impact of the officer's statement shook Michael considerably. He suspected Matilda would react violently to being arrested and had hoped the authorities would surprise her and give her no chance to ponder it. For that reason he had made no effort to confront her himself. Slate had escaped and run into her insane wrath. He had paid with his life, and now they would all suffer the consequences. "Where is Matilda Lancer now?" he asked.

"No one knows. She went screaming out of the house, swearing that she would get revenge on all her tormentors. By the time the servants had recovered enough from the shock to follow, she had disappeared."

"How long ago was that, Lieutenant?" asked Michael, rubbing his chin as a deep furrow crossed his brow.

"I'd say it must have been two hours or more by now," he figured aloud.

"Well, it's pretty safe to assume she is not coming this way then, for she would have been here by now. But where else could she have gone?" Michael wondered.

"The servants must be thoroughly frightened and confused. I believe I'll have Morgan hitch up the carriage and fetch them here with me. I'd feel much better if they were safe here with us," volunteered Sir Phillip.

"Yes, I agree. They will surely be better off with us than with neighbors. But first we must find Matilda. I'll fetch my coat," said Michael. "Christy, come inside and lie down," he said and took her arm to lead her up the steps. "I will be with you in a moment, gentlemen," he called over his shoulder to the two waiting officers.

Moments later, Christy and Sir Phillip stood at the study window watching the three men ride off. Both prayed silently for the safe return of the man they loved. As the riders disappeared from sight, Sir Phillip turned to address his daughter-in-law. "Come sit down by the fire, my dear. You've had a bad shock and are pale as snow. Why, you're chilled to the bone from standing outside so long," he remarked in concern as he touched her arm. "Perhaps some brandy will warm you," he offered and poured a substantial glassful.

"Thank you, Father," she said, gratefully accepting the soothing drink. She suddenly felt exhausted and in need of something to calm her shaken nerves. She sipped slowly, allowing the liquor to warm her stomach as it brought a soft flush to her pale cheeks.

Noting these encouraging signs, Sir Phillip settled down himself and sipped contentedly. "You've been through much, my dear. And now, to have your uncle brutally murdered . . ." he mumbled in pity. "I'm so sorry about all of this."

"You are too kind, Father," said Christy, her sparkling eyes attesting to her happiness.

"A thousand pardons for intruding upon such a touching scene. Had I but known, I would have timed my visit for later." The cold, hateful voice filled the room, and they spun to face a bedraggled and wild-eyed Matilda Lancer.

"Matilda!" cried Sir Phillip, nearly choking on the exclamation.

Matilda seized upon her surprise entrance with gusto. "Yes, Father dear," she crooned with forced sweetness. "You're not happy to see me?" she pouted dramatically.

"Well I guess not, since now you have a new little daughter to fondle and spoil, one who is sweet and docile and attentive to your powers," she seethed and sent Christy a withering glare.

"Matilda, really . . ." began Sir Phillip.

"Oh you needn't try to weasel your way out of this one, dear," she interrupted and began to pace about the room.

Matilda's eyes grew black. "I'll get right to the point. I'm here to settle a little debt I owe you and that interfering little bitch cowering behind you," she cried. In a flash her hand dipped deep into her pocket and reappeared clutching a deadly black gun. With cold, white fingers, she pointed the gun directly at her approaching father-in-law.

Christy gasped in horror at the lethal weapon, and Sir Phillip jerked to a halt in mid-stride. "Put that gun down, Matilda. You are in enough serious trouble already without adding to it. Now give it to me before you hurt yourself," he demanded, hoping his forceful, commanding tone would temporarily confuse her into turning over the weapon. He took a determined step forward, never taking his gaze from her blazing eyes, and reached for the gun.

His steely composure momentarily confused her. Her hand wavered in the air. Uncertainty flickered across her face. Seeing her weakness, Sir Phillip grabbed for the weapon. His quick movement startled her back into control and she jerked the gun out of his reach.

"Get back, you wretched old man, or I'll gladly put a

hole in that fancy suit of yours!" she exploded in anger.

Sir Phillip drew back instantly, appalled by the insanity he detected in her voice. "You are crazy, Matilda."

Matilda snorted and cocked her head arrogantly as she fingered the gun's trigger anxiously. "Crazy am I? Well, I'm not crazy enough to let the lot of you banish me to some stinking prison to rot. Oh, they may catch up with me and drag me off to jail, but I can assure you of this. Before I go, I have a debt to repay. For I promise you, as long as I stand with this gun in my hand, you'll both precede me to hell!" she screamed and waved the gun threateningly at them.

"Matilda. Listen to me. Whatever quarrel you have with us can surely be worked out. Let us sit down and talk it over like civilized adults," pleaded Christy. As soon as she spoke, she realized her error in bringing Matilda's wrath upon her.

"Oh yes, my girl. You play the sweet, innocent mediator very well. This gun has mellowed your reasoning, for you never before cared how you manipulated me or ruined my plans. Oh yes, this little black hunk of iron makes all the difference, doesn't it?" she oozed. "But it's too late now."

Christy stared helplessly into the cold black barrel of the gun. "No, Matilda. Do not do this. What purpose will it serve?" she pleaded. "It will not bring Michael back to you, and it certainly will not undo what has been done. Think it over. You may be acquitted of Slate's murder if you can prove it was self-defense. But if you kill us, there can be no question as to your guilt. Don't throw away the rest of your life. Let us help you," she pleaded desperately.

"Help me? Help me, you say!" she spit back, incited anew by Christy's reasoning. "You cannot help me, you little bitch. I need no one. Do you hear me? No one! I'm going to kill you all, and you will be the first to go," she screamed and eased her finger back on the trigger.

"No, Matilda. No!" cried Sir Phillip. Frantically he lunged at the deranged woman in an effort to deflect the bullet. Matilda staggered back as his arm struck her. A shot exploded. Sir Phillip groaned aloud and dropped to the floor, clutching his shoulder as blood spilled down his arm.

"Oh my God!" cried Christy as he fell. Her hand flew to her throat as she struggled to catch her breath. Heedless of Matilda, she raced to his side and cradled him in her arms, searching his ashen face for signs of his condition.

"You damn fool!" cried Matilda savagely, regaining her balance and watching the proceedings with marked agitation. "She was my target. Not you. Now you've only delayed her death," she spit at him.

"Matilda, he's bleeding badly. We must summon a doctor at once," said Christy, ignoring her threats as she tried to stop the flow of blood.

"Miss Christy! Master Phillip! Are you all right? What's going on in there?" came a frightened cry. The door shook on its hinges as Bertha tried to enter.

"Get away, you black witch, or I'll kill them both!"

cried Matilda through the door.

Christy turned abruptly away from Matilda and devoted her complete attention to Sir Phillip. There was little sense in arguing further with the woman. But at least now the servants were aware of her presence, and perhaps they might bring help.

"Please don't move, Father. Save your strength. You will only agitate the wound more," pleaded Christy as he lay heavily in her arms.

"The wound is not serious, Christina. I shall be fine. But you are in great danger. She's gone mad. You must devise some means of escape," he whispered. The effort cost him precious strength and his breathing became more shallow.

"I will not leave you," she whispered back as a tear trickled down her cheek.

"Escape? Leave you say?" cried Matilda and then laughed without mirth. "You underestimate me, dear sir. The little lady will not escape a bullet in her breast. There is no one now to stop me," she cried and waved the gun menacingly at them.

Christy shot a glance at Matilda. "You are a vile and evil human being Matilda, to do this horrible deed. You may well kill Sir Phillip and myself, but Michael will not let you get away without punishment."

A crooked smile touched Matilda's lips. "Oh, you'd best not count on your precious Michael, my dear. He can do me little harm now," she smiled, as if savoring some memory.

"What do you mean, Matilda? Why, he is out looking

for you right now," she rallied, yet the tone of Matilda's voice sent a quiver up her spine.

Matilda regarded her defensive face with mock pity. A burst of laughter suddenly shook her shoulders grotesquely. "Do excuse my amusement. But your words struck me hilariously funny. You see, 'tis highly unlikely that your dashing Michael shall come to your rescue now, for I put a bullet through his head only a short time ago." Again she broke into a renewed fit of laughter, a cross between misery and hysteria.

Christy's heart leapt to her throat. "Michael . . . dead? No! It's not possible. It's not true!" she cried in horror. Forgetting the danger, she jumped up and rushed toward Matilda, ready to wipe the sneer from her face and force her to retract her words. "You're lying! He's not dead!" she cried, near hysteria herself.

"No, Christy!" cried Sir Phillip as he watched Matilda's face contort into a wicked, ghoulish grin as she watched Christy advance. But his warning fell on deaf ears. Christy plunged headlong at Matilda. A stinging slap across her face stunned her, and Christy fell weeping to the floor beside Sir Phillip, filled with despair.

Matilda looked down at the heartbroken girl with a total lack of pity. How she enjoyed bringing despair and destruction to the little bitch. She smiled and continued her heartless barrage of bad tidings.

"Yes, it certainly was a simple task to shoot the invincible Michael Lancer down. You see, I heard him coming down the road with those two bastards from the sheriff's office. I figured they were looking for me, so I hid in the woods. When Michael rode by, I just couldn't resist the urge to put a nice, neat bullet hole through his arrogant head. It was a joy to watch him fall from his horse into the mud." She laughed heartily, enjoying her moment of glory. "It's only what he deserved for spitting in my face and turning me over to the law."

"Why, Matilda? You claimed to love him," questioned Christy, still overcome with grief.

Matilda's face shone mean and ugly. Her eyes blazed and again she shook her fists at the two on the floor. "I killed him because he turned me down as unfit to wipe his boots. I killed him because I could not bear to leave him to you."

"You are indeed insane, Matilda," uttered Sir Phillip.

Again Matilda's mood suddenly shifted from hateful to jovial, a fact which frightened Christy even more. "Insane am I, dear Father? I beg to differ with you. In fact, 'tis quite the contrary. I have not experienced such elation since the day Henry, my late husband and your eldest son, met his convenient and timely demise."

"What do you mean? Are you saying Henry's death was no accident?" cried Sir Phillip. With great effort he raised himself on one elbow and met Matilda's gaze.

"You stupid old fool! You never guessed Henry's carriage accident was a carefully planned and executed plot, did you? I had you all fooled," she boasted eagerly. "Why, he was even more of a wretch than you—always demanding, domineering, and stingy. It was degrading to have to beg for every new dress or hat. And those two little brats were the first of many he planned. It mattered not how I hated being pregnant. He cared nothing for me and yet showered them with money and affection," she said with renewed hate. "So I carefully planned an 'accident' for him. It was so easy to sabotage the carriage. And no one ever guessed or even suspected that his death was anything but a tragic mishap."

Christy's nails dug deep into the flesh of her palms. Memories of another identical "accident" flooded her mind. She tried to block out Matilda's hateful words, but they pounded on with renewed force.

"But even in death he found a way to punish me with his hate, for he left a great share of his wealth to those two brats of his, and fixed it so that I could not even touch it. He did it purposefully that way, because he knew it would crush me to have the money so close, yet be unable to spend it. Oh but he hated me dearly, and I him."

Christy's stomach churned in nauseating fear. How could she ever hope to overcome or outwit someone whose thinking was as distorted as Matilda's? Perhaps the only way was to play along at her game. A plan was beginning to form in her mind as Matilda spoke again.

"Now dearie, your time has come. Enough of this idle chatter. My finger grows anxious on this trigger. Move over there beside the window and away from the gallant Sir Phillip. You wouldn't want me to miss and hit him again, now would you, dearie?" she laughed viciously and motioned her away with the gun.

Christy moved slowly to the place Matilda indicated. There was little doubt she fully intended carrying out her threat. By her own admission she had already killed three people. It was unlikely she would feel remorse at adding two more to her list.

"Good. Good," came Matilda's croaking voice as Christy moved into place. "And now, before I shoot you, I want to savor the sight of you down on your hands and knees. Before you die, you will apologize to me for all my ruined hopes and dreams. And after you tell me just how sorry you are that you were ever born, then, my dear, then I want to see you crawl to me and beg me to spare your wretched life. Get down and crawl to me on your belly. Let me see how you can plead for your life," she hissed.

Christy forcibly stifled her fear and anger, and masked her true feelings under an expression of utter dejection. Heart pumping wildly, she lowered her eyes to the floor and spoke in a low, completely despondent voice.

"Matilda, my parents were murdered and cruelly taken from me when I was very young. I was then left in the hands of my wicked, hateful uncle until I ran away, unable to withstand his abuse any longer. A few months ago, I found a man who brought me the love and happiness I have lacked all these years. Because of your treachery, I have lost his child. Now you tell me you have murdered him whom I love. You have left me with no passion for living. You have taken from me all desire to go on. Shoot me now, Matilda, and free me from this heartache, for I cannot bear to go on."

Matilda was surprised at Christy's response. She had expected defiant resistance to her demands, not utter surrender. She bristled in anger.

"Oh, you sniveling bitch! Do you not see this gun pointed at your breast? Don't you realize I can kill you instantly where you stand? Now do as I say. Get down and plead for mercy!" cried Matilda wildly.

Christy's voice was low and stubborn as she turned her back to the woman. "No, Matilda. I will not even grant you that small bit of satisfaction. If you shoot me, then you must shoot me in the back as you did Henry Slate and Michael, for I will not turn around to face you."

Sir Phillip glanced first at Christy, stunned by her words and actions, and then to the enraged Matilda. Fighting pain and dizziness, he struggled to his knees. "Matilda, do not do this. Please, let Christina go. I will see that you are generously taken care of, and given every opportunity to prove your innocence. Whatever you want, just tell me."

Blind with rage, Matilda began to curse them. "There is nothing I want from you, old man. Nothing! Do you hear me? I . . . want . . . her . . . dead!" she shrieked, barely able to extract the words from her tightly contracted throat.

Christy heard the trigger cocked. Her hand flew to the table beside her. Icy fingers clutched a brandy decanter. Without warning, she whirled around and heaved the bottle at Matilda just as the woman was ready to fire. Unprepared for the attack, Matilda staggered back as the bottle struck her arm and then crashed to the floor.

Instantly Christy lunged across the room for the fallen gun. Her fingers clawed across the floor in desperation.

Another inch—just another inch! Stretched beyond endurance, her fingers closed around the weapon. The metal felt cold in her hand.

"Look out!" Sir Phillip's warning cry penetrated the room.

Christy spun about just as a sharp pain punctured her side. She fell to the floor, wincing in pain.

"You'll pay for this, you bitch!" cried Matilda as she raised her foot to kick again.

Lightning quick, Christy heaved herself across the floor, missing Matilda's boot by fractions. As her attacker attempted to regain her balance from the missed kick, Christy jumped to her feet.

Three pairs of eyes simultaneously focused on the gun lying just out of reach beside the door. Sir Phillip, powerless to move, watched as both women raced toward the weapon.

Matilda's fingers locked about the gun. Before she could turn, Christy lunged at her and both women tumbled to the floor. Matilda shrieked madly and clawed at Christy's hair and face as they rolled about the room in mortal combat. It would be a fight to the death, and both knew it.

Matilda smashed Christy's head against the leg of the heavy desk. Stars danced before her eyes, but she blinked them away. Her fingers clenched in a tight fist and she landed a stunning blow to Matilda's unprotected jaw. The attack left Matilda momentarily dazed, and Christy struggled to her feet.

Panting heavily and still dizzy from the blow to her

head, Christy grasped the desk for support. Her eyes darted about the room in search of the pistol. Where had it gone? Under the sofa? Her glance flew to Sir Phillip, struggling to stand. "Where . . . where is the gun?" she panted.

A growl sounded behind her. Clawlike hands gripped her arm and spun her about. Christy gasped in terror as her eyes focused on the hissing form converging down upon her.

"Stop, Matilda. Stop!" Sir Phillip cried helplessly. Matilda never heard him.

She grabbed Christy by the shoulders and hurled her across the room. New pain shot through Christy's head and back as she slammed against the wall. Frantically she blinked away the darkness which threatened to render her helpless. Her mind cried out for flight, but her sluggish movements suddenly seemed to be in slow motion.

Helplessly she watched as Matilda raised her arms high and brought them down with crushing swiftness. Her head exploded with pain. Blinding lights flashed before her eyes, blocking her vision. Instinctively she raised her arms to protect her head from another destructive blow. The crippling thrust came within seconds, but this time in her stomach. She groaned aloud as Matilda landed another punch, and then another.

Slowly, ever so slowly, Christy slipped to the floor. She could endure no more. She closed her eyes to block out the sight of Matilda's deadly glare. Pain pulsed through her and she was unable to distinguish when one blow struck or ended.

Matilda began to laugh. Her delicate hands, unaccustomed to being used as weapons, thumped painfully. But the ache bothered her not as she stared at her devastated adversary. With a joyful sneer, she scanned the floor and pounced on the gun.

"My God, Matilda!" shouted Sir Phillip, hoarse from his cries of horror at what he witnessed.

"Get back, you fool," she hissed as he stumbled at her. "My moment of triumph has come at last." She eased her finger on the trigger. . . .

Somewhere deep in the recesses of her mind, Christy heard a resounding crash as glass shattered across the room. Sir Phillip's cries were slowly fading. Sights and sounds were a blur of confusion. Blackness was enveloping her. Matilda shouted hysterically. Another familiar voice sounded from the darkness. Michael?

"Drop that gun, Matilda! Drop it right now!" commanded a voice from amid the flying debris.

Matilda spun in astonishment. Her eyes grew wide as saucers and she stared, utterly dumbfounded, into the cold brown eyes of Michael Lancer. His clothes were caked with mud, but he was alive—very much alive.

"No! You're dead. I killed you. I watched you fall with my own eyes!" cried Matilda in confused panic.

Michael forced himself under control and stole a look at his father, bleeding on the floor, and at Christy, lying motionless. Hastily he riveted his attention back to Matilda. "As you can see, Matilda, I am very much alive. Your shot only grazed me slightly. You should have taken better aim," he said with intentional dryness. "If you do not believe me, then perhaps you would care to touch me and prove to yourself that I am not actually a ghost. Come closer and I will show you," he said in a convincing tone. His finger nervously tapped the trigger of the gun he clutched in his sweaty hands. Slowly, very slowly and deliberately he edged ever closer to his wild-eyed sister-in-law.

"Old man, why do you stare at me so? Do you not see your son come back to torment me?" she cried.

"Matilda, are you truly gone mad? Whom do you speak to? I see no one save you and Christina," he said. At last he had succeeded in propping himself against the sofa for support. "What is it frightens you so?" he asked in open astonishment, playing along with Michael's game.

"No. No!" she cried in confusion, hesitating momentarily and beginning to question her own sanity. "You're trying to trick me into thinking myself mad," she accused, darting her wide eyes from father to son. "Somehow you are making me see what is not there." She yanked repeatedly at her hair and stepped away from her apparition.

"I'm real, Matilda. See me. Touch me. Come closer," said Michael as he moved steadily closer.

"Stay away from me," whimpered Matilda like a frightened child. The gun slowly lowered to her side as she again clutched at her throat.

"It's all right, Matilda. Here. Give me the gun. Everything's all right now," soothed Michael.

She jerked her head from side to side. Slowly, cautiously Michael reached for the dangling gun.

Suddenly the study door burst open. In rushed the police lieutenant and his assistant. "Drop the gun, Mrs. Lancer. We've got you covered!" he ordered. "We've heard your confession of murdering your husband and Slate. You are also guilty of attempted murder. We're going to take you in," he said roughly and stalked toward her.

Matilda's head jerked around to stare, wild-eyed, at her accuser. Instantly she jumped back, just out of Michael's reach. "So it was a trick!" she seethed, swinging the gun wildly at them, her eyes again alert and deadly. "You played me the fool, Michael Lancer! But it's too late for your father and your precious little wife. And it's too late for you. You'll never take me alive!" she shrieked wildly. A piercing scream shattered the room and instantly she bolted for the broken window. Before anyone could intercept her, she disappeared into the yard.

Michael watched the law officers pursue Matilda but turned away quickly. His face was contorted in concern as he bent over Sir Phillip.

"I'm fine, Michael. Go after her. Stop her. Bertha will tend to me and Christina," he said and waved his son after Matilda. "You must stop her before she kills again!"

Michael's gaze rested on the small, crumpled form of his wife. Gently he lifted her still body into his arms. "Christy, my love," he whispered as he brushed away a lock of bloody hair from her face.

"Go on, Michael. You can do nothing for her now. For Christy's sake, catch Matilda," urged Sir Phillip.

Pounding hooves raced past. Michael's eyes flew to the window as Matilda rode recklessly by mounted upon Alyn. In close pursuit followed the two officers.

Bertha's horrified cry brought Michael's attention back to the room. "Send Morgan for the doctor at once, Bertha. They're both hurt badly. Hurry now." He jumped to his feet.

Thirty-Seven

"Christy . . . Christy . . . wake up, my love."

The words drifted in and out of Christy's consciousness. She smiled. It was Michael's voice she heard, speaking softly, lovingly to her. She could feel his arms about her, and deeply savored the sensation; content in a world just outside of sleep. She took a deep breath yet refused to open her eyes, fearful of waking from the pleasant dream.

"Come on, love. Wake up. You have been asleep nearly four hours, and I grow impatient to see your sparkling emerald eyes," he said.

Christy's eyes were heavy and she was reluctant to open them lest this feeling of euphoria vanish. She ignored the persistent demands and luxuriated in the security of her sleep. A moment later, she felt warm, teasing lips upon hers. She had never experienced such a lifelike, sensual dream. Very slowly, she opened her eyes.

"I thought that might bring you around," laughed Michael playfully as he outlined her lips with his fingertips.

"Oh, Michael," she breathed softly and reached up to clasp his hand in her tiny fingers. They felt warm, powerful, and so alive. Alive!

She sat bolt upright as full memory came flooding back with vivid clarity. Blinding pain shot through her head and she grabbed her temples in agony.

"Easy, little one. Relax and lie still. You had a very bad bump on the head. You must rest," he said and gently eased her back onto the pillow.

"Oh Michael, Michael. You're not dead! Matilda told us she had killed you. I was mad with grief. I wanted to die rather than live without you," she cried as tears of joy streamed down her pale face. Her grip on his hand increased, as if she feared letting him go might cause him to disappear once again.

Neither spoke for a moment. Their eyes met and silently conveyed the intensity of their emotions.

"How is your father, Michael? He was badly hurt."

"The doctor left just a short time ago. I'm afraid he had his hands full here, with you, Father and Matilda. But don't worry. Father is weak but in good spirits and will be up and about in no time. It takes more than a flesh wound to keep a Lancer down."

Christy shuddered at the memory of Matilda's crazed attack. As long as she lived she would never forget the look of insanity she had seen on the woman's face.

"What has happened to Matilda? I remember little after we began struggling. Did you capture her? Where is she?"

Michael gently stroked his wife's face. He wanted to choose his words carefully, for the news would no doubt be a shock to her, and she had had enough trauma for one day. "Matilda will bother us no longer, darling."

Christy regarded him with questioning emerald eyes. "Has she been arrested then, and taken away by the two officers?"

"In her haste to escape, Matilda grabbed the first available horse, Alyn. Alyn was hurt and confused and ran totally out of control. When Brutus, that huge pup of yours, saw the chase, he thought it was some kind of game and raced after them. He ran right at the frightened horse, causing her to rear and stop abruptly. Matilda lost her seat and fell, headfirst, to the ground. She . . . she died immediately. A broken neck," said Michael as gently as possible.

Christy squeezed her eyes closed and shuddered at the brutal ending to the vengeful woman. "Oh, how terribly tragic." Silence hung heavily.

Christy gazed silently up at Michael. The nightmare was over. It was time to forget the past and collect the shattered pieces of their lives, to make a new beginning. Looking back could only bring more heartache and pain.

"Oh, Michael, despite all of life's heartaches, it truly is good to be alive. We all have so much to be thankful for. Praise God we still have one another. Our love has carried us through this nightmare. It is time to forget the past and begin again."

A deep sigh passed her lips. She focused shining emerald eyes upon Michael, eyes filled with a determination that nothing fate could throw at her would ever get her down again.

"Michael?" she whispered softly, her featherlight touch upon his face was warm and gentle, yet demanding his attention.

"Yes love, what is it?" he asked, his pulses already aflutter.

"Michael, I love you. I love you so very much. Promise me we will always be together."

"That, my love, is a promise I shall gladly fulfill for the rest of my days," he vowed solemnly. A broad smile touched his lips. "Do I sense my beautiful wife's need for some love and affection?" he asked lightly.

Christy said not a word, but nodded her head and looked up at him with wide, pleading eyes. It had been a day full of tragedy and sadness. Though she possessed a renewed determination for the future, she sorely needed his reassuring love and comfort right now. Without a word, he wrapped her in his arms. Ever so slowly, ever so gently, they left the cares and worries of the past behind and escaped to a world of passion and ecstasy. And in this their finest moment of love they sowed the seed for a bright, shining future.

Epilogue

The weather was cooperating completely as the Penn-crest household and staff bustled about making final preparations for the christening party of its youngest member. However, Phillip Michael Lancer, just three months old, cared not for the fuss being rendered on his behalf. His main concern was a dry bottom and a full stomach.

It was an entirely different story, however, for Eleanor Diana, almost three years old. She in no way shared her brother's lackadaisical attitude about the coming party. Her wide green eyes and silky dark head appeared in the most awkward of places as she whipped like lightning about the house, desperately worried she would miss some small bit of excitement.

Eleanor, named after Michael's beloved mother, was a truly beautiful child, and looked the perfect picture of her mother, with soft curls and striking emerald eyes. Though little Phillip was only a few months old, his hair, in contrast, was brown like his father's, and his sturdy features promised to resemble Michael's.

Matilda's children had grown too in the past four years. Oliver was a handsome and likeable young man of twelve, and Michele, almost as much a tomboy as her brother, was an energetic ten years old. Both were handsome children and though they somewhat resembled their mother, their temperaments were even and pleasant.

It was their job to locate little Eleanor and keep her out of everyone's way. But thus far the little toddler had been uncooperative. At last they were all captured and placed in the capable hands of their nursemaid. Christy was ever grateful that Nadine, Matilda's servant, had willingly agreed to take charge of Oliver and Michele when their mother had been killed. Now, with Eleanor and young Phillip, the woman had really proven a godsend.

With the children at last tucked away for a nap, final preparations were completed without further incident. Bertha, always in her glory when it came to such affairs, had things well in hand. With an air of authority, she shooed her mistress off to her room to dress for the gala picnic.

Christy was glad for the brief respite and sank heavily into a chair as Milly prepared to do her hair for the party. The little maid would soon be leaving to marry a young man from the neighboring house, and Christy knew her presence would be dearly missed. They had practically grown up together at Penncrest. But the lad seemed nice enough, and she wished Milly much happiness.

As Milly brushed and coiffed her long, silky curls she relaxed somewhat and let her thoughts wander. It was hard to believe that nearly four years had passed since that devastating day in February when Matilda had held the Lancer family in terror. But when it was over and things had settled down, the years had brought much peace and happiness for everyone at Penncrest.

Sir Phillip's wound was only a memory, and he once again presented a welcome sight about the docks in Charleston. Upon the urgings of his associates and family, he was becoming increasingly involved in politics and thoroughly enjoyed the salty debates waged in the Colonial legislature about taxes, English domination and the like.

Theodore Joanace had been sent back to London where, after a lengthy trial, he had been found guilty of numerous crimes, including his part in the Pattersons' murder. They received word that he had been locked away in prison to serve a life sentence. Everyone hoped they had seen the last of him.

A good many of the Pattersons' belongings, confiscated by the former lieutenant governor, had been sent to Christy after the trial. Thanks to Sir Phillip's expert lawyer, she received a tidy cash settlement from Joanace's confiscated estate. It did not bring back her parents, nor erase the years of suffering, but it did prove that justice had at last been served.

And most important of all, the name of her parents had been completely cleared of all treason charges. She felt her parents could now rest in peace, and she could once again be proud of her family name.

Milly's tug on a stubborn curl brought her back to the present. Good-naturedly she teased the girl that her fingers, usually so steady and precise, were trembling and clumsy—no doubt due to distraction over her coming marriage. Milly laughed happily.

Her hair at last finished, Christy slipped into a bright yellow gown which fit her superbly, flattering her slim waist and swelling breasts. Michael loved her in yellow, and she had chosen the gown especially for him. He still often complimented her beauty and admired her curves. She no longer had the figure of a girl, but had blossomed into an even more tantalizing woman. Though they had been married five years, they were still very much in love.

As Milly finished fastening the last button on the gown, a knock sounded at the door. With a show of dignity, Michele, Oliver and Eleanor entered the room, closely followed by Nadine. Proudly they presented themselves before her for her inspection. Christy complimented them all on how grown up they looked, gave each a kiss, and sent them on their way as she herself headed for the kitchen to check on final preparations.

A brief word with Bertha assured her all was running smoothly, and she went out on the lawn to join Michael as the first guests began to arrive.

"You look lovely, my dear, as always," he whispered in her ear as they paused in welcoming the first guests. "You have a talent for turning our female guests green with envy. I must forever be mindful of the many wistful male appraisals directed at your radiance."

"Oh, you greatly exaggerate, Michael. But thank you anyway," she said and squeezed his hand in gratitude. "I never grow tired of your flattery. Your words always make me feel like a queen."

Tables had been set up under delicate canopies on the lawn. The temperature was pleasant and in no time the grounds were crowded with gaily dressed ladies and leisurely clad gentlemen. The children romped and played happily in the sunshine.

Everything was going smoothly, and even young Phillip cooperated by gratifying his onlookers with a toothless grin.

Christy crossed the lawn to see to the comfort of Becky Anderson, at long last swelled happily with child. Becky and Pete beamed from ear to ear at the coming birth. Pete seemed likely to burst with pride.

As she once again headed for the house, Christy spied an old familiar figure. With a cry of delight, she hurried toward the lone man standing leisurely under the roses, diligently attempting to light his pipe.

"Paddy MacDonough? Is that you?" she called excitedly.

The hefty Irishman lowered his pipe and watched with a sparkle in his eyes as Christy approached almost at a run.

"Lord o' mercy, Miss Christy! Why just look at you. Prettier than I remember and quite grown up now," he said as she hugged him warmly.

"Oh, Paddy. When did you get here? I didn't see you arrive," she cried breathlessly. "It's been years, but you've not changed at all. Even your hair and beard are as flaming red as I remember. Life must be treating you well," she commented with enthusiasm.

Paddy's blush matched the red of his beard. To cover his embarrassment he again attempted to light his pipe as he addressed his beautiful hostess. "Yes, it only seems yesterday when we fished you out of the ocean. You were just a little girl then. Now look at you. A grown up lady with two children of your own. And you've done quite well for yourself and must be good medicine for the captain, for I've never seen him fitter or happier. Can't help but call him 'Captain.' An old habit," he apologized. His eyes twinkled merrily as he finally abandoned his attempts at lighting his pipe and slipped it into his pocket.

"I'm right happy for you, Miss Christy; or I guess it's Mrs. Lancer now," he chuckled.

A little girl's head popped up beside her, and Christy bestowed a happy smile upon little Eleanor who presented her with a wild daisy but would not stand still long enough for her mother to place a grateful kiss on her cheek.

"I've never been so happy in my life, Paddy," sighed Christy.

"Oh, you deserve it, lassie, after the rough start you had," reasoned Paddy. "Nobody worked so hard or is more entitled to a little happiness than you."

It was Christy's turn to be slightly embarrassed by Paddy's forthright praise. She smoothly changed the subject. "But enough of me, Paddy. What have you been doing? I'll never forgive Michael for not telling me you were coming," she said. She turned to the crowded lawn and caught sight of her husband, mingling among the guests. He looked even more dashing than usual. Her fluttering hand caught his attention and he headed toward them at a leisurely gait.

"Here he comes now. The two of you haven't changed at all, have you? Still conspiring against me, aren't you?" she said happily as the two men shook hands and exchanged greetings.

"Michael Lancer, why did you not tell me Paddy was coming?" stormed Christy in feigned anger.

"I wanted to surprise you, my dear," he explained and put his arm around her lovingly. He winked secretively at Paddy, for though she did not know it, her surprises were not yet over.

"It certainly was a pleasant surprise," she acknowledged. "Now tell us, Paddy, how are you?" she asked again. "How are things at sea?"

"Why, Miss Christy, I couldn't be happier, myself, I'm glad to say, though I gave up the sea nearly a year ago," he explained.

"But Paddy, I thought you loved the sea! What made you change your mind?" she asked, genuinely astonished.

"Well," began Paddy awkwardly. "You see, lassie, I met me a lady, and suddenly I knew it was with her I wanted to be. I had me fill of the sea and wanted to spend the rest of me days with her," he said.

Christy clapped her hands in delight. "Oh, Paddy, that's wonderful. I'm so happy for you. Have you settled here in Charleston?"

"Well, I met me wife in a little town just outside Charleston. She'd been working for a family named Baxter, looking after their young ones. Not wantin' to up and leave the children all together, we decided to settle there and she still visits them once or twice a week. It's a nice little place, and we are very happy," he concluded, his face evidence of his contentment.

"Oh, Paddy, I'm genuinely happy for you. I always thought you needed a woman's gentle presence, though you put up a good front of loving the sea more. But where is your wife? I'm just dying to meet this woman who turned your head from the sea," she said with enthusiasm.

Paddy looked past his host and hostess to the tables set up under the trees not far away.

"Why, here she comes now, Miss Christy. She stopped by to pat that big dog o' yours and get some punch. That's her, in the gray dress," he pointed out with pride to a rather plump woman heading in their direction.

As the woman approached, Christy strained her eyes to get a better look at Paddy's new wife. She must be some woman to have landed Patrick MacDonough. But there was something about the way she walked . . . the way she held her chin high and proud. . . . She seemed so familiar to Christy.

The woman smiled and waved. Christy's heart stopped. Was it possible? But—no, that would be too much to hope for. Her eyes must be playing tricks on her. But the woman looked so much like Elizabeth, her childhood nanny. The resemblance was uncanny. It was Elizabeth who had played with her, wiped her tears, and taught her the many graces of being a young lady. How painful it had been to lose Elizabeth when her parents had been killed.

But surely it couldn't be . . . after all these years . . . and here, in her own home . . . as Paddy's wife!

Hardly daring to express her suspicions, and unaware of the two smiling men behind her, Christy took a step toward the approaching woman.

"Elizabeth? Can it be you?" she called across the lawn breathlessly.

The large woman stopped not far from the bewildered young woman. A soft gentle, familiar smile touched her lips. "Yes, child. It's your Elizabeth," she said softly.

Christy's eyes grew wide in wonder, and for a moment she stood rooted to the spot, unable to move. "Elizabeth . . . Elizabeth . . . Elizabeth!" she repeated over and over. Her eyes were not deceiving her! With a muffled sob of joy, Christy raced toward the woman, feeling like a child again as Elizabeth threw open her arms and enfolded her tightly in a loving grasp. Sobs of joy and happiness intermingled as the two long-separated women embraced.

Both Michael and Paddy watched silently, each filled with their own happiness at having brought the two women together. It was a sight to touch any man's heart. After their wives' tears subsided somewhat, the two men walked over to them to join in the reunion.

"Oh, Michael, you never cease to amaze me with your surprises. I am truly the happiest woman alive," breathed Christy and hugged all three in pure joy.